THE CULLING

By Tricia Wentworth

THE CULLING

By Tricia Wentworth

Published by Tricia Wentworth

ISBN: 9781549849282

Cover design by Vila Design

viladesign.net

To my family and friends who were in on the secret.

Without y'all this would still be a bunch of jumbled thoughts in my notebook.

Prologue

150 Years Ago

Dr. Pak

The irony was not lost on the scientist. The birds were chirping. The sun hit the water at a forty-five-degree angle and made the light dance across it as it wove its way further downstream. It was one of those spring mornings that give people hope. And there they stood, about to release a deadly weapon into the world, about to destroy all semblance of hope.

What they didn't understand, what he couldn't make them see, was how deadly Trident will be. She's too unpredictable. Too erratic. Too brutal. And she will be just as brutal to people as she is to bacteria. She blinds. She paralyzes. Then she shuts down the host organ by organ. Trident. The triple headed spear of death. There will be no exceptions. Not even children.

This wasn't his intention. He had wanted to create a water transferable virus capable of destroying bacteria and purifying the increasingly polluted waters. In doing so, he came across a worst-case mutation scenario that was unfolding into his worst nightmare. Biochemical warfare and a virus named Trident. This was not his war. He wanted no part in this, yet somehow landed a leading role.

"Doc, do it or I will."

The no-nonsense voice snapped him back to reality. The weight of the medical briefcase in the scientist's hand felt like it would pull him six feet under. And it would, just not today. He crouched down and opened the briefcase as commanded. The click of the clasp may as well have been a gun cocked to his head. Holding the first vial in his hand, the only thing he thought of was the death storm that would surely follow. He brought his free hand up and brushed two shaky fingers across his brow. Blood was about to be on his resume and there was nothing he could do about it.

He couldn't stop this. The people in charge were too evil. Too power hungry. In too much of a hurry to prove themselves. This was the last thing he wanted. What started with good intentions was being used for the evilest of purposes. Going to the authorities like he was supposed to had done nothing. He was sold, like a slave, in an effort to unify Korea once again. And what a lost effort it was, as he stood on the riverbank about to send the virus to citizens of his own country.

If he didn't do this, he knew his body would be dumped in the river along with the vials of his creation. So he led this trial run in hopes of preventing them from overusing a weapon they didn't yet fear but should. He opened the first vial and poured.

As Trident hit the water, nothing changed. The water was still blue and continued slowly meandering downstream, delivering the virus to the unsuspecting first victims. The birds still chirped. The sun still shone. The world as the scientist knew it continued on.

But not for long.

The deed done, the scientist had only one thought, "God help us."

Chapter 1

150 Years Later

The lead of my pencil shatters again. Go figure. What I want to do is chuck the stupid thing across the room. Instead, I quickly put that piece of crap down and pick up a fresh pencil to fill in another empty circle with what I only hope is the correct answer. I try to do it more lightly this time, going easier on the shoddy writing device.

My mind is beginning to feel like the remaining circles on my paper, empty and full of nothing. I continue on, answering dozens of questions. I've been taking tests like this every day for the past five days, six hours each day.

Today is the last day of pre-qualifying testing. Thank goodness.

I'm not even sure if I want to qualify for the Culling. I know what it would mean for my family, but I don't know if it would really be worth it in the end. Is life in Omaha really so bad? It would make life different, that's for certain. Good different? Bad Different? I'm not sure, but I'm tired of doing the same old thing every day devoid of any significance. I'm also tired of these hateful pencils and circles.

I finish the last question. I know I should spend the remaining time going back over my answers and double checking, but after doing this for so long, I just don't care anymore. I'm numb. Done for. I gave it my best effort. It is what it is. I tuck my hair behind my ears and then rub my temples as if massaging my brain will help erase away all the stress of these tests.

Was it enough? Am I good enough?

****

I work in the fields in the late summer sun stopping only for a drink and to wipe the sweat from the back of my neck. After waiting two excruciatingly long weeks, today is the day that I will find out how I fared on the testing. Having stopped working again thinking about it, and refusing to keep thinking about it, I take another quick drink of water and get back to work. The sun is making me hot and I am glad I ditched my long-sleeved shirt for my tank top. The only thing that matters in this exact moment is this field and this crop, or so I'm trying my darndest to convince myself.

The soil crumbles with each beat of the hoe I drive into the ground. It's hard work, but it's oddly gratifying. It's like the weeds among the plants are the insecurities I'm currently trying to keep at bay. I'm determined to find them and take them down one by one. *Not good enough. Not smart enough. Not pretty enough.* Yep. These suckers have to go.

"Dude, those carrots and radishes look better than all the crap in the greenhouses. Let up a little would you? What did the weeds ever do to you?" a jovial and familiar voice soon interrupts.

"Well, we don't have long before harvest and then we are stuck in those stupid, sticky greenhouses for winter, so I had better enjoy it while I can, Ash," I respond back without looking up or ceasing my work.

"So the fact that your testing results are broadcast throughout the entire country in a few hours has nothing to do with your incessant hoeing?" he retorts with a snort as he walks over to me. I look up and see his all-knowing expression.

He sees right through me as usual. Our family dog, Shepp, is with him and trots over to me wagging his tail.

"Hey, boy," I greet him. I stop a moment, putting down my tool again and look at Ashton guiltily, "Look, it isn't for another couple of hours. Leave me be." I shrug and reach to fix my hair bun, which probably resembles a bird's nest at this point.

My brother Ashton doesn't say a word but somehow seems to understand that I am borderline freaking out but can't stop working or then I really will freak out. I'm not sure if the freak out will entail ugly tears, punching something, verbal vomit, or maybe even a combination of the three, but it is best to steer clear of it altogether. Instead of leaving me alone like I asked, Ashton picks up a hoe and works beside me. Meanwhile Shepp finds a spot off to the side in the shade to lie down while we work.

Ashton doesn't say anything. I don't say anything. We just keep working. We pull up weed after weed as we turn the soil of the huge field of vegetables and the time on the clock slowly ticks away. The harder and longer we work, the better I feel.

We don't stop until Mom calls us in to shower, an hour earlier than usual. I'm not sure why this annoys me, but it does. Heaven forbid I actually have dirt on my pants when I get my results? Seriously?

Normally Ashton and I would race to the shower or play some sort of juvenile game to see who got the water first. Not today. We walk to the house tired from our work. I reach down and scratch Shepp behind the ears as he finds his spot on the porch. Ashton and I go inside and the screen door slams behind us. He walks the short distance to the bathroom door and bows before it, saying, "You first, Your Highness."

I roll my eyes, walking in and slamming the door shut much harder than necessary.

All showered and sporting sweats and a t-shirt with my long hair pulled back in a braid, we sit down to a quiet but cordial meal of turkey and biscuits for what feels like the fifth time this week. I'm feeling much more comfortable out of my work clothes, although I'm not sure I'm ready to know the results yet. Mom brings out a special dessert of angel food cake and canned peaches. It isn't every day we get dessert, so at least one good thing came from this. I savor the deliciousness. We need to plant more peach trees in the orchard next year. I wonder if I make it to the Culling, if they have a lot of peaches in Denver.

No, no, no.

Best not to think that way. No use in getting my hopes up. Just a little bit longer and I will finally know for sure that I didn't make it and then life can go back to normal. No more "what ifs".

After taking entirely too much but yet not enough time, we turn on our television to await the results. We don't get to use the machine for recreational use like they used to, just Fridays when they broadcast an old movie for us after the weekly news reports. I wonder what movie they will play tonight after the results. I guess there is something to look forward to. Dad turns the flat screened television on, and we watch the bright blue screen waiting for the inevitable, the broadcast.

"I'm sure you did wonderful sweetheart. No matter the results, I know you did your very best," he tells me proudly.

I look away from him and back to the TV without replying. He has said the same thing to me at least a dozen times in the last two weeks. For some reason, instead of making me feel better, it actually makes me feel worse, and I have the overwhelming feeling of just wanting this to be over.

Ashton flicks my ear and comes to sit on the couch next to me, stretching out his long legs in front of us. I hear Mom scold him for his bare chest and not putting on a t-shirt with his sweats. Somehow that feels better than Dad's words of wisdom. Listening to them harass one another is familiar.

It feels like hours pass as we sit there watching a blue screen and just breathing. Dad thankfully gives up on his words of wisdom and mom sits there busying herself by crocheting something. I can't help but wonder exactly how my family would be compensated for my making it to the Culling. I know they would get something because that is what we were told before the tests. They wanted to make sure we were motivated.

I take a deep breath and swallow down the insecurities lodged in my throat. I am only 18 years old. I am in my last year of school and have just been assigned my specialty. I have my whole life ahead of me. I will start working full time in my career next year. Within three or so years, I will be married and starting a family; it is law after all. Someday I will think back on this day and laugh at how nervous I am. There were others in my classes that didn't even get the letter that I did, so at least I made it this far. Being so young, I probably wouldn't make it very far anyway.

"Good Evening."

The screen comes to life and interrupts my mental pep talk as President Maxwell begins speaking. He is wearing a striking blue suit with a red plaid tie. It has been a while since he has been on the newscasts personally, and he looks thinner and paler than I remember. And old. When did he get so old?

"For only the fifth time post-Trident, I am pleased to be here today to announce to you the list for the State of the Union's Culling. These young people are the best of the best. They are our future. They are our most prized possession. I won't keep you waiting any longer with formalities. This is why we are all gathered together tonight as one nation. The following are the 50 young men and 50 young women chosen for the State of the Union's fifth Culling."

The screen changes to a list. Boys are listed first, by township, and then alphabetically. I don't care to look at it, or look for Omaha even. I find I'm holding my breath and take one more deep gulp of air.

This is it.

I feel Ashton playfully put his arm around me and am glad he is there holding me up. I am just sure my body has turned to mush and would be on the floor in a heap if he weren't supporting me. Good thing he is considerably bigger than I am. Having a big brother comes in handy sometimes, but mostly they are just a pain in the butt.

After a full minute or two of seeing the boys' names, the screen changes to the girls' names.

I immediately slam my eyes shut. This is finally it. I can't bear to look. None of my small family is screaming. No cheers or applauses. Mom isn't doing her signature super-excited squeal.

Sooooo, I didn't make it then.

I sigh. We will be stuck where we are for the rest of our lives. Working, working, working. I was our last chance for something better, if such a thing even exists anymore. I have failed them. We live in a world where dreams are just a whisper on a cold wind. Why did I even let myself mentally go there? I was stupid to have hope. I should've known better. I want to facepalm myself into next week.

Ashton squeezes my shoulder rather roughly and I open one eye, then the other. I see three sets of eyes staring at me. One set of which, my mother's, are filling with tears while she holds a hand over her mouth.

"Mom?" I ask, feeling horrible.

She must be upset I didn't make it. I let her down. Why else would my normally emotionally stable mother be crying? I've seen Dad cry more times than she, so this is unnerving. Mom teaches junior high students during the day. She's a rock.

She can't seem to stop though. She isn't sobbing, she just stands there quietly while tears spill out of her eyes and down her cheeks. She doesn't bother to wipe them away either. Unable to find words, she points at the TV. The names are still up so I am confused.

Then I see it under "Omaha." Two names.

Mine is one of them. Reagan Scott.

I'm in.

Chapter 2

*I*s *this real life?* That is the only thought running through my head as I look at all three sets of eyes again. Am I happy with this? Excited maybe? Maybe that nervous feeling I am feeling is just because I have to pee. I don't have time to decide. The screen switches back to the President.

"I would like to congratulate all the candidates, whom I can't wait to personally meet. I know, firsthand, what it takes to lead this nation. I will take great care in helping to choose our next leaders. There are 100 of you now. Yet by the end of the Culling, only two will remain. Congratulations for making it to this point. Some of you are only 18. Some of you are 21. All young. All vibrant. And our best hope. Remember this moment and then prepare."

Then he gets more serious as he takes a deep breath. "The responsibility you have just been given is not to be taken lightly and you have a long road ahead of you. We will push you and challenge you to your greatest capacity in order to find our greatest leaders. We need leaders in this day and age not for four years, or eight years, but hopefully for forty years." He pauses a moment then smiles again. "So without further ado, let the Culling begin." He ends it with a nod.

The screen is then on the Speaker of the State, who takes over. "To all the candidates aforementioned, please say your goodbyes and pack only a small bag of personal possessions. Within two hours, you will be escorted from your home to leave for Denver, given another routine blood sample first, of course. The Culling starts immediately. Because all of the candidates obviously weren't around for the last Culling, here's a quick reminder that it has no time requirements. It may take only a matter of months. It may take a year. It may take two. Say your goodbyes accordingly. The State of the Union has called on you for its highest honor. We will have a new Presidential Couple by the end of this."

There were a few more announcements made that I didn't really pay attention to after that and then I was again staring at a blue screen.

I really did it? I made it to the Culling?

"Well, what are you waiting for, Your Highness?" Ashton says, snapping me back to reality. "Let's get you packed." He stands and curtsies, bare chest and all.

I try to keep it together. Feeling weirdly and unusually emotional, I think I might cry right there on the spot. Mom's emotions must be rubbing off or something. But before I burst into tears, laughter instead escapes my lips. First a giggle, then a laugh, then a snort from trying to contain it, and then a harder and uglier laugh. And then there really were tears, but the laughing kind.

Through my tears and fits of laughter, it takes a while but I manage to get out, "Me? The Madam President? Essentially royalty? Can you imagine? That's so...*ridiculous.*"

Though I am fairly certain my family thought I was nuts, they smile and shake their heads like they would expect nothing less from me and then we get to work. Mom hands me a small bag before I even know she has left the room. She is clearly over her emotional fit and has herself back together and barking orders, barely pausing to breathe between one command and the next.

"What should you take? Do you need a full change of clothes? A dress? Oh my goodness, what should you wear? I suppose you should dress to impress? Which shoes would be most practical? I wonder what the weather is in Denver. Is it chilly? It will be soon. I suppose you need your good coat. Oh, and how should we do your hair? I need to go find my makeup kit. Do you need anything to drink? Eat?--ASHTON! Stop standing there and get her some tea from the fridge.--I wonder what they will feed you. Ah! I bet there will be chocolate! And the boys! I bet they will be handsome. Don't fall for their charms though," she pauses only to shake her head and point at me. "Be the strong girl we raised you to be. Don't settle for anything less than the best--ASHTON! THE TEA!! AND FOR PETE'S SAKE GET A SHIRT ON."

She just keeps going and going. It's impressive really.

"Ummm, Mom?" I ask quietly while Ashton walks to the fridge shaking his head and barely hiding his smile.

She hardly takes a breath. "Yes, dear? What do you need? How can I help? Oh, your hair is still wet. Well at least you put it in a braid. We can work with that. I'll get--"

I grab the hand she is gesturing with and squeeze it, cutting her off. "Mom, just chill out a minute, would you? I will look fine, and I'm sure if I don't, they will have something for me or tell me what to do. I just want to spend the last few hours that I can with you guys. I'm sure I will be back soon anyway, but still."

"Please just let me be a mom and take care of you one last time," she pleads quietly with a smile and looks like she may or may not be on the verge of tears again. "I'm not sure I will ever get to again after this."

"Geez. Okay, Mom," I say, unable to deny the loving woman that has raised me. "What do you need me to do?" I take a sip of the iced tea that Ashton returned with, having also donned a t-shirt as told.

I let my mom dress me in black slacks with a tucked in loose cream colored blouse. It is one of the two fancy shirts that I have, but hey, at least it's designer. I guess there are a few perks to having a fraction of the previous population; we all get the good stuff. For our good clothes anyway. Not for work clothes. That would be frivolous and wasteful, two things life in Omaha never is.

My brunette hair is down past my shoulders in waves, mostly from my braid and a little from the natural wave my hair already has. I put on a pair of black flats and pack my favorite tennis shoes in my small bag along with my other belongings. I don't take much--a picture of my family, a journal, a favorite book, and my watch. I take one last look at my reflection and see that my forehead is a little sunburnt from our work in the fields today. I can't believe so much has happened since then. That was just a few hours ago.

The goodbyes are typical. It's not like I'm going off to military training like Ash did for a summer. We had a proper goodbye then because we knew how long he would be gone. It's hard to say goodbye when I don't know when I will be back, but since it's the first time I have ever left home, I do the best I can.

Dad tells me how proud of me he is. Mom tells me I am all grown up now and to try my best and hold my head high no matter what. She once again tells me to "settle for nothing but the best" and lectures me on boys and always being on time. Ash is the only one not entirely happy for me. He is trying to put on a good face, but because I know him well, I realize he is a bit withdrawn and looks a little anxious.

He gives me a hug and whispers, "Trust only yourself."

Before I even have a chance to ask him what he means or wonder why he said that, we hear Shepp barking to alert us someone is here and then shortly after there is a knock on the door.

My ride has arrived.

How do they even know where I live? And how did they get here so fast? There are just so many unknowns about this whole Culling business.

Two uniformed military men greet my father at the front door.

"Good Evening, Mr. Scott. We are here to gather Ms. Reagan Scott. Congratulations on having a daughter make it to the Culling."

One man is older in what I assume is his late 30s or maybe early 40s. He reaches out and shakes my dad's hand. The other man is younger and probably just a little older than Ashton. The older one is very obviously in charge. Neither are smiling or looking happy to be here. My dad asks them to come in, but they kindly tell him we have to get going immediately. We have a plane to catch.

A plane? Holy crap!

I give a quick goodbye hug to Mom and Dad again and try to look Ashton in the eyes quizzically to find out what he meant by his comment but he avoids eye contact. Oh well, I'm sure I will be back in mere days. I have nothing to worry about. Right?

"I love you guys. See you next week," I joke with a smile as I turn and walk out the door, giving Shepp a pet goodbye on the porch before I go.

I feel weak when the tears pool in my eyes. I haven't ever left home for more than a few hours unless you count going to Offutt. I blink away the tears and don't dare let them fall. I don't want to be a bawling mess in front of these two intimidating men in matching military uniforms.

I take a deep breath. *I'll be back next week. I'll be back next week.*

Sitting on the driveway of our family farm is a fancy car. Yet another perk in the aftermath of Trident I guess. Lots of cars; not a lot of people. There were so many cars left empty and sitting there after Trident, that there is no need to even make very many. The manufacturing plants rarely run anymore. In Omaha, we really only have two types of cars. Old pick-ups I refer to as "the clunkers" and small cars that get good gas mileage that we use to go between subdivisions. None are even remotely new.

This car, however, does seem new. And pretty. If a car can be pretty. Although it is getting late in the evening, I can still see that the car is black and sleek and you can just tell by looking at it that it must have been one of those "luxury cars".

"Woah," I say impressed and the younger of the guards smirks.

He moves to open the back door for me. They both get in the front seats of the car with the one in charge taking the wheel and just like that we are on our way and I have left the only home I have ever known.

"We are heading to the airport in Offutt. It is a four-hour drive, followed by a two-hour flight to Denver."

The younger guard hands over a folder while the older one explains, "Here is a packet of information about the Culling and the other competitors. With only three of you from the Omaha township, we shouldn't have to wait long for our flight. You will have a blood test when we arrive at the airport, which is really just a formality at this point. We hope to be in the air quickly and land early in the morning at 0300 or 0400 hours."

"Competitors?" I repeat with raised eyebrows, looking at the older of the two guards.

I have only ever heard the word "candidate" when referring to the Culling. I should be more alarmed by the plane flight I am about to take, my first ever, but I'm caught off guard by the verbiage used in regard to the Culling.

"I am sorry, Miss, but to think of the Culling as anything other than a competition would be unwise," the younger man talks this time.

The other man gives him a look as if to shut him up and he just shrugs.

"Any other words of advice?" I ask bluntly but trying to be polite to the two guards. Neither of them look at me while we drive, they just keep facing forward.

This time it is the older man who replies, "Everything is a test. Everything."

"What exactly does that mean?" I ask somewhat surprised.

Isn't the testing part of the Culling over now? Why don't I know more information about the previous Cullings? There have only been four before now, but I feel like I have literally no information or previous knowledge on how the process works. How is that even possible? One of the most used clichés post-Trident is the whole "knowledge is power" gambit. It seems odd I know nothing. Zip. Zilch. Nada.

"You will soon find out, my dear. You will soon find out," he smiles sympathetically while looking at me in the rearview mirror and I feel relieved that the two men before me are turning out to be not as intimidating as they first were.

I peer out the window in the moonlight at field after field of crops. Omaha has to feed the country, after all. I wish I knew my neighbors more, wish we weren't all too busy and overworked to spend any time with one another other than at work or at harvest.

I also wish I knew which other two candidates--or competitors-- were from Omaha. I was so shell-shocked when the list came on, that I only knew of one person, myself. Well two people I guess, but I don't really know the other, just know of him.

There has been speculation from the beginning that the only reason President Maxwell is retiring now, is because he wanted to ensure his son takes the throne, so to speak. It wouldn't be the first time a president did so. And it probably won't be the last.

I don't even know what the kid looks like though I vaguely remember a light brown haired kid standing by the President in the presidential family pictures on the broadcasts. That thought reminds me of the packet I hold in my hand, but with the surrounding darkness and my exhaustion from this day, I can't will myself to focus on the material before me. The moonlight provides enough light to see, but not light enough to read, so I don't even bother.

My back aches a little from my hard work earlier today and I again can't believe that was just a few hours ago. I lean back against the cool leather seat and look across the fields and close my eyes while resting my forehead on the cool window. I feel exhausted both physically and emotionally. It was a long two weeks of waiting.

Better to sleep now and stop thinking about things that are out of my control. I have never had a problem sleeping despite distractions. I can just flick a switch and shut it all off. If I don't, I get too emotional and then my temper flares up. And I can have quite the temper so it is best just to not "wake the beast", as Ashton says.

I turn the "switch" off and hope to get a few hours of rest while we drive in the dark. I shut off thinking about the terrifying plane ride and what that will be like. I shut off thinking about the other competitors and the fact that I apparently will be tested some more. I shut off thinking about how far I will go in the Culling. I just shut it all off.

****

"Ms. Scott, we have arrived at the airfield," the young officer announces as we pull up to a huge plane sitting on a runway.

I have never seen a plane or a runway before, I have only been taught about them. Despite the poor lighting, as we pull up closer, I can tell the plane is massive. The thought of flying so high in such a machine gives me a bit of the heebie-jeebies. Are these things even safe anymore? Suddenly, staying in Omaha and never ever leaving doesn't seem like such a bad idea after all.

"Ms. Scott?" the officer repeats.

"Yes?" I reply shyly.

I'm disappointed in the fear and uncertainty I hear in my own voice. I should be stronger than this. I want to impress people, not the opposite. *Get yourself together, Reagan!* Mom isn't here to scold me, so I mentally do it to myself.

"We will be boarding the plane after a quick blood test. We are all here and accounted for," the older officer says while the younger officer opens my door so that I can step out.

I have to admit, I could get used to this whole having doors opened for me thing.

"Thank you," I say more confidently this time as I smile at the younger officer.

I see the two other competitors right away as we seem to have been the last to arrive. One boy and one girl. The boy I slowly recognize in the lights from the blood drawing station as he finishes up. We had school together in the same subdivision, but he was a few years before me. His name is Benjamin Carter. Only the cool kids call him Benji. So I definitely will not be calling him Benji.

The girl I know immediately. She is a year older than I am but a sweetheart through and through. She is from the neighboring subdivision to mine, but our subdivisions share buses when we have to go to Offutt for yearly testing so I have seen her on numerous occasions. Although I don't know her well, I know her enough to know she is a genuine person. Her name is Agnes. Her long dark braid seems to give her an approachable look. It suits her well. I'm happy for her that she made it to the Culling too.

"Hi, Agnes," I smile and wave.

"Hey, Reagan!" she greets in return. "Good to see you."

"You too!" I say and mean it. Competitors or not, I am glad she made it.

Before we have a chance to small talk with one another, she is ushered into the big plane with her two military guards. I head over to get my blood drawn. I sit down and the military man wearing gloves ties the elastic band around my upper arm. The only word he says to me the entire time is "poke" as the needle goes in. I'm sure he doesn't like having to do this at this time of day. It seems a bit silly anyway. Trident and all similar strains of the virus have been gone for over a hundred years. Not that they would ever let up on the blood tests. We are tested weekly and before any travel between townships, which is pretty much never.

Finishing with a cotton ball and a band-aid, I then get to walk up the steps and enter the massive air chariot. Inside, I am impressed with all the seats and the roominess. Three seats line one side of the aisle and one on the other with maybe twenty or so rows. The plane smells a little stale, but nothing too horrid. It's probably because it rarely is used. It seems silly that we are taking a huge plane for the three of us, well nine of us if you count guards.

My guards lead me to my seat. The three candidates are separated throughout the plane with at least five rows between us. The seats are huge and there is plenty of space. I'm in the rear row. Seven rows ahead of me and to the right is Benjamin. Then back on my side of the aisle, and five rows ahead of him, is Agnes.

I guess they don't want us conversing? Then again maybe they are just trying to intimidate us.

Yep. It's definitely working.

I fidget my feet as I sit in my seat between my two guards feeling a little anxious for the plane ride. The cloth seat beneath me is comfortable but not as comfortable as the seats in the car. I wonder why my guards have to sit on either side of me when they very easily could sit in a different row.

"Here," the younger of the two hands me a thin piece of something in a wrapper.

I look at him confused.

"It's just gum," he explains.

"Okay." I try not to sound suspicious. I hear Ash's words in my head about not trusting anyone. But, I guess if they want to knock me out for the plane ride, I am okay with it. I take off the wrapper and pop the gum in my mouth, glad for its cinnamon flavor. I turn to thank my guard and realize I still don't know their names.

My mother would kill me for being so impolite thus far so I don't hesitate to try to remedy the situation and ask, "I am sorry but I never asked your names?"

"I am Corporal James Cane," the younger one says and then nods in the other's direction. "And this here is Sergeant Kirk Sargent. Yeah, Sergeant Sargent. So, we all just call him Sarge."

"Thank you, Corporal Cane?" I ask, trying to use propriety but not knowing the correct terms. I know military ranks are a big deal and I want to be respectful.

"Oh, puh-leeze. Call him Jamie. We all do," the older one scoffs. "You go around calling him 'Corporal Cane' and he is going to have a huge head. Then what would we do with him?"

I laugh lightly, glad my guards are becoming more likable. "Fair enough."

At that point, the pilot comes over some sort of sound system saying, "Please make sure you are buckled up and stay seated for takeoff. Thank you."

I grip the armrests and hold on for dear life. Sarge apparently takes notice. I have the feeling not too much gets by him.

"It won't be too bad hon'. First we drive a ways, then there's take off. The engines will sound loud and you will feel a little floaty. Then you won't feel any different than if you were on the ground while we are flying," he says quietly and lightly pats my arm in reassurance.

"Thanks, Sarge," I respond and release the breath I was holding.

"It's not so bad. You'll do great," Jamie takes over, obviously trying to get my mind off it and matching Sarge's quiet tone. I thought Sarge was going to tell him to stop talking, but he lets him carry on. "Can you believe that before Trident people used to fly all the time? Not just for military purposes, but for leisure activities. For vacations..."

I feel the plane start moving forwards. It feels just like the car ride, only bumpier. I know my guards are trying to make this easier for me and I am immediately loyal to them. I look in front of me and to the right. It seems the guards for the other candidates aren't really talking.

"Heck, they had flight after flight EVERY DAY. That's why we all fit at DIA. There is terminal after terminal after terminal. It was centralized in location and just plain easy to set up a communications and military center there in the aftermath of Trident, not to mention the elevation gives us an advantage too."

I feel the plane stop and the engines turn on full blast. I'm pleased that I don't jump though it's loud. I grip the armrests tightly again and keep listening to Jamie rambling on over the powerful hum.

"Not that you will be spending too much time there…"

I feel the plane take off at a rapid pace. Ready or not, here we go. I take a deep breath and close my eyes for a moment.

"You will be at Mile High for the most part."

"Mile High?" I open my eyes and ask as I feel a little floaty like Sarge explained.

I'm assuming we are lifting off. I feel a slight pressure in my head and am sure that the chewing gum is helping with the effects of that. I am very thankful for this cinnamon, taffy-like substance in my mouth.

"Yeah. It's the name of the old stadium that used to be there. Not to worry though, the second and third presidents fixed it up real nice since it's where the presidents always live and work out of. It was the shape of an oval with the middle cut out for a field for people to come and watch football. Can you imagine? 80,000 people watching a football game together? And they all had that much free time? And they served hot dogs and nachos! Hot dogs. And nachos," he says in amazement while shaking his head. "I got to watch footage of an old game once during training. It was pretty cool."

I feel the pressure ease off and don't feel so floaty anymore. Sarge was right again. I don't even feel like I am thousands of feet above the ground. If it was light and I could see out the window, I am sure I would be thinking differently.

"Anyways, that is where you will spend the majority of your time, but you may go to DIA on occasion," he shrugs.

"I haven't heard about Mile High before," I state rather confused.

Why haven't I heard of it if it is where the President works? I release my hands from the armrests. The worst of this plane ride seems to be over. Or at least for now anyway.

"Of course not. It's on a need to know basis," Sarge chips in.

"Why? Before Trident, everyone knew where the President was, 'The White House'. Granted, the name seems a little silly but still. And to my knowledge, it was so well protected that a president never died there. Well, except the last one, and that was Trident." I am going through information in my head trying to process why it matters. I'm saying these things rapidly out loud, although it feels like I'm just talking to myself. "And what do they think someone will do? Go to Mile High? Like Jamie pointed out, we don't fly anymore. How would we even get there?"

I take a deep breath. Crap. That was a lot of words. I am turning into my mother! *Callllm it down, Reagan.*

"Just another precaution in the wake of Trident," Sarge shrugs. "Just wait until you see it all. Now, let us quit jibber-jabbering your head off and let you get to your packet." He clicks a light on just above my head.

I run my hand across the smooth and thick packet that has been on my lap since we got on the plane. I have been carrying it around like it is my only link back to Omaha. I inhale deeply and open it. Inside I find a yellow folder for the girls and a blue folder for the boys. My guards just look at the seat in front of them and don't glance once at the information I have. I'm assuming they have been told that it is not information for them. They won't be a bit of help as I go through all of it, but I am still impressed with their discipline in not even glancing at the papers before me.

Making a quick decision, I assume I will be dealing more with the girls at first, so I will begin there. After all, there will be only one boy and one girl at the end of this. I need to get to know these other 49 girls if they are my ultimate "competition".

I start with the girls from the Denver township because their files are on top and it's easy, but also because if this really is a competition, they will be the hardest to beat having grown up in our capital. Never mind the fact that there are more girls from the Denver township than any other township. They each have a picture in which they are smiling on what looks like an oversized flashcard. Under their picture is their basic information, such as their ages and specialties and any special projects or achievements. I read what information I am given on each girl while trying to memorize their names. I'm shooting for first names only. I can't pronounce some of these last names, so why even bother?

Some of these girls are years into their careers and almost all of them have immediate family members in the military ranks! Holy crap. That's intimidating. A few seem to be of influential families with parents serving as cabinet members for President Maxwell. One girl looks far meaner than the rest; her name is Marisol. She is beautiful and smiling, but her smile doesn't quite reach her eyes and she has an air about her that reminds me of a catty girl I went to school with. Maybe it's just the way she sits with her pretty little nose high in the air, like she knows she's better than everyone else. Or maybe it's the way her hair and makeup are done perfectly, like she knows she's pretty. Another girl is far prettier than the rest though; her name is Elizabeth. I'm not sure how this process works at all, but I already think that she will definitely win. Both Elizabeth and Marisol look like they've been taking make-up classes because they are flawless. Flaw-less.

Crap, crap, crap.

Wait, why do I care? And why am I feeling more intimidated by the pretty girl than the one who looks mean?

I decide to turn to the Omaha section of the girls' folder after the intensity of the Denver township. I see my own picture and description. I remember the day we took those pictures. It was the first day of testing right before the blood tests. I look hopeful and maybe even a bit smart? My smile looks way more confident than I really am. I'm glad Mom insisted on doing my hair that day, as my brunette hair is in curls down past my shoulders. I don't look drop dead gorgeous like Elizabeth, but I look pretty enough and I look happy.

I take another deep breath and read my description, "Taking part in the Omaha township's production of Agriculture, Ms. Reagan Scott is not only top of her class, but found time outside of her studies to help her father create a more efficient means of irrigation being used in half of the Omaha area. She is our youngest candidate at the age of 18, and has only just begun her specialty in irrigational engineering."

Great. Now everyone knows for sure I am the baby. I wasn't sure that I was the youngest, but I knew I would be one of the young ones since I turned 18 not that long before the letter for the Culling arrived. I don't know if being the youngest will help me fly in under the radar or put a target on my back. No sense in wasting time thinking about it. It is what it is. Plus their use of "irrigational engineering" makes what I do sound sophisticated. It isn't. I water the crops. I'm pretty good at what I do and have made a few shortcuts to help us do it faster, but it seems rather insignificant compared to the Denver girls.

Next I move to Agnes, or Ms. Agnes Warren, as the packet tells me. Her picture makes her look very approachable, just like she is in real life. Her dark skin matches her dark hair, but her honey colored eyes are what give her that kind look. That and she doesn't lack in the smile department as she supports two perfectly placed dimples. She is 19 and through the description I find out she has been working with the genetic breeding of cattle trying to produce better herds. She isn't just a nice person, but a smart one too. And we are two of the youngest candidates as I compare us to the Denver girls.

Should I be worried about Agnes now? I look up and see her head cocked to one side as she sleeps on the plane. I shake my head and put it out of my thoughts. If it isn't me, of course I would want her to make it far, if not win the Culling. Of course I would want someone from Omaha represented. Since Benjamin can come off a bit arrogant at times and is what I call a "closet jerk", I would rather it be her and not him. For that reason alone, I will not and cannot look at Agnes like an enemy. The girls from Omaha must stick together. I sigh and keep going.

Eleven girls are from the Vegas township. That makes a ton of sense considering other than Denver, it is the second biggest township and our science and medicine powerhouse. The bad news about that is all of these girls are smart, and not just common sense smart, but each seem like geniuses at things I have never even heard of before. I try to memorize names and faces. I'm not sure I will remember anyone, other than Agnes and maybe Elizabeth, once we get to Denver.

I move on to the Galveston township where ten more girls are from. I'm impressed with what some of the girls are working on in Natural Resources, except for water and water purification, which is the focus of Seattle. One girl named Haley has managed to work on growing better plants using solar panels and the journals from the Bunkers as resources and has gotten a tomato crop with very good yields. Being from the township of agriculture, I am impressed. I realize that some people might think of her work as insignificant, but I find it interesting. Another girl named Honor is working on a less labor intensive means of oil purification. Almost all of these girls have their specialties, are in their careers, and at the oldest ages for the Culling at 20 or 21. I find them having a definite advantage over me, but respect it all the same. They just have more experience.

Next is the Seattle township, where eight more girls are from. The very last file I look at is a gorgeous dark haired girl named Marcia Sanchez. She is 20 and working in water purification. Too bad I'm not here to make friends because I think we would have some things in common, starting with working with water.

And just when I think I can't look at another face of all these girls that are smarter than me, better than me, and prettier than me too, I get to the last township, Detroit, where only four girls are from. They are all working in their township's focus of engineering except for one named October who is teaching nuclear design classes at the collegiate level at the young age of 20. The packet tells me she is the youngest professor Detroit has ever had. She seems impressive to say the least. Finishing up the final few from Detroit, I close the yellow folder and close my packet.

I cannot take anymore faces. There is no way I can memorize all this information anyway.

"Can I get you some water?" Jamie asks.

"Absolutely, thank you," I nod, feeling both parched and a bit overwhelmed. If this is my competition, I better put my big girl panties on now.

"Anything else? Anything to eat?"

"No thank you," I reply, still chewing my gum from lift off. "What time is it? How much longer do I have?" I ask Sarge while Jamie stands to get my water. I want to stay productive, but not be burned out by the time we land.

"We still have about an hour," he says and checks his watch.

"Do you have any more basic information I need to know?"

I wasn't sure I would ask this question and wanted to earlier but decided against it. I want as much information about this process as I can, but I don't want to sound weak and needy or even demanding. Are asking questions a sign of weakness in Denver? Not where I'm from, it's just a way of life.

I hesitate before continuing, "I mean there is a ton of information here. I can't get through it all so I'm focusing on the girls because I'm assuming we will be spending a lot of time together and they don't just throw all 100 of us together or anything."

"I am not at liberty to discuss this with you. However, I will say that I am confident in your abilities," Sarge says with a slight smile as Jamie brings back a bottle of water from somewhere behind us.

So yes but no? I think he was trying to tell me I am on the right track without actually telling me so.

"Oh, and I forgot to tell you, if you need to use the restroom, there is one on the plane," Jamie adds as an afterthought and gestures somewhere behind us with his head.

"Excuse me?" I ask, completely taken aback by the thought.

"You heard me." Jamie smiles.

"On the plane?!" I ask with lifted eyebrows. Sarge holds back a chuckle.

"Yep."

"Well, I don't. Even if I did, I don't think I could." I was just getting used to this plane business as it was, in my seat and not moving.

Jamie laughs. "It's kind of cool. The engines are louder in there."

I shake my head. I'm completely disturbed by a toilet being available on a plane. I mean really? Even if I ever fly on a plane again, I don't care to use the restroom while flying above the ground. It's just weird!

At this point, I flip back open the girls' folder, thinking that from Sarge's comment I am correct in my narrowing down the information to girls only. I try to flip through them and look at pictures only and use the pictures like the oversized flashcards they remind me of to try to practice names. It feels like this takes forever, but I am sure it has only been 15 or 20 minutes.

I think about opening the thick blue folder for the boys but avoid it. I am just not ready to see 50 more smiling pictures with names. Plus, boys and I are like oil and water. Boys in Omaha just don't see me. I have zero experience in the romance department. *Zilch.* So the fact that there will be 50 boys, and the very small chance that I could be married to one at the end of this, is unsettling. I just cannot mentally make myself go there…yet anyway.

Mad at myself for packing my watch instead of wearing it, I figure I have about a half an hour left on the plane, so I shut off my light and try for a 20-minute power nap. It's better to be rested than exhausted when we get there. Since I have only gotten about three hours of sleep thus far and don't foresee any more sleep tonight after we land, this is my last chance for a bit of a nap. The boys can wait.

****

"We will be landing in five minutes. Thank you, and congratulations on making the Culling," the pilot comes over the sound system again.

I jolt awake as he starts speaking and realize I am still on this stupid plane but at least I was able to get a little rest. I see the other two candidates in front of me start to slowly move around in their seats.

"Hey, Sarge?" My voice sounds a bit groggy.

"Yes. Ms. Scott?" he answers immediately. I realize neither one of them got any sleep at all tonight, nor seem the least bit tired either.

"Any words of wisdom for this landing part?" I ask, already gripping the armrests and chomping down on my gum.

"I think it's easier than lift off. We will come down on the runway and there will be an initial jerk when we touch down, then it will be like a car again as we make our way to a terminal. We will actually use a terminal this time since part of DIA still works like an airport."

"Thanks." I try to smile at him. My hands have gone sweaty. I'm not sure I care for this whole flying business.

Sarge is right again though, and it happens exactly like he said. I still grip the armrests, but after we land, I let go and relax. I look at the other two candidates before me to see if either of them is affected by flying or if I am just being a whiner. Agnes seems normal, but Benjamin's neck muscles and shoulders seem tense.

Good. I wasn't the only one.

As the plane rolls to a stop, I hold onto my packet. From somewhere above us, Jamie takes down the black rolling suitcase that holds my small duffle bag from home.

"May I put the file in the suitcase for you, Ms. Scott?" he asks but is really just telling me to hand it over as he takes it before I can even respond.

I realize I still haven't let go of it since we left, but in a quick glance, I see that the other two don't have their files either, so I just go with the flow. Although Ashton said not to trust anyone, I feel like Sarge and Jamie are only trying to help me. They were intimidating as heck at first, but have been nothing but helpful since.

"Shall we?" Sarge gestures towards the exit as Agnes is already making her way off the plane.

From there, we walk off the terminal down a hallway and into DIA. There isn't much going on at our terminal in the dead of the night, but lights are on everywhere, almost blindingly so. I wonder what is going on in other parts of the airport and where all the other candidates flying in are. Other planes would be much more filled than ours was. The Vegas plane was probably completely full with 11 girls plus their guards. Crazy!

Sarge quickly leads the way down an escalator, around a few corners, and out a sliding door. Three black SUV type vehicles sit waiting with no other candidates or no one else around. I am kind of relieved. I'm not sure I'm ready to meet anyone else just yet.

As we prepare to get loaded up, I look again at the building behind us. The lights on in the middle of the night at DIA are impressive and I wonder what all goes on here. The place is *huge*. Huge doesn't even begin to cover it.

Sarge opens the door and lets me in the third SUV. Since there is already a driver with another man sitting in the passenger seat, Sarge and Jamie sit on either side of me in the next row of seats in the SUV, just like we were sitting on the plane. But the cheerful and helpful mood radiating from my guards on the plane has now been replaced with a somber, quiet one. I pick up on the cue that now is not the time for small talk although I really should have asked how long it is going to take to go to Mile High, assuming that is even where we are going.

I think about what is to come and meeting the girls. I also ponder about meeting the boys and when that will be. Romance is bound to ensue since there will be a Presidential *Couple* at the end of this. So, I'm sure boys will be chasing girls and I'm sure it will even be encouraged. Not girls like me though.

Oil and water. Oil and water. Boys in Omaha always seem to go for girls that aren't very smart, or at least play dumb, and never argue back. They go for the type of girls that are calm, look flawless, and exude grace. Since I have never been that way, I have never had a boyfriend. Eventually, it is going to have to happen though since if I haven't married by the end of being 21, on my 22nd birthday I will be assigned someone to marry. It's yet another curse of Trident and the curse of trying to grow the population. Oh well, I have three years. A lot can happen in three years, right? The thought of being assigned someone to marry makes me want to projectile vomit so I hope it doesn't come to that.

We keep driving in our assigned SUV and I get sleepy. Since it seems we are not stopping anytime soon, I let myself nod off. I need to get as much rest as possible for whatever is to come in the future. I'm just glad I'm on solid ground and not on that stupid, flying porta-potty.

Soon I am lightly bumped and find that I slumped over on Sarge's shoulder while I was sleeping. Jamie seems to have bumped me, and judging by the fact that we were still driving, he must have done so without wanting to make a scene. I find it odd that literally not one word has been spoken since we left the plane. My guards seem to be back to how they were being when I first met them and was intimidated by them.

As we pull up, I see it is only a short distance to what I assume is Mile High. It looks like what I pictured when Jamie told me football games used to be played there, but far prettier as the outer building is all glass. Instead of the middle holding a football field, the middle now holds a monster of a building towering up above the outside circle of the stadium. Even in the dark, it is more than impressive. Lights on in the middle of the building guide our way. I can also see a few lights in the outer circle of the stadium. I haven't seen such a tall building post-Trident look so extravagant and modern. It looks sturdy too, like it has been there for forever, but I know it hasn't.

Since we are the last SUV to pull up, we sit and wait while Benjamin and Agnes get out and head up the sidewalk toward the huge buildings. I find it funny that no one is awake, and there is nothing going on. Not that I was expecting a welcoming committee or anything, but we have arrived in the dead of the night so there is nothing and no one about.

Then it's my turn. Jamie and Sarge unbuckle their seatbelts and open their doors at the exact same time. I unbuckle mine and turn to the right toward where Jamie was sitting at the open door. While Sarge goes around back to get my suitcase, Jamie is holding the door open and offers a hand to help me out. I take it. I take a deep breath and then straighten my clothes, silently wondering how messy my hair looks right about now.

We walk the 30 or so yards to the entrance of Mile High. Unable to keep up the silence and feeling like a bundle of nerves, I jokingly whisper, "Ready or not, here I come."

Although neither of my guards says anything, I am fairly certain if I looked at them they would be smiling. Or I hope so anyway.

They lead the way through two doors where another pair of guards are standing. After the three of us put an eye in this weird laser thing, we go through two huge metal doors. Then they lead me through a couple of hallways and around a few corners and then we are outside again, walking up to the very tall building in the middle that nearly attaches to the outer building.

As Sarge uses a special key and code, we enter through huge metal doors. This time it takes a fingerprint from all of us to go through two more doors. I am about to think we are never going to get there, when on the other side of the metal doors are two more doors, but pretty and not the usual metal. These are instead intricately made of iron and wood. Inside the pretty doors is an entry room beautifully decorated with couches and even a water fountain. White columns are everywhere and there is even a chandelier over the center of the foyer. I don't feel like I am here for a political competition, I feel like I'm a guest in some sort of castle.

This is Mile High! I have never seen anything like it and the feel would be homey, except for the military station right inside the doors and the guards that seem to be around every nook and cranny. Sarge and Jamie lead the way to the elevator, which is also a first for me. I would have liked to stay and look at the artwork placed along the walls, but apparently we have stuff to do.

The doors slide shut and they push a key in and hit the button "12". We slowly move upwards and my stomach feels a little dip, and then it is over. When the doors slide open, I again have never laid eyes on anything like what I see. I have read about places like this, places called hotels where people used to stay when they traveled. There used to be a hotel in almost every city. I just cannot imagine that many people needing to stay somewhere that is not their home and I cannot fathom the need for so many rooms in one building.

Outside the doors is a small sitting area with huge, fluffy couches covered in matching pillows and the biggest television I have ever seen. In the corner of the sitting area is a fridge with bottles of water or soda, and a pantry. There is also a table with coffee containers and coffee cups.

There is a woman standing with a clipboard in a skirt suit that greets us as we walk out of the elevator doors. Her hair is pulled back and if I had to guess, I would say she is about 30 years old. She looks important. Just the way she holds her clipboard demands respect.

"Welcome, and congratulations on making it to the Culling. My name is Elle. I am going to show you to your quarters and then later you will be going downstairs for a meeting with the other girls during breakfast." She gives me a tight smile.

"Thank you, ma'am." I smile at her, ready to see where I will be staying and get that first meeting with the girls over with.

"Please call me Elle. You are Ms. Reagan Scott, correct?"

"You are correct, uh…ma'am," I stammer, unable to call someone who seems so important something as casual as their first name. My mom would be beside herself if I did.

She smiles again and leads the way down the hallway walking purposefully in her three-inch heels. We are about halfway down and pass four doors before she stops and says, "Here we are. Home sweet home."

The lights are already on and I realize we are on the floors that I saw lit up when walking up to the building. All other coherent thoughts leave me as I'm looking at the most amazing room I have ever seen. It's HUGE. In the corner, I have a small kitchen sink and fridge across from a decent sized closet.

Across from the small kitchen area, I have a closet and a beautiful bathroom with a huge shower/tub. The tile is gorgeous and the bathroom countertop is a creamy tan with dark, almost-purple streaks and swirls in it. In the main living area along one wall is a mammoth of a bed with a white fluffy comforter and about a dozen pillows of all shapes and sizes. A small couch and a couple of gray upholstered chairs with colorful pillows sit around a beautiful, dark wooden coffee table in-between the bed and the bathroom area. A large picture window with curtains separates that wall from the opposite wall, where a dresser, a desk with drawers, and a chair are found. The desk and dresser are both in the same dark wood as the coffee table.

I'm not sure if I'm more impressed with all the fluffy pillows or the insanely soft carpet beneath my feet. I smile as I realize if I were by myself I would consider making what we call in Omaha a "snow angel" on that soft carpet. I girlishly giggle thinking about it and turn bright red in embarrassment.

"I'm sorry," I say trying to compose myself. "I just have never seen anything like this before."

"So it will do?" Elle smiles amused.

"It will more than do," I nod in agreement.

"Please take your time then and unpack. It is almost 5:45 am right now. Breakfast will be served at 6:30 downstairs. One of your guards will remain outside of your room and will escort you down when you are ready. Oh, and the gift on the bed is yours to open and keep. See you soon," she smiles once more and swiftly leaves the room, closing the door behind her.

The woman just walks like she dominated the world. I wish I had that much assertiveness.

Trying to act my age, I decide to unpack my things. Upon opening the dresser to put in my belongings, I see it is already completely full of clothes that are exactly my size with one drawer left empty for my things. Jeans, shirts, pajamas, and more fill the drawers. I walk to the closet by the bathroom and find the same thing. Dresses and skirt suits in different colors fill it full in exactly my size as they lay in clear protectors and all are without a single wrinkle. I put away what little I brought and stow the suitcase away in the closet while I itch to play with all of the new clothes. I look at the time and see that I only wasted about ten minutes.

Unable to help myself, I then walk over to the gift on the comforter and pull the ribbon on the bow. I open the box and find the most beautiful watch I have ever seen. It is silver with a big face and roman numerals for numbers. Although it looks heavy, I pick it up and am surprised to find that it's just as light as my plastic watch.

There is a handwritten note with the box that reads, "Congratulations and welcome to Denver. Please wear this as my gift to you. Sincerely, President Maxwell."

Considering the vagueness of the letter, I am assuming all of the girls got a watch or something similar. I rub my hand over the handwriting and feel the little bumps telling me that the note is real. Even if all of the girls got the same gift, he still took the time to sign the letter in my possession. I debate putting it on now or waiting until later and determine that I absolutely do not want to come across as ungrateful, so on it goes.

I then go to the bathroom and wash my face, brush my teeth, and apply a light and natural looking layer of makeup which was provided for me in one of the drawers. How did they know what colors I would need? I try to fluff up my hair but it seems like a lost cause so I leave it. I look at my watch to see that the time is just past 6:10. I feel myself starting to get sleepy, and finally give into temptation as a means to keep me awake.

I run over to a clear area in the carpet and lay down on it while moving my arms above my head at the same time my feet go in and out thus making a snow angel on my carpet, or a "carpet angel", in this case. Laughing, I get up and fall back on the bed letting the pillows suck me in with a giant "poof". I sigh, thinking it will be wonderful to sleep on this bed for however long I last. As comfortable as this bed is, I hope it is more than just a night.

I walk back to my huge bathroom mirror, poke my cheeks a few times, and seeing that I look more awake now, decide that I will just head down to breakfast early. My mom always says, "If you are on time, you are late." I figure I might as well get this initial meeting with the girls over and done with. It is time to meet the competition. And hopefully just the girls today. I don't want to deal with that whole boy thing right now.

I open my door and peek my head out to find Jamie standing outside my door. I look up and down the hall and see numerous other guards outside of the doors. Is it really necessary that we have a guard at all times? Weird. Where do they think we will go?

"Ready to go down, Ms. Scott?" Jamie asks with a smile and I wonder how he is still smiling and in a jolly mood when he has had even less sleep than I have.

"Yes, I think so," I reply.

He offers his arm and I loop mine in his.

We take a quick elevator ride and walk a short distance to a cafeteria. We pass four or five guards outside the door before we turn the corner to actually enter the room. Five long tables are decorated as if royalty really was here and real flower arrangements even rest on each table. There isn't food on the tables yet, but the smells! I know it is around here somewhere.

Five girls are already here. Two are talking and seem to know one another. They are dressed in dresses, have fancy makeup on, and curled hair. The other three girls in the room have sort of isolated themselves but are sitting all at the same long table.

"May I get you something to drink, Ms. Scott? Coffee? Water? Tea? Orange juice?" Jamie asks, pointing to the drink station behind us in the corner of the room.

"Some hot tea as well as a bottle of water would be great, if you don't mind," I smile at him politely while still trying to figure out the game plan of where I should sit.

This is like school all over again. I don't really want to interrupt the two girls already chitchatting. I remember one of the two right away. Marisol. The mean looking one. The other one is from Denver also. I think her name starts with an "S".

"Here you are, Ms. Scott," Jamie hands me the tea in one hand and the bottle of water in the other, still sounding awfully chipper. He must be a morning person. He then quietly adds, "I'll be just outside the door, good luck."

Going with my gut and deciding it would be rude to interrupt the chatting girls that stopped only to give me a look over and then kept going, I move to the second table where the girls are spaced out. I sit down and set my tea and bottle of water down across from one of the girls, thinking it is already a small miracle I didn't spill anything. The thought makes me smile.

"Hi, I'm Reagan." I try to keep smiling though I'm very nervous.

"I'm Attie," the girl with the baby blue eyes and soft looking light brown hair smiles back.

"And you are?" I say to the other girl sitting about ten feet from us.

"Cadence," she says even more shy than Attie, if that were possible.

"Do you want to scoot down and sit with us? If I don't talk to someone, all I am going to think about is that smell, and I may try to eat someone," I say only half kidding. I'm not sure why I always use humor in intense situations, but it could get me in trouble here if I'm not careful.

This time Cadence smiles while scooting closer to Attie. "Yeah, I will sit with you guys."

Phew. Two down; Attie and Cadence. Only 47 more girls to go.

I try looking at the far end of the table where the other girl is sitting, but she has her head in a book and very obviously is not interested in making friends. I remember from our packets that her name is October. She is the genius one that teaches at the collegiate level.

"So, Attie, where are you from?" I ask.

"Vegas, you?"

"Omaha," I smile and then turn my attention to Cadence, "And how about you Cadence?"

"Detroit," she answers. It makes sense that the three of us were spaced out in the cafeteria since we are from different townships. Why October and Cadence aren't sitting together, both from Detroit, I don't know, but I'm sure it has to do with October giving off the vibe that she doesn't want to be here.

Trying to keep the conversation going I say, "I don't know about you guys, but our rooms are huge."

"Oh my goodness. I don't know what to do first, take a bath with all of those amazing smells they left for us, or take a long, hard nap in my bed," Attie giggles, rubbing her hands together as she does and I begin to think that she isn't that shy at all.

I laugh, take a sip of my tea, and look at my watch to see the time realizing that a whole bunch of girls will be arriving very shortly. Then I notice the other two girls wearing their watches. Attie's is gold and Cadence's is a rosy pink color. It is apparent that we all have received watches from the President. What a kind gesture.

"I wonder what's on the agenda today or if we get to take a nap," I offer, keeping the conversation going again.

We all look to the door as another girl arrives. I think she was from the Seattle bunch but I'm not sure. As her guard gets her a soda, she turns to go sit by October. That is what I would have done also in seeing two groups already talking. I also see her watch is bronze in color. What is the significance of the difference in colors, or is there any?

Three more girls come in, one right after the other, keeping our attention. One must be from Vegas because she knows Attie and heads on over to our table without hesitating, sitting in the empty spot between Attie and Cadence.

"This is Renae, guys. Renae, this is Reagan and Cadence," Attie introduces her.

"Hey. And oh my goodness. That smell. What is it?" she asks.

"My guess is bread, chocolate, something fruity, and either pancakes or waffles," I say sniffing the air. The bread smell reminds me of our bread factories in Omaha and makes me realize how far I have come in just the last 24 hours.

"The girl is from Omaha, so she would know," Attie tells Renae and I like her even more. I wish I could remember information like she is though. She seems to immediately know everyone. She is shy at first, but very charismatic. I already completely adore her.

Two more girls come in. The taller one I recognize as being from Denver. Thinking she will obviously go sit with the other Denver girls, I am surprised when she waves at the two other girls then sits down right beside me.

"Vanessa," she holds out her hand to me.

"Reagan," I say, shaking her hand rather surprised.

She takes a sip of her coffee like it's her lifeline and whispers, "I so need this."

Five or six girls come in but don't sit at our table. The last one makes all of us stop and stare. It's Elizabeth, the pretty one. She doesn't even seem to notice the whole room looking at her, but I'm sure she's used to stunning a room with her beauty. I'm glad the boys aren't here. I wouldn't get to talk to a single one with her in the room. She graciously accepts a bottle of water and sits at the end of the table where Marisol and the other girl are forming a little Denver group.

A girl named Trinity comes and sits at our table, and Agnes joins as well, sitting beside me on the other side. I see the girl named Marcia come in and hope that she sits at our table since I wouldn't mind chatting with her, but she sits more towards the middle of our table with a few other girls. Too far away to hold a conversation with.

As more and more girls come in, most of us are gathering in clumps but with different people from different townships in each clump. I'm trying to keep up and quiz myself as each girl comes in on who they are and where they come from, but I finally give up and just drink my tea and listen to the girls around me. I have determined that Attie is a genuine sweetheart, Cadence is very shy, and Renae seems to be a bit of a chameleon just agreeing with whatever Attie says. Before I know it, we are all accounted for and present.

"Good morning," Elle begins as she gets our attention standing at the front of the room. "I have met you each individually as you came in last night and early this morning. Welcome to Mile High, where you will be staying the duration of the Culling. We will get to the food in just a moment as I'm sure some of you are famished. Immediately following breakfast, you are welcome to rest as the first part of your second round of testing begins this evening at 1700 hours, or 5 pm. We know some of you have been traveling through the night and want to give you an equal opportunity to be rested. Lunch will be served to you in your rooms whenever you are ready. Just let your guard know. You are not expected anywhere before 5 pm, at which point, your guards will deliver you where you need to go.

"Now, some quick rules before we eat. First and foremost, for those of you wondering about the boys, yes, they are obviously in this building too. You will not meet any of them until the Canidatorial Ball. Only approximately half of you will be remaining at that point. Trying to meet them or find them in this building before that point will be grounds for dismissal and your families will receive demotions." She pauses a moment, letting that sink in before carrying on, "You are to stay at Mile High and you may not leave. There will be a guard with you at all times. The two assigned to you will remain with you throughout the Culling. You may not contact anyone outside of this building. On the bright side though, the clothes in your room are for you to not only wear, but also keep."

This gets some smiles as she keeps going, "For those of you wondering how this works, you will be getting schedules of our day to day activities after your round of tests this evening. We will be testing you in a manner of different ways before we get to the final four girls. At that point, the country votes for who they would like as President and Madam President. As stated on the evening of the initial results, there is not a time requirement for the Culling. This could last a week. This could last a year. Generally in the past, it usually lasted somewhere between three and six months. Tomorrow you will begin two history classes as part of your training, one of which will be to learn about all the past Cullings, the other more in-depth about Trident. You are all part of the fifth Culling. Being chosen for this is an honor. Making it farther is even more so. Congrats, girls."

She then leads us in a toast and we clap afterward, looking and feeling hopeful. Before we are even done clapping, servers bring in tray upon tray of glorious food. Muffins, fresh fruit, waffles and syrup, eggs, a variety of bagels, hash browns, ham, sausage, and bacon are served to us. There is even a small chocolate fountain placed at each table in which you may dip your fruit. I've never seen anything like it.

We all dig in and chitchat back and forth. "I wonder" and "do you think" seem to be the trending statements of the morning. Vanessa appears to be falling asleep despite her coffee. I kind of wonder why, since being from Denver she didn't even have to travel, but I don't want to sound rude so I don't ask.

Before I know it, I am stuffed clear full. I overindulged in the fruit dipped in chocolate AND a wonderful chocolate chip muffin AND a piece of warm ham AND hash browns. It is some of the best food I have ever had. I don't remember the last time I had that much chocolate. And if chocolate is indicative of our time at Mile High, I hope I make it a long ways in the Culling.

Attie seems to be becoming less and less shy as we eat. "What do you think the President's son is like? Vanessa! You're from Denver. Have you seen him? Henry that is? I mean we have all seen his picture, but...oh my word. Is he nerdy? Weird? Domineering?" she giggles excitedly. "He just seems so dreamy."

"Yes. And none of the above I don't think," Vanessa is looking at Attie like she grew three heads. She is clearly not taken in with all of the Henry hype.

"Is he as cute as his picture? Sometimes people take a good picture but aren't really that good looking in real life. But is he? He's the President's son so I'm sure he is, isn't he?" she looks hopeful. Renae can't help but laugh because Attie seems so pathetic about him.

"I guess?" Vanessa smiles, shaking her head and her short, dark, almost-black hair.

"What do you mean you guess? He is or he isn't. Which is it?" Attie is apparently not easily deterred on the Henry subject.

"He's cute. I just don't really know him. Even in Denver Henry keeps to himself for the most part. He doesn't really leave Mile High. We only see him and his sisters in public with his father or for our yearly tests."

"Bummer. I thought you would be able to give me all the dirty details about him," Attie sighs disappointed. "I mean, he is like royalty."

I suddenly feel guilty for not even looking at a single boy in my packet. I will get some rest after breakfast and then go ahead and start going through all of the boys' information. They keep talking about the boys and which ones they find cute. I nod and laugh if need be so it isn't obvious I haven't looked at a single boys' picture yet.

"Well, gals, it's been nice to meet you, and I will see you at 1700, I mean 5, but I am spent. Sleep calls. See you later."

We all say our goodbyes as Vanessa gets up and leaves the room. She is the first girl to go. She just kind of walks to the beat of her own drum. I find myself totally respecting her for it.

"Cadence, what time did you get in?" I ask, trying to keep the quiet girl roped into our conversation and knowing Detroit is farther away than Omaha.

"My plane landed just after 5:30," she informs me with a slight smile.

"Goodness gracious, girl. You need some sleep," I say, thinking to myself that I need some sleep too.

"Yeah, and I didn't really like the plane," she admits honestly and then blushes. "I took a course on engine mechanics a while ago. Knowing how powerful they are and what can happen if anything goes wrong is a bit intimidating."

She has just said more words in that explanation than she has all morning.

"Oh, but Cadence you have a greater chance of dying from an upper respiratory infection than a plane. Especially these days!" Attie states, trying to make Cadence not feel as bad.

"Well, I think I am going to head back to my room and try on all my clothes," Renae announces. "Anyone on floor 16 and want to walk with me?"

"I am. And sure!" Agnes hops up. I know her well enough to understand that she is very polite but likes time to herself as well. An hour worth of being social is plenty for her and me both.

"I think I am going to head out too. Anyone on 12?" I ask.

No one says anything at first but then Trinity says, "I'm on 13, I'll come."

We walk through the doors and pick up our guards as they walk down the hallway beside us.

"So, you're the youngest and from Omaha, is that right?" Trinity asks, running a hand through her straight and super thick blonde hair while we load into the elevator.

She is very pretty, but I have a hard time seeing it through the cloud of pretentiousness she wears. A few things she said at breakfast were red flags for me.

"That's right. You are from...Seattle?" I ask, straining to remember everyone and where they are from. 49 new names are hard enough without having to remember any other information.

"Correct. I am 21 and will be 22 next month. I'm not sure, but I might be the oldest," she says with a shrug. Even the shrug seems a bit condescending.

"Then you will be the wisest," I offer, trying to be nice.

"I would hope so. I've been training for the last five years. We all knew it was a matter of time before they called for the Culling. I take it very seriously. I can't wait until they start kicking out the people that shouldn't be here," she says matter-of-factly as the elevator dings at my floor.

"Oh. Well, this is my stop. Have good day," I smile and try not to let her bother me, but I feel like she was implying that I don't belong here.

What did I ever do to her?

"Yeah," she says coldly as the elevator doors close. No smile. Nothing.

I let out a heavy sigh as I walk down the hallway to my room.

"Get some rest. Forget her," Jamie says quietly.

As he uses the card key to open my door I whisper back, "Thanks, Jamie."

This is only the first day, cue the girl drama.

Feeling completely and utterly exhausted, I quickly change into some soft fleece pajamas and set an alarm on the clock on my dresser for four hours which puts me waking up at noon. This will give me plenty of time to delve into the boys' packet and make myself presentable for the evening test. I fall into the fluffy pillows and am out in no time.

Chapter 3

At noon, I roll over, hit the alarm, and snooze it for an hour. Then at 1, my stomach decides I'm too hungry to continue sleeping the day away. I throw a robe over my pajamas and open the door to my room to find Jamie. Instead of Jamie being there, I find Sarge.

"Ready for some lunch, Ms. Scott?" he asks nicely.

"Indeed I am, Sarge." My stomach is dying for more of that delectable food.

"Sandwich or salad?"

"Definitely sandwich." I shrug like it was a dumb question. I probably should be eating salads, but I have always done enough hard labor to indulge in food other than what Ashton and I call "rabbit food".

"Tea or lemonade?"

"Tea," I shrug the same way. As if it were even a question.

Sarge smiles and grabs a device from his pocket. "Lunch will be up in 10 minutes."

"Thank you," I say and smile back, remembering my manners at the last moment before I turn to go back into my room.

I grab my packet and sit in one of the gray chairs and try to get comfortable. In a few short minutes, I decide that the chairs are here more to look good than to actually use because they aren't comfortable at all. Deciding it doesn't matter, I quickly give up and go to the bed. I prop up a whole bunch of pillows behind me and lay down the packet in front of me. I decide to first go back over the girls since I will be seeing them again and want to know all their names. I am halfway through when lunch arrives.

I take a break and eat in the uncomfortable chairs because I absolutely do not want crumbs in my precious bed. I eat a sandwich, chips, and a cookie. I'm most impressed with the chips. Chips are not something we normally get nowadays and I am wondering where Denver is getting all of this processed food. When I'm done, I grab the rest of my iced tea and head back to the bed.

I sit staring at the closed blue folder awhile. Boys. I'm imagining all their faces. What if I don't ever get to meet them anyway? Elle said half of us would be gone by that point. The chances aren't good that I get to meet a single one. Even worse than not meeting them though, what if I find none of them interesting or attractive just like in Omaha? Well, to be fair, some boys in Omaha are attractive, but the attractive ones aren't interesting at all or like girls that aren't like me.

I stare at the folder some more. I almost open it once. Then I do open it to the cover page with the list of all the names. I look at all the names but can't seem to bring myself to look at any of the pictures. A certain fear keeps gnawing at me...what if I am smart enough to do this, but none of the boys like me anyway?

Oil and water. I don't have a good track record with boys. It started in second grade when Gregory Banks chased me around the playground telling everyone we were boyfriend/girlfriend. I was faster than him so I just ran away, but he just wouldn't stop chasing me and so when I finally got sick of it, I turned around and punched him in the nose. That was my first and only detention. Boys have stayed away from me ever since. Giving up on the boys' file, I slam the folder shut and decide a nice bath is what I need.

I run the water so it's extremely hot. In Omaha, we get lukewarm water at best. I then sniff all the lotions and potions and find the soap smell I like best. I add soap until bubbles are all around me. I just sit there, soaking in the water and bubbles. If I go home tonight, this whole trip would have been worth it, just for this bed and this tub. I would rather take them with me than the stupid clothes. What will I do with the clothes back in Omaha anyway? Work in them? Ha. I think not.

I stay in the tub until the water is no longer hot. I jump back into my robe and panic slightly when I realize that we don't know what we are supposed to wear or where we are going at five. I paw through the clothes in the dresser. I rifle through the nicer clothes in the closet. Just when I think I am going to freak out and have to ask Sarge of all people, I think about my mother and what she would do. "*Dress to impress*," she always says.

I decide to mix and match what is in the closet and the dresser. I take out a long black pencil skirt and black heels from the closet. How did they know my shoe size for Pete's sake? I then take out a sheer looking white top that is short sleeved and a deep red tank top for underneath. I put it all on and tuck in the shirt. I get out the suit jacket that matches the skirt and decide I'll take it along in case I get cold or am underdressed compared to the other girls. I check myself out in the mirror. I think I don't look half bad until I realize the battle is only half over. Now for makeup and hair.

Ugh.

I dry my hair using a hair dryer and decide wearing my hair in a loose bun, sort of like Elle's, looks most professional. I do my best with my makeup, wanting to look nice but not overdo it like a few girls I saw this morning. I add the finishing touches: a splash of perfume, my watch from the President, and my necklace from home. I look in the mirror. Not bad. Unless everyone else is wearing a formal dress or something. I shake my head and smile at my reflection thinking that sometimes it might be easier being a man. I look at my watch and find that it is 3:45 already.

Afraid to get too distracted by the boys' packet before whatever tests we have at five, I decide I shouldn't look at that packet until later when I have more than enough time to go through it. Or that's my excuse anyway. This might come back to bite me in the butt later, but surely whatever we are doing tonight has nothing to do with them.

Not knowing what to do with my time, I decide to start a journal to my family about this whole experience so they can read about it when I get home, which may be in just a few days from the sounds of it. I write down anything and everything. Checking my watch and seeing that it has only been fifteen minutes, I write down even more and include the chocolatey fountain and my ramblings on where they get chips and then close the journal and put it back. I go over the girls' pictures a few more times and before I know it, it's 4:40. I look myself over in the mirror once more and decide I look good enough.

I open the door to find Sarge. Being late is the last thing I want to do.

"Ready to go, or did you need something first, Ms. Scott?" he asks.

"I'm ready now," I say, unsure if it is best to be early or almost late, but eventually deciding early is always the way to go. Being late or close to late gives me a bad taste in my mouth. I'll thank my mother for that later.

After just a bit of walking and an elevator ride up a few floors, we arrive at a huge room that has tables and pencils and looks like the testing rooms we were in for the initial tests back home. Only three girls got here ahead of me, one being that Marisol girl. I quickly notice that there are name tags for assigned seating and thank Sarge while quickly trying to find my seat. I manage to find it, then go to the back of the room and get a bottle of water. I don't drink it but keep it for later as I don't know what time the test will be over or how long it is. I read the name tags of the girls next to me while I wait. Chrysanthemum Harper and Julia Collins. Chrysanthemum is from Seattle. Julia is from Galveston. I smile thinking I was correct in studying the girls more.

Just as soon as the smile hits my face, it disappears as I wonder for the hundredth time if any of the testing tonight will be over anything in the boys' packet. What if the test is just facial recognition of all of the candidates? And I only studied half of them? I need to make sure I don't take a huge gamble like this again.

Before I have time to truly panic, a few other girls start showing up. I find I know most of their names as they go to their seats. I look at the name tags around me and mentally quiz myself to see if I remember the faces of the girls that will sit in those empty seats. I am pleased to find that I am dressed differently from everyone else but am not overdressed or underdressed. Most of the girls are wearing a skirt suit. Technically I am too, since my jacket is over the back of my chair. I'm glad I look different though. I don't want to be just another face in the crowd. Maybe that's my problem though. Maybe that will get me sent home soon.

Soon everyone is in their seats. I introduce myself to both Julia and Chrysanthemum, who goes by "Chrys". They seem nice, but everyone is nervous and waiting for whatever test we are about to take to begin. Soon Elle enters and stands at the front of the room, clipboard in hand again.

"Good evening everyone. I trust you are all well rested and ready to go. This evening will begin the second round of your testing. You will have one hour to complete a written exam. Following the written exam, we will take you one-by-one for a short verbal exam. After the verbal exam, your guards will take you to the cafeteria for dinner and then you are to be in your rooms until morning. You may talk in the hallways or lounge areas on each floor, but no going into one another's rooms." She pauses. "Let's get the written exam over with, shall we?"

She passes out the packets and gives us quick instructions. I take a deep breath and focus. I shouldn't look around. I shouldn't think about the verbal exam or what it will be like. I need to focus on this and this only. It is a 60 question test and we have 30 minutes to answer it.

I'm through the first five questions before determining this test sucks. It's all subjective and on the topic of leadership. Questions like

"Which of the following characteristics are most important for a leader to have?" fill this stupid test. Unfortunately for me, with the time limit we have, I don't have much of an opportunity to think them over. If I did, I can usually come to some sort of logical conclusion with these questions.

Instead, I just keep answering with my gut and ignore all thoughts about how they would want the Madam President to respond. I look to my watch a while later and see that I have about eight minutes left and only a handful of questions. I take a deep breath then stop to take a sip of water before finishing the last questions. Thinking I will go crazy if I double check my answers, I leave them be and close my test packet.

I look around and see that maybe ten girls were quicker than I was, but for the most part, most of the girls are still working on their tests. Not long after I'm done, maybe three or so minutes, Julia finishes and then Chrys shortly after. We all wait in silence, half glad this test is over and half nervous for the verbal part. I again hope it has nothing to do with the boys' packet. Regardless what it will be over, the verbal portion seems a bit more intimidating.

After the time is up and the tests are gathered, we are informed by Elle that we will be called individually to go for a one-on-one verbal which will last 5-10 minutes. There will be two testers so two of us will go at a time. Unfortunately, we are going in alphabetical order of last names, so I will be waiting a very long time. The first two girls are called out and I look at my watch seeing how long it will take them. One is done in just under eight minutes, the other takes only six minutes.

This would be a great time to sit and talk to some of the other girls, but since no one told us whether we could talk or not, we all assume that means we can't and don't. We just sit there. Some girls I notice are getting more nervous the longer we sit in awkward silence. I keep track of the girls and how long it takes so it gives me something to do. I drink my water slowly. It would be embarrassing to have to excuse myself to pee while taking the verbal.

I start to quiz myself on both first and last names of the girls remaining as I continue to time them. I'm afraid if I don't keep my mind moving, I will fall asleep. I can hear my comfy new bed calling my name.

Halfway through and over an hour and a half of silence in, only one girl has almost taken the full ten minutes and that was Elizabeth. Not surprising. Her beauty was probably distracting.

I find Agnes a few rows over and up and smile at her understanding that we both have waited a while and have a while more to wait, her more so than me since her last name begins with a "W."

I then look around the room and realize the Culling has all different types of girls. There are skinny and pretty girls like Elizabeth. There are short, curvier girls like me. There are tall and bigger boned girls. There are tall and skinny girls like Vanessa. There are short and bigger girls. There are girls with black, blonde, red, and brunette hair. Some of us have light colored skin, some of us have dark colored skin, and every shade of color in-between. There seems to be every combination possible present. So far, the Culling is apparently just judging us on our intelligence level. I like that. I want the next Madam President to be smart enough to handle the country, even if it isn't me. Looks aren't everything and it is comforting to know that up to this point they are more concerned with our minds than our looks.

Before I know it, we are to the "R" last names and I'm close to going. I look at my watch and realize it is almost 8 pm and I'm also starving. Since arriving in Denver, I have been constantly ravenous. Those darn chocolatey fountains are getting the best of me.

"Ms. Reagan Scott," Elle calls my name and I stand and walk over to her.

She leads me out of the room a short distance to another room. Sarge follows behind us and waits outside the door. Elle opens the door for me and I walk into the other room, which is much smaller than the one we were just taking the exam in. There is just an older looking man, if I had to guess probably in his sixties, with a clipboard sitting in a chair with an empty chair across from him. He wears a suit and tie, and glasses, which I assume are for reading with the way they are perched on his nose. Elle leaves me at the door, closes the door, and leaves. Although I'm pretty sure I'm supposed to sit down, I wait to be told to do so. He hasn't said a word but he doesn't look happy to be here. His eyes match his hair and are gray colored and cold looking, just like his demeanor seems to be.

"Good evening, Ms. Scott. Have a seat." He gestures and I do as he says. "This will be relatively harmless. I am going to ask you a series of questions and you are to answer. Some are yes and no, and some will take a sentence or so of explaining. Please don't over elaborate as we only have 10 minutes. We will start out easy and work our way to the hard questions," he recites this beginning part as I am sure he has said it over and over again this evening.

"Thank you," I smile politely. I place my bottle of water on the floor, put my jacket across my lap and cross my ankles, all the while thinking that I am not thankful at all for his vague directions and don't have any idea what I am going to be asked. The verbal tests we had in Omaha were over our classes. What will this verbal entail?

"Is your name Reagan Scott?" he starts.

"Yes," I smile amused. By easy he meant real easy.

"Are you from Omaha?"

"Yes."

"What is your job there?"

"Nutritional supply specializing in irrigational engineering." I give the textbook answer. I don't think he was looking for me to say, *"I water plants."*

"How old are you?" He keeps quickly asking me question after question with no hesitation between them.

"18."

"Does that worry you?"

Oh crap. Here comes the subjective nonsense.

"Yes," I answer honestly and he smirks showing the first hair of emotion I've seen since I entered the room.

"Do you miss your family?"

"Yes."

He asks me what has to be close to a hundred more questions that really have no purpose or meaning. At six minutes in, I am somewhat confused on what the point of this even really is. Why ask a bunch of dumb questions? To what purpose will that serve? No test questions? No academic content whatsoever?

"Did you have a boyfriend before coming to the Culling?"

"No."

"Do you have anyone in mind for the required age to marry?"

"No." I almost have to laugh at that one.

"Do you find any of the male Culling candidates attractive?"

Crap!

"Umm...probably. So yes?" I answer uncertain, thinking that I'm sure I will, but I haven't looked at the packet so how would I really know? Was I supposed to lie and say yes?

"You aren't sure?" he asks, looking at me over the glasses on his nose.

"Correct. I am not sure."

Crap. Totally should have just lied. I'm sure I'll be attracted to at least one of the fifty, right?

"Why aren't you sure?" he asks, paying more attention to me than the list of questions for once. His gray eyes look like they are drilling into my soul, just waiting for me to trip up and make a mistake.

"Because I haven't looked at the boys' packet yet?" I admit embarrassed. I'm sure I'm also blushing.

"Why?" he asks, looking straight at me, maintaining eye contact with those evil gray eyes.

I think it was easier when he was just looking at the dumb paper. Plus his hair is oddly the same color as those eyes. Maybe if he would smile for once it wouldn't be so obvious.

"I didn't want to be distracted and I wanted to make sure I knew the girls' names and information first," I say honestly along with a sigh knowing that I probably messed that up. I should have just lied. Or I should have just looked at the stupid boys' pictures and stopped avoiding it.

"Interesting. Why do you think that is important?" he is still watching me intently.

"Knowing the girls?" I ask for clarification.

"Yes."

"Because I was sure I would be spending a lot of time with them. They are my competition. So that's half of it. Even as my competition, they are still people though, and I believe you should treat people right even if you might secretively want them to lose. So, I need to know at least their names and where they are from." I stop, then nervously add, "I'm sorry. That was much longer than a sentence."

Why can't I shut up? I'm sure I'm failing this stupid thing. That was not at all a short answer like I was instructed to give. I went way off in the rhubarb patch, as we say in Omaha.

"Do you believe any girl here could be the next Madam President?" he asks, getting back to the clipboard questions.

I think of Marisol and her whispering and snobbery. "No."

"Could you?"

"I believe so, yes. Or at least I'm hoping," I smile shyly.

"Last question, which you may use more than a sentence for if needed, how are you different from the other 49 girls here? What makes you specifically different?" With this question, he sets the clipboard in his lap and waits for my answer.

I think for a moment or two before answering. "I have the will to succeed above everything else. I don't do things halfway. If I am going to do it, I will do it right and it will get done, and I will treat people right in the process too. I do things wholeheartedly or not at all," I say, looking him in his creepy eyes while I do. "I'm not afraid to work hard either, it's kind of just how I roll."

No smile. Nothing. Why can't he be nicer for Pete's sake? We sit there a moment, and I refuse to look away from his eyes though all I want to do is look down as fast as possible.

Finally, after what feels like five minutes of an awkward staredown, he says, "Thank you. This concludes the verbal part of the exams tonight. You are dismissed."

He then goes back to looking at the clipboard, thank goodness. The gray eyes are majorly freaking me out.

I check the time to see my verbal exam was right at ten minutes, probably because of my long answers. I quickly leave meeting up with Sarge in the hallway, hoping I answered the questions like I was supposed to.

Everything is a test, after all.

****

Down at supper, it's already quiet and winding down. Over half of the girls seem to have already gone back to their rooms as it is after 8:15 pm, or 2015 hours as Sarge would say. I spot Marcia Sanchez, the girl that I learned is working with water purification from Seattle. The one that I thought I might actually have something in common with.

I go to the huge heated containers of food in the back of the room and fill my plate with some of the pasta with a white creamy sauce and two fresh bread rolls. Making my way, I wave at Renae but choose to sit by Marcia and introduce myself.

"Oh hey. How are ya? Not a good night to have a last name towards the bottom, huh?" she says, striking up a conversation and immediately being less reserved than most of the girls I've met.

"Nope. This food smells delicious though." I stop to smile. "It may make up for all the waiting."

"Oh, I know, girl. I am going to go home fat and happy with the way they feed us. And that bed? Oh. I would rather go home with that than the clothes," she laughs.

I laugh too. "I don't even know how to use all of the stuff in the makeup kit."

"Ah. Well, I don't think it matters too much yet. Besides, my mama always says that you can't hide ugly. Inside. Outside. It doesn't matter. Eventually ugly always rears its face." She uses a thick Spanish accent and gestures when imitating her mom and it makes me laugh again. "Not that you are ugly, hun. You will do just fine," she adds.

"I can see someone must have passed their verbal exam. You are too funny." I give her an honest smile, still somewhat laughing.

"Oh, please no. I got that stuck up man with the gray hair and matching devil gray eyes. These fancy heels I'm wearing have more feelings than he does." I find myself giggling a little too much as she gestures, "Girl, eat that before it gets cold."

"Well while I do, will you please tell me about your project? I've been working on a few irrigation projects myself in Omaha and would love to hear what you are doing in water purification."

Her very brown eyes light up with my interest in her. I get the impression that she makes it a point to be interested in everyone around her but the feeling isn't always reciprocated.

She takes a deep breath and begins, "Oh, girl. It's nothing really. I'm from Seattle, obviously. Since Trident, water purification of the rivers and lakes has been the main priority. Obviously, we need water to drink first to survive, and then to grow crops and use for everyday living. I have been doing tests on portions of the ocean and figuring out a simpler means of purifying the water in areas where the toxins aren't as dense. The salt in the ocean water is providing a shortcut in the normally lengthy process of water purification because of the chemical makeup of the salt and the oxygen already present in the water.

"We have to go about 50 miles out into the ocean to get away from the toxic shore, to where there are just traces of any toxins, but even considering all that and getting the water and transporting it, it's still quicker and more effective in the end. Purifying is such a chore, not because of the viral contamination itself, but because of the contamination of everything else imploding because of Trident. No one will go near water that isn't completely purified. None of the water we drink hasn't been completely purified at least twice. Which is silly, but that's just the way it is."

I drop my fork when she is done. "Marcia, that isn't just a big deal for irrigation, it's a big deal for all water, for the entire country. This is huge. Call me ignorant, but I didn't realize we could even drink water that was once ocean water."

She nods. "We can. They did it a little before Trident but it was expensive. Now that money isn't an issue and we have more technology and all the time in the world, no biggie! Ha. I would like to think it could be huge too, but many do not agree with me. We could use our method for drinking water and irrigation water both, but everyone is just too scared. Since Trident mutated and spread across the ocean, people don't like to trust the water, and especially not ocean water. I mean I understand that since the initial contamination was through a water source how everyone would be skeptical, but still. Our waters have been clear of any remnants of Trident for decades now.

"People just don't understand the basic components of ocean water and how we can use them to our advantage. The team I'm working with is having a hard time getting the people with the power to listen or learn. It's literally safer for us to drink purified ocean water than water from the rivers and lakes. Since Trident, the same water purification techniques have been used on all water and that is the only thing the officials trust. Our process is essentially the same process, we just incorporate the metallic components of the salt into it. But because it looks different and isn't the traditional way, no one will listen, especially any bio-medics," she pauses to groan in frustration. "The best part of all though is the batch size we can make. How many trucks of water do you get delivered to Omaha at a time?"

"In my subdivision, four big tankers. Two for rationed drinking water and household use and two for agriculture. Which takes care of our crops for like two days but has to last us a week. So if we don't get rain, the crops suffer." That is why I have been working on designing hoses that let out droplets every so often instead of all at once and specialized for each crop.

"One batch size for this process we created can fill all the tanks on a train. So you would be able to get at least what, ten tankers to just your subdivision? We would literally have to double if not triple the trains just to haul all the water," she explains proudly but not boastful.

"Ho-ly crap. Omaha as a whole only gets twenty tankers. I'm glad I asked. This is *so* amazing. If we had that much water, we could almost double our yields or expand the orchards," I say excitedly. I also feel a little pang of jealousy that she is so darn intelligent to have created such a thing or even be a part of a team making such impactful changes.

This could fix a lot of issues. No one is really starving, but since there is always a push for a population increase, more mouths mean more food. And despite all our technologies, our yields are staying steady. This concept could be huge. Monumental!

In almost a whisper she says, "Just between you and me, I could care less if I become the next Madam President. What is most important to me about being here is to find someone who will listen to me. The team I work with can help make all of our lives easier. We found an easier way to fix something broken because of Trident, but no one will listen because they are still scared of it. When will we stop cowering to Trident? We have everything to gain and nothing to lose from this."

"Wouldn't someone in engineering agree with you though?" I ask, trying to think of a way she could get more support.

"Yes, but as we all know, the townships don't mix much. No one from engineering ever comes, just the deliverers. If they did, I'm sure they would agree," she shrugs.

"You need to tell someone like October and see she what she thinks. I know I am sold," I suggest.

"Ahhh, Reagan girl. I already thought of speaking to her. You and I will be best of friends here," she winks at me.

"Thank you. I feel the same," I smile back.

We talk about anything and everything until almost 9:30 and find that Marisol is the only other girl in the cafeteria by the time we are getting ready to leave.

As we stand up to go, she storms by us annoyed and says haughtily, "It's about time."

Since when does she have to be the last person to leave? Is it a rule or something? Come to think of it, she's always the first, or one of the first ones in a room, and the last to leave.

Marcia whispers to me, "Who peed on her pillow?"

I let out a loud laugh in surprise and try to stifle it with a cough. Seeing right through me, Marisol whips around and glares at us both.

"Excuse me?" she says glaring at us, "Do you have something to say?"

"Yeah. I said I can't wait to sleep on my pillow. No need to get your panties in a bunch, girl," Marcia says fearlessly while playing with a strand of her chin-length hair.

I stand with my mouth open in disbelief. Though it's the first day, everyone knows Marisol is the mean girl. She looks the part and acts the part, except around Elle of course. Marcia just doesn't care that Marisol is a jerk. She's got a backbone and she doesn't let anyone push her around. And I love her for it.

Seeing she can't bully Marcia, Marisol turns to me and stares me down. Unwilling to bow down to someone like her, I immediately stop laughing and stare back not blinking. We stand there for what seems like minutes, and I realize this is my second staredown of the day. As I look into her beautiful blue eyes with super fake, over the top eyelashes, I can't help but wonder if a bird has ever pooped on those suckers. They stick so far out! I mean, they probably pick up their own internet signal.

Marcia takes a moment to yawn exaggeratedly and I have a hard time being serious and not cracking a smile. Marisol squints at me one last time with her super long eyelashes like determining I'm not worthy of being in her presence, then suddenly whips her long blonde hair back around and storms out of the room stomping all the way.

We wait until we hear the elevator door ding before moving to get our guards, and then I am laughing so hard I don't think I can breathe. Sarge just shakes his head unable to keep from smiling at us. Marcia's guard also seems amused. I'm pleased to find out, Marcia is down the hall at the end on the same floor as me. We say our goodnights and go to our rooms.

I enter my room in good spirits in finding a friend. Other than Ashton and my classmates, I don't really have time for friends at home. As I turn on the lights, I see another file looking like the packet I was given with everyone's information. This one has the country's seal on it. I kick off my heels which are making my feet numb and don't hesitate to walk over to it and open it.

Inside is a letter congratulating me on making it to the Culling. I find out that there will always be a running rank of us girls from 1-50 and we will be eliminated as such. There is a little of the information I already knew, like at the final four boys and girls, the voting will begin. What I didn't know was at that point a quarter of our score will be from the Board of Directors and the rest from the votes from the citizens. This is to help the most deserving person become the leader, not just the most charismatic. It also says that the first five girls will be eliminated by Friday. Upon reading that, I get that nervous pit in my stomach.

I don't want to go home just yet. I just got here. I just made friends.

The information also tells me that we will have three classes of training and one written test per day for the first six days, beginning tomorrow. The first class from 8:00-9:45 am will be "Culling: Past and Present", the second class from 10:00-11:45 am will be "Trident Training", and the last from 1:00-3:00 pm will be "Social and Practical Etiquette". It doesn't give a definite time for each daily test but says that times will vary.

Next is a letter stating that all our families will be receiving compensation and other perks for our being absent. It says, "We understand that family is a big part of the candidates' upbringing and will reward those families in raising the leaders we need in the wake of Trident." It goes on to explain that if we make it through the first two cuts, our immediate family members will receive a promotion. If we make it to the halfway point, they get another promotion. If we make it to the final eight couples, they will get "reevaluated as to be determined for leadership within the township". At the final four couples, the candidates have the opportunity to stay in Denver or relocate to one another's home townships if we should choose to do so, thus staying together. And if we make it to the final two couples, our families have the option to join the candidate in Denver "to help serve on committees, possibly even cabinet positions, to better our nation". If we win, they will "assist the President or Madam President however the Presidential Couple deems necessary".

And now I have even more motivation. I have to do this. I have to help my parents. Not everyone in Omaha has the same level of jobs, and there isn't much moving between the levels of jobs. Ours isn't the lowest level since we have been allocated our own acreage to work, but it definitely isn't the top level of jobs either, the leadership and management jobs. If I can make it through the first two cuts, we will be automatically moved up to more important work. The thought of my family being able to help with the leadership in Omaha, which is all older families who are quite lazy, is more than motivating. Moving to Denver? I cannot even imagine. I don't even know if they want to leave our home, but I know I have to get them as far as I can. At least give them options.

I then think of Marcia. That is what she needs. She needs to be here to talk to the people of power and influence to get them to hear her out. Or she needs to become one of those people herself.

The only downside is that we will all be thinking the same thing. Every single girl is going to want to make the first two cuts. Thinking of Marisol's brash cruelty and superiority complex, I realize that there are some girls who will do whatever it takes to win. I am grateful for my guards always being here with me so no one can mess with me or try to take me out of the competition. Sarge was definitely correct in warning me that this is a competition. All this really is, is one big game. And the stakes are high.

But, I like playing games. And more than I like playing the games, I like winning them.

After slipping into some amazing silk pajamas and getting an evening cup of hot tea, I decide it's time I look at the boys' folder before I am caught unaware again. It's almost 11 pm, but I know that if I don't do it tonight, I never will, and I'm not sure when I will have the time tomorrow. I want to be as informed as possible going into classes tomorrow morning. I've just been delaying the inevitable because I know my track record with boys. I am more confident in my own abilities than in my ability to be woo-worthy of the boys.

I lay the folder on the bed in front of me, put a fluffy pillow or two behind my back, sit cross-legged, and open the ominous blue folder. I decide to start with Benjamin and Omaha since he is the only one. His description does make him sound notable, but if you really knew him, you would understand that he is a bit of a jerk.

I once watched him and a few of his friends pick on a small boy from our township on our lunch break because the kid was very quirky and nerdy. Benjamin is just a glorified bully hiding behind a mask of machoism. He looks good on paper and in a picture, but he sucks as a person. I don't like bullies. Not my type…if I have a type.

I decide to then go to the Seattle boys where only two candidates are from. The one named Ajax looks like he could be Marcia's identical twin. He isn't because they have different last names, but still. Maybe they are cousins of some sort. The other is completely opposite looking, blonde hair, blue-eyed and named Oliver.

All three boys I've looked at so far have been smiling and look handsome. I wonder what they think when they look at my picture? What is my first impression? Well, I probably don't have one because they got stuck on Elizabeth's picture and never even turned to mine.

Already deciding to save Denver for last since a whopping 20 boys are from there and because the unofficial heir to the presidency is somewhere within those 20, I decide to go to Galveston next where 11 boys are from. Most of them work in fuel or energy. Although the description is completely over my head and I understand nothing, a boy named Knox seems extraordinarily smart. I don't know his height from his description but I see him being tall, on the skinny side, and smart enough to beat the pants off anyone in a battle of wits. Another one of the 11 catches my eye because his eyes seem to sparkle. If pictures could laugh, his would be laughing. His name is Trent. He has dark tan skin, his hair is a shade between blonde and brown, he has honey brown eyes, and he just seems to be so happy that it's jumping out at you. From what I can tell from a lousy picture, he seems more muscular as his neck is more defined. He must have to do some sort of manual labor like we do in Omaha.

Next, I move to Detroit, where seven boys are from. Quite a few of them are working on transportation projects. One, in particular, is working on a chemical purification bomb that I find interesting. His name is Joshua. He has dark hair, dark skin, and dark brown eyes. He seems to be the seventh boy I've found moderately attractive.

Take that Mr. Gray-eyes!

With this pool of boys, I am sure I would have had a boyfriend by now in Omaha. If they would notice me that is. Finding most of the engineering jargon a bit over my head again, I quickly move through and finish Detroit as it is starting to get late and I would like to go through all of them this evening.

Onward I flip to Vegas since I'm saving Denver for last, where nine boys are from. Most are going through pre-med classes and have a focus area. One named Sean is going to deliver babies. One is focusing on vaccinations and immune system rehabilitation. One has majored in biochemical warfare, his name is Maverick. He has a kind smile even though he is an expert in a dangerous and touchy subject. Another of the boys named William looks kind and has volunteered to be one of the doctors trained and relocated to another township. He is one of the rare people that are allowed to experience two townships. I smile and think of Omaha's doctor. It takes a special kind of person to do that and I immediately respect him. Yet another boy named Adam is working on the biomedical sciences of animals and will eventually end up in Omaha as a veterinarian since we have the most animal population. I like all the boys from Vegas it turns out. They will be a force to be reckoned with, competition wise.

This brings me to the final township, Denver. Not surprisingly, 20 of the 50 boys are from Denver. Normal male citizens have military training at the age of 21. Denver boys start at 16 since most of their specialties will be in the military anyway. So almost all of them have had multiple years of training and are climbing the military ranks. I start in and see face after handsome face specializing in things like "weapon advancement", "tactical advantages", "technological weaponry", and "communications intelligence". I have no idea what any of it means, but I am impressed by all of it. If I thought Vegas boys were going to be tough to beat, these boys are going to be even more so.

One boy named Bronson has so many muscles I have no idea how his face even fit in the picture. I stop for a while at one boy named Lyncoln. All of the Denver boys are smiling, albeit half smiling in some, but smiling nonetheless. Lyncoln is not, and unapologetically so. His blue eyes pierce through the paper, but he doesn't seem cruel or mean like Marisol either. He just seems rough around the edges and has a confident and aggressive air about him. I take in his dark hair contrasted with his blue eyes for a moment and wonder if he was being intentional in not smiling. It's just a picture though, so maybe I am letting my imagination run wild. I move on to the next picture. I see three more of these military boys, and then I come to the very last picture knowing exactly who it must be, none other than Henry Maxwell.

Our country now works as a democratic monarchy because of necessity, but if it were a true monarch, Henry would be the rightful heir. He has honey colored hair and deep emerald green eyes. He's smiling like he knows he's already won. He has dimples also. Dimples for crap's sake!? I remember what President Maxwell looked like last night and think that Henry must have gotten more of his looks from his mom, the former Madam President. Regardless, he is just as handsome as Elizabeth is pretty. He's a catch. I can see why Attie is so enamored with him.

I sigh, shut the folder, and put it on my nightstand. Well, judging by the pictures, Henry has it in the bag. I think over all of the boys I saw and the questions my tester asked me tonight. Am I attracted to any of them?

Ah, yes.

They are just pictures but yes indeedy, to probably half of them! Then again, I would be attracted to Benjamin's picture if I didn't know him. I remind myself that I must get to know these boys and find out their true colors. I don't want to get wrapped up in a jerk like Benjamin and not even know he's a jerk until it's too late. In the words of my mother, I can't "settle for anything less than the best".

But at the same time, worrying about these boys is stupid. I'm not here for a boyfriend. I'm here first and foremost to do the best I can on these tests, and then I will deal with the boys. If I make it that far and a single one pursues me or shows any interest at all given my track record with boys, I will be pleasantly surprised.

Chapter 4

"What you are about to see is not pretty. We have real pictures of Trident victims and events following the first cases of the virus. You may have seen Trident pictures before, but not like what you are about to see today and in the days following. Since pictures are worth a thousand words, my hope is this is the best way to instill in you a deeper empathy and begin our course on Trident," Professor Zax begins and I realize I am not going to like what I am about to see.

I'm sure they are going to be testing us on our reactions too, which means I need to prepare myself. This is going to suck.

"The population of earth before Trident was approximately 7 billion people. 7 billion. After Trident the population was a weak 150,000, with North America having the most survivors and 100,000 of that 150,000. After doing search and rescue for years across the oceans, we only found about 50,000 surviving people on the other continents.

"This means there was a fraction of a percent of the people left on earth. Not even one percent was left living! We have risen the population current day to roughly 1.5 million split across our six townships, although not exactly evenly of course.

"This one virus almost completely took out the entire human race. It was originally created for good, as a means to purify our waters. Then it turned into a weapon. It was deadly and volatile, mutating again and again. You know the phrase 'spread like a wildfire'? This was more like random violent waves of the ocean. There would be a few incidences, then silence for a day or two. Then another wave would hit. People would leave their homes for food and water thinking they were safe, and then another wave would hit. Just wave after wave after wave leaving nothing but death and destruction in its wake.

"Enough of my chatting ladies, without further ado, here are some pictures of Trident and what the world used to be like. I'm going to remain quiet while the slideshow plays to show my respect for the lives lost. That and I'm not sure I could talk during it anyway." He rubs his graying mustache and hits a button on a remote moving to the side of the classroom. The blinds on a few of the windows in the classroom come down as the drop down screen begins playing.

The slideshow begins and we see things we have all already seen before. Booming huge metropolises with cars everywhere and tall buildings called skyscrapers. And people. There were people everywhere. We see pictures of the big cities: New York, Los Angeles, Chicago, D.C., Houston, and more.

Then come the pictures of the hospitals as the first cases developed. Following right behind those pictures are the pictures of the hazmat suits we are all used to seeing and isolation tents as Trident reached full blown pandemic. From there the pictures just get more and more grotesque. People were dying so fast, and the world was in such chaos that everything imploded. Some of the not yet infected even tried to burn neighboring cities that were contaminated hoping to save themselves. There were isolation areas of citizens that killed anyone who tried to come near. And then there were the brave souls that tried to help the infected and learn from the virus, even if it meant their own lives. It was the best and worst of humanity.

In the next half hour we are shown picture after picture of what Trident did and picture after picture of people infected in the different stages of the virus. The details in these pictures are unlike anything we have ever been shown before. It feels very real and is very frightening. I would be able to hear a pin drop in our classroom. We are shown a picture of all the dead bodies in a mound outside of a hospital, limbs laying every which way with no way of knowing where one body ends and the next one begins. The next picture is that mountain of hair and limbs lit on fire. One girl runs and vomits in a trash can. I can't say I blame her.

I look around and see many girls crying, one of which is sobbing and sniffling quite loudly. Marcia sits beside me on one side and Agnes on the other. Both are sniffling and struggling to cry in a dignified manner. I'm trying to be strong and take it all in while maintaining what little poise I have. I've seen death before in the animals we raise in Omaha. I was also around when my pops, my grandpa, died. Death like this though is entirely different. This is both surreal and completely brutal.

Then I see a picture of a little girl, she must be four or five as she holds on to her teddy bear for dear life. She looks very ill and very still. There is a man in a hazmat suit holding her hand while I assume she dies. He has tears streaming down his face inside the suit. I feel my eyes sting and allow just one tear to roll down my face, not even bothering to wipe it away. No little girl should die that young. But as we always say, Trident didn't discriminate. Young or old. Male or female. Black or white. Trident just didn't care. There was nothing anyone could have done. That is one of the most brutal parts of it all.

We are shown probably two dozen more images before the screen stops on one picture. An old man looking in the distance at a city where smoke is billowing out of the sky. The look on his face is pure anguish and grief; it's the look of a man who has lost everything and everyone he has ever known or cared about.

"Okay ladies, I think you get the point," Professor Zax says after giving us a moment or two to compose ourselves. "This virus was originally created to kill bacteria. When it was discovered that it was potent enough to kill people in the same manner, that information, along with the scientist who discovered it, was sold to an evil government. The ironic part is that the virus was too intelligent and it outsmarted and killed them all first, just like the creator warned them it would. But, it eventually did what they wanted it to do; it came to the United States and created widespread destruction. They just weren't around to see it and they definitely weren't around to come in and take over our country after the fact.

"As bad as Trident was here, it was worse overseas. They tried the virus on the country of South Korea as a trial run of sorts. There was no looking back at that point as the virus seemed to explode. The world would never be the same from the moment Trident touched that river in South Korea.

He pauses to smile while switching gears. "Now, let's do a little testing of your knowledge on the virus. Who can tell me the first United States city where Trident showed her big ugly face?"

Many hands raise and he points to one girl who says, "New York City."

"Correct. It was a tragedy for it to hit our biggest city and made it all the more devastating though it really wouldn't have mattered in the long run. Washington D.C. wasn't far behind. This brings me to my next question. How long after the first cases of Trident was it before the entire communications and government shut down?"

More hands raise and another girl says, "Two weeks."

I quit raising my hand as it's obvious he's only asking questions he knows we already have the answers to. None of us are outshining the others with our answers because we all know these answers.

"Correct again. It took a measly 14 days for the virus to completely destroy a prosperous and well-working country. 14 days to break through all the plans we had in place in case something like this ever happened. That isn't to say everyone was dead in 14 days, some were hiding, others trying to help others, and others fleeing. But in a mere 14 days there were no means to communicate to the people to organize any sort of protocol. There was no television. No phone lines. No cell phones. No radio. And while what used to be the east coast was dying off, people were moving to the west coast. Then Trident hit a city on the west coast. Can anyone name that city?" he asks.

More hands raise.

"San Francisco," Marisol answers when pointed to.

"Very good. And this is roughly how she spread," he nods to the screen and shows us a map of what used to be the United States. He hits a button and red dots start to pop up and spread until they eventually cover the entire map. I can't imagine living through that and I'm glad I didn't have to. Few survived, and the few that did had to live with some pretty serious survivor's guilt.

"And a tidbit of information that you may not already know is although the exposure of Trident in New York was as far as we have ever been able to investigate an accident, the San Francisco exposure was not," he adds.

We are all silent for a moment in confusion but he keeps going. I'm sure he did it to make sure we were all paying attention.

"How was Trident spread from person to person?"

Before we can raise our hands, he points to October who answers intelligently, "They initially dropped it in a water source of a South Korean river, and then eventually it mutated and spread airborne from the initial cases. The idiots also used a river as a water source, which greatly increased the death toll on their so-called trial. Instead of their test plot being a village, it was eventually all of South Korea. Then it spread to their own country since they share a border with the country they tested on. And then it took the world by storm. "

"I agree. They were idiots. Very smart idiots," he responds with a smile. "They were smart enough to have in their possession a viral strain with two different vehicles for spreading; I just think they didn't know the magnitude of the strength of the virus they were dealing with. Nor did they understand the magnitude of contaminating the water source they used. The virus mutated and was so highly concentrated that it came back to bite them.

"In their contained trial runs on mice, the scientists managed to manipulate the life of the strain so the water was only contaminated for a short amount of time. By the time they took the virus to South Korea, it was mutating again, growing stronger and stronger and thus staying in the water source longer. This is why, to this day, we purify every drop of water we come in contact with from the water in your shower to the water used to grow the food you eat. Although Trident spread more so as an airborne virus, the water contamination was where it all began."

I look at Marcia and smile. The first day of classes isn't the time or place to start a ruckus, but what she has been working on is so revolutionary and unbelievable that it will help our country immensely. If one of us could win for contributions to the country, it should be her. I water plants. She waters the country. Or she could, if they would let her. But I do get why everyone is still so squeamish about water. Something in the water changed the world forever. And we won't and can't ever forget that.

"Though initially created for a good reason, the result was a virus so ugly it could spread using two different avenues, which is kind of magnificent from a scientific perspective. But, in their haste to prove themselves and become a world power, North Korea destroyed everything in using this creation too soon. We have letters and even videos of the scientists they held as prisoners warning everyone of what was about to happen. But because of greed and politics, they didn't listen."

He stops to shake his head sadly then adds, "By the time the rest of the world knew what was going on in North Korea with the scientists and the weapon they had, it was far too late. Even worse, South Korea had sold the scientist who created Trident to North Korea for peace and a unification of Korea once again. But North Korea turned on them and disagreed with their opinions on how to use the weapon, so they used it on them first. Their brutality was only outmatched by Trident herself. One creation, originally intended for good, altered the history of the world forever when it fell into the wrong hands."

"Now, why is Trident called Trident?" Zax continues with the questions. I get distracted by how often he touches his mustache. It's a very nice mustache though. Ashton tried to grow a mustache once, but he just ended up looking like he got into a fight with tweezers.

He points to Attie who properly responds to the question, "Trident attacked her victims in three phases, Sir."

"And what were those phases, my dear?" he asks, falling for her charm immediately.

"The first was blindness, the second was the loss of arm and leg functioning essentially paralyzing them, and the third was, of course, multi organ failure leading to death," she answers matter-of-factly.

"Very good. This is possibly the worst part of Trident. It wasn't enough she killed almost all of us. It wasn't enough she took the whole world by storm, but death by Trident had to be slow. You knew it was coming and you knew there was nothing you could do about it.

"First came the loss of sight. At that point, you knew Trident had her hooks in you. There was no cure. There never would be. You knew you were going to die. But, you had to wait a few days before you would become paralyzed. Then a few more days before your organs would shut down one by one and you would actually die. This is why some convinced their loved ones to give them a more peaceful means of dying.

"What would you do, if one of your loved ones had it? Would you help them die peacefully or at least more quickly? Or would you make them as comfortable as they could be while you watched them become more and more less human as Trident took her time taking over their bodily functions one by one? What if it was a child? Killing a child is abhorrent. Watching one suffer in that manner is too. And if you were by yourself, you were just screwed once you got to the second phase, lying there hungry, thirsty, blind, and unable to move, sitting in your own feces just waiting for death to overtake you."

He pauses but no one says anything. He's doing a very good job of painting the picture of how ugly and devastating Trident was. I feel a shiver run up my spine. Thank God Trident is gone for good.

"I think that is enough about death for today, my dears. The interesting part for you ladies will be that you get to learn a bit more about the topic than the general public knows. We will look at some case studies, the clean-up, look at the Bunkers and the transition to the townships, and of course, we will discuss why all of us are still here if Trident was unstoppable. Have a good, and hopefully less depressing day, and I will see you tomorrow." He smiles at us as he dismisses us, but none of us really feel like smiling back given the information we just went through and the vivid picture he painted for us.

We stand up whispering to one another and start to file out the door for lunch. We have been through almost four straight hours of class time at this point. The first session in the morning was on past Cullings and we basically went through the first Culling list of male names, how it was determined and formed, how the tests were made, and all of that nonsense.

We did learn in past Cullings upon making it to the final 16, or final eight couples, many boys and girls paired up with the person of opposite sex they liked the most, or who they most wanted by their side, making the country vote for a couple instead of a person. It gave them an edge to gain votes from their counterparts. All of the Cullings since have worked in the same manner. Ours more than likely will too, though there are no official rules decreeing it.

I'm not sure I like that. I think it should be the best man and the best woman, no feelings attached. But, as we all already know, in all four previous instances, the President and the Madam President were traditionally married. It started off that way as a means to promote families and thus population growth. Now, it just seems like tradition so no one questions it.

As if this process wasn't enough to deal with on its own, now we have to worry about that? *Great.* Let's go ahead and add hormones to the already insurmountable task of running a country in this day and age. I kind of just assumed if you got the madam presidency that you were going to have an arranged marriage of sorts. I didn't realize we had any choice in the matter, and although we still sort of don't, there is just more pressure added to the mix. I feel like I have enough on my plate in even thinking about running a nation, that I have no idea what it would be like to find someone I actually want to spend the rest of my life with, within this process. And if by chance I do find someone, will they even be good for the job? Or reciprocate my feelings? It all just seems so farfetched. And too fast. How long will I even know this person before marrying them?

We head for lunch and grab our warm plates of manicotti. I find I'm sitting by Agnes, Marcia, Attie, Renae, and Cadence. Trinity hasn't been back to sit with us since the first day and none of us seem to mind. Vanessa comes and goes as she pleases; she's just a free spirit type of girl. Renae, Ms. Size-zero-and-dang-proud-of-it, is commenting on how much weight she is going to gain by the end of the Culling because of all the pasta they are feeding us. I can tell Marcia is about to bluntly tell her to shut up. I smile. We may not all get along swimmingly all the time, but I do like the bunch of girls I sit by.

"I feel like the Trident class was more interesting than the Culling class," Attie offers up to get Renae off the topic of herself, which is a topic she likes to approach often.

"Me too. Although it was a bit graphic," Cadence adds as we all nod our heads in agreement. She is becoming more and more talkative since joining our bunch. I like her intelligent input. She is the polar opposite of Renae and helps balance us out.

"I feel like some of us may have issues with the etiquette class, myself included," I smile and look playfully but purposefully at Marcia.

"Just what is that supposed to mean, girl?" She pretends to be upset and look surprised.

"It means we all know you aren't very…ahhh…filtered?" Cadence chips in, resulting in the rest of us giggling.

Between giggles Attie says, "That's putting it mildly. And this is coming from the quiet one of the bunch."

"Yeah, yeah!" Marcia says, pretending to be mad.

"Hey, I would much rather put up with your blunt comments than Marisol's whispers and glares," Renae offers.

This gets Attie going. "This is the first day of classes! I mean, come on. Why does she have to be so mean? Did you see her chastise that girl for crying so hard during Trident class? And the constant whispers and rude stares? I'm going to have to talk to her. Kill her with kindness and see how that works. Maybe she's just misunderstood. Maybe she has a reason she's so mean. I don't get it."

Attie is the softie of the bunch. Granted, she's a nurse, but she also didn't handle the pictures well this morning. I'm sure it was hard for her to see so many people hurting and know there was no way to help them. So in other words, she's the total opposite as Marisol. Kind. Compassionate. *Nice.*

"You go, girl, but I won't be joining you. *That* girl has somethin' stuck up her butt!" Marcia says honestly and we all laugh again.

We finish our lunch, grab a cookie, and head to our rooms to freshen up. As Jamie drops me off, I kick off my heels and dive face first into my bed of fluffiness. When I go home, I am so going to miss this bed. As I lift my head up off the comforter, I see the boys file on the nightstand.

Since I have about fifteen minutes before I have to leave for etiquette class, I grab the folder and try to do the flashcard thing and memorize the boys' names. An odd fact about them is that the majority of them are 21 or 20. There is only one under the age of 20 and he is 19. I'm a lot younger than all of the boys. They seem to be much easier to memorize than the girls as they have more distinct features, like muscles for example.

I hope I make it to the halfway point to meet some of these boys. But, I need to be honest with myself, the boys I am most drawn to never return the feeling. I had all of one crush in Omaha and he never even noticed me, despite my doodling "Mrs. Reagan Cooper" a zillion times in my notebook at school. In fact, until the Culling list was announced, Tommy Cooper probably didn't even know who I really was. One time I thought he waved to me in class and I waved back excitedly. Much to my dismay, I turned and found he was waving to the pretty girl behind me. That right there is just how my love life has gone so far: awkward. Very awkward. Like a turtle trying to hurdle a log. Slow and boring. Not a lot happening.

As the time draws nearer, I put the boys' folder away, try to fix the bun my naturally wavy hair is escaping from, and then straighten my pants suit. I open the door and have Jamie take me downstairs. I wish we could fast forward this week already. I want to know if I make the first cut. I will do my darnedest to make sure that I do, and make it past the second one too, so that my family can get promoted.

****

"Rough night?" I ask the normally quiet Vanessa as we are sitting around eating breakfast the next morning.

"No. I mean yes. I'm just used to working nights so this…" she waves her hand around for emphasis and smiles, "has me all messed up. I'm scared to death to sleep at all because I'm afraid my body will resort back to what it's used to and then I will sleep through something. I could've used the day off yesterday to catch up on sleep."

None of us seem to care or take notice that yesterday was a Sunday, the one day we normally have off, but Vanessa seems to have a different perspective on all of this. It may be because she is from Denver, or it may just be the way she is.

"I know how you feel about missing out on something; my mom always taught me that if you are on time for something, you are late," I shrug and take a sip of my tea. "I'm terrified of being late."

Attie smiles and quotes our etiquette instructor from yesterday, "A lady is never too early or too late. A true lady knows when and how to make an entrance." She uses a frilly hand motion as she ends it, making me laugh.

We all survived yesterday, but our etiquette instructor seems to be the mean one of the bunch.

"I swear if it were up to that old hag, we wouldn't be able to vote. Does she even know she's a woman too?" Marcia plops down and is up to her usual bluntness.

"She told me I was too short in her 'initial assessment'." I use finger quotes for the term and then roll my eyes.

"She told me I was too quiet and didn't use enough makeup," Cadence shakes her head in disgust.

"She told me my body was not proportional." Agnes rolls her eyes. "Tell me something I don't know."

"And I am too talkative," Attie chirps.

"I am too vain," Renae pouts.

"She told me I was too independent and hard to predict." Vanessa shrugs then whispers, "How would she know that after a two-hour class? I swear to you they are watching us."

We are all quiet and look around nervously until Marcia says, "Girl, I hope they are. Then she heard me call her an old hag. Maybe she should try telling her face to smile. That's my initial assessment."

We go from nervous to laughing just like that and Agnes laughs so hard she cries. One thing about it, Marcia is just good for morale.

We finish our breakfast and chitchat back and forth starting to know one another better. I don't want to leave my new friends, and I don't want them to leave either. And for some reason I keep looking around the room trying to find cameras. What Vanessa said validates something I was already wondering and suspecting. Are they watching us? Everything is a test, after all. I can't shake the feeling that since I have walked into Mile High, my every move has been watched. Even when I'm alone, I don't quite feel alone.

As probably 15 girls have already left for Cullings class, I decide I'm ready too. I dismiss myself and walk more slowly than usual, looking around. Jamie picks up on it right away.

"Ms. Scott, are you looking for something? Can I help you find something?" he asks.

"Yes I'm looking for something, Jamie, but I'm not sure what, or where, or if I should even be telling you at all….or talking about it at all," I stammer, realizing I must sound off my rocker. "I do trust you though," I add as an afterthought.

I keep looking for cameras at places they would have the best angles and Jamie must know exactly what I'm doing, for as we round a corner, he stops and grabs my wrist so tight I think it will fall off. At first, I'm scared he's trying to purposefully harm me.

Then he leans over and very quietly whispers, "The watches."

When I understand he's trying to block whatever the watches are doing instead of hurt me, I relax. We keep walking and I try not to look around anymore but still feel like someone is watching me. I want to know if the watches are it. Are they just listening to us through them? Watching us through our watches? How ironic! Or is it more? Are there cameras everywhere? What have I done on them thus far? And who is on the other end watching me? Is this what Sarge meant by telling me that everything is a test?

I don't know why, but this upsets me. I am not an animal in a cage. I deserve more than that. I try to think of a discreet way I could ask Jamie if there are cameras. I'm sure he would be honest and tell me if there were. The guards, or at least my guards, don't seem as wrapped up in the Culling as everyone else. They have moments where I can see them as friends, instead of just guards.

Finally, after we leave the elevator, I think of a way to ask. "Hey random question. So remember when you told me there were sports played here, specifically football," I say kind of pointing to my watch with a weird look on my face, trying to communicate with him that I'm speaking in code.

"Yes ma'am," he responds with a smile and a nod. I know he either thinks I am a lunatic, is thinking of the nachos and hot dogs he seemed obsessed with, or he caught on to what I am trying to tell him.

"So *are*, I mean, *were* there other…" I look at the corners of the hall and back to my watch quickly, so quick I hope he notices, "*Other sports? Here?*"

He thinks for a moment as if trying to figure out how to answer both of my questions.

"I don't know for sure. But I would definitely bet that there could be," he says and nods his head up and down in an exaggerated way that makes me think there are definitely other ways we are being watched.

Great. It really is all just a competition, an ongoing and everlasting competition. How long before I do something I shouldn't? Or have I already? They have obviously been watching us since we got here. The more important question is, why?

****

The next few days fly by in a blur as we are overloaded with new information. The good news is, the time is getting shorter and shorter until we find out about the first cuts. After chatting at dinner and laughing with some of the girls about our ridiculous etiquette class and how to do all things proper, I go to my room to unwind. We haven't had our written test yet today since etiquette class ran long. I'm hoping we will skip it since they are completely dumb just like the first day.

I change into pajamas until I'm told otherwise. I'm not used to having to look this nice all day, every day. My feet definitely aren't used to heels. It's exhausting! I don't know how Elle does it. If I'm the next Madam President, I'm going to wear slippers everywhere. I will demand it.

I lounge on my fluffy bed and go over the boys' packet again. I'm fairly certain over the last few days I have managed to memorize them all. I sip on some tea for a while. Then seeing that it is 9 pm and being exhausted from all the hoopla this week, I decide to go to bed early and avoid thinking about the cut that should be announced tomorrow.

I jolt awake to a knock at my door. The clock on my nightstand reads 1:45 am. Before I have time to answer the door or move at all, Elle and the same man that did my verbal test a few days ago come in my room, turn on my hallway light and the lamp beside my bed, and help themselves to sit at my chairs by the coffee table.

"Sorry to interrupt your sleeping, Ms. Scott. Another verbal exam will take place now for the next ten minutes," Elle informs me and then as if reading my mind adds, "No cuts as of yet, but this is the last big thing before the first cuts."

Feeling tired and not in the mood for games but relieved I'm not yet going home, I retort, "Okay. Might as well call me Reagan. No need for formalities since you are in my bedroom and seeing me in my skivvies. Boy am I glad Fridays are my nude sleeping nights and not tonight."

I just couldn't seem to stop myself and as soon as it's all out of my mouth, I silently blame Marcia for rubbing off on me. I only joke around like that with Ashton. I wouldn't be surprised if they throw me out of the Culling immediately. That is definitely not what we just learned about "meet and greets" in etiquette class. I should have just said hello, for crap's sake. But when I'm tired, I get weird. And obviously inappropriate.

Elle stifles a giggle but is having a hard time being serious, and the tester man with the gray eyes, who is normally emotionless, smiles a half-smile.

"Shall we begin, Ms. Scott?" he asks and just like that is back to being all business.

"Yes, sir. We shall," I say, sitting up straight against my pillow and using a hand gesture in the attempt to get professional while trying my hardest not to yawn. I'm sure they're trying to see how we answer things tired. I'm obviously a bad tired person, so this may be interesting.

"Is your name Reagan Scott?" he begins just like the last time.

"Yes."

"Are you from Omaha?"

"Yes."

"What is your job there?"

"Nutritional supply specializing in irrigational engineering," I respond exactly like last time, trying not to yawn in the middle of it.

"How old are you?"

18."

"Does that worry you?"

"Yes." I smile, still answering the same as before.

"Of the Culling Candidates, which person do you think is most suited to be Madam President?"

"Elizabeth," I say without hesitating, fighting another yawn.

"Why?" he asks.

"Isn't it obvious? She's beautiful, always poised, and unlike myself, knows how and when to keep her mouth shut." I smile shyly trying to make up for embarrassing myself earlier.

"Is there anyone who you think is unsuited to be Madam President?"

"Yes."

"Who?"

"Marisol, Trinity, and Bethany," I offer. I could probably give more, but those are the three that stand out the most.

"Please explain your reasoning for each."

"Marisol is too cruel hearted to be a leader. I venture to say she would do anything to become Madam President. She just wants it too much and doesn't care how many people she will hurt or truck over to get there. Trinity thinks highly of herself and looks down on others. Entitled and egotistical leaders become disastrous leaders as we have all learned if we look to the past, and both of those girls would fall into that category. Bethany is a total sweetheart but is the complete opposite of Marisol. She was uncontrollably sobbing in class during the Trident slideshow. She is too empathetic and too emotional, too tender hearted. She is a wonderful person, but wouldn't do well with the responsibilities the presidency entails. She wouldn't ever be able to say no to anything." I am quite proud of myself for thinking of that entire spiel spur of the moment as well as tired.

"Have you looked at the boys' information?" he asks, trying to hold back another smile but I see it there hiding in the corners of his mouth.

Maybe he isn't so bad after all. But for real, he should color his hair or something. The hair matching the eyes is just plain weird.

"Yes," I nod and can't help but grin.

"Were you attracted to any of them?"

"Yes." I'm sure I'm probably blushing now.

"Would you like to tell me who stands out?"

"No."

This surprises him as I see his eyebrows slightly raise. I'm finding that he does show emotion, it's just so quick you have to really pay attention to pick up on it. He must not be trying to intimidate us as much now either because I can pick up on it, even in my tired state.

"Why not?" he inquires.

"I personally know for a fact that some individuals in that packet look great on paper, are physically attractive, but are actually kind of crappy people. I don't want to judge someone by a picture, as I hope they wouldn't judge me. We all look good on paper and in a picture. What really matters is who you really are as a person, what makes you tick, and how you treat others. And if you were wondering, on looks alone, I would date about half of them." I shrug as I finish.

He quickly looks at Elle then looks back down at his clipboard. "What has been your favorite part of this experience thus far?"

"The friends I've made, the food, and my fluffy bed here." I pat the bed beside me.

"We will now be going over some questions you answered on your written exams as we want you to elaborate on why you answered the way you did."

He continues and asks me questions like, "Why did you pick integrity over honesty as the characteristic most needed in a leader?" There are probably fifteen questions I give short but definite answers to. I hope I'm answering them how I'm supposed to be, but really I'm just trying my hardest not to yawn. I feel like yawning during a verbal will dock me points or something.

"In regards to the question about government, you were asked if you think our government is doing a bad, fair, good, or exemplary job, and you said fair. Why?"

"Well, in defense of our government, I don't know much insider information. What I do know though is sometimes we are shooting ourselves in the foot. We are too afraid to change much of anything that was set in place following Trident. I know for a fact there are projects out there that can make our lives easier that just need some collaboration from other townships. Overall, I think we are doing okay, but I don't think it's our best effort. Anything less than our best effort after Trident seems wasteful. We owe it to all those people who died to make our country flourish again, not just survive, but flourish," I explain soberly, thinking of that little girl in the picture who died.

I must have answered one question correctly because Elle gives me a nod of approval and takes a sip of tea while the tester man scribbles. The feeling doesn't last long though.

"Do you have any concerns about the Culling thus far?"

I'm sure most girls are going to answer "making it further" or "doing my best" or something of the sort. I decide to wade into the deep waters and see what happens. I can't shake the feeling that we are being constantly watched. I have discreetly searched my entire room and haven't found a thing. No cameras. Nada. I will go crazy if I don't figure it out. And it's just creeping me out. Someone is watching me. I just know it.

I simply answer, "Yes."

"What are those concerns?"

I let out a sigh and put my hair, which I am sure is a total mess, behind my ears before beginning. "I'm going to just be honest here…I can't shake the feeling that I am being constantly watched. I understand as part of the Culling we need to be monitored. Given how some girls act, I even understand wanting to monitor us unknowingly. I just can't help but feel that since I've been here, there hasn't been one instance that I haven't been watched in some way or another."

"This is a concern?"

"Yes. My concern is my basic right to privacy. We all know I never sleep naked, you knew I didn't when you walked in here, which is why you didn't hesitate to come in. If I did though, is some creep watching me sleep in some control room? See what I'm saying? It's just a bit unnerving." I stop and look at both of them in the eyes. "Can you just tell me I'm right? Or that my concerns are only that of a young paranoid girl?"

Elle looks at the tester and the tester looks at her. "Some of you are discovering that yes, you are being monitored," she admits.

"How often?" I don't hesitate to ask my next question and the other two look uncomfortable with me being the asker of questions now. This obviously isn't part of the script that they usually use which means that I'm probably way out of line. They look at one another and back to me.

"Please, sir. How often?" I plead with the gray-eyed tester man.

"Completely off the record, and believe me when I say we will know when and who you tell if you do, you will not get any of your coveted privacy back until you either go home or become Madam President."

"Okay then," I say nonchalantly.

"Okay then?" the tester asks.

"I'm fine with that. I mean I have to be, but I do understand why you would want to do so. I just needed to know so I could quit looking over my shoulder. It was majorly creeping me out. I'm even glad in some instances that you are watching to see how cruel some people can be when they aren't kissing up to certain people. And on the plus side, now I know I need to wear pajamas tomorrow night," I smile, trying to help ease up the tension that had been in the room when I was getting mouthy.

This time Elle doesn't even try to contain her smile.

"Any other concerns before we leave?" the tester asks.

"Only that I'm concerned about my performance if you keep waking me up in the dead of the night. I'm an imbecile tired and obviously don't know when I have crossed certain lines," I shrug trying to stifle a yawn again as I take a deep breath.

"No harm done and no need to get up. We will see ourselves out. Goodnight, Ms. Scott." Elle picks up her tea and walks to the door with the tester man.

"Goodnight," I respond, sinking back into my pillows in relief as they shut off the hall light and the door closes.

Now I know someone is watching me at all times. I look around and salute to whoever is watching and shut off the lamp. They really shouldn't wake me from sleep. I am much too impetuous. I even think in big words I don't know the meaning of.

****

"Mine was at four in the morning," Vanessa spits out upset. "I mean, come on. How rational will I be at four in the morning?"

"I'm sure I looked like a total crazy woman!" Attie chimes in.

"Don't you always?" Marcia laughs before adding, "Just kiddin', hun."

"When do you think we will find out about the rest of the cuts?" I ask, feeling a bit nervous about my behavior the night before with my verbal.

In the light of day, I would've never been that blatant or brave with my comments or my questions. As we are all sitting at lunch, we notice that Bethany, the girl that sobbed uncontrollably at the video, and a Denver girl are missing. At this point, it's probably safe to assume they went home although there has been no announcement or anything.

"I don't know, but I just wish they would tell us already," Attie pouts.

"Like they will send you home, you're the sweetheart." Marcia rolls her eyes.

"What?" Attie asks confused.

"You're the sweetheart. The closest thing I have heard you say bad about anyone was when you stubbed your toe on your desk leaving class yesterday and said 'gee willikers that hurts'."

This makes us all laugh hysterically as not all of us heard it. Cadence seems particularly quiet this morning. Vanessa must pick up on it too.

"Hey Cadence. You alright?" she asks while the others are busy eating and discussing the boys again.

"Yeah. I mean yes. I'm just ready to know if I stay or go home. I would really be okay with either. I'm starting to think I would be more okay with going home than with staying," she says with a sad shrug. I wonder if she misses her family or just isn't dealing well with the way in which this whole thing is set up. I do know she really enjoys her specialty in chemical engineering.

"Well, we would miss you," I say with a smile while trying not to sound too cheesy but cheer her up all the same. She might not be the most social girl, but she still gives valuable input to our little group.

"Yeah. We need a Detroit girl in this group and October down there," Marcia says nodding to where October always sits and reads, "won't ever get her nose out of that book."

She smiles with a sad expression on her face. "Thanks, guys, I just sometimes miss home I guess."

I think of my own home and family. I miss my dad and his consistency. I wouldn't ever go to him with a problem, but his presence is always known; he is always there. I miss my mom as she is always taking care of us all and making it look so easy. And probably most of all, I miss my brother Ashton. He is who I would go to with a problem. I can't help but wonder what he meant when he told me not to trust anyone. I miss them more than they know, but I just don't want to go home yet. The worst part is that I feel that way not necessarily out of duty for my country, but for me.

Now that I'm here, I want to see what I'm capable of.

****

Friday leaves as swiftly as it arrives and Saturday drags on but marks a whole week away from home. The most interesting thing we learn all day is that the first Culling was initially just men. There were so many babies out of wedlock post-Trident that in order for the President to promote traditional families, which they determined was the best way to grow a population, he decided to do another Culling later on of women and incorporate it into the guidelines for future Cullings. This worked well since he needed a wife anyway. The first Culling for the madam presidency took place a few years into the first post-Trident presidency.

Other than the interesting Culling class, the day absolutely drags on. Most of us are apprehensive about the cut. Two are gone? How many more will go and when? None of us really want to go. It has only been a week.

I manage to halfway pay attention in etiquette class and make it to dinner. I sit with my new friends and chat with them, but all of us seem to be a bit quieter than usual. Well, with the exception of Marcia, of course.

Saturday finally comes to a close and we don't get any announcements about the cuts. Instead, we do get an announcement that there will be a physical fitness test the next morning. No list. No one leaves. No one mentions the cut. Nothing. We have all been on edge the last few days, and still, there is nothing.

We all go to our rooms after dinner feeling confused as to why the ominous cut hasn't occurred yet. How many more days must we walk around on egg shells? Will someone come at night like our verbal test a few days ago but dismiss us? When is the cut happening? And are they trying to drive us crazy and test our reactions since "everything is a test"?

Sunday morning I wake up with a jolt and look around to see that I'm still in my fancy bed. No one came in the night to dismiss me. I find myself somewhat excited for the physical fitness test today, as I know that I have done more hard work than some of these girls. I'm also more so excited because I'm still here. Does this mean we have made it past the first cut and are that much closer to our families getting promoted? Or has the cut even happened yet?

Down at breakfast, Cadence is nowhere to be found along with two other girls. We have a two-hour break before our fitness test so we sit in the sitting area of the floor Attie is on and wait it out chatting with one another. It's a relief that some girls are gone because it means that the cuts are happening, but since there isn't a clear dismissal procedure, it's unnerving that any of us could go missing next.

"I'm sure she's fine. She even said she wasn't sure she wanted to be here," Marcia offers about Cadence.

"I know. It just sucks that we never even get to say goodbye or anything." I shrug soberly.

"Oh, I agree with you totally, Reagan." Attie sighs. "I thought there would be an announcement at the end of the day, or even a small ceremony, or just something with closure. Then those people would pack their things and say goodbye. Like they said, it's a big deal they made it even as far as they did."

"Yeah, that's just not how we roll in Denver," Vanessa says as if it explains everything.

"Well, how do you roll then? And why do you sit with us when you could be sitting with the Denver girls?" Renae demands, borderline haughty-like.

The stress of the last few days has obviously been getting to her. She looks worn out and the dark circles under her eyes prove it. For some reason, she doesn't seem to like Vanessa very much. Probably because Vanessa is very pretty. But unlike Renae, Vanessa doesn't seem to know she is pretty. She wears her dark brown hair shorter in a cropped style and always wears a light layer of makeup. It's almost like she's trying to hide that she's that beautiful, which messes with Renae's insecurities big time. Renae is all about flaunting it if you've got it.

Vanessa smiles at Renae, not at all mad. "I sit with you all because half of those girls were raised knowing they were the same age as Henry so they could be a potential bride for him, thus are here for him and him only. The other half probably have hidden agendas from their fathers in politics or the military. Plus, you misfits are way more entertaining." She automatically looks towards Marcia.

"So which one are you? Here for Henry or here with an agenda?" Renae asks rudely again.

"Neither. Or I guess you could say an agenda. My dad would kill me if I didn't give it my best, and he would hear about it too. So here I am. It's not like we can quit if we wanted to. They tell us when we leave if you haven't noticed," she responds, ignoring Renae's continued rudeness.

We all know now that Vanessa's dad is some sort of important military man. She hasn't really been all that forthcoming in telling us what he does, but she hasn't been trying to mislead us about who he is either.

Attie's eyebrows raise and she leans in closer in excitement as we broach her favorite topic. "So how long have they been training or whatever to be with Henry?"

"Since grade school. When he would come for yearly tests, all the girls would throw themselves at him, and I mean we are talking since first grade! I know you fancy him Attie, and I hope he likes you because you are a total sweetheart, but know that some of those girls would literally claw your face out in order to have him," Vanessa says truthfully and quickly glances at Renae as if thinking that it sounds like something Renae would do.

"Thanks for telling us, Vanessa," I say and mean it.

I would rather know that now versus later if I make it very far in this. It seems I'm already behind if people have been training for this. Even the other townships have been training for the Culling apparently.

The topic of conversation then leads to the other boys and Attie runs down the hallway to get her packet of information. We have the great debate on who is the most handsome from just the pictures and get insider information on the boys from the girls in the same township. We avoid Henry as everyone knows if they want to be Madam President, Henry is the best shot. Attie just holds on to his picture as we go through the rest.

When we get to the picture of Maverick, Vanessa actually sounds interested for once.

"Now there is a boy that I would chase," she says proudly. "He's got brains and looks. Hopefully, he's taller than me."

"Nope, I want this one," Marcia picks up the picture of the very muscular boy named Bronson from Denver and imitates him by flexing her muscles, or trying to.

Vanessa snorts a giggle, knowing but seeming uninterested in all the Denver boys.

Agnes picks the almost laughing guy from Galveston named Trent. Renae picks Benjamin and winks at me knowing he is from Omaha. Everyone but me has sort of picked someone at this point. Marcia looks at me and gestures with her head for me to choose.

On a whim, I decide to pick Lyncoln, the lone man not smiling. Mr. Blue-eyes. I figure I will get teased the least about him. Like someone this intimidating and attractive would even talk to me anyway.

"Oh, really?" Vanessa smiles with raised eyebrows in surprise.

"He looks confident and… dangerous? Maybe mysterious? I want to know who 'peed on his pillow'," I explain, borrowing a Marcia phrase and wink at her.

"Go figure. Well you've got that right about the dangerous," Vanessa laughs.

"What do you mean?" Attie asks intrigued although she holds on to Henry's picture for dear life.

"You will just have to find out for yourselves." Then she looks at me and shakes her head while smiling.

****

"I wish I never had to pee. Ever again!" Marcia groans, "My legs are killing me."

I giggle as we leave to go back to our rooms after breakfast Monday morning. Since the fitness test on Sunday was quite long, the rest of the day we got free time to get to know one another and study up on our classes and the load of new information. I rather enjoyed the fitness test as afterward we were escorted by our guards out to the gardens around the inner building of Mile High. It was the first sunlight I had seen for a week and I loved it.

"So since it's Monday, we have officially made it past the first cut, don't you think?" I ask, still doubting I really made it.

"I would assume so. I better have. I can't move. They'd have to wheel me home," Marcia shrugs dramatically as we wait for the elevator.

Neither one of us comments on how we are that much farther to helping our families, but knowing how much Marcia adores her family, I know we are both thinking it.

"I just wish they would make an announcement of some sort or something. Like, 'Hey, you made it!'"

"Screw that! I just wish I didn't have to wear heels every day," Marcia laughs. "I mean, come on!"

I laugh too, "Good point. How did the Madam President do it?" I shake my head in wonder. I have had to soak and massage my feet numerous times. Yesterday was fabulous as I wore my new tennis shoes we were given for the fitness test all day long. Glorious. Who knew tennis shoes could be so therapeutic?

We board the elevator and go to our rooms to freshen up. I'm really growing close to Marcia, more so than the other girls, and I hope for both our sakes we stick around for a while.

After adjusting my skirt suit, fixing my hair and makeup, and putting my heels back on, I'm ready to go with plenty of time to spare. I journal a little bit and then decide to head to Culling class.

Since it's morning, Jamie will be delivering me to class as he has been doing the day shift for now. I've made it a point to ask my guards questions every day to get to know them better. I know that Sarge has three children already and wouldn't mind a few more, and not just because the country strongly urges it; he just genuinely likes kids. I know that Jamie is the youngest of four brothers who are all in the military at some position or another. Jamie reminds me so much of Ashton that it seems to help me not miss him as much.

"So are your brothers stuck here for the Culling too?" I ask.

I know Sarge says he's missing his family because he barely gets to see them until we are done, or until I'm done, but he told me he wants me to make it as far as I can anyway.

"One other brother, yes. But not as a guard," he says stiffly.

"Well can you tell me what he does?" I ask.

"No," he responds, unusually short-lipped.

"Would I even want to know?" I ask with raised eyebrows. I'm finding there is a lot more going on behind the scenes to the Culling than I ever would've thought.

"No."

Hmmm. Okay then. Time to change the topic so he doesn't seem so tense.

"So does your mom like all of you being in the military? I know I said it before, but I will say it again, that poor woman!"

"She doesn't have much choice, but yes she loves it. My oldest brother and his wife are expecting their first baby, so she is currently over the moon. I think she wants it to be a girl so she isn't so outnumbered." He lights up when talking about this brother, much unlike the other one.

"I can't wait for my brother to get married and have kids," I say thinking of Ashton. He is almost 23. Men have seven years to find a mate and must be married by 25, while women have only four years and must be married by 22. It seems a little odd, but since the men have military training and the women are strongly urged to have at least three children by the time they are 30, it's just the way it is. Most women get married around 20 and most men get married around 23.

"It's something special. Marriage that is," he says and smiles.

I know from our previous discussions that Jamie was married when he was 20 to his childhood sweetheart and then his wife sadly passed away from a brain aneurysm shortly after. He hasn't yet remarried, although by law he will have to when the allotted five years is up since he doesn't have kids.

"You'll find her," I smile sadly, full of empathy for his having to lose his wife so young. "She can never replace your wife, but you'll find her."

"Thanks," he says and reaches over to ruffle my hair even though he probably shouldn't. We are becoming more and more like brother and sister every day.

He leaves me at the door like usual. I grab a bottle of water, sit down, and quietly wait for class to begin. After waiting for what seems like forever, I look at my watch and see that our class should have started over five minutes ago. That just never happens. We all look around at each other wondering what we should do and if this is another test of some sort.

About that time, our instructor, Professor Bennett, and two guards arrive at the front of the room. Sometimes Professor Bennett is dressed in his military uniform, some days in a suit and tie. Today he is in his military uniform. For some reason it makes the gray hair he is starting to get look more noticeable.

"As you can see," he begins very obviously upset and all business, "we are late in starting class. We have an issue that needs to be addressed." He loudly calls out, "Ms. Julia Collins."

We all stop and stare at her. From the tone of his voice, she's in deep trouble. She's the girl I sat by for the first written exam. In what little conversations I have had with her, she seems very intelligent, shy, but intelligent nonetheless.

She looks nervous but gives a confident, "Yes, sir?"

"Did you or did you not try to contact a boy in the Culling from your township?"

"I did. I jus--" she doesn't even get to finish trying to explain.

"A simple yes or no will suffice. Did you or didn't you?" he says more rudely than I have ever seen the professor. His voice is boomingly loud. Borderline yelling. He's about to blow a gasket.

"I tried to," she says honestly and looks a little ashamed. "I didn't, but I did try to."

"Did you or did you not know it was against the Culling rules, the ones which you were told and received on the day you got here?" He begins walking towards her.

"I did," she says looking nervous and worried.

He slams his hand down on the corner of her table, making us all jump. "You are dismissed from the Culling. For not following directions, your family is demoted from your original positions in your township. You will serve a week in jail and three months community service in your township. You will never see Denver ever again. Do I make myself clear?"

Holy crap! That's a bit harsh.

Julia's face turns red and tears start to form as she struggles to keep herself composed. "I'm sorry. I just had to warn him..."

"ENOUGH!" he yells and grabs her by the arm harder than he needed to as he forces her to stand up.

I have never seen him lose his nerve like this, or be so...*violent.*

"You are done here. If any more discussion needs to be made, I should remind you that jails and community service aren't the only forms of punishment this country has in its arsenal," he says quietly as he moves her forward to the guards. I happen to be sitting near the wall by the door, so I hear every word of it. A shudder moves through me as I realize he's talking about expulsion.

It's a cruel form of punishment really only used immediately post-Trident for those trying to disrupt the balance of the new government. Expulsion meant you were on your own, no food, no water, in the middle of nowhere, and more than likely would find death by the populous numbers of predators in the wild. It's basically a death sentence, but a seemingly more humane way of doing it. And it's beyond harsh, even if he is just threatening her.

"Please. I will do anything. Just not my family!" she begs him, tears now streaming freely down her face.

"Too late," he glares then gestures to the guards, "Go ahead and take her."

They quickly remove her and we can hear her crying all the way down the hallway to the elevator.

He turns back to the rest of us. "Let that be a lesson to you all. You are not here for you. You may not do as you please. You are here to be molded into the next leaders of the country. You will participate, you will do your best, and you will follow the rules, or there will be consequences." He looks around the room at every one of us as his threat settles in, and then his face softens for only a moment. "This isn't an easy process. I should know, I was a candidate in the last one. But this is a matter of national security. We have to be able to trust you to run our country. If you can't handle this process, you definitely won't handle the presidency. Oh, and you all have officially made it past the first cut. Class dismissed."

Our Culling class only lasted a few minutes.

No one moves until well after he storms out of the room and down the hallway.

What the heck just happened?

Chapter 5

L ater that night, I can't help but think that Julia knew something that I don't. Who was she trying to warn and why? I look through my study guides over the things we are learning. Since I doubt it's about etiquette, I study the other two classes thoroughly, coming up with nothing. We have a test on the second Culling coming up, but that's mainly names and people. Something just doesn't add up. The little I knew of Julia, it seems uncharacteristic of her to blatantly disregard the rules like that.

I then go to my packet and look through the Galveston boys. Which one was she trying to get to? She said she had to warn him about something. What was it? If it wasn't something she learned from class, she must have heard it from someone. Who were her friends? I make a conscious decision to try to get to know Honor and Haley better as they were both from her township and might know more. Maybe not tomorrow because I don't want to seem snoopy, but definitely soon. What had that girl so concerned that she took such a huge risk? I don't sleep well that night, tossing and turning about Julia.

The very next morning my week gets worse as Agnes is missing from breakfast. I try to tell myself that she just overslept and is skipping breakfast, but then she misses both morning classes and in Professor Bennett's class we have the test on the second Culling. Then she is still absent at lunch. It would make it easier if there were more girls missing.

I would know then that more cuts were being made, but the end of the first set of cuts was just yesterday.

After dinner, I finally summon up every ounce of courage I have and catch Elle in the hallway after our written exam.

"Elle. I know I'm probably out of line, but can you just tell me if Agnes is gone? Can you tell me that she's okay? She isn't in any sort of trouble like Julia is she?"

"You know I can't, Reagan." Elle smiles sadly which makes the tears well up in my eyes. She puts a hand on my arm and says, "Just trust the process."

"Some days that is easier than others." I shrug and leave to get in the elevator with Sarge. I'm almost in tears by the time I reach my room. I don't want to go in there. I love my bed, but today this place seems more like a jail. First Julia and the way she left. Now Agnes? And no one can even tell me she's okay? What the heck?

As I get to the door to my room, Sarge tries to give me a smile of confidence but I'm not in the mood for everyone and their empty support. I let myself in my room, change into my pajamas, turn out the lights, hold onto the picture of my family from home and hug it to my body as I cry.

****

The next morning, Professor Bennett is back to his usual calm and kind self. This is the first time teaching us since Julia left because we had a test yesterday.

"Good morning ladies." He lets out a huge sigh and pauses. "I need to apologize for losing my cool on Monday. I realize now that it must have scared some of you. As a member of the Culling Board of Directors,

I take this very seriously. What you may not know is that not all presidents were properly suited to run our country and the results were not always satisfactory. It has taken a while to perfect the process of the Culling. A lot is at stake here. We can't afford to have the wrong person at the helm of our country."

We all kind of look around confused as this is the first any of us have ever heard of this. All four presidential couples have been well esteemed. Until now, anyway.

"You see, the Culling has a lot of built-in tests and precautions we take in getting to know the candidates on a personal level." He looks at me as he says this and it makes me wonder if he knows about my concerns with the monitoring. "It has to be this way because we have come across some huge mistakes in the past. It will be harder for you this time around than it ever has been before. Why? Because we don't want to make the mistakes of the past. Madam Johans and President Kane were not very good people. Neither of them cared about the affairs of the country or what state of ruin we were in. They only cared about themselves and the title, essentially royalty. Their power-hungriness was a disaster and almost tore us apart. In fact, the Johans retired only because they were about to be impeached.

"That's all I can tell you for now, but understand that as in all governments, there are parts of what goes on here that are not known by the general public. You are not allowed to know everything at this point. But please understand that the farther we get in this process and the more we come to trust you, the more you will learn. When you make it to the final eight, you will be sworn in and under oath to not disclose this new information to the public. Punishments for doing so will be of the highest regard. Those so called 'secrets' keep our country safe. Those secrets can be the difference between life and death for some of our citizens so we take it very seriously. The only reason I'm telling you this now is because I don't want you to doubt your country because I lost my cool over Julia's actions. I don't want you to doubt this process. We are just trying to weed out the ones that aren't qualified and find the few that are." He pauses and runs a hand through his jet-black but graying hair.

"That being said, we are going to fast forward a bit and then go backward. President Maxwell, our fourth post-Trident President, is an amazing leader and man. I would know as I was in the final four of our Culling with him. We could have been adversaries, but instead, I consider him a friend for life. He has served our country greatly. He has made great advances. But, he is aging. We both are as you can tell." He smiles and gestures to the gray in his hair before continuing, "Running a country comes with a weight of responsibility. Running one such as ours in the condition of the world today is even more responsibility. This job isn't for the faint of heart. The Maxwells have done their best and made great strides in putting our country back on its feet. The President is getting up there in age and rather than become ill or die, leaving us without a president for the duration of the Culling, he has decided he would like to help find the next leaders with a sound and still working mind. Unlike his predecessor who served until death.

"Today, we will begin learning about the Culling that I was in with President Maxwell and President Kane's son too. Since I was there, I will be able to offer you an insider's point of view of the whole thing. I have been in your shoes, and I know it can be hard. Before we begin though, I have one announcement I need to make." He pauses again and smiles, apparently about to deliver some good news.

"The Fifth State of the Union Canidatorial Ball has been scheduled for next Friday. And yes, that means you will finally meet the boys." He stops to wiggle his eyebrows and multiple girls gasp or make excited noises. "Some of you have shocked faces, and yes, that means we will be down to 25 girls or less at that point, the halfway mark. The end of the second cuts will be this Friday. We have made enough observations thus far that we are fairly confident in our pool of 25. Many of you will be going home. You should know that you should still be proud of what you accomplished here. You have served your country well. It just takes a special type of woman to run the country."

He looks up as if remembering something, "Oh, and on the topic of the promotions for your family. We have decided to change the original guidelines and reward your families once if you make it to the final 35, and again at the halfway point so there are still two promotions involved as promised. We did this as it gives a clearer guideline since the cuts are running together. It should give more families overall the promotions. So lots of exciting stuff in the next few weeks. Ladies, ready or not, the Culling is moving forward."

Gasps are heard throughout the room as he finishes and it sinks into all of us that this is happening faster than any of us ever thought. We are already down seven girls counting Julia. That means 18 of us will be going home in the next week and two days. And we've only been here 11 days. I guess I thought it would take more time than that. I miss my family and would love to check up on Agnes, but I'm not ready to leave yet.

I'm a little surprised that I fully and wholeheartedly want to stay, and then there is also the part about the boys. I give myself a pep talk and try to calm down. It's best not to get my hopes up. I will more than likely be home by next Friday, I just hope I make it to the final 35.

****

"I just don't understand how they can already know the 25, or 35 for that matter," Attie says saddened as we sit around chatting at lunch.

The monitors. That's how.

I glance at Vanessa while Attie is speaking, wondering if she knows what I know. I can't be the only one in our group that has caught on about the monitors. As Attie continues talking, Vanessa doesn't say anything but just nods when it's appropriate. I haven't gotten to know Vanessa like I know Marcia or Attie, but I still think the world of her.

She's harder to get to know because she has a backbone that most girls don't. Some of the Denver girls are quite prissy or vain being raised their whole lives to be proper politicians' wives, but Vanessa is different. Stronger. More guarded. Like she's in the military herself, though I know that isn't possible.

Attie ends her rant by getting choked up and saying, "I don't want to say goodbye to you guys yet."

"Now, now." Marcia pats her on the shoulder. "You won't even have to say goodbye. They don't do goodbyes here." She grins.

"Oh. That so does not help," Attie says stifling a sob but giving her a slight smile. "Promise me you will email?" She takes a moment to look at each of us individually.

Vanessa perks up. "And this is about the time I wish we still had cell phones. Can you imagine how people used to be able to communicate every day to one another using phones while being hundreds of miles apart? There was even this program that let everyone see other people's pictures and keep in touch with them constantly. Like every day! Multiple times a day even," she thinks out loud while shaking her head. We all know that she works in communications and is fascinated with both new and old uses of it.

"Well steal us some phones, girl!" Marcia is being typical Marcia and keeping the mood light to help cheer Attie up.

"Even if I could, and I can't, and I wouldn't, but even if I could, the signal towers would have to be back into working order and they are definitely not. Do you know how long it would take to fix every tower between our townships? We hardly use them here and it took a long time to get what we do use here up and going," Vanessa elaborates. "That's why we use a radio system over Wi-Fi."

"Vanessa. It wasn't a serious suggestion." I look at her smiling. If you mention anything about communications, the normally laid-back Vanessa just rambles on for days.

"Oh. Oops. Well then heck yeah I will," Vanessa throws her hands up and smiles as she says it.

"Thanks for that, Vanessa." Attie smiles, getting over her bout of sadness.

"On the bright side, we get to meet the boys in a week and a half!" Renae chips in. "I can't wait for my attendant. I'm sick of doing my own hair and makeup."

I shouldn't be surprised by her statement, but I can't help but be. I can't think of a reason why Renae would be here while Agnes got sent home, but I guess it isn't my place to make those inferences.

"Oh. I did consider that," Attie smiles excitedly.

"Here's to making it to the 25, ladies!" Marcia says, putting her soda bottle in the air in cheers. We all put our bottles or glasses up with her and then take a drink.

As we all laugh, Marisol rudely storms away and says under her breath, "Fat chance."

We roll our eyes or shake our heads. That girl better be going home soon.

****

"So as we have been discussing in more detail than you ever thought you needed to know, some of our DNA is just naturally immune to Trident. It's even more mystifying than Trident's complex makeup that some people are simply immune," Professor Zax explains the next morning in our classroom turned into a laboratory complete with microscopes.

"As you learned the past week, some of the survivors are genetically immune, we call those people the 'resistant'. Others test positive to Trident, but yet have had zero symptoms. We called them the 'receptors'. It's like these people had the virus but lived, except for the fact that they didn't have any symptoms at all, not from any of the three phases. The virus just laid dormant within their body. And of course, there was the very small population of people that weren't immune but never contracted Trident either. We called them the 'susceptible', meaning Trident susceptible." Professor Zax pauses, gathers his thoughts, and absentmindedly runs a hand through his mustache.

"Now you should know, as freaked out as everyone was post-Trident, as soon as the scientists figured this all out, they moved everyone around and kept the receptors, resistant, and Trident-susceptible in different Bunkers. Which weren't underground as the name implies but rather were old military bases. There weren't as many receptors, so they were isolated in one bunker. The group that was neither resistant nor receptive was also in a separate Bunker, the smallest of them. Please understand that this group of 1,000 people or less were just never exposed to Trident and still ran the risk of getting it. The implications of that were very intense." He stops and shakes his head a moment before continuing with this information we all have never heard of before.

"There was just wide-spread panic afterward and though most people were finding out they were in fact immune, they were still frightened of it after all the death they had just lived through. Or what if the virus mutated again and they were no longer immune? At that point, it felt like Trident was a permanent fixture.

"You should know that the Bunker segregation was not at all a happy one, especially from the receptors. Their blood cultures looked identical to the resistant and they posed no threat to spreading Trident. They were just as immune as anyone else. Husbands and wives, if they even both survived Trident, could be separated if one was a receptor and one a resistant. Even worse, mother and child. Can you imagine?" He pauses again for emphasis, allowing us all to consider that.

"Now the other group, the Trident-susceptible group, they were even more so the hot topic of the time. What were we to do with a group of people that ran the risk of carrying Trident on? We couldn't dispose of or kill them after so much death already. We desperately needed them for the gene pool too. Since everyone else was immune, they shouldn't get sick, but they were trying to choke out Trident, not slowly keep it going." He stops again. "And if a single one of the susceptible contracted Trident, it could potentially kill them all."

"So what happened?" a girl named Morgan from Vegas asks.

"After two years of complete and total isolation, the susceptible were allowed to finally join the State of the Union."

There is an audible, collective gasp in the room at that. "I'm sure that is new information to most of you, that we didn't just welcome with open arms everyone from pre-Trident, even if they were United States citizens. In fact, the whole situation brought about by fear and tragedy brought out the ugliest in people. It is not a time period to be proud of, but definitely a time to learn from.

"Now. Moving on. Eventually, some crazy person in charge thought it would be a good idea to produce offspring from resistant and receptors. Their line of thinking was that it would double the immunity." He stops, shakes his head, and I can see a few Vegas girls fidget in disapproval.

"Medically, we know that once you are immune, you have full immunity. There is no such thing as double immunity. But because of this crazy idea from a politician, not a medic or a scientist, they mixed two bunkers and there were babies like crazy because the people wanted to ensure there was no way they would have to see their children exposed to Trident. Some were made in a lab artificially and some…" he pauses and blushes, "Well, I think you have all had biology, you know how it works.

"Also, the Trident-susceptible were required to only reproduce with resistant through artificial insemination regardless of their marital status pre-Trident. This caused more strife because not many resistant women wanted to carry a baby from a susceptible and vice versa.

"So there were babies everywhere and it was a mess. Enter the first President, President Walters. A few short years in, it was becoming quite clear that the Bunker system as it was, was going to lead to a civil war. How could we have a war with so few people and so soon? We were making headway on helping the population increase, but it was a total disaster. Babies were hot commodities but families were becoming extinct.

"So President Walters did away with the rules when starting to create the townships that they would transition to a few years later. He did a trial township of those willing and mixed all three groups. The people in this group couldn't disclose which group they came from. It thrived. He then slowly started making townships one by one, using mixed groups from the bunkers. He emphasized the family dynamic and did away with artificial inseminating. People even got to choose their townships.

"The almost five years of the Bunkers were rough. Trident left people resentful and scared. Being stuck in the Bunkers for so long didn't help matters. They didn't need to stay in the Bunkers that long, but everyone was too afraid to come out of isolation. That and there was nowhere to go and death everywhere they could go. There was not a single city that they could occupy without having to clean up the death and destruction first. Trident impacted us for many years after the pandemic and is still impacting us today," he finishes intelligently.

"Now. We will be doing lab work today to look at and test your blood to see which of the three groups you have more similarities to. This, of course, is a test because we have documentation of all babies born post-Trident and have the documents for all of your lineages. Please break into groups of three and let me show you how we are going to go about this." He slaps his hands together excitedly, finally ending his teaching.

We quickly shuffle to our stations in groups. He shows us the tests and test order used that tells us to pour in different chemicals and look for reactions. The more reactions for one way, the more lineage in that group. It is actually quite complex if you have all three in your lineage and your blood won't respond to many of the tests. We have vials of the different chemicals in front of us, as well as small vials of our blood. They have taken our blood numerous times, so they must have saved some for this.

"Well this is weird," I say to Vanessa and Marcia that I naturally grouped myself with.

"Totally irrelevant. We are all immune to Trident now. And Trident is gone." Vanessa rolls her eyes as if annoyed.

"True, and I think I would rather not know if I have a long line of Trident-susceptible people in my descendants," Marcia adds.

"I'm just glad things are more organized now," I say, shaking my head at this new information.

"So you mean you're glad you get to bump uglies to make babies the good old fashioned way?" Marcia wiggles her eyebrows and winks making Vanessa burst out laughing.

I blush bright red and am glad when Professor Zax interrupts with more instructions.

A few short hours later, the three of us have determined that Vanessa and Marcia have more receptive in their bloodlines and I have more resistant. We pass another meaningless test with flying colors.

****

Friday, only three more girls have gone home, so that means in a week there will be fifteen more of us leaving. We have another short fitness test at 6 am before breakfast and are told to report to Cullings class immediately after. We all look tired and nervous about the upcoming week. Only five more girls to the 35 mark and that means promotions for our families. And if we survive the next week, we get to meet the boys. It's exciting but tremendously nerve-wracking too.

After waiting for what seems like forever for class to start, Professor Bennett comes storming in the room wearing full military gear again. I'm immediately nervous. The last time class started late, Julia was forcibly removed from the Culling. The way he's standing today isn't quite that intense though.

"Ladies. Cullings class is canceled for today, along with all other classes. You do have a different sort of test taking place. As you know, you have had numerous verbal tests. We will now be giving you another verbal test but this time it will be a lie detector test. As long as you answer truthfully, it should be a breeze. You are dismissed to stay in your rooms until you are retrieved for your test. No socializing. All meals will be brought to you. Unfortunately, you will do a lot of waiting today," he explains all business.

We look around nervously and one by one file for the door. There isn't much chatting going on. This is a big deal and we all know it. Who will survive this test? And why do I have such a pit in the bottom of my stomach about it? Probably because with fifteen of us leaving in the next week, this test is going to carry some heft to it.

Jamie is also unusually quiet and drops me off at my door. I decide to quick shower then journal for a while. When I am done with that, I decide to study up on our classes. In etiquette we are having a test soon on full dining propriety. Before coming here I didn't know a salad fork from a real fork. A fork is a fork. I study place settings for a while but can no longer take it. I finally resort to reading the book I brought with me though I'm distracted and have to backtrack and re-read sentences more than once.

Exhausting all things to do, I go to the window in my room where I frequently spend time and look out. From my window, I can see a few trees from the garden below, the outer building of Mile High, and also the sky and area around the stadium with the mountains in the distance. Today is a partially cloudy day. If Ashton was here we would be making comments about the shapes of the clouds and what they look like. The trees in the garden are just starting to change colors for fall and it makes me miss home even more.

After that I decide to lie down. I don't feel that tired after the three-mile run and weights we just had to do, but I should try to at least relax. I may not sleep, but at least with my eyes closed, I know I can think without being monitored. Even then I know the cameras are still there somewhere. After what feels like an hour, I drift off. I wake up hours later, a short half hour before it ends up being my turn for the big test.

Sarge delivers me to the testing room. He doesn't talk or say a word the whole way which doesn't ease my fears. Neither does the room itself. It's a huge, dark room with what looks like rubber walls. Elle is there along with the tester I have had before and another angry looking tester man. When they did the verbal in my room, it was much less ominous. There is tension in the air and it's as if this entire room was created to intimidate the crap out of us.

Mission accomplished.

They hook me up to all sorts of cords and set up the lie detector and inform me to keep to yes and no answers. They also inform me that I may not repeat or discuss anything from this test with any of the girls. In no time at all I'm all hooked up and ready to go.

This time the other man is asking the questions.

"Is your name Reagan Scott?" he starts.

"Yes." I don't even smile. This test seems more serious.

"Are you from Omaha?"

"Yes."

"Are you 18?"

"Yes."

"Do you miss your family?"

"Yes."

"Did you have a boyfriend before coming to the Culling?"

"No." It would be interesting to know if anyone has lied to this question.

"Do you have anyone in mind for the required age to marry of 21?"

"No."

"Do you find any of the boys attractive?"

"Yes."

He asks me stupid question after stupid question about my family, Omaha, people I know, my friends at home, my friends here, the other girls here, the boys here that we haven't even met, things from my classes, if I still have my innocence intact or how many people I have slept with, you name it. I've been sitting in the chair for at least ten minutes when the questions take a turn and start to get more interesting.

"If a family member of yours were to do something against the State of the Union, would you disown them completely?" the sinister tester man asks. I used to think the other tester with the matching gray hair and eyes was evil but have now decided that he's a cup of tea compared to this guy.

I look at him confused. This is irrelevant. And a stupid question.

"Depends," I say.

"Yes or no only," he reminds me quite rudely.

"Well, the question is irrelevant," I answer rudely, returning his attitude and quite surprised with my guts as I have the nerve to stare him down. I'm glad my voice doesn't portray how nervous I really am.

"Yes or no," he says this time almost yelling at me.

In an act of pure defiance, I just continue to stare at him and say nothing. Five or six seconds pass of total silence. I'm sure I'm going home soon anyway and I will not give him an answer he wants just because he wants it. I will not change for anyone. I will not lie and say I will disown a family member of mine. I would never do that, no matter what they did.

He stands up and slams his clipboard down causing Elle to jump. I don't flinch and am proud of myself for it. "Yes or no!" He does yell this time.

"No. I would never disown my family," I answer honestly and quietly.

Screw this test. I don't care if I fail, they are being jerks. I won't be disloyal to my family just to make it further in the Culling, promotions or not.

"Yes or no answers only," he reminds me and sits back down.

For just a slight moment I think I see a hint of emotion there. He seemed...amused? I'm sure I didn't catch it right because the man was just screaming at me. Gray-eyes is a walk in the park compared to this guy. He takes it to a whole other level.

"If someone formerly banished from the State returned seeking assistance, would you provide it?"

These questions are getting hard. I know what I'm supposed to say, but I just can't make myself do it.

"If they were rightfully banished with cause and a threat to national security, then no I wouldn't provide it," I offer seeing as that is the answer they are looking for, but add, "But case by case I would try to see if there was a way to provide help by some other means."

"Yes and no only," he snaps annoyed.

I lean forward and look him directly in the eyes. "I heard you the first time."

Is my temper getting the best of me? Sure is. But this guy is just a jerk. I see that flash of emotion again but don't have time to process it because he keeps going. How can he be amused and pissed at me at the same time? I'm not amused at this point. I'm just pissed. And it pisses me off even more that he is amused in my pissed-off-ed-ness.

"If you found the people responsible for releasing Trident, would you punish them?"

Finally an easy one. "Yes," I smile sarcastically while giving my proper one-word answer.

"If someone was a threat to the country and had valuable information that was needed to protect the people, would you approve of doing anything necessary to get the information?"

"No."

"Well, would you approve threatening them?"

"Yes."

"Would you approve inflicting any personal harm to them?"

"Look. Just threaten their lives and make sure they know that you are serious. If they want to live, they'll give it up. If they don't, then no matter what you do, they won't talk and the information will just die with them," I explain.

"You seem to have an issue with following directions, Ms. Scott." This time it isn't a question.

"Yes," I answer, my voice dripping in sarcasm. I smile while looking him dead in the eyes.

I don't know how I channeled this courage, but I'm glad I have it for this test because this test sucks! I just want to punch him in his evil face. Then roundhouse kick him in the nuts just for good measure.

"Do you think it's appropriate for a government to withhold information from its people?"

I think of the monitoring and how they withheld that information, but how it will hopefully be used to find the best-suited leaders. "Yes."

"Do you want to become Madam President?"

"Yes."

"Will you marry anyone in order to do so?"

I shrug thinking of Benjamin. I wouldn't even be allowed to lead with a jerk like that at my side. "No."

"Would you work against your friends in order to become Madam President?"

If it were absolutely necessary, but not in a degrading way. I might work against them, but I wouldn't tear them down in the process. That's what I want to say, but I'm trying to play nice and get back on this evil man's good side, so I just reply with a simple, "Yes."

"If becoming Madam President meant that you could never talk to your family again, could you do it?"

I smile and shrug. "Well if I had that much power, I would do it regardless."

He rolls his eyes before moving on to the next question. "Would you do anything to protect your family?"

"Yes."

At this point, they turn on a light in the room next to ours. What looked like a rubber wall is actually glass. I see Ashton bruised, battered, and tied down. He barely looks conscious and I would be worried he was even alive, but I see his head limply roll to the side. He's sitting in a chair in a side room by himself. The ropes around his wrists are so tight his wrists are raw and look like they've been bleeding. His face is bruised and he looks awful. What did they do to him? An even better question, why?

What is going on?!

I'm out of my chair before I even know I'm moving. I pull all of the cords attached to me with me, tearing some off my hands with my sudden movement. I hear my chair drop to the floor with a bang. I run over to the glass and bang on it trying to let Ashton know I'm here.

Dear Lord, is he even alive?

"Ashton, Ash. Can you hear me?"

He can't even see me. I feel tears burn in my eyes and begin running down my cheeks, but I don't care. None of this makes any sense. Why? Why would they do this? Was it because he told me not to trust anyone? I immediately become enraged.

WHY?

I wipe the tears away and spin around looking at the testers, who obviously know why Ashton is here and why they beat the crap out of my brother. Through them is the only way I get to him. And I will fight them all if I have to.

"What did you do?" I ask them. I try not to look behind me at Ashton otherwise the tears will come flooding back. "I know he didn't do anything so why? Why would you hurt an innocent man?"

I walk over to where they are sitting, pick up the evil man's clipboard, and slam it down just like he did with me. "Answer me!" I yell and throw his clipboard to the ground breaking it in the process. None of them say anything.

"Let him go," I plead and command both. "I'll do whatever you want. I'll quit. I just don't get you people. You monitor our every move. You test us and test us and test us. Then you beat up my brother? Why?" I'm so angry I feel like it's about to take over my body. "I NEED TO KNOW WHY!" I scream at them.

No one moves or says anything. They all just sit there watching me.

I see that amused look flash across both testers' faces this time and I lose it. "What is so amusing about this gentlemen? And you Elle. *You* had me fooled. I didn't think you were a cruel woman but what do I know? Turns out you are if you would allow this to happen."

I hear her suck in a breath and it looks almost as if she wants to cry. She wants to cry, but it's my brother in there beat within inches of his life? How does that even make sense?

"You just sit there rudely asking me all sorts of questions and you beat up my brother and can't even give me the courtesy of telling me the reason?" I ask confused. I'm about to just head for the door and find a way to get to Ashton but...

That's when it clicks.

Elle almost crying. They're not saying a word. None of it is logical reactions. Sarge told me everything is a test. This is a test within a test. They aren't saying anything because they want to see what I do. They want to see how I react. Of course. If Ashton was really in trouble, they wouldn't show it to me during a test. This situation is staged. They must have beat him up to see how I'd react.

I shake my head looking at them and let out a snort. "Well, this has been a sick and twisted little test within a test. I hope my reaction has been entertaining enough for you." I gesture with my arms then pick up the chair and sit back down, crossing my legs and folding my hands like I've been taught in etiquette. "This test is over. Let him go." I glare daggers at the three of them.

More lights turn on in the room and the tester moves to get the pieces of his clipboard. Elle actually smiles at me.

"Congratulations. You passed," my original tester, gray-eyes, informs me.

"Great. Give me my brother," I spit out at them.

"And in a most impressive way, remarkable really," the other one adds and smiles, also ignoring my comment.

All three of them then clap which seems to irritate me even more.

"Most impressive, Reagan," Elle nods with the other two.

I'm sitting there somewhat confused and still angry but not really paying attention to them as my head is turned and my eyes are on

Ashton. I see a door open in the room Ashton is in and a guard walks in and removes his ropes. I'm standing again and move over to the glass which is cold against my hands. I hear the other three making comments about how fast my test was completed.

I snap at them. "You all make me sick. All you are concerned with is my test time when there is a man bleeding in the other room? He may not be your brother, but he is still a human being that you beat the crap out of for a test. Did you do that to everyone's siblings or was this a privilege you extended to just me?"

"Regs! They didn't really hurt me." I turn at the sound of his voice to see Ashton enter the room smiling at me.

I fly across the room and into his open arms. Now I'm crying again and I can't seem to contain it even a little bit. "Are you sure you're okay?" I look him over. He is smiling and seems his usual self, not like someone that just got the crap beat out of him.

"Yeah. It wasn't real. I'm fine." He smiles and puts his hands out for me to see.

"Are you sure?" I reach up and gingerly touch his face where the bruising is.

Elle walks over with a bottle of water and a paper towel and rubs it across his face. Sure enough, it wipes away just like makeup. I reach down and look at his wrists which looked almost like they were bleeding. It all wipes away too. It looks so real. I could have sworn it was. Why was I smart enough to figure out they were testing me, but I wasn't smart enough to know that both parts of the test were staged? I should be disappointed, but am still mostly just angry.

Still crying and not even trying to hide the tears, I look to my instructors. "I'm sorry I lost my cool here, but I'm still not okay with this. Not even a little. It looked so very, very real."

The evil tester man, the new one, smiles at me sympathetically. "That's fine. And don't feel remorse for not knowing it wasn't real." He nods toward Ashton, "Our testing techniques are not at all usual and we have an exceptional makeup artist that is supposed to make it look real. Know that you did very, very well though. This one test tells us volumes about our candidates, and sadly we use it to weed a lot of you out. It tells us how you will react in the worst of circumstances. I would like to say this is our last test of this nature," he gestures to the other room, "but it probably isn't. You definitely passed with flying colors though."

Elle smiles again and it's as if I didn't just call her cruel about sixty seconds ago. "For the next hour or so I will bring you to a room so you may spend some time with your brother before he flies back home. I may be out of line for saying this, but it may be a very long time before you see him again, so enjoy. And, congratulations. You have made it to the final 35."

This time I do smile.

****

"I wish I could've seen your face. I bet you freeeaked," Ashton laughs, all cleaned up and looking normal. Well, as normal as he can look.

"How can you joke about this? I thought they had tortured you," I say, still trying to shake the image out of my head.

He smiles and nods. "Honestly though Regs, if this were reversed, if it was you and they did that to me, I would have killed every one of them. I'm sure you handled yourself well."

I look around the small conference-style room that we are sitting in while eating some dinner. "I wouldn't categorize my reaction as 'well'," I smile.

I know I can talk about the horrifying test I just took with Ashton and Ashton only as I am not to speak of it with the girls. I just wonder where the camera is in this room because I'm sure they wouldn't leave us completely unmonitored. Otherwise I'd ask him why he told me to trust only myself before I left home.

"What did you do?" He smiles slowly as if imagining all the terrible things I could've done.

"Well, first I flew to the window," I begin while rubbing the tops of my hands where the pulse patches were ripped off. "Then I demanded answers and got a little feisty. One of them had the nerve to look amused and I lost my cool. Then it just clicked. If it were real, those wouldn't be normal reactions. They didn't say a word. Not even when I insulted them or yelled. So they had to be doing it just to gauge my reaction."

"A little feisty? I can't wait to tell Mom and Dad. You and your infamous temper." He laughs out loud. A little too hard.

"Hey. I've been keeping it in check," I offer. "Until today, anyway."

"Yeah, you must be if that hot chick said you would be around for a while." He wiggles his eyebrows.

I fidget and avoid looking him in the eyes. This process is more difficult than I assumed. If my performance on that last test taught me anything, it was that I may not be tough enough to win. Or smart enough since I didn't realize it wasn't real that Ashton got beat up. And the evil tester man said this probably wasn't the last test of this nature. What's next? I feel like I'm in over my head here.

"Regs. You can do this. You would make an excellent Madam President." He looks at me like a proud older brother, oddly serious.

"Thanks. I just don't think I'll really get to that point. But thanks anyway. I appreciate the vote of confidence, bro."

He shakes his head at me in that way that tells me a scolding is coming. "Don't give up. This country needs someone like you and you aren't a quitter. Think of it as a game of Monopoly between the two of us. You never gave up on that. If you were going to lose, it would take me six hours to take your money, every last dollar. I'm sure it's going to suck. You are probably going to hate it at some point or another, but you deserve this. You deserve the chance to do something great. Mom and Dad agree." He reaches over and squeezes my hand.

"I made it past the first two cuts now, so we get promoted. So there's that. We might get promoted again if I make it to the halfway point," I say proudly. "That's only ten more girls away."

"Regs, don't put that much pressure on yourself. I mean, it's awesome and it sounds like you'll for sure make it, but you have to quit doing it for us. We're fine. Thank you, and the promotion will be awesome, but do this for you and don't be too hard on yourself. You are a perfectionist through and through," he says seriously before adding, "Sooooo, tell me about these girls?"

I laugh. "That would be the one reason they would have you in jail. You need to find a woman already, Ash. Have you found anyone in the time I've been gone? You are Omaha's most eligible bachelor, you know."

He is well over six foot tall, has strong shoulders and arms though the rest of him is lean, and has sandy hair and greenish-hazel eyes that all the girls swoon over. The girls are always interested; he just hasn't picked one yet and doesn't seem in a hurry to do so.

"No. All the girls I date are just...surface level. All they do is talk about themselves. I need someone...I don't know...a bit deeper than that crap." He shrugs. "Blame mom, she's the hopeless romantic that always spouts off that 'don't settle for anything less than the best' crap."

"Tell me about it," I nod in agreement and smile. Our mom has always wanted us to find love. Law requires us to marry, but she has always told us that instead of finding someone we can live with, we should find someone we can't live without.

"Whatever. You don't even have to worry about it. You'll be Madam President and all grossly in love with our next President," he says with a wink.

I don't tell him that I'm worried none of the boys will even be interested in me. I quickly change the subject. We talk for a half an hour more and eat our meal of steak and potatoes, which Ashton got to request and was quite pleased with.

He fills me in on life in Omaha. After I left, apparently a note arrived from the President thanking them for raising "a fine young daughter" with certificates for keeping a bunch of our harvest food and even some of our meat. I'm glad that we get some benefits for my being here. Although I have only been gone two weeks, he tells me about harvest preparations for the gardens, specifically the tomatoes and cucumbers, and that soon they will be making the switch to working in the greenhouses for the winter. Neither of us like the greenhouses as much, so I know he isn't looking forward to that. We laugh and talk about past harvests and the weather that never seems to cooperate. Before I know it, our time is up.

Ashton leaves and Sarge delivers me back to my room. I change and fall into my fluffy bed. I'm going to miss Ashton now more than ever. I can't help but keep thinking, what else is a test? Is there anything they won't do?

Chapter 6

The next morning at breakfast, five girls are gone, including the girl named Trinity that tried to intimidate me on that first day. I can't say I'll miss her. I'm pleased to see that no one from the group of us, well other than Cadence and Agnes, has gone home. It's bound to happen eventually, but I will take it while I can. It could be any one of us. At any time. Ten more girls will be gone by Friday. But, in officially making it down to the final 35, I should have at least gotten my family a promotion. That is a definite perk in what will be a stressful next week.

"I'm like Vanessa. Just sucking down the coffee today," Marcia says as she slurps her coffee.

She looks miserable. We all do. This leads me to believe that it wasn't just me they used a family member on for the lie detector test. We can't discuss it though, so there is a definite elephant in the room. I don't get why we can't talk about it if we all had a similar test, but whatever.

"Anyone know what we are doing today?" Attie asks cheerfully though even she is looking a little rough.

"Hmm. Hopefully sleeping," Vanessa offers.

Much to our dismay, we have another fitness test with a ton of pushups and squats. I'm not sure what the point of this is, but I enjoy it because afterwards we get to walk around the gardens outside. Later after we shower up, we are taken to etiquette for a final review before yet another stupid test.

Much to our surprise, Professor Dougall has given us a real life scenario for our test. She has invited numerous people for a dinner this evening and we are to dress and act accordingly and she will grade us based on our performance. The Board of Directors will be there as well as two current cabinet members. If there was ever a class I thought I may fail, it's this one. As she keeps explaining how everything will work, I keep getting more and more nervous.

We review everything we know and she walks us through a proper meal setting. She lets us know we are expected back in five hours. We are to eat a light lunch and get ready for this evening. We get to wear one of the gowns in our closet and are allowed to get ready amongst one another.

"This will be fun!" she says in the best mood we have seen her. "It's time we put into practice all of this stuff we've been learning. But don't think that you can shrug this off. This is not a party, it is still a test, my dears. This is making sure you are ready to meet the boys."

Am I?

****

Hours later, I'm ready to go wearing a beautiful, dark green square cut sleeveless dress that is long and to the floor. Marcia and Attie convinced me to flat iron my usually wavy or curly hair. Completely straight, it drops down past the middle of my back. One side of it is pinned back a little bit. I am wearing more makeup than usual, but still keep it natural looking. For the first time since the first day, I'm not wearing my watch. Not that it matters. I know they will be monitoring us one way or another. Everything is a test.

Attie is dressed in a lovely navy that complements her light blue eyes, while Marcia wears a burgundy dress that looks like the color was created just for her skin tone. Since we have only three dress color choices and a variety of styles in each, we choose to look different wearing both different colors and styles. One more glance in the mirror and we are ready to go.

As we enter our normal cafeteria, my breath is taken away. The room has been decorated and transformed into a beautiful dining area complete with music playing softly in the background. There is even a vibrant and quite ostentatious chandelier in the center of the room. Our normal three rows of tables have been resituated into two long rows. Men serve champagne in lovely glass flutes along with some hors d'oeuvres. I have no idea what those are or what they are made of, but they look fancy.

Smiling and saying thank you as I have been taught, I accept one glass of champagne and barely sip it. I'm not even of the old legal drinking age, but I guess they figure if we are old enough to be elected Madam President, we should be able to handle a glass of champagne responsibly.

I talk with Attie and Marcia for a while since we came down together. Attie is giddy and babbling a hundred miles a minute about the room, who she thinks will be here, if we will pass our test, etc. Marcia looks like she would rather be elsewhere and I catch her looking at the door a few times like she wants to escape, but she's in good spirits nonetheless. Compared to our test yesterday, this one should be easy peasy.

It's just the Culling girls for the first hour. I notice some girls are taking more than one glass of champagne and wonder if that is wise since this is a test. I still have my first glass and am sipping it at a pace that will allow me to still be holding it when our guests arrive without the need for another. We haven't really been taught how much alcohol to consume, but I think it's pretty much common sense not to make a drunken spectacle of ourselves.

"I love your dress," I hear the sweet voice of Elizabeth say. I turn and in utter horror see that she and I are wearing the exact same dress. It looks much better on her than on me. Her gorgeous, dark brown hair is in ringlets down her back almost to her butt and her body shape makes the dress look like it was made for her and her alone. She's a vision.

I know she sees the panic on my face, but I have to make the best of the situation. "It looks so much better on you," I smile truthfully.

"Well thank you. I think it looks great on you too!" she pats my arm and then we chitchat for a little bit. I'm finding there is more to this girl than meets the eye and that's frightening. Someone who has just her looks alone is intimidating in this competition. If there is depth to her too, I think we should just call off the whole thing now and give it to her.

"Oh and look, you two aren't the only ones," Marcia interjects and we turn to see Marisol staring down October as they are both wearing shorter versions of the same navy color that Attie is wearing.

"Well at least *we* are acting our age about it," Elizabeth blurts out then puts her hand over her mouth. "Did I just say that out loud?"

"You did," I laugh. "Don't worry about it. Those of us around Marcia here tend to have that characteristic rub off on us."

This makes her laugh and then she and Attie talk about Denver for a while. Renae comes over wearing a poufy burgundy dress and looks to be on at least her second glass of champagne. I see the girl named Haley, from Galveston same as Julia, off to the side and approach her.

She's also wearing dark green, but the tighter version of it with one shoulder strap. She looks flawless. I wish I were confident enough to wear it like she is. She must not try very hard with her appearance most days because she's looking considerably more beautiful tonight. I can appreciate that. She was keeping her beauty in her arsenal to use at a later time. She reminds me of Vanessa, who I still haven't seen yet tonight.

"Reagan, right?" Haley smiles.

"Yep. Haley?" I ask politely.

"Yes. You have such a pretty name," she compliments me.

"Thank you," I say, not used to getting compliments. "How do you like Denver?"

"It's a bit colder than home, but I'm getting used to it. It's not like we have to go outside much anyway." She shrugs.

"I know. It makes me a bit claustrophobic," I say honestly.

"I wonder if we will ever see any other parts of Denver, or if we will just stay here," she thinks aloud.

We talk back and forth for a little bit. I don't want to blatantly drill her for questions about Julia in this setting, but I would like to find out if she knew anything more about why Julia was kicked out of the Culling. Vanessa then comes in wearing a tight-fitting burgundy dress, the same style as Haley's, and looking fabulous. She just has this amazing skill of doing it without trying. Seeing Haley and me first, she comes over to us. Marcia comes over also, with the girl named Chrysanthemum that sat on the other side of me for that first test. She introduces her as Chrys and we all comment on how unique her name is, which matches her dark red hair.

I look around our group and am suddenly proud of the girls I have become friends with. We are a close-knit bunch, but we don't exclude or deny anyone who wants to become part of our group, unlike Marisol and her following. And although I miss Agnes and Cadence, I'm looking forward to making more friends and getting to know the other girls for however long I am here for.

"Hey, guys. Mind if I make proper small talk with you? You seem a bit more welcoming than them," October says interrupting my thoughts as she joins our group. She nods over to where Marisol is standing with her group of friends, all six girls being from Denver. They are definitely not inviting or friendly. Until someone important is around.

"Sure," Marcia says kindly followed up by, "WAIT! Where's your book?"

Knowing how extremely intelligent October is, I'm surprised Marcia doesn't hesitate to goad her. Then again, that's Marcia for you.

"Well, Professor Dougall is displeased with me enough as it is." She shrugs and rolls her eyes.

"Welcome to the club," Marcia laughs.

"What are you always reading, if you don't mind me asking?" Attie smiles at her using her charm.

"It varies. This week? Quantum particle physics," she shrugs and we all just stare at her.

"I have no idea what she even just said. Was that in English?" I joke. She laughs along with the others.

At this point, all three of our Professors arrive. The two men in their official military formal wear, while Professor Dougall wears a beautiful silver gown that is tight to her hips and then flares out. The silver color seems to exactly match the color of her hair and sparkles as she moves. They have barely entered the room before Elle arrives, along with the two testers.

"Good Evening, Ladies," Professor Dougall nods as she makes the rounds.

"Your gown," Attie stammers. "It's amazing!"

"Why thank you, dear," she smiles. "Don't be too jealous. You will get to choose your gown from thousands of gowns if you are to make it to the Canidatorial Ball. Your attendant may even choose to have one specially made or altered to your liking."

I hear a simultaneous gasp from the girls close enough to hear what she just said. It's nice to get dressed up for a change, but we only had a few options. For meeting the boys, we get to wear what we want, as well as take in the handsome men. A bunch of faces flash across my memory of boys I want to meet. I really hope I make it, and I know that is what everyone else is thinking too.

Our big group breaks up to talk to the guests, knowing that if we all approach one guest at the same time, we will fail our test. I briefly greet our other two professors before I stalk down Elle. I approach her while she is getting an appetizer and speaking to the man serving it. Once he leaves, she turns her attention to me.

"You look fabulous, Reagan," she smiles kindly.

"Thank you. I am really, really sorry again for saying what I said to you yesterday." I sheepishly shake my head and double check to make sure that we are by ourselves.

"Hey. I took it as a compliment. I'm the one you felt most comfortable with, so of course you would feel most betrayed by me. I get it." She shrugs and pats my arm, "All is forgiven."

"Thank you."

"Now if you'll excuse me, I must go find Dougall about our surprise guest," she winks and walks off leaving me thinking that it's too bad she's just over the Culling age or I think she could win this herself.

I go next to a small group talking to the tester man that I normally had and I realize I don't even know his name. He knows me better than I might even know myself at this point and I know nothing about him. I can tell from the groups I have seen talking to him and leaving him quickly that most girls are still uncomfortable with both of our seemingly emotionless testers.

When Chrys greets him and leaves, I find myself alone with the man.

"Hello. Okay, so I know we've met on numerous occasions, sir," I smile as I begin, "but I still don't know your name."

"That's okay. No one really does, dear." He doesn't smile but the use of the word dear can't be too bad.

"Would you care to enlighten me?" I raise my eyebrows in anticipation.

"Herman Winters." He almost smiles and takes a sip of his champagne.

"Pleased to meet you, Mr. Winters." I smile, hoping my charm can work half as well as Attie's. I wonder why he didn't give me his military rank like Zax and Bennett did, but don't know how to ask. Knowing that most girls would just walk away at this point, I decide to ask him a question. "Do you have kids, Mr. Winters?"

"Yes. I have two sons and one daughter," he responds, eyeballing me suspiciously since I'm the only one who has stuck around to make small talk with him. His eyes are a very distinct shade of gray which I hadn't seen before in an eye color. Or a hair color either, for that matter, since his eyes and hair weirdly match. It's very disorienting, even when he's being nice.

"And what do you do when you aren't quizzing us for the Culling?" I ask the next question that comes to mind not thinking that it might be a little personal.

"Military work in special forces," he says without emotion again.

"Well, I think I speak for all of us when I say that you definitely specially force answers out of us," I smile.

This time he actually chuckles and I have accomplished my mission. I don't think the testers are as bad as they portray themselves to be. They purposefully try to get under our skin and they have to be intimidating. It's part of their process.

"Well I suppose I should go find the ev--" I stop myself realizing I'm going to refer to the other man as "the evil tester" out loud. I only ever call him that in my head. What was I thinking?

Stupid, Reagan!

He looks somewhat amused. "Who, dear?"

"Well, if you must know, in my head I call him 'the evil tester'," I honestly whisper to him and he stifles another laugh.

"And what did you refer to me as, in your head?" he inquires.

"I would tell you, but then I would have to kill you," I playfully whisper again and am relieved when he takes it well. He was who I referred to as the evil tester until the other guy overtook that title. But I will just keep that little detail to myself. Gray-eyes here doesn't need to know that.

He gives me a genuine smile and gestures for me to leave. "Always a pleasure, Reagan."

Vanessa and Marcia happen to be talking to the man I'm looking for, so I join their group and say hello in a break in conversation.

"Ms. Scott. And how are you doing this evening?" he says rather emotionless as usual.

"I would be better if I weren't about to fail a test, I'm afraid," I joke and the other girls laugh with me.

I see that quick look of amusement, but I don't have time to say anything more because the two cabinet members along with none other than the President himself arrive, all wearing proper tuxes.

I remember Elle saying there was a surprise guest. I think I know who that is now. Knowing the girls will swarm to the three new guests, I stay put even though I don't necessarily want to. I need to find some courage and not put another foot in my mouth before meeting the single most powerful man in the nation. I was friendly but not as formal with Mr. Winters as I should have been. This is a test and I need to focus.

"Ahhh. There he is. Ladies, please excuse me to find some appetizers as I am sure dinner will take a while now," the evil tester man says and I realize I didn't ask his name.

I ask Vanessa in case we happen to be tested on that information later and she says his name is Marvin Alexander. She saved my butt there.

Out of the corner of my eye, I watch girl after girl meet the President. When I see Marisol woo the President with her false facade, I want to vomit. I take a large sip of my champagne and turn facing the other direction. Maybe not watching would be better.

I only have time to meet one of the cabinet members before Professor Dougall makes an announcement. "Ladies and Gentlemen, please find your seats. I realize all of the introductions have not yet been made, but this is hardly your normal dinner party." She smiles at the President and we all file to our named seats.

The President, of course, is at the end, and then about five or six girls down is another guest, and so on for the two tables. I'm pleased to find I'm sitting right across from Mr. Winters and five girls down from the right side of the President. Elizabeth is two girls down from the President, and to my selfish dismay, Renae is sitting right next to him. I sit down and place my napkin properly in my lap and sit the appropriate way. Maybe I will pass this test after all.

Yeah right.

"Ladies. I trust you've had a good stay here," the President makes small talk as we eat. I notice his rather large watch and smile wondering if there is a monitor in there. Probably not!

Elizabeth pitches in with the appropriate answers and realizing five people away I won't really get a shot to say much, I decide to talk to Mr. Winters instead. He seems to be making this hard on us as he is only giving one-word answers to the girls around me as they try to get him to talk. I like a good challenge so I decide to take a turn.

"Mr. Winters," I begin. "Do you know if the mountains are already getting snow?"

"I don't," he says shortly.

"You mean you don't take skiing trips when you aren't testing us?" I ask sarcastically while I finish up my salad and wait for the entrée. I know no one skis much anymore and that those resorts on the mountains are a thing of the past, but I know in order to pass our test we must be able to make proper small talk with our guests. I have no idea why I just asked about skiing of all things, but carrying on small talk with Mr. Winters is a feat! His short answers are tormenting to an ongoing conversation.

"No," he responds with one whole word but his eyes are dancing with amusement. Is he trying to get me to fail?

"How old are your kids?" I squint my eyes at him not giving into his dismissiveness.

"28, 26, and 24," he responds shortly.

"All married off I assume?"

"Yes."

I swear if he gives me a yes or no answer again I am going to kick him in the shins under the table.

"Any grandchildren?" I keep going but realize that I'm rapidly running out of questions and have no idea what to say next.

"Yes," he says almost smiling. Now I've about had it. No more of this yes or no answer business.

"Planning any more late night visits to us, Mr. Winters?" Anytime another girl would pitch in, would be great. Neither girl on either side of him seems willing to hop in and help me out.

"Actually, yes," he nods his head.

"Fabulous," I say with sarcasm then try to harass him back. "I would like to dress accordingly. Not on a Friday?" I smile knowing that only he knows the inside joke.

"I cannot disclose that information to you, Ms. Scott." He smiles and gives a soft chuckle. "I think you will be readily prepared regardless."

I laugh and then in a voice that is completely polite but entirely sarcastic I say, "Now, Mr. Winters. A simple yes or no would have sufficed."

He shakes his head and tries not to laugh. I hear a chuckle from the end of the table and see the President watching our interaction looking quite entertained.

"And this delightfully sassy young lady giving our Mr. Winters grief must be Ms. Scott," he smiles and I'm immediately embarrassed. Especially if he knew the inside joke about the pajamas…or lack thereof. I blush what I am sure is a bright red.

"Yes. Pleased to meet you, President Maxwell. Thank you for the lovely watch," I smile knowing he has probably heard that line numerous times tonight.

"You are most welcome." He winks. "Are you liking your stay here?" he asks genuinely.

"Yes. Of course I miss my family too. But, this is the opportunity and chance of a lifetime." I think of seeing Ashton and how good it felt to talk to him when he was here. "And those beds you have for us make up for missing my family! It's hard to miss them when I am so spoiled." As I finish he laughs along with a few of the other girls, Elizabeth being the only one who really seemed interested in what I was saying. I already appreciate her kindness.

"I remember the feeling well," he begins, "I came from Galveston so I was not used to being pampered either."

"Your Culling took only three months if I remember correctly?" I ask, trying to keep the conversation going.

Elizabeth nods her head in agreement with me.

"Yes. It went rather quickly once I finally won over the heart of my dear Essie, may she rest in peace." He smiles. "Ahhh. To be young. Are you ladies looking forward to meeting the gentlemen?"

I smile at the other girls while we all nod our heads yes. "I think I speak on behalf of all of us when I say that the answer to that question would be a resounding 'yes'."

He chuckles and winks at me again, "I think they are all raring to meet you as well."

The way he says it makes me feel like he's talking to me specifically. Like the boys would want to meet me in particular. How odd. He's a charmer, that one. I almost want to believe him, too! No wonder the people love him if he goes out of his way to make everyone feel special.

We all smile, all taken in with him. Renae asks him a question about Henry being in the Culling and then someone else chimes in and I lose his interest. I'm glad I got what little time I did have with him.

****

Exhausted, I take off my heels and flop on my bed. I think I greeted everyone. I used the correct silverware when I needed to. I only got to talk to the President for a little bit. And when I did, he called me sassy. I'm not sure that is a good start, but at least it's a start. From appearances, I should have passed my test. If Professor Dougall could listen in, and I know she can and more than likely will, I'm sure I utterly failed. She threatened us beforehand about proper conversations and how to properly maintain those conversations and told us our grade was dependent on it.

Ugh.

I take off my dress and change clothes. I have only slept a couple of hours when we are called for another fitness test. I quickly change and follow the girls to our training room for a run. Although the lights are blaring inside, it is completely dark out the windows.

Soon after, we are called for a written test at 5 am over the evening before. We are asked questions about our guests along with the basics. None of us have slept much after having a fitness test at 1 am and only sleeping a few hours. I'm not sure what the point of all this is, other than to make us tired.

After that, we are given another written test, this time on each other. Then we are given a light lunch and another fitness test. At this point, I'm positive they're trying to wear us down and see how we do when we are tired. Unfortunately for me, that isn't good. I'm a monster tired.

We have classes all afternoon and then dinner. Most of us are very tired and ready for bed, but then we are called to Professor Zax to work in groups on a lab regarding Trident DNA. All of us are tired, and girls, so biting people's heads off is standard operating procedure and there is a bit of tension in the room.

After completing that and all of us riding on maybe three hours of sleep, we finally get back to our rooms at 10 pm. I collapse immediately. At midnight we have another fitness test. At 2 am, directly following the fitness test and a shower, Mr. Winters and Elle arrive for a verbal. At 6 am we are given another written test on leadership and past Cullings. It lasts four hours. By noon I'm drinking iced tea like I need it to survive, willing the caffeine to please enter my bloodstream. In our afternoon classes, we are told we will have a cumulative test at 8 pm.

I take my time through that test knowing there will be some girls who will rush through it and finish quickly just so they can finally get some sleep. Tensions are high and we are all deliriously tired. The Canidatorial Ball is only a few days away and ten more of us will be going home, yet all we do is test after test after test after test. I hope I passed. I really want to make it to Friday.

Just four more days.

****

On Tuesday morning, five girls are missing: two from Vegas, one from Detroit, and two from Marisol's group of friends, but not Marisol herself, unfortunately. Chrys and October have officially joined our group and sit with us at lunch now. We are all weary but all happy to have made it this far. I wonder when the other five of us will be going. At this point, I just really want to know if I'll make it to Friday. I know Elle alluded to the fact that I would be around for a while, but I'm still nervous. Making it to the halfway point means my family is promoted again, and as a bonus, I get to meet the boys.

Yes, there's definitely *that*.

After lunch during etiquette class, Professor Dougall gives us a long speech about what is and is not allowed with the boys during the rest of the Culling. She informs us that we will all be going on contraceptives immediately. Apparently in the third Culling, there were two girls that wound up pregnant. So they are putting us on birth control for extra prevention. Seems a little much to me, but I obviously don't have much experience in the boy department. I can't imagine going that far with someone I've just met, but I guess for the other experienced girls here it must be a conversation that needs to be had.

We then start our dance lessons for the ball, which seems to put life back into us after the uncomfortable spiel we just had to sit through. We learn the basics and dance with one another since there are no boys to practice with. Professor Dougall stays on us and more than once picks on me critiquing my "hold." Not letting her get to me, I head to dinner feeling somewhat rejuvenated and excited for the ball. Contraceptives and all.

Sitting around eating brownie sundaes for dessert, I feel grateful that my circle of friends has made it thus far. And giddy too, as I think about what Friday brings.

"Do you think they will tell us which 25 boys are still in it?" Attie asks excitedly.

"I hope so," Chrys says in matching excitement.

"I can't wait. Y'all are great and all, but I'm ready for some better-lookin' scenery," Marcia laughs and wiggles her eyebrows.

Vanessa is sitting across from me and has her eyebrows furrowed watching something. I turn to see what she is staring at and apparently Marisol and Elizabeth are having a bit of a disagreement. Elizabeth turns to walk away but Marisol grips her arm rather hard.

They are loudly whispering to one another although not loud enough to hear.

"Those two don't really get along. Never have," Vanessa explains to me.

"I can't imagine why," I say sarcastically while seeing Elizabeth try to turn away again. She looks on the verge of tears. I'm sure Elizabeth's beauty has been a major source of jealousy for Marisol.

Without even really thinking about it, I'm suddenly moving. I understand what Marisol is doing. Marisol knows Elizabeth is her biggest threat. So she is trying to get Elizabeth to act out, maybe even hit her, in order to make her look bad or even get kicked out of the Culling. I'm not sure what she is saying, but it can't be pretty. I hear Vanessa on my heels as back-up as I hurry to make it in time.

"Your mother was a *SLUT*," Marisol spits out at Elizabeth as I come close enough to hear.

Elizabeth lifts up her free hand like she is ready to either slap her or deck her, but I grab her elbow from behind, giving it a sound squeeze and letting her know I'm there.

In surprise, Marisol loses her grip on Elizabeth's other arm. I take advantage and quickly move so I'm standing between them.

"Oh, imagine that. Perfect little Reagan to the rescue," Marisol glares. "Stay out of this and mind your own business."

"Oh," I begin, using the same exact tone with her that she just used on me, "You mean saying hateful things trying to make Elizabeth hit you because you know she's prettier than you and you can't win against her, so you want her out of the Culling before we meet the boys? You mean that business?"

She glares at me venomously and I return it not backing down an inch. I am *so* sick of this girl. Why the heck is she even still here? She's fake from her eyelashes to the stupid nice girl she portrays. From day one she has acted holier than everyone else and has looked down on everyone. I'm not sure if her nose is naturally angled upwards at the tip or if it got stuck that way after carrying it so far in the air all the dang time. She's stuck up and a snob. Those are not opinions, they are facts.

Finally, she breaks our staredown saying, "You are making a *HUGE* mistake, Reagan." She gestures with her hands at the word huge and storms out of the room.

Vanessa is standing beside Elizabeth and lets out a chuckle. "Here I thought you would need backup, Reagan. Turns out, she might have. You just destroyed her."

I turn and smile at them both, taking a big inhale of air as I do. "I am just so sick of her insolence."

Elizabeth is still fighting back tears but tries to smile at me, "Thank you."

"You're welcome. Did you get a brownie? Would you like to sit with us?" I offer. "Don't let her get to you. She is one of the meanest people I have ever had the dis-privilege of meeting."

She nods. "That'd be nice. Thanks."

And just like that, our group befriended the beautiful girl that will beat us all.

****

The next day, we have more tests. I have been tested on everything from my favorite color to the complex DNA structure of those of us showing immunity to Trident. Thursday and Friday are prep days for the ball, so we have comprehensive tests all day on Wednesday. By the time I finish what feels like my thousandth test since leaving Omaha, I don't even care if I passed or answered the questions correctly. At the end of our etiquette test and after five straight hours of testing, Professor Dougall hands out our contraceptives and stops us for a quick announcement before we leave.

"Tomorrow at varying times, you will be meeting with the Board of Directors for a panel to review your performance thus far in the Culling. Those of you who will not be making it will be immediately dismissed. Those of you that have the privilege of continuing on will be given an attendant to help you properly appear at the Canidatorial Ball. Please get your rest and be on time tomorrow. Congratulations in advance for those of you moving on. This week has been hard, but it's about to get better." She cocks her head to the side and smiles, adding, "For a little bit anyway."

After dinner Marcia and I are walking down our hallway feeling rather sober, excited to meet the boys, but still sober about the panel.

"In all seriousness Marcia, I don't want to go home yet. And I don't want to say goodbye to any of our friends either. Especially you. Of all the girls here, you just seem to get me," I say dreading the next day.

"Reagan. You aren't going anywhere, hun," she stops me and holds onto my arm looking at me seriously for once. "You deserve this. You are a leader without trying to be. Who organized the bunch of us who sit together? Who aces every test we have to take and scored the highest on our stupid etiquette test? Who stood up for Elizabeth yesterday? That's all you. You'll make it."

Sniffling back some tears, I smile at her, "No need to get all girly on me. Cripes."

This makes her smile. "Now, if one of us goes home, it's me. So I'm going to go change into some jammies and you are going to invite me in for some tea and we are going to stay up chatting, girl. We are both nervous for tomorrow anyway."

Even though we are both exhausted from the week, we do just that, staying up laughing and sharing with one another. We talk about our families. We talk about the other girls. We talk about the boys. Marcia tells me that although the boys from Seattle are funny and intelligent, they aren't the type a woman just swoons over. I warn her to stay away from Benjamin. The only thing we don't talk about is the Culling itself. We both seem to know that we are being monitored or at least that we shouldn't say anything too bad. We do laugh and joke about Dougall and the sex talk she had to give us before handing out birth control like candy though.

By the time she leaves my room, she has me rolling in fits of laughter and I'm feeling much better about tomorrow. I mean after all, if a girl like Marisol is still here, then chances are good that both Marcia and I will make it to Friday. I know what it would mean to our families and for Marcia's project. And I know what it would mean to me.

I want to stay. For my family, and for me.

****

"So you have known about the monitoring for some time now?" the evil tester man, Mr. Alexander, is asking me what feels like hundreds of questions. We've been at this for almost a half an hour. Both testers are there as well as all three professors and Elle. The full Board of Directors. It is late in the afternoon and I'm getting hungry. I didn't eat well all morning in nervousness for the panel.

"Yes," I nod, giving simple yes and no answers to the questions.

"You seemed upset about it at first. Would you please explain?" he smiles and gestures for me to elaborate. He's a ray of sunshine this time compared to the last time.

"I just felt lied to when I first found out, so initially I was angry. Then I thought of how some of the girls are and realized it might be necessary. There are girls here who are angels to you fine folk, but to the other girls are downright barbaric. I realize it might be needed in order to see someone's true colors. I just wish it didn't have to be all the time. Every time I go to sleep, I go to sleep knowing that someone somewhere has me on a screen watching me. It's just not at all what I'm used to and seems a bit...creepy." I shrug.

"Your performance on the lie detector test was the fastest and placed you second among all the girls. How did you figure out the test within the test?" He almost smiles.

Second? My freak show and temper tantrum?

"Wow. I had no idea." I shake my head before I continue, "I guess I'm just good at reading people. When I insulted Elle she looked upset even though it was my brother in there. There was no guilt. No remorse. Then you, sir, looked quite amused at one point. I knew those wouldn't be the emotions or reactions if it were real. Plus, the timing of it all. Why would you take that moment to tell me my brother was a supposed traitor? Why during a test? It just didn't add up. Unfortunately, I just didn't connect the dots that his getting beat up was also staged and not real."

This time it's Elle who speaks. "The manner in which you handle yourself has impressed many of the Culling directors albeit sometimes you are brash and blunt. You helped form a little family out of the group of girls you sit with, which is something we look for in a Madam President, a motherly or family minded woman. But, there are also times you just care about others too much. Mentally, you are tough enough for this. Your intellect and basic reasoning are astounding. Emotionally, we are not yet totally sure. And yes, you are young so that is part of it, but you seem to be loyal to a fault sometimes. Predictably so. And your temper can get the best of you."

I catch and hold my breath thinking this is the point when she sends me home, second on the lie detector test or not. Maybe being so young is even cause enough for them to give me the boot.

Professor Zax runs a hand over his moustache before he begins speaking, "You are a very intelligent and perceptive young lady. With your scores and current ranking, we have no problem moving you on to the next round. Congratulations, Reagan Scott. You are going to the Canidatorial Ball."

I immediately grin and let out the breath I have been holding.

I am going to the ball!

"May I?" Professor Dougall, whom I think doesn't really like me, looks at the others seeking approval. She gets a nod from the evil tester man, I mean Mr. Alexander.

"Ms. Scott, you're very much a frontrunner in this and it is time you start acting as such. The only thing I am truly concerned with is not your knowledge of silverware placing, but rather your own self-confidence. You need to know that you can do this and you need to start acting as such. You have amazing gut instincts. Trust them." She smiles with an affection I have never seen before. More than once she has singled me out in class much to Marisol's amusement.

"A…a frontrunner?" I stammer in shock. I was just sure I might be going home a few seconds ago.

"Of course we cannot disclose to you your ranking throughout this process, but know that it has always been quite high," Elle nods. "Your lie detector test only confirmed that."

"Thank you," I manage to say, looking at each of them in the eyes. "I don't want to let you down. I will try to work on my emotions and my temper. I will do my best."

"Of that, we have no doubt." Mr. Winters smiles with a nod.

Down the hallway, I can't help but do a little dance in front of an amused Jamie.

"I made it!" I whisper to him, "I'm going to the ball!"

Ready or not, I'm going to meet the boys!

Chapter 7

After eating in my room again since all our meals today are to be in our rooms as the panel is going on, I decide to see if Marcia is back yet. I open up the door and greet Sarge and we walk down to her room. Her guard isn't there so I know that she isn't either.

Feeling restless, tired from the week but still excited for the boys, I change into my pajamas and read and journal a little before there is a knock on my door. I run to it knowing that only one person would knock on my door at this time. I have a huge smile on my face as I swing open the door only to completely lose it in surprise.

"Darrrrrling!" a skinny little man wearing thick rimmed glasses greets me. "I am to be your attendant. Now, let me in and let's see what we can do. I know some attendants are waiting for tomorrow, but not me. You have Stephen Frank as your attendant and Stephen Frank does not lose or waste time." He bows down before me and gestures with his hand.

"Lovely to meet you," I say, regaining my composure at his not being Marcia. I'm sure I look completely shocked and confused.

"Now let's have a looksee at you. My assistant will be joining me in the morning." He has me stand in front of my mirror and turn around slowly.

"A short, curvy little thing. I can definitely work with this," he says thinking out loud to himself as he starts to ramble, "Your legs are absolutely fabulous and will look even more so in heels. Your eyes are a perfect mixture of green and those specs of honey are just lovely. But, the torso is so very short. So nothing poufy or you will look like an elf. Oh. Your feet are amazing. You would be surprised how often ugly feet can ruin an outfit or pair of strappy sandals. I love the hair."

He stops only to gesture. When his mouth isn't running, his hands are. "We need to keep that natural wave and add some more curls to it. Face is a little mousey but pretty nonetheless." He stops and walks forward. "What is this?" he asks, pointing to my eyes. "Dark circles under the eyes? No, no, no, my dear. That will not do. You have a ball tomorrow night. I'm going to order your breakfast delivered in tomorrow morning at nine. You are to sleep until nine. Sleep until I am here. Do *not* go anywhere. Do you understand?"

I manage to nod and add, "Okay."

I'm somewhat amused with this character of a man. I can't help the dark circles though. When you are a part of a process like this, you are bound to experience a little stress. But his enthusiasm and the seriousness with which he takes his job are amusing.

"Now. What color did you wear at the etiquette test the other night?" he continues on, flipping open a small notebook the size of his hand and starting to scribble. I wonder how long he will be here.

"The emerald green."

"Ohhh. Not only do I have a lovely candidate, but I have one with brains. Excellent choice, my dear." He smiles affectionately and I can't help but think that although he was just totally critiquing my body, I am going to have a hard time not completely loving this fellow.

"Now. Most girls will be wearing a shade of white like a wedding gown or a bold shade of red or something like that to draw the attention of the boys. I am going to draw their attention also, but you will not be wearing white or red." I raise my eyebrows intrigued as he continues. "Most of the time I would say a purple or a blue, perhaps something of a silky material. Soft and inviting, like your eyes. This time though we are going to go bold and daring. I would like to put you in black. Nothing too sexy. You aren't on your honeymoon yet, my dear," he chuckles at himself and blushes, "But definitely something that accentuates your assets. What do you think?" He bounces his eyebrows. I can clearly see that he loves his job. He can barely stand still he is so excited.

"I think whatever you say is best. I'm really not that good at it. Black seems a bit morbid, but if you can make it work, I'm all for it. I don't want to look like all the other girls. So I'll trust you," I nod.

"Ahhh. Yes. You and I will get along just fine. I'm leaving you now. My assistant and I will be here at 9 am sharp. I will have your breakfast with me. Sleep. Sleep, darling! You need it!" He rubs my arm, gives me a side hug, and leaves just as quickly as he came.

Standing at the door trying not to snort out a laugh as he quickly turns down the hallway and heads for the elevator, I ask Sarge, "Is he for real?"

Sarge smiles back, "He definitely is." Then he shifts uncomfortably from one foot to the other as if he needs to tell me something.

"What is it?" I ask, trying to read him. He looks a little worried. Whatever he's about to say I'm not going to like.

"While you are at the ball tomorrow evening, your room will be moved to a different floor," he says almost sad.

"Well do I still get my bed?" I smile but he isn't smiling in return.

What's the deal? What is he really trying to tell me here? If it were just the rooms he wouldn't be acting like this. Like he is about to deliver bad news.

"Yes. The…uh…the only reason it's necessary, is because you are the only girl left on this floor." He reaches out and puts a hand on my shoulder.

I feel my heart skip a beat. Marcia. He's trying to tell me that Marcia is gone? Less than 24 hours ago we were laughing and joking about the boys and the ball. I hold onto the door frame or I'm going to fall over.

I will never see her again?

Sarge grabs my arm in one hand and holds tightly onto my watch with the other. "I thought you'd want to know as soon as I knew," he whispers. "Before you got to breakfast or the ball and she was just gone. I didn't want it to ruin tomorrow for you."

"Thank you," I manage to whisper back.

At this point the tears start falling. I feel horrible. There I was enjoying my success. Enjoying making it to the next round and getting an attendant. I was looking forward to meeting the boys. Marcia won't be going. She won't be there. I never got to say goodbye. And what about her project? How could she make it this far just to go home right before another big milestone? Her family was so close to having another promotion, and I know with there being six of them, it was important to her. We got so close in such a short amount of time and now she's just gone? Just like that? And I'll never see her again? She's just...gone. *Forever.*

"Can I get you something from downstairs to help? Tea? A brownie? You know I hate crying and I would hug you if I could." He is still holding onto my arm to steady me.

I have tea in the fridge and am not in a brownie mood without Marcia to eat them with. What do I need? I need to get out of here a moment. My room feels like a jail cell again. I feel like I'm getting claustrophobic. I need to move. I need to walk. I need.....*air.*

"Yes, there is something you can do. Maybe. I need fresh air. I haven't had fresh air in days. If I don't get outside soon, I'm going to freak out. The thought of going back into my room, on an empty floor without my best friend sounds horrible. Will that look bad? Will I fail some stupid test I'm not aware of?" I blurt out as I sniffle the tears away. "Can I go outside for just a few minutes?"

"I'm not sure if we're supposed to, but we'll do it anyway. You will need a coat and shoes though," he smiles supportively.

I quickly grab my coat, slip on my bright neon pink slippers, and try to dry my eyes. We go down the elevator and when the door opens, we immediately weave through people, dodging them left and right until Sarge stops at a communications center of sorts.

"Wha--" the man starts to say to him before Sarge cuts him off.

"We're going outside. She's on the verge of a panic attack and needs air." With that, he grabs me by the arm and we walk towards the door. He leans in close to me and whispers, "Don't worry. I just said what I had to say to get you outside. You shouldn't be in trouble of any sorts or docked for anything."

"You need that approved. You need more men!" the man yells after us.

"So get them," Sarge says as we walk out of the door into glorious, fresh, crisp, cold autumn air. I couldn't love him more for getting me outside, all the rules be damned.

Outside, I feel much better. A panic attack might have been a bit of an exaggeration, but if it allowed me outside, I'm cool with it. I find a bench on the path about 100 or so yards from the building. I look up at the stars and immediately feel better. The cool air on my face feels amazing. I will miss Marcia more than she knows, but I know she wouldn't want me to throw a fit. She would want me to kick butt in this stupid game we call the Culling.

Two more guards come outside and stand beside Sarge keeping watch. I greet them both and ask one, "Is it really necessary for so many guards to be on one person?"

"Yes," he replies, looking strict and annoyed.

"Why?" I ask somewhat rude. Hearing and watching my every move isn't enough?

"You could be the next Madam President. Our country cannot afford to lose you and so we take every precaution necessary to keep you safe at all times." He doesn't seem too happy about being here. That's my bad.

"That makes sense but this isn't like the days before Trident. No one is threatening my life or anything." I watch them look uncomfortable after my statement and I realize I have come across something that I shouldn't have.

Interesting.

I look Sarge in the eyes and his look seems to tell me to let it be.

I sigh. "Just five more minutes please, guys. I have to try to find some shapes in the star constellations. It's an Omaha thing. See that moose over there?" I map it out for them as a joke and everyone seems to be relieved I have dropped the topic. The one I was rude to even looks somewhat entertained.

Who is threatening me? I know it can't be me specifically, but someone is threatening the President or the Culling members. Why? All three of them were uncomfortable with what I said. It can't be coincidence. Is that what Julia discovered? My gut tells me it has to be related. There's just something going on here that's more than what meets the eye. More than just being monitored. I just know it.

As I look up at the stars, I feel much better knowing Marcia, Agnes, and Cadence are all actually safe from whatever is going on here. I trust Sarge and Jamie literally with my life, but I still feel better knowing that my friends are safe at home. A movement interrupts my thoughts and I tense up.

"Ms. Scott?" Sarge asks worried. He knows me well enough to pick up on my body language right away.

I see a figure on top of the roof of the building just standing there as if they are watching us. This could be a perpetrator, but he isn't threatening at all, he just stands there with his arms on the ledge. Not a stance a guard would have either. The person is so far up there that I can't see much other than their outline.

I wave two fingers at whomever it is, wondering if they are in fact watching us, while I say to Sarge, "There is someone on the roof. I didn't know we could go up there."

"You can't," he says in return, smiling because he knows I will ask why.

"Why not?" I ask. If the other two weren't here he would have just told me why not in the first place.

"The roof is part of the Presidential Quarters," he informs me.

"You mean I just waved at the President? And not a graceful or beautiful wave either. It was a 'hey, dude, what's up?' sort of wave," I blurt out embarrassed and one of the extra guards chuckles. "Dougall would kill me."

"It could be someone else in the President's quarters," Sarge shrugs trying to make me feel better but it makes me feel worse.

Oh gosh. That could have been Henry. My fun is over. I'm ready to go back inside now. I may have just messed up with the boys and I haven't even officially met any of them yet.

"Let's go inside before I make a bigger fool of myself, shall we?" I sigh, wondering who I waved at.

I would almost rather it be the President than Henry. Dressed in pajamas, slippers, and a coat isn't exactly how I envisioned meeting him. Nothing screams "romance" or "date me" like my current attire. I can't even relax out here in the fresh air under the stars where I usually feel the most at ease. Please, oh please, let that have been the President I just waved awkwardly to. Fortunately, I'm so far away, whoever it was shouldn't recognize me. Or I can only hope.

Way to go, Reagan. Way to be.

****

At exactly nine the next morning, Mr. Stephen Frank knocks at my door wearing the same thick framed glasses. I open the door to find him and a woman of about the same age with him and a cart with my breakfast. He is wearing a color of blue I have never seen in a suit before. It's almost teal, almost baby blue. He has a white dress shirt on underneath. His assistant has her gray hair short and spiked to the side and is wearing a purple velvety suit matching him. Together, they are quite the pair. I have never seen clothes like the ones they are wearing. Eccentric would be a good word to describe them.

"Good morning, Mr. Frank," I smile, looking the two of them over and wondering if I got the best attendants or the worst.

"Good morning. Darling, this is my personal assistant Gertrude. We all call her Gertie. And everyone calls me by my last name of Frank. Stephen is also my father's name, so I've always gone by my last name instead."

"Nice to meet you." I shake Gertrude's hand, which is the softest hand I've ever touched.

"First things first. You need to eat breakfast. You need to have strength for tonight." I nod to him as I grab the plate off the cart he wheeled in and head to the couch while he continues, "Good girl. Ah! Just think, tonight you may find the man you marry." He and Gertie share a dreamy look.

It's almost nice to think of it that way. Truth be told, I'm not looking for love, I'm looking for an ally or two. Love seems like wishful thinking at this point in the game. I know some presidential couples found it, like the Maxwells, but others did not. Is love a requirement to become the next presidential couple? Definitely not. And for me? Oil and water. Oil. And. Water. That's me and boys. And isn't this whole process difficult enough without opening that can of worms?

"Now! We are going to wax you and then bathe you in our special mixture. Your skin must be soft to the touch so we will start with the waxing and then move to the special butter bath. And don't you worry, my darling Reagan, no one else knows the ingredients!" he winks at me, obviously proud of himself.

"Is that why Ms. Gertrude's hands are so soft?" I smile. I'm a little worried about the waxing as it sounds painful.

"Please, darling, Gertie, and yes, that's why my hands are so soft. I'm glad you noticed," she smiles.

Having brought in a foldable table with them, they move my furniture to the corner and get to work. An hour later, I have smoother legs (although I shave them often), arms, and better shaped eyebrows. I handled it like a champ except for the eyebrows which made me jump and made my eyes water. Sheesh. The things we do for beauty.

Gertie runs the bath for me and tells me I must stay in there for one hour exactly. I know Frank jokingly referred to the bath as a "butter bath", but it smells amazing and looks exactly like butter. Gertie shuts the door so I can undress and tells me she will knock in one hour to help get me out of the mixture.

A whole hour for a bath? Holy crap.

I lie in the amazing smelling stuff and can't wait to tell Marcia about it. She will have all sorts of funny things to say about my bathing in butter. *Dang it.* I did it again. Marcia isn't here anymore. As I continue to just lie there, I wonder how tonight will go. My biggest fear is that no one will be interested in me, love interest or otherwise. That fear is putting a damper on the giddiness I have about meeting the boys. And if tonight sucks, I don't even have Marcia there to laugh with.

Oil. And. Water.

In an hour, Gertie knocks and tells me to wear a towel while they come in and remove the special mixture from the tub. I then shower and rinse off the film left on my skin. My skin already feels great. I put on a special tank top without straps and some shorts they brought for me to wear.

In two more hours I have my fingernails and toenails painted a dark beige color, my hair is treated in some sort of softening cream, and I have had three different creamy mixtures on my face. I then receive the most amazing back massage I have ever had in my life from Gertie. I feel like a million bucks! Bring on those boys.

Lunch is delivered and I sit and talk to my attendants getting to know them better. They both seem very excited about the dress, no, *gown*, they have chosen for me to wear. I can't wait either. I hope I won't be wearing the same dress as anyone for this event.

After lunch, Gertie takes some creams and massages my hands. She tells me my hands need to be the softest with all the dancing we will be doing. Sometime later, between more hair products and teeth whitening, Elle knocks on my door.

"Ms. Scott, here is your information packet on this evening." She hands it over to me and I know exactly what's in there.

I barely say thank you before I bring it back into my room and tear into the envelope.

"Oooooh. Do tell, darling, do tell!" Stephen Frank says excitedly.

I find the list of the boys who have made the cut, all 22 of them. Then I find the list of the girls who have made the cut and there are 24 of us. I smile finding my own name on the list. This means I officially made it to the halfway point and have gotten my family another promotion!

Boom.

Resisting the urge to do a little victory dance, I quickly scan the list looking for my friends and am relieved to find both Vanessa and Attie. I am surprised to find Marisol, a few girls from her group, and even Renae. I thought for sure they would be going home soon. How do girls like that get to stay while girls like Marcia go home? It just doesn't make any sense. I see Elizabeth, as expected, and am pleased to find that October, who recently joined our group, made it as well. In my entire circle of friends, Marcia and Chrys were the ones to go. Two of the six leaving yesterday were my better friends. I'm sad to see them go. It feels like Marcia took a small part of me with her.

I then focus in on the boys list. I'm rather surprised to find that most of the boys we jokingly picked last week are still in the running. Most who are gone were from Denver or Vegas. Only three from Detroit are left, and only one from Seattle remains. Perhaps even most surprising though, is the fact that Benjamin is still in it too. Two of the three Omaha kids made it to the halfway mark.

"This is the list of people that made it to this evening. May I study this for just a few minutes or do we need to be doing something?" I ask my attendants. I want to practice putting faces to the names before me, but don't want to be rude either. Apparently getting ready for this shindig is a whole day's worth of work.

"Oh we have plenty of time, dear. It's only 3:30. Take a half an hour or so while we get everything set up for makeup," Frank says as they busy themselves. Gertie is kind enough to drop off some iced tea on the nightstand before me. I'm fond of both of my attendants already. They're hard not to like.

Twenty minutes later, I hear Gertie catch her breath. She is looking at some of the pictures I have strewn across my bed while I sit cross legged practicing names. I know she is just itching to pick a few up so I nod to her.

"Are you sure it's okay?" she asks excitedly.

"I am sure." I smile. It's not her fault. It was impossible for her not to notice them since I have them spread all over the giant bed.

She picks up a few and is commenting on how handsome they are and then Mr. Frank gets into it with her. I sit back enjoying their banter and advice on which ones I should approach.

"Ahhh. Henry. Poor thing has practically been locked up his whole life training to take over the country. I have heard he is very kind despite being spoiled rotten." Gertie sighs looking at his handsome face wistfully.

"What about this one? His eyes are laughing!" Frank laughs, looking at Trent.

"Aww. This one works with animals!" Gertie swoons looking at Adam's picture. "Oh my. This one is quite muscular," she switches to the picture of Bronson.

"Oh. This one is just too macho!" Frank says in reference to Christopher, imitating his face and throwing the picture on the bed before laughing.

Gertie catches her breath for what must be the tenth time. "This one. Oh my. Look at him. He looks dangerous. Yet there is kindness in those eyes. He looks like the type of man who knows how to kiss a woman, if you know what I mean." She winks at me and I blush knowing she has to have the picture of Lyncoln, the only one not smiling. "It reminds me of someone else I know," she adds and winks at Frank this time, who swoops in for a quick kiss.

"Wait! You guys are a thing?!"

"Oh yes, darling. I have loved and been married to this woman for the past 25 years of my life," Frank smiles affectionately.

"Well now I love you guys even more," I grin. No wonder it seemed like they worked so well together.

"She's going to make me cry!" Gertie fans her face.

"Enough of this. Let's get to the hair and the makeup, darlings," Frank commands and we move to get back to work. "There will be no tears today, my dears. Not for ball preparations. No way!"

****

In a few more hours, I don't even recognize my face in the mirror. My hair is down and is curled in the most amazing way with just a few pieces pinned, making it possible to see the gorgeous earrings dangling from my ears. My makeup was put on with something Frank called an "air brush" and looks flawless. I have more eye shadow on than I normally do; it's a light sparkly tan towards my tear ducts and a smoky gray around the outside corner of my eye. I have on black eyeliner that I'm not used to. They were going to put on fake eyelashes too, but decided against it and I'm glad. I look enough like me that I don't feel fake, and beautiful enough that I feel confident. It's perfect and I tell them so almost bringing Gertie to tears again. Apparently, she's a crier.

"Now. For the grand finale! Are you ready to see your gown?" Frank asks, practically bouncing on his heels.

"Absolutely." I smile, feeling nervous for more than one reason.

Frank opens my closet and brings out my dress that was delivered earlier. He wouldn't let me look at it, telling me it was a surprise. He tells me to turn around while he gets it out of the package and then hangs it on the back of the door.

"Ready, and go!" He gives me the go-ahead.

I turn back around and am left speechless. It's perfect. The dress is made of a smooth black material. There is one strap, which swoops across my back to a very low cut above my derriere. The dress looks like it will fit somewhat tight around my torso and waist, and then flares a little as it reaches the ground. Perhaps the best part, other than the back, is that starting at my waist there are ever so slight black sparkles. The farther the dress goes down, the more of them there are, so the bottom of the dress is solid sparkles. There is a long slit up one leg also.

"Do you not like it?" Frank asks, startled by my lack of words.

"No!" I exclaim, "I mean yes, I like it! Oh my word, I love it. Where did you find such a thing? I'm not sure I'm worthy enough to wear it, but this is amazing. This is a masterpiece." I reach out and touch a sparkle. This *is* amazing. I feel the shoes too. The shoes are a black suede heel adding at least three inches to my height.

"Let's get it on you, my darling!" Frank claps, very pleased with himself. "The slit and the sparkles should make you stop them in their tracks. You will outshine all the others, my dearie."

I head to the bathroom and Gertie helps me slip it on. It's skin tight at the top around my chest just like I thought, and then more flowy once it reaches the hips. And it's light as a feather. I have never worn anything so beautiful. My bare back makes me almost feel...*sexy*? I'm not sure because I've never used that word to describe myself before. I'm glad my hair is down to help with the naked feeling though.

When I come out of the bathroom, Frank and Gertie both clap and make happy noises. Frank has me sit down and puts on my heels for me before helping me back up. I stand at the mirror ready to go. A million different emotions go through my mind. Above all, I'm nervous. Borderline terrified.

Please let them like me.

Frank puts his arm around Gertie and they both smile. "Our princess is ready for the ball."

Chapter 8

I am about to open the door to leave with Sarge for the ball when Elle shows up at my door with her clipboard in hand. "Oh my goodness. That gown. You look amazing!" she says honestly.

"Thank you. I was about to leave. What can I help you with?" I ask.

"Oh yes, I need you to sign this," she says politely, remembering that she brought a paper and a clipboard.

"What is it?" I wonder.

"Dougall already addressed this with you all, but these are the rules for what you are allowed to do with the boys. The future Madam President has a reputation to uphold and we won't hesitate to dismiss anyone who disregards the rules," she says sternly but like she has said it a million times. Then she smiles. "Don't worry dear, I have had to tell all the girls this and give them the rules in writing. Just routine procedure! You are one of the last to get to. I'm glad though. That gown is worth delaying you a little. Just sign here so that we can prove you understand the rules."

I sign her paper immediately. Who would lose their innocence or sleep with someone they just met at a ball, just like that? With someone they didn't really even know? I have to take those stupid pills because of this too. I know we haven't seen a person of the opposite sex for almost three weeks now, but you would think we would have more restraint than that.

"Thank you," I say, holding a copy of the stupid rules in my hand. Seems a bit overkill if you ask me, but whatever.

Elle puts her clipboard back down at her side. "You still have fifteen minutes. I would definitely wait too. Make an entrance," she whistles and nods her approval.

Liking her idea, I smile. "Yes, Ma'am."

Exactly eleven minutes later, I look in the mirror and give myself a spritz of my favorite perfume, and then make my grand entrance upstairs. I don't remember feeling this nervous before in my entire life. Sarge gives my arm a squeeze of support as he drops me off at the door.

Other than a glare by Marisol and a few sighs from the other girls, my dress wasn't as big of a hit as I thought. But I am a bit distracted. We all are. I can feel the hormones bouncing off the walls.

I barely even notice the lavishly decorated room I didn't even know existed here at Mile High, complete with a huge, intricate fireplace tucked in the corner. Extravagant bouquets of white flowers in vases taller than me line the outer edge of the room. A boisterous chandelier stands at the center of attention. Men in suits again come around with appetizers and champagne. The lighting is soft and a real life small orchestra plays in the background. I barely notice any of that.

The boys are here.

Getting extremely nervous, I look around shyly. Immediately seeing Vanessa in a lovely floor length, dark red dress talking in a group of people, I head in her direction not noticing or caring who is in her group, just glad for a familiar face from my circle of friends.

"Hey, Reagan," she smiles warmly.

Not normally a huggy person, I reach out and give her a quick hug which she returns. "I'm so glad you're here," I say softly.

"I'm glad you're here too, although I'm not really surprised," she winks at me and makes room for me to stand next to her while whispering, "Sorry about Marcia."

I nod my head in thanks. As I look around the group, I realize Elizabeth is here too and I am the only one not from Denver. I just ruined their little Denver pow-wow. Whoops.

"Reagan, this is Christopher." I already know his name so it's just a formality, but it's still nice to be introduced.

"Call me Chris," he says and shakes my hand. And holy crap he's tall. He might be the tallest person I've ever met.

"And Bronson," Vanessa gestures to the next boy.

I reach out my hand to shake his, but he laughs. "Nope. Bring it on in for a hug." He gently lifts me into a bear hug. I turn bright red.

"And Lyncoln," Vanessa says.

I reach my hand toward him, but am trapped for a moment by an amazing blue and brown mixture of eyes staring into mine. I knew from his picture his eyes were blue, but I didn't notice the specks of brown also.

Holy crap. This man is...intense...scary...hot? Definitely hot. His eyes are just so blue, a deep cobalt, almost navy, blue. Then at the centers near the pupils, there is an explosion of dark brown. It's the weirdest eye color combination I have ever seen. Lyncoln doesn't take his hands out of his pockets where they are lazily resting but instead just gives me a curt nod.

Okay then, Mr. Sassy-pants.

"Reagan, your gown is amazing!" Elizabeth smiles, moving to stand on the opposite side of me as Vanessa.

"Thank you. Yours is amazing as well!" I respond with a smile and mean it. Elizabeth is wearing a pale yellow dress that is skin tight to her thighs and then spirals outward in chiffon with one side having a slit showing off her legs. As usual, she looks just perfect. So perfect it would be sickening if I didn't know her, if I didn't know her inner beauty matches the outer one.

"Ladies, ladies, ladies! Come on now. We all know that I'm the best dressed of the bunch," Bronson says, giving his lapels a tug and making us laugh. I blush a little. I've never seen someone so naturally outgoing. Or handsy! He's always reaching out to touch one of us girls whether it be a hand on the back or something like that. And it isn't just with me, it's with all of us.

The group of us talk for a while. Soon I'm laughing and feel more at ease. I notice Lyncoln isn't talking much, but the way he looks at me is almost as if he knows me. *Weird.* Dark and mysterious it is then, just like the flashcards and the conversation with the girls. Before I have a chance to drill him with questions until he cracks like I did with Mr. Winters, Professor Dougall makes the announcement that the dancing will begin. I resist the urge to run and grab a champagne glass and down it.

As she explained to us earlier in the week, we are to line up and all dance with one another as it apparently is the best means to do introductions, or at least the most awkward anyway. There will be one song per match up with the boys rotating around to the girls. In a few short hours, I will have met and danced with every boy in the room. Tonight I will go from zero dances with boys to twenty two.

Ready or not.

"Oh, and due to the difference in numbers between boys and girls, Professor Bennett and none other than the President himself have offered to step in," she says and the girls all give surprised noises along with applause.

Make that 24 dances then.

I turn to move to my spot and as I walk by Lyncoln, he clenches his jaw. I try to think back to the conversation we all just had and wonder if I said something that upset him. Do I smell? No. I remember putting on perfume right before I left. Who knows what his problem is. Maybe he and Marisol are two peas in a pod, moody and full of attitude.

Oil and water though. Here we go!

The room is in movement as the girls get to our assigned positions we practiced earlier in the week. Benjamin happens to be the first boy I get to dance with. He holds me properly, but I can't help but be a little stiff at his hand on my bare back. This boy is a bully. Granted he looks good in a suit and bowtie with his amazing blonde hair, but he's still just a dressed up bully. A very good looking bully, but a bully nonetheless. It would do me well to remember that. His baby blues do nothing for me. I can't ever forget the look on that poor kid's face that he and his friends made fun of.

"I hear you've been kicking butt," he smiles that killer smile that every teacher we have ever had falls for.

"What?" I ask, taken aback for a second.

"At my panel, one of our testers alluded to the fact that you beat my lie detector test score," he shrugs.

"Oh." That seems to be all I can come up with.

"I'm not really surprised though."

Is he actually being nice to me? What is this? He's talking with me like we are old friends.

"You aren't?" I sound like a dumb fool. I need to snap out of it. I need to act like a girl worthy of wearing the dress I have on. It's just weird that we are from the same township and he's never given me the time of day before, but is now acting like we are all buddy-buddy.

"No. You were always quite astute."

I look into his eyes trying to find a hint of him trying to play with me, but he seems like he actually means what he says. Is he actually trying to flirt with me even? Or am I just hormone drunk?

"Uh. Thanks," I say and move on. Of all the people I thought I would get attention from tonight, never in a million years did I think Benjamin would be so...*nice*. "Do you miss home?" I ask, changing the topic.

"Yes and no. I feel like I'm more myself here than I ever was at home." He shrugs.

I'm not sure what to think of that so I just nod. "I miss my family."

"I'm sure you do. You and your brother have a great relationship."

I'm trying not to be shocked again. How would he know that I'm close with my brother?

"Yes we do. It mainly consists of driving one another crazy," I say, trying to recover from my shock. I think it works as he laughs. I just don't know what he's doing. Is he just trying to be nice and stick together because we're from Omaha? Or is he manipulating me somehow? I don't trust him. Not even a little. I remind myself that there are 23 other dances, and that I just have to survive this super confusing first one and then I will be onto the next one.

We laugh about what we think is going on at home with harvest approaching and the song ends shortly after. I have officially survived the first dance. And it was quite the dance. Quite confusing. Quite odd.

Next up is Oliver, the only remaining boy from Seattle. I tell him how much I like Marcia and ask if he knows her.

"How do you not know a girl like her?" he laughs and tells me a few stories of going through school with Marcia and I'm laughing fairly hard as we dance in our allotted area on the dance floor. Marcia was correct in that he isn't the most attractive of the bunch, but I like his demeanor anyway. He gestures with his head and our joined hands a lot and I find him entertaining.

Next up is the boy named Adam who works with animals. He seems a bit uncomfortable in the setting but loves to chitchat about different animals. We are cordial and have a common love for animals, but neither one of us seems to light the other's fire, so to speak. And I'm okay with that. I'm still recovering from Benjamin being so nice.

Next are two boys from Denver. They are named Abraham and Douglas. Both ask the proper questions and make small talk, but twice I catch Abraham watching Elizabeth out of the corner of his eye. And

Douglas just kind of lets off the vibe that he doesn't want to be here period.

Cool, guys. It's fine, I'm used to it.

After Douglas, I dance with Trent, who lives up to his picture in that he is animated.

"Holy mackerel girl, what did you do to your skin? Because it is softer than a baby's bottom," he asks as soon as we get into hold while smiling that same huge grin as his picture.

"And have you been feeling babies bottoms as of recently?" I ask with a smirk, trying my best to look serious.

"Oh. I like you already. You cheeky little beauty."

I smile at that and am starting to relax a bit. It's hard not to have fun with Trent. I do realize as outgoing as he is that I'm not the only girl he has probably called beautiful tonight, but I appreciate the gesture all the same. We talk about the decorations and the weirdness of the Culling Canidatorial Ball and he has me almost in tears of laughter with his impersonations of the professors.

Next is the boy named Joshua from Detroit. He's somewhat boring other than his comment about being hard to follow after Trent that makes me laugh. I tell him how much I enjoyed Cadence and he says he is sad she had to leave. I remember being drawn to his picture, but in real life, though he's attractive enough, he doesn't seem to be doing much for me. I'm interested in him as a person, just not in a dating sort of way. And I'm kind of beginning to be nervous at this point that even with the overabundance of hormones in the air, I'm not going to have a romantic connection with anyone at all. Not that you *have* to or anything, but it's definitely encouraged.

Dancing with Bronson next is like dancing with a ginormous teddy bear, but I manage to handle his touchy feely thing well. He's never inappropriate, it's just obvious that he's more touchy than most of the others. I'm laughing about a story he's telling about someone beating him up in grade school when the song ends and the next begins. Still laughing, I turn and find myself face to face with none other than Henry Louis Maxwell.

He smiles.

Those dimples though.

He takes my hand and we get into proper hold. His hand on my back makes me feel nervous.

"Hi. I'm Henry," he says kindly with the most amazing green eyes I have ever seen.

"I'm Reagan."

Wow. I am shocking myself with my own embarrassment. All I can manage is an "I'm Reagan"? Maybe if he weren't so good looking in a tux it wouldn't be so dang hard to form words. A bow tie? How can a man look *sooo* good in a bow tie?

"How have you been liking it here?" he asks, looking at me with his deep emerald eyes penetrating all the way down into my soul.

"I really like the bed?" I say almost as a question and he busts out laughing which only makes him more attractive and makes those dimples bounce into action. I'm glad he's a good sport so I gather all my courage and both boldly and nervously ask, "And how do you like all these girls throwing themselves at you this evening?"

He laughs somewhat surprised and cocks his head to the side saying fancifully, "I am not one to over indulge in such frivolity."

"Well that is a striking disposition," I respond, using large and fancy words back to him. I am trying to treat him like I would anyone else, but obviously I'm afraid to say much of anything in his presence and what I do end up saying is awkward!

Why am I so embarrassing!? *UGH.* My heart is thumping rapidly in my chest and might just explode from nervousness.

He laughs again. "My father did say you were a spitfire."

"Probably not the best thing to be pointed out for," I note.

"Ahhh. But I would much rather marry someone with a little fire in her." He smiles and winks right at me as he says it and I almost fall over. Good thing he is holding me up. He just used the word "marry" in a conversation with me. Did that really just happen or am I dreaming?

"Is that so?" I smile and try my hardest not to blush though I'm sure the heat is there in my cheeks anyway. Heck the heat is everywhere for that matter. He's just so...*beautiful*.

"Quite so," he says. He pulls me just a little bit closer as we turn and my heart rate accelerates even more.

Okay, I have to be dreaming. This cannot really be happening. Is Henry flirting with me? ME?! I tell myself not to read too much into it. He is probably flirting like this with all the girls. Right? Has to be. That would be the most logical explanation for this turn of events. He is probably just like his father in that he likes to make other people feel special. It's part of his natural charisma. That's all. *Right?*

I try to keep him talking to me, wanting to get a better read on him. "Well, there may be such a thing as too much fire also. You should know that I have a bit of a temper."

"Is that so?" he grins looking down at me while maintaining eye contact with those smooth emerald green eyes. He is so animated, even when I'm talking, that it's intoxicating. And I could listen to him talk all day.

"Quite so." I use the same phrase he used and he smiles once again and shakes his head.

"By the way, your dress is my favorite of the night," he squeezes my hand while he says it to let me know he's serious. I hope my own hands aren't getting sweaty. My whole body feels a bit feverish.

"And how many other girls have you said that to?" I joke.

"Well, none. But I should confess that I am only about nine girls in." I laugh at his banter before he continues, "Regardless, it will be my favorite."

"Thank you." I try not to blush again.

Is the stinking heir to the presidency really flirting with me right now? And does he really do this with all the girls? Am I losing my mind? Maybe it's the hormones. I am hormone drunk and so I am reading more into what he is saying than I should be. That must be it.

"I would say the same to you, but all of you look alarmingly similar in your suits." I try to keep the mood light.

"But how will I know you won't forget me then?" he pretends to look broken-hearted.

I squint at him. "Oh, I think you're quite memorable."

"Is that so?" he spins me around happily and I laugh.

"Quite so," I flirt back.

I am flirting. Actually flirting! I wanna high five myself right now. I have never flirted before in my life. I hope I'm doing it right. He's just so…drawing.

"I have a bit of a secret, Reagan." He bites his bottom lip to keep from laughing.

"Do tell." I gesture with my head not realizing our heads would be even closer than before. I can even smell his minty fresh breath. For the first time in my life, I find myself wondering what it would be like to kiss someone. I haven't ever kissed anyone before and am sure my first kiss will end up being an embarrassing slobbery mess. Lips just seem like a weird part of anatomy anyway. His lips are nice though. They look soft. Like little pillows.

"I like your bright pink slippers," he whispers, interrupting my inappropriate and rambling thoughts.

"Wha--No!" I exclaim, suddenly horrified as I catch on. Has he been messing with me this whole time? I try to pull back but he holds me in place. I can't believe it was him that I waved to last night, *in my slippers!*

"Not to worry, beautiful. I found you fascinating." He smiles and my fears start to fade.

"Is that so?" I ask, wanting to know if he's serious. He saw me in no makeup, pajamas with a coat thrown over, and slippers. Though from the distance, I hope all he picked up on was my bright pink slippers. I could barely see him so I hope he could barely see me. How did he even know it was me?

"Quite so," he responds with a grin and playful eyes. Before I have a chance to say anything more, the music ends and it's time to switch. Before he leaves, he steps back and waves at me with two fingers just like I did to him last night. I am both thrilled and embarrassed equally.

The next four boys didn't even have a chance as I found myself jittery and distracted from Henry. Never in a million years did I think I would have a chance. I'm still not sure I do considering the glares I was receiving from every female in the room. If looks could kill, I would be dead at least a dozen times now.

Over halfway done, I then dance with the President and find myself focused and back on my best behavior. He asks me some strange questions like my favorite food and favorite color. I ask all the silly questions back and find myself relaxing with the most powerful man in the room. Before I know it, and before I have time to really dwell on any stupid things I'm saying, I move on to the next man.

I meet Knox from Galveston who is very intelligent. We are having a discussion involving Omaha's harvest yields when the song ends. I move on to a boy named Grady, who has seemingly already drank too much champagne and is a little touchy with me. More than once I move his hand higher on my back. *That* song cannot get over soon enough.

Next is a boy named Pierce who just talks about himself and how good he is doing thus far in the Culling. I get that he's trying to find someone as an ally, but he needs to settle down a little bit. No one likes a narcissist. The song is less than three minutes long and I feel myself already not liking the sound of his voice.

Three boys later, I am turning to switch partners at the end of a song and feel the back of my dress catch. Afraid it will rip at the slit and I will be naked showing the whole room my bare bottom or more, I willingly fall back onto my butt, trying to save my dress at the cost of my pride.

So I almost made it through the ball without falling.

As I look up, I see Marisol grin her evil grin as she sashays away. I know right then and there that she stepped on my dress on purpose. *That girl!* I want to waltz across the room and punch her in the nose. Maybe a head-butt too. Just to be sure to break her face. But as I look around, I see the whole room has stopped and everyone is looking at me where I sit on the ground.

I squint my eyes at her but before I can even finish glaring daggers at Marisol, I am lifted up by some strong arms. People are watching and I hear a gorgeously deep and raspy voice say, "It's okay, she just tripped on a crack in the floor." To which people laugh and smile and then continue dancing. Magically, everything is back in full swing like I didn't just fall flat on my butt.

The floor is wood and has no cracks though. Jerk.

I turn and find myself in the very muscular arms of Lyncoln and his piercing blue and brown eyes as he still holds me in his arms like an overgrown child. How is it possible both colors can be so prevalent in an eye color? I want to confront him about embarrassing me in front of everyone but am distracted by how good he smells. He smells like heaven. And he's looking at me like he knows me again. It's super unnerving. Other than seeing his picture, I know I have never met him before.

We stand there like that for a second or two and then he gently puts me back on the ground and says, "Hasn't anyone taught you to keep your friends close and your enemies closer?"

He picks up my hand and brings me in close as we begin to dance. Grady may have been a little touchy feely, but even we didn't dance this close. Grady made me feel uncomfortable, like he was going to inappropriately try to grab my butt or something. This, however, is different. Wayyy different.

"So I take it we are enemies then?" I joke as the feel of his hand on my back is sending heat throughout my body. He places his hand in just the right spot. It isn't high like it properly should be. It isn't dipping too low like grabby Grady. It definitely covers some surface area of my back too. And I'm glad I'm wearing the three-inch heels as he is definitely at least eight inches taller than I am.

This time he does smile almost completely. "Probably should be." He rubs his hand across my back with his thumb ever so lightly and I'm left with a tingly feeling traveling all the way down to my feet.

An entire minute passes without him saying a word. We just dance and he keeps rubbing his thumb on my back.

"Why didn't you smile in your picture?" I blurt out, finally thinking of something to say. I find myself not even wanting to talk to him. His hand on my bare back is making it hard to think, let alone form a sentence, as I try to avoid those mysterious blue and brown eyes which seem to already know all my secrets.

"I only smile when given something to smile about," he shrugs amused. "Plus, it made me look intense." He bounces his eyebrows once for effect.

"Nope. Had you pegged as dark and mysterious," I say playfully but completely honest.

"Oh. Even better." He rubs his thumb up and down my back again and for the second time tonight I'm glad I have someone to hold me up.

What. Is. Happening.

Hormones everywhere that's what! I remind myself that I haven't even drank any champagne so I shouldn't be feeling wobbly like this.

Seeing my serious expression, he asks concerned, "You okay? Did you hurt anything when you fell? Ankle or wrist or something?"

Uh, oh. Here comes the word vomit again. I just can't contain it. I just cannot stop it.

"No. I'm just nervous. What would you care anyway? I understand I'm not as pleasing to look at when Elizabeth is right beside me, but you didn't even say a word when I got here. Not one. You didn't act like you wanted to shake my hand either. Now we are dancing like we definitely know each other. Can you see how that's a bit disorienting?" My nervousness does away with any filter I thought I had. Why am I telling him my every thought?

Just shut up, Reagan!

"Interesting. Elizabeth? You think I want Elizabeth?" he asks.

"She's very beautiful." I shrug. "And smart. And kind."

"She is." He shrugs the same way.

"Okay then. I guess that's settled." I feel flustered. One minute he rubs his hand across my back and I want to swoon. The next he is calling another girl beautiful. And why are we dancing this close again?

He half-smiles as if knowing the effect he has on me and enjoying making me squirm. "I don't want Elizabeth."

"You don't?"

"No." He shakes his head once for emphasis.

"Well why not?" Suddenly I feel like I'm talking to Mr. Winters again. He has very short answers and I'm doing all the muttering and asking. What is it with the stuck up Denver people? At least Henry can carry on a conversation.

"She's great, I just don't see her that way. I have my eye on someone else," he explains and I'm astounded by both what he said and the number of words he said. That was two whole sentences! And is he implying that I am the someone else? Surely not. Yet here we are, with our bodies practically bumping uglies in the middle of the dance floor.

"Oh," is all I can manage.

"How about you? Do you have your next boyfriends all lined up yet?" He takes a turn asking a question now. Thank goodness.

Remembering what Gertie said about him knowing how to kiss a woman I admit, "Next implies I would've had one before." I stop to shrug uncomfortably. "So that'd be a no."

He shakes his head and with one nod says, "Even better."

Before I can ask what he means, the time is up. He removes his hand from my back and I feel my skin instantly go down a few degrees. I can already breathe more comfortably again. He leans in and squeezes my hand before whispering in my ear, "See you later, Regs."

I'm in shock at both his kind gesture and his using the name "Regs" for me, which my brother Ashton always uses. It reminds me of home. I'm not sure if that man is precociously precarious or precariously precocious. Danger. Danger in a hot muscular form. Danger I need to stay clear of.

The next boy doesn't have a chance as I am an emotional train wreck yet again, this time after Lyncoln. My second to last dance is with Christopher, who reminds me a lot of Lyncoln in that he is more reserved and...calculated? Maybe it's just the military training thing. He towers over me, but he's nice and not near as confusing as Lyncoln. He also does nothing to my hormones. My last dance of the evening ends up being with Professor Bennett and I'm beyond glad to have a carefree conversation with him about the evening and our upcoming classes.

When we are done with our introductory dances, Professor Dougall tells us we have twenty minutes to socialize before President Maxwell will close out the night. I know it's not much past nine, but I guess they know the later we stay out, the more likely something inappropriate is to happen. I guess that's why I had to sign that stupid piece of paper and why I have to take the stupid pills.

I grab another flute of champagne and go find Vanessa, who is all smiles.

"Maverick is totally like I imagined," she whispers dreamily which surprises me since she isn't exactly a girly girl. "What were you doing with Henry? I thought Marisol was going to kill you on the spot. And pretty much all the other girls, too."

"I don't even know." I look at her confused.

"Ladies." Bronson returns to those of us he was talking to before we departed to dance.

"Bronson. I swear. If you hug her again, I'm going to deck you," Vanessa warns with a smile. She must know how uncomfortable I was with his touchy-feely-ness.

"Wouldn't be the first time," Bronson says seriously and then turns to look at me, "Not even kidding."

"No way." I smile.

"Way." Bronson smiles back. "She packs a mean punch."

"Well, I've got to hear this story." I look at Vanessa who just rolls her eyes amused.

Bronson goes into story mode and has us both laughing. A few others come over to our group and join us. About halfway through, Henry joins our bigger laughing group also, and is followed by at least five girls. I'm not sure if I should be jealous, but I kind of am. We had a great time, but maybe it was my imagination and maybe he's having a better time with the other girls having had the chance to meet everyone. He literally has a line of girls waiting to get his attention. I can't compete with that.

Feeling goosebumps like someone is watching me, I spot Lyncoln from across the room. He's keeping his distance but is definitely watching me as he talks with a Denver girl. Though he talks to her here and there, every so often he looks back over at me. He's just a completely frustrating man already and I don't even really know him. Though he's talking to one of Marisol's friends, I haven't seen him near her at all. I thought at first he was in cahoots with Marisol over the whole tripping fiasco. Now I'm not sure.

A few stories and conversations later and nearing the twenty minute mark, I realize I have gotten as much time with Henry tonight as I will get and my feet are killing me. I'm not so sure that I didn't sprain something after all as one foot hurts much more than the other one, the one I had my weight on when I fell. I excuse myself to walk over and switch for a fresh glass of champagne even though my current one is over half full and then head towards the people chatting on the large couches in the far corner. I just need to sit down a moment.

I find Renae and a few others and decide to sit there with them for a bit while absentmindedly rubbing my ankle. All of a sudden I can tell by the sizzle of danger in the air, or maybe it's the amazing smell, that Lyncoln is here. His cologne is kind of a woodsy and outdoor smell like at home, but much, much, *much*, better.

Not even caring about the others or if he is interrupting, he sits down beside me and looks at me concerned, "You okay?"

"Yeah, I'm fine." I place my hands back in my lap.

Without asking, he squats down, carefully moves my dress aside, and reaches for my ankle. He lifts it up resting it on his knee. He then presses on it lightly while rubbing the top of it. I'm in a little bit of pain, but he is definitely making me forget about it. Good thing Frank told me I have pretty feet.

"See. No biggie." I shrug, jerk my ankle back, and place my foot back on the floor, trying to get him to stop before we cause a scene. Renae is talking to Adam but gives me raised eyebrows noticing the tension between Lyncoln and me. Another boy/girl pair is on a couch on the other side of us, but pay no attention to us.

"You good?" Renae asks after a minute.

"I'm fine. Thanks, girl." I nod to her and she goes back to her conversation.

"I don't think it's sprained badly, but you may want to ice it," Lyncoln says bossily not even looking at Renae or giving her the time of day. "I'm sure they'll make you wear heels again tomorrow."

He leans back against the couch putting one leg across the other and an arm along the back of the couch way too close to my back. Is he marking his territory by trying to put his arm around me? Or is this just his usual way with the ladies? Even relaxed he has a laid back air of confidence about him. He is so very confusing. I wish I had even a little experience with the whole flirting thing so that maybe I knew what the heck is going on.

Using every last ounce of courage I have, I put a sarcastic, sweet smile on my face, turn to him and say, "Lync, honey dearest, what do you think you are doing?" I turn sideways towards him and gesture with my head to his arm behind me, letting him know I see right past him.

"Just sitting here, *babe*. What are you doing?" He says "babe" sarcastically and grins an actual grin making me wish he hadn't. He looks to die for when he grins. It almost makes me catch my breath. And his calling me babe shouldn't make me feel as giddy as it does, especially when he said it with thick sarcasm.

"You are frustrating. Do you know that?" I stand up and am about to leave as he laughs, but Professor Dougall calls for our attention for the President's speech so I sit back down.

I gesture for him to move his arm but he just grins again and doesn't move. Anyone who would look over here would think that we were definitely pairing up. Is he really an enemy after all and trying to make it so that no one else approaches me?

The President begins talking about what an honor it is for us to be here and how proud we should be and lets us know that it will only get harder, but he is confident that the new Presidential Couple are in the room. I get the gist of what he is saying, but am so bothered by Lyncoln and what his true intentions are that I'm only half paying attention.

When it's over, we all slowly begin departing. We know we're supposed to go back to our rooms, but none of us really want to go yet, so we lollygag as we head for the door. This is the first time we have seen the boys, or any boys, in three weeks. Renae and Adam are standing and shuffling toward the door. I feel exhausted and just want my bed and this night to be over. Like a sugar crash, I think I am having a hormone crash.

"Goodnight, Lync," I say, using a nickname for him since he used one for me. I stand quickly and turn to leave.

Before I can get away, he leans in placing his hand on the small of my back, but appropriately so. "Sweet dreams, Regs," he says softly. He then allows me room to breathe by letting me walk a few feet in front of him. I feel his gaze on my back and it gives me chills. I fight the urge to turn back and look at him.

We are starting to file out the door now, but it takes a while as there are almost 50 of us and each of us has a guard standing outside the room. I say goodnight to Vanessa and Attie and a few others while we make our way out. Benjamin makes it a point to say goodbye and I am mystified by his actions yet again. I smile and wave at Oliver, who playfully salutes back. I'm almost to the door and chatting with Renae when I feel a warm and soft hand gently squeeze mine.

"It was a pleasure to meet you." I hear Henry's voice and feel his breath on the side of my neck. "Better go find those slippers." I can't see his face, but I know he's smiling. Before I have a chance to say anything back, a girl named Katie from Denver grabs him by the arm, pulling him in her direction, and starts talking to him.

I finally get my turn at leaving and am quick to find Sarge and take his arm. We are in the elevator about to go down, but before the door shuts, an arm sticks in the door and Lyncoln boards the elevator with us. He doesn't have a guard with him which is weird. Sarge and I scoot to the back of the elevator and I keep my hand looped in Sarge's arm so Lyncoln has no reason to be near me. The door dings at my new floor first. Lyncoln steps aside and does his half-smile thing which I am beginning to think is his signature thing. He rarely fully smiles, but when he does it's something magnificent.

"Lync," I look him in his dark and mysterious eyes as I acknowledge him and then quickly leave the elevator.

"Regs," he nods and puts his hand on my back again to help me leave. The spot where his hand touches feels very bare and very hot once again.

Sarge walks me to my new door. I'm rather quiet and he picks up on it right away. "Are you alright, Ms. Scott? Do you need anything?"

"I...uh...yeah. I just...I--I don't know what happened back there?" I explain blushing.

He chuckles. "Well, it has been awhile, but I believe they call it flirting." He cocks his head to the side and smiles sheepishly, very much amused in my discomfort.

"Yeah, but I was flirted with on more than one occasion, I think," I whisper, totally dumbfounded.

"Reagan Scott, everyone in this Culling knows that you are a catch and a force to be reckoned with. Everyone, it seems, but you." He uses the keycard and opens my door for me. The way he is talking to me reminds me almost of a scolding from my dad.

I rub my temple not knowing what to think. Maybe I do need Tylenol after all. Is there a hormone hangover cure?

"I know you will choose wisely. Just go with your gut, hun." He gives my arm a squeeze, opens the door for me, and I walk in.

Will I choose wisely? Choose? Since when do I have options?

I don't even notice my new room or look out the window to see where I was moved to. I just take off my gown, change into pajamas, and collapse onto my bed. It's early for going to bed, but I am exhausted.

What just happened back there?

Why is Marisol the spawn of Satan and still here?

Why was Benjamin so nice to me when he never was when we were in Omaha?

Was it my imagination or did Henry and Lyncoln *both* seem interested in me?

Sleep finds me a few hours later and I dream of boys wearing suits that smell exceptionally well.

Chapter 9

"Good morning, my dear!" Frank and Gertie are at my door at the ungodly hour of 5:30 am.

"Morning. What are we doing today?" I manage to mumble sleepily.

"You get to keep us until the Culling is over, so we are here to help you prepare for your day, darling!" Frank slaps his hands together excited and comes in with a rack of clothing.

Morning people.

"But it's Saturday," I yawn.

"Honey, you get us every day of the week from here on out until we have a new Madam President." Gertie gives my hand a squeeze.

"Now, I know Saturdays are more casual, but I still have ideas. Let's get you ready for the day," Frank nods and gets to work.

****

I'm relieved to find that Jamie delivers me to breakfast with just the girls. I'm not ready to face the boys again just yet. Jamie teases me on the way down about my night and how it went, but I just answer yes and no to his questions. I don't know how to process last night so I try my best not to think about it.

I'm wearing a soft, magenta colored sweater, skinny jeans, boots, and my makeup is done nicely by Frank and Gertie. My hair is down and curled. I will confess that it's nice to be pampered and not have to worry about my attire for two days in a row now.

I grab a glorious chocolatey muffin, some fruit, and a bottle of water and plop down by Vanessa in our usual spot.

"Okay, spill it," Renae demands the moment I sit down. She does smile at me though, so there's that.

"Good morning. Spill what?" I ask embarrassed and already feel the heat in my cheeks.

"I was sitting there when Lyncoln was putting moves on you so don't play silly with me, missy." She playfully shimmies for effect as Attie sits down next to her obviously interested in my answer too.

"I--um…well, Marisol stepped on my dress on purpose when I fell and he was worried I might have sprained the ankle I fell on, so he just checked it out for me. That's all." I take a drink of water trying to play it cool. "Other than Marisol trying to disrobe me, I don't even know what happened, so I don't know what to say."

"Well, your ankle wasn't all he was checking out. Just saying." Vanessa smiles and winks exaggeratedly making us laugh.

"I'm surprised you noticed. You were too busy making your own moves." I look at her knowingly.

"Speaking of that, what's the deal with you and Bronson?" Renae asks and I think it's pretty clear she didn't miss a thing the entire evening. Now that I think about it, she was always placed to watch things going on around her. She may be more perceptive than I give her credit for.

"We've been good friends for a long time. Our parents are friends. It's not at all like that. I do love him, but not at all like *that*," Vanessa explains.

"Oh," is all Renae says. Attie seems quiet so I look to Vanessa for help. I know Henry was "hers" and I didn't mean to flirt with him and make her mad…it just kind of happened. I can see she is clearly bummed and it makes me feel guilty.

"Attie, did you have a good time?" Vanessa asks, saving me. I give her a "thank you" look.

"I did. There are so many cute boys! I'm afraid I might not have made a good enough impression on Henry," she shrugs and avoids looking at me. "I was just so nervous."

Welllll, this just got awkward. Before I can figure out what to say, Elizabeth sits down next to me and we ask her about her evening. October loudly plops down on the other side of Elizabeth.

"I think everyone in the room was jealous of you, including me!" Renae says nicely to Elizabeth, much to my surprise. I'm sure mentally she's trying to sabotage Elizabeth, or trying to figure out a way to one-up her.

"Thanks. I was rather surprised by some of the boys. I don't know what I was expecting, but it exceeded my expectations." She smiles and blushes a bit. Then she adds, "I saw Marisol step on your gown, Reagan. I am so sorry. Part of that is my fault."

"Don't be," I say honestly and reach across to squeeze her hand for extra emphasis. Marisol was mean before I came to Elizabeth's rescue.

"October. How was it?" Renae asks. I'm not used to a cheerful Renae and a moody Attie. Normally, it's the other way around.

"It was, meh, satisfactory I suppose. Interesting to learn about the other townships and stuff." She shrugs and we all laugh. October would probably have had more fun reading in her room.

Before we have a chance to chitchat more, Elle greets us and tells us that after etiquette class this morning we will have a joined class with the boys all afternoon as well as joint dinner this evening. Most meals and classes, except for etiquette class, from here on out will be with the boys. They were just giving us a minute to decompress after the ball in separating us this morning. I find myself excited to see the boys again, then scold myself. I am not this girl. I am not the girl that loses focus over a boy. I need to get serious if I really want this.

I'm not here to find a boy. I'm here to win a presidency.

****

After lunch, we meet in the usual classroom and find Professor Zax looking quite pleased with himself. He gets excited about the weirdest stuff. We're sitting as assigned alternating boys and girls. There are long tables along the back of the room but no lab setup for today.

The tension of having the boys with us is making it difficult to function and Professor Zax knows it. I know Henry is a few rows in front and to the right of me and Lyncoln is somewhere behind me. I'm sitting in my assigned spot with Abraham on one side and Trent on the other. Trent has me laughing while we wait for class to begin.

"Alright, ladies and gentlemen. Welcome to your afternoon class and your first class together. Congratulations on making it to the halfway point of the Culling." He claps for us and we join in. "Now, today I bring you a very interesting assignment." He pulls down a map at the whiteboard at the front of the room.

"What we start today could potentially be used in the real world. You will work in groups of five, except for the one group of six, and will be assigned a city that has yet to be cleared after Trident. Don't look surprised either; we just haven't had the time or resources for every single city, town, and village. The bigger cities are of course already done, but some of the smaller ones we aren't using were left as is. So you will create a plan of action for cleaning the city. The idea is to find what is useful or valuable, if anything, and go from there. You will be graded on your group's work as well as the time and resources used to clean your city. The winning group will also receive a prize." He pauses to let us think on that for a moment but doesn't enlighten us as to what the prize is.

"Now. I have selected the nine group leaders. The group leaders will choose their second in command and the second in command will choose the next in command and so forth. So who you chose is very important. The only requirement is that the groups have both male and female group members. Though I am sure you are excited about that part, I should warn you this test carries a lot of weight. We are not here to flirt.

"The following nine people please come with me into the hallway to the neighboring classroom while the rest of you await their first round picks. As you wait, think about the teammate you will choose." He pauses a moment and adds seriously, "You will be graded on every aspect of this assignment. Good luck."

He lists off nine people but I am not one of them. He does call Bronson, Lyncoln, October, and Benjamin though. Four of the nine people I know. This should prove itself interesting. I feel like I'm in recess getting picked for kickball all over again. I wasn't ever picked dead last because I was too competitive, but I didn't get picked first either. I have a feeling this will be a lot like that.

"I bet you five cookies at dinner you go first round," Trent smiles and nudges me.

"If they are smart, I will go second or third round. Deal." We shake even though we know it's an empty bet. We can have as many cookies as we want.

Ten minutes later, Professor Zax comes in looking excited. I have a feeling who we pick is just as important as how we do on this project. It's just another test within a test, but this is one that's out of my control. I can't decide who picks me and when. I can only decide who I pick next.

"Will the following nine people please come with me…" Professor Zax calls off nine names, my name not included.

Trent pouts and I smile victoriously.

"I win," I laugh.

Not surprising, Henry and Knox both go first round. What is surprising is that Marisol does too, and I have a hard time not being jealous. I understand why the boys will pick another boy first; they know them better. But I don't understand the logic behind picking Marisol. Who would pick her? Someone who must know how cutthroat she is apparently. Someone trying to use that to their advantage.

Ten more minutes pass and Professor Zax walks back in and again says, "Will the following nine people please come with me…"

Trent is called first this round and to my own surprise, I am the last name called. I get up and walk to the next room wondering what group I will be a part of. Hopefully not Marisol's, or we might as well just forfeit now. I'm not sure I have it in me to work with her civilly.

Please, any group but hers.

Since I'm the last one in the room, there is only one group standing around a table in the corner without a third person. Much to my dismay, that group is consisting of only Lyncoln and Henry at the moment. They are laughing about something and I realize they must already know each other, and by the looks of it, quite well.

Well isn't this just peachy?

"Hey, Reagan," Henry greets me while Lyncoln just stares me down in his dark and mysterious way.

"Hi," I say even though my thoughts are screaming, *"ARE YOU FREAKING KIDDING ME?"*

"Choose wisely, you have our next pick." Henry gestures to the names on the wall.

"What pick do we have?" I ask and kind of ignore them both as I focus on the task at hand and read the names.

I try my hardest not to be distracted by the fine male specimens before me. Henry is dressed in a sweater, jeans, and cowboy boots. Lyncoln is in a tight v-neck t-shirt with jeans and military grade boots. Both shirts fit too good on their muscles. What sort of fitness regimen have these Denver boys been on? Lyncoln is just a bit bulkier in muscle mass than Henry, but both are tall and lean and look like they are in amazing shape. Like can run for 12 miles non-stop, or do 200 one-armed push-ups, good shape.

"We just went first, so we will be last," Henry informs me, looking me in the eyes affectionately.

Lyncoln still hasn't said a word, just stands there.

"Are you serious?" I look at one in the eyes and then the other. They picked me first pick of the third round?

"Quite serious." Henry grins this time, using the phrase from last night, and shows off his dimples in the process. You would think they would make him look more childish, but they offset his muscles and lean build to make him look more approachable. I mentally slap myself back to reality and the task at hand.

FOCUS.

My pick? This is just dandy. I better not screw up. I better pick someone way more capable than I am, or we are doomed. I will be no help in this entire exercise because I will be too distracted. What are the odds that I would be in a group with the both of them? Really, there are 20 other boys here besides them. Hormones. These hormones will be the death of me. Or at least the end of my being in the Culling unless I'm careful.

I look at the list of available names and know I'm screwed. Attie is still on the list, but if I pick her, it will be to save our friendship, not because she's my ultimate choice. If I don't pick her, will she be offended and think I'm just boy crazy? Two picks later, she is erased off the board. I no longer have to feel guilty about it as choosing her becomes irrelevant. I quick look around the room and am shocked to see Marisol and October in the same group with Maverick.

Again, it's defying all logic; I just don't get it. That means October picked Marisol? Why? What was her motive there? It reminds me of Lyncoln telling me to "keep my enemies closer" last night. Maybe that's October's angle?

As two more names are erased off the board, I'm getting more nervous. I don't have time to think about October and Marisol right now. It doesn't help that my two companions are just watching me think and fidget and not saying a word.

"Any suggestions?" I ask, looking at the names of available people again, avoiding looking at either one of them.

"Can't. Professor Zax says picks have to be made without help." Henry shrugs. "Sorry, beautiful."

"Ugh," I groan and try not to blush at Henry calling me beautiful.

I look at the list. Logically, I should pick another girl as I know them better, but every last one of my friends are already in the room in groups already. I look over the remaining names once more and decide what I will do. I'll pick Oliver. He is quiet but very intelligent, just like Marcia told me. Of all the boys left, I would trust him most. Better to pick someone a friend trusts than to just blindly pick. And as an added bonus, I'm not attracted to him at all romantically, which is nice in comparison to the other two.

"Ms. Scott. Please come forward with your pick," Professor Zax states.

Without hesitating, I walk up to him. "Oliver George, please."

"Thank you. You may return to your group," he dismisses me and erases Oliver's name from the board. I can tell he's a little surprised with my pick, though he doesn't say anything more.

Back to my group in the corner, Henry smiles and nods his head up and down in approval. "Good choice."

I choose to stand by the window as I am a safe distance and across the table from them both. They both smell so good and their smells colliding are giving me high blood pressure. I look at Lyncoln who has yet to say a word, but has his half-smile smirk thing going on. This annoys me more than anything and I feel my temper start to flare.

"Cat got your tongue this afternoon, Lync?" I ask sarcastically, using my nickname for him.

"Dude. She called you Lync. No one does that. That's great," Henry busts out laughing and slaps Lyncoln on the back while Lyncoln just glares at him. After trying to contain himself, Henry turns to look at me and says, "Reagan Scott, you really are a spitfire. No one in their right mind talks to Lyncoln like that."

With fake confidence, I smile at him and lie, "I'm not afraid of him." My rapid heart rate and sweaty palms would indicate otherwise, so hopefully they can't tell how nervous he really does make me.

They both look at one another, smile, and at the exact same time say, "You should be."

****

Much to my dismay, I end up being the only female in the group. Although I'm thankful for the opportunity to talk to Henry without five or six different girls butting in, I'm very certain that I'll now have a huge target on my back, especially where Henry is concerned.

My group along with three others move back to the tables in our original classroom while the other half stay in the room where we chose teammates. At least now I have half as many daggering glares to ignore. Professor Zax bounces between rooms and we have a military chaperone in each room as well. I'm not sure what they think we are going to do in a room full of our peers, but whatever.

Our group decides to split up. Lyncoln, Joshua, and Oliver are discussing safety precautions and trying to prioritize the to-do list on the cleanup for our city. While they do that, Henry and I brainstorm places that need to be searched and things of value that we would need to locate. We sit at one corner of the table with some maps of the town. I purposefully turn my back to Lyncoln so that I can focus on Henry and our project without hyperventilating or wondering if Lyncoln is ever looking at me, or worse, catching him looking at me with that weird "I know you" look. Henry sits closer than he needs to and our legs brush up against one another often.

An hour later, I'm happy with Henry and my list, especially since he makes it rather hard to focus. Our city is about halfway between Omaha and Denver, so I'm pleased that I know the basic terrain of the area. Having finished our part while the others are still deep in discussion over more maps, Henry and I make small talk as they finish up.

"So who do you miss the most?" Henry smiles at me while leisurely leaning over the table with a hand tucked under his chin and asks me questions about Omaha. He looks entirely too good in his jeans and sweater.

"My brother Ashton. I only have one brother since my parents couldn't have any other children after me. We're pretty close." I look off into the distance as if looking for Ashton.

"You're fortunate, Reagan. I have two sisters but we don't get along that great. We don't hate each other, but we aren't very close either. When mom was sick, we all kind of just grew apart while we each dealt with it in our own way," he says, bringing my attention back.

"I'm sorry." The way he says it makes me want to reach over and give him a hug, partially because I feel bad for him and partially because I have hormones and like being close to him. "How was growing up here? I'm sure it wasn't easy," I ask, trying not to blush at my own thoughts.

"No, but it had its perks. I have so much respect for my dad. He would do anything for this country. Sometimes I wish I could be normal. Half of these girls would leave me alone if I were." He laughs kind of embarrassed and runs a hand through his light brown hair. "But normal just isn't my dad. I've lived my whole life wondering who is my friend because of the presidency, and who truly likes me for me. I try to do it with a good attitude though because I would do anything for my dad."

"That sounds awful." Always having to be suspicious of other people's motives? How exhausting. Though kind of sad, I feel glad I get to have a one-on-one conversation with Henry like this. I have a feeling there won't be too many chances. He's a hot commodity.

"So how about you, beautiful?" He smiles and lightly elbows me. "Do you like me because I'm the heir or do you like me for me?"

"Who said I liked you?" I blush and he laughs before I add, "I don't know you well, Henry. But, what little I do know, I very much respect."

"Then I can't wait for you to know more," he says seriously while looking me in the eyes. His eyes are a very distracting color of green. I have green in my eyes but they have specs of brown too. His are just all that smooth emerald green color. It's kind of remarkable.

As if sensing the seriousness of our conversation, Lyncoln rudely interrupts with, "You two done canoodling over there?"

I look at him and roll my eyes. "Canoodling? Really?"

"Jealous, much?" Henry jokes with Lyncoln, and surprisingly Lyncoln just grins over at Henry.

Well, this is nice.

Poor Joshua and Oliver sense the lighthearted tension and try to keep serious faces but they aren't doing the best job of it. I can tell that not many people fire back at Lyncoln, which is probably why I keep doing it. I'm glad Henry doesn't seem to be afraid of him either though he does seem to really respect him too; it makes me wonder how it is they know one another. Must be a military thing.

I reposition myself so we are facing the group again and I feel Henry's hand on the back of my chair as he scoots closer to the group also. Across the room, Attie sees his hand and looks like she's about to cry. I feel a little guilty, but it isn't like I asked for him to put it there either. I'm completely novice at this whole flirting and dating game. And for all I know, he could be doing this stuff with all the other girls too.

As our group leader, Lyncoln starts in about things needing to be cleared and threats to the area. Henry pitches in with priorities of materials we need to find and use. Then starts the big debate about the area and how much we will need to destroy. Joshua tells us destroying everything after we remove the valuables would be cheapest and easiest, but definitely won't win us the competition.

We are all looking over our budget and rubbing our temples wondering how we can use what little resources we have and fix the town. It just isn't possible, especially since there wasn't a focal resource in our town. None of our ideas seem to help. If we prioritize, we can fix some of the nicer and bigger buildings, but then buildings next to them will remain in ruin. It has been at least a hundred years since anyone has stepped foot in the town. We really don't even know what we are working with. And having a fixed up and nice building next to one that is eroding away seems a bit wasteful.

Suddenly I think of an idea but don't know if it'll truly work. Construction just isn't my forte.

Henry notices my head snap up and smiles. "Reagan has it." Both seeing and hearing the affection in his tone causes my heart to skip a beat. He gives my shoulder a squeeze for confidence while Lyncoln seems to be staring me down.

"This ought to be good," Joshua playfully jokes while Oliver rubs his hands together preparing for my spiel.

I avoid looking at both Lyncoln and Henry and look at our information so I can get my thoughts together before I begin. "I'm not entirely sure this will work so just hear me out, but what if after doing numerous and extensive sweeps of the area, let's completely demolish the north side of town. We can salvage what materials we can and use that to completely restore the southern side of town from the interstate south, or at least a decent portion of that area. Doesn't it make sense to have a smaller town that could be fully functional if we ever need it? Like an emergency or backup township of sorts." I turn and look at Joshua. "You're the demolition expert. Am I crazy or does that make sense?"

"Actually, it's genius." Joshua shakes his head. "I'm just mad I didn't think of it first. Duh."

"Plus, all the other groups on this same budget will be revitalizing one certain area of their town, maybe only recreating what was once a street or two, or a resource within the town. By destroying part of the town that isn't used anyway, we can make a smaller functional one." Oliver nods in agreement. "So we clear out and build up simultaneously. It's magical."

Before someone else does, mainly Lyncoln, I argue against my own idea. "But to truly do it, we need to go all out. The bad news is, the buildings will need swept top to bottom before we destroy everything. Anything and everything found will be used in revitalizing the other half of town. A huge portion of our time and resources will need to go towards that, which isn't exactly logical. Our project will need the most time overall."

"Not logical, but still worth it." Henry smiles and looks to Lyncoln for final approval. They both exchange a look like the two of them know a secret and then Henry shrugs with a grin.

In looking at Lyncoln, I see he is smirking. He glances at me then towards Henry. "It should work as long as..." he stops himself a moment. "But with the safety precautions...well, we can make it work." He looks at me again. "And just like that the woman makes the men look like idiots."

The others nod and laugh at that. I just feel relieved he likes my plan.

We discuss timeframe and budgeting our resources and are so lost in our own group and our idea that I barely notice the girls in the room looking like they want to murder me. And what was with the look between Henry and Lyncoln?

The only thing I'm not confused about at this point is that I know I have absolutely no idea how to handle these boys.

****

Though everyone seems excited and geared up for the rest of our day with the boys, afterward we have a break and then all meet back with Professor Zax to view a case study on Trident, which pretty much kills the mood. We have to watch footage of someone with Trident on a time lapse. So basically, we have to watch someone die. It only takes a few hours, but is still pretty gruesome.

It sucks having to watch it with the boys around. Henry manages to somehow sit beside me, with Katie on the other side of him. Vanessa sits on the other side of me. I don't know where Lyncoln went to, but I'm sure he's around.

The worst part is hearing the man tell us what he's experiencing in a series of interviews with himself. It's just so sobering. The man knows he's going to die, but is still taking the videos and staying in a contained room to be monitored with cameras and microphones. Case studies like this were done with a hope that in learning more about Trident they could somehow stop it. But they never did stop it. Trident just ran her course, killing as many as fast as she could.

An hour and a half in, and day three for the man in the video, the man starts to lose function of his arms and legs. It is horrifying watching him try to use his appendages but not having control of them. One minute he will be walking around normally, and the next he can't even lift himself up off the ground. He can't see either, which makes matters worse, and now he can't even control his own body. It doesn't take long for him to start begging for them to just kill him already.

I can barely take it. What is the point of this? Making us watch the footage makes me almost want to cheer for the man, but yet I know his fate. It seems cruel just sitting here watching him suffer and eventually die. I try to find Attie but can't see her from where I'm sitting. I know if this is hard on me, it's even harder on her. She likes to save lives, not watch people die.

I feel tears sting my eyes when he is completely paralyzed and lying there but still talking to us and describing what is happening to his body. He sounds defeated. Miserable. Hopeless. Trident was cold-hearted. The way in which she killed is unheard of in its level of barbarism; it was a slow torment.

By the time we finish, watching him essentially slip into a coma he never wakes from, it's right before dinner time. Many girls can't help but sob when he finally dies. Some of the boys are taking it upon themselves to be a hero and console the criers. I want to cry my eyes out, but I'm an ugly crier and Henry is right beside me so I'm trying my hardest not to. As if sensing that I'm about to lose it, he puts his hand across the back of my chair and lightly gives my shoulder a squeeze before trailing his fingers over my shoulder in a circular pattern.

His distraction works and my focus switches to the fact that he's comforting and touching me. In front of everyone. As the video wraps up, Professor Zax moves back to the front of the room.

"Today we saw this poor man die. I wanted you to see first-hand what it was like to see Trident's ugly face. We must never forget Trident. You must always keep the mistakes of the past in your minds as you embark on a journey of leading our country. The only way I could truly make you understand what happened and what it was like, the only way for you to truly have empathy, was for you to experience it like this. Harsh? Maybe. But I don't believe any of you will ever forget this. I think now you understand the seriousness of what Trident was." He nods for emphasis. "That's all for today though this is not our last case study. Class is dismissed."

****

Somewhat off by ourselves in the back of the pack of the dinner line, Lyncoln stands behind me and touches my back leading me forward when the line moves. I'm not sure he does it because he wants to touch me or because he's polite. Whatever the reason, it seems he's always touching the small of my back.

"You did well today," he tells me and I assume he is referring to our group project and not the case study. This is the nicest he has been to me all day. Come to think of it, this is the most he has talked to me all day. I didn't even really see him after our group project.

"Thank you, I think. We better win because I'm fairly certain there is a pretty big target on my back since I'm the only girl in our group," I confide.

"As there should be," he says honestly.

I spin around to look at him, wondering exactly what he meant by that statement. Is he a friend or enemy? Frenemy? I can't figure it out. At first I thought he was in cahoots with Marisol. Now, I'm not so sure.

"You're dynamite. Dynamite I should be staying far, far away from." He smiles softly while looking me dead in the eyes as if that explains everything.

"Dynamite?" I stammer.

He looks down at me and grins, "You know, small package, big delivery."

"Oh?" Oh is all I can come up with. I have never been called dynamite before and the way in which he says it makes me believe it's a compliment I wouldn't mind hearing again.

"Yet, here I am, a glutton for punishment. I just can't seem to stay away from you." He half-smiles with a shrug and turns me back around since the line is moving again.

"I'm sorry," I say, not really sure what on earth I am apologizing for, or why he thinks he needs to distance himself from me. Also, he is talking to me. In full sentences. How about that?

"I'm not. Don't forget a peanut butter cookie. They're my favorite," he nods to the desserts as we get to the end of the line.

I go to our usual table on autopilot and am both happy and jealous to see Henry sitting by Attie, talking to both Attie and Renae. Maverick is across from Elizabeth and Vanessa and Bronson are there as well. I wave Oliver over to join our group also.

Lyncoln puts his tray down directly across from mine. As he sits down, he leans across the table and whispers, "Future boyfriend?" He nods at Oliver.

"I don't kiss and tell," I whisper back, laughing at my boldness. I don't kiss period, but he doesn't need to know that.

Fortunately, Christopher sits down next to Lyncoln and starts asking him some questions. This gives me time to chat with Vanessa.

"How are you holding up?" Vanessa smiles like she knows I'm caught in a testosterone cyclone.

"Um. I have no idea what I'm doing here," I whisper and she laughs so hard I have to add, "Rude."

"You're doing just fine," she whispers back with a wink and gives me a nudge of her elbow in support.

****

Two days later, though we have a full set of classes, the priority for everyone seems to be the group project with Professor Zax. All having our own parts to work on in our group, I haven't had to deal with the tension with both Henry and Lyncoln because we have all been busy. Lyncoln has seemed to withdraw from me anyway. He still sits with us for dinner and I catch him looking in my direction often, but he hasn't been touchy or talkative the last few days. Surprise, surprise. Mr. Dark-and-mysterious is at it again.

Oliver has been my partner for the second half of our project and I'm pleased to work with someone without the extra stress. I'm usually either trying to get a read on Lyncoln and who he is and if he's making a move on me, or am freaking out about Henry and the fact that every girl here wants him. But, I'm beginning to really like Oliver the more I get to know him. The fact that I am not attracted to him at all probably helps enormously.

We are finishing our model on our city as others have long since filed down for dinner. We have glue stuck to our hands and though we look slightly disastrous, our project model looks favorable. We finish up, and as I glance at the clock, I realize we almost completely missed dinner altogether. We leave later than usual and are walking behind two girls who are in Marisol's circle of friends, Sapphire and Jade.

"I mean a group of boys to herself?" the one named Jade says and rolls her eyes. It doesn't take a genius to figure out who they're talking about.

"Henry doesn't even like her, I bet. He's just stuck with her and too nice to tell her no." Sapphire shrugs.

"I don't know who she thinks she is. I mean, she really isn't even that pretty," Jade says as they round the corner.

Unable to take hearing anymore, I slow down until I'm barely walking. Oliver stays with me and asks, "Holy crap. Are you okay?"

"Yeah. I just need a minute. Go ahead." I do my best to smile at him.

"Just for the record, you are very pretty and none of us feel stuck with you. Those girls are just impertinent." He gives me a quick hug and leaves me to my thoughts.

I am emotionally drained and fighting off tears. I can feel the evil stares all the time so I know that some girls here do not care for me, so that's not news, but it's completely different to overhear some of the things that are being said about me.

"Give me a second, Sarge," I stop against the wall and hold my hands over my face rubbing my temples while taking deep breaths.

I tell myself not to take it too personally. Girls turn monstrous when they are jealous. I try to remind myself that this isn't about me and who I am as a person, this is about them and their own insecurities. And if I can keep my emotions in check watching a man die from Trident, this emotional crap with the girls should be a breeze. Right? Never mind the fact that I'm about to go down to dinner where I will see both of those girls and have to act like nothing happened.

I stand there a few minutes rubbing my temples to calm down. Suddenly I feel a hand on my shoulder and another one over one of my hands. Knowing it isn't Sarge, I take down my hands surprised to find Henry's eyes staring into mine, just inches away.

"What happened?" he asks with his emerald green eyes in concern while his hands rub up and down my arms. My skin goes from being somewhat chilled to tingly as soon as he starts rubbing my arms. It just feels too darn good.

"I just overheard something I didn't really care to hear, that's all." I shrug.

He looks at me knowingly. "Something with the girls?"

I nod.

"I'm sorry." He says it almost angrily and brings me in for a hug, and we just stand there for a few seconds. Since he's quite a bit taller than I am, my head is level with his heart which I can hear beating. He feels safe. And warm. And smells good. And his muscles are definitely nice, especially his pecs. I could get used to this. I don't know where he came from, but I'm glad he's here.

"Thank you," I say as he pulls away. I find I am no longer concerned about crying, but am more concerned about falling over from all the feelings he makes me feel while in his presence. He's a lot to take in.

He grabs my hand, rubbing his thumb back and forth along my hand while starting to walk slowly towards the elevators. Sarge and his two normal guards follow closely behind. They give us enough distance to talk in privacy, but as usual, they are ever present.

"I have a feeling you being in my arms will never be a burden, no matter the reason. So let me know if you ever need a shoulder to cry on," he smiles and I almost fall over in shock.

"Why me?" I ask honestly, thinking out loud. "Sorry," I immediately add, trying to save face.

He stops walking and turns to look at me while still holding my hand. "Don't be. I like that you are direct." He smiles and adds, "It has been you and only you since you waved to me in your slippers. I'm not sure how or why, I just know that at the ball you were the only one I wanted to keep dancing with, the only one that kept my attention. I know that I have to humor these other girls and see what else is out there, but right now, I only want to spend time with you. I don't see that changing any time soon. Just to be honest with you, you had me at the slippers."

He reaches down, gives me a kiss on my hand, and then we get in the elevator.

****

After dinner, I purposefully leave right when Attie is leaving. I need to talk to her to clear the air. I need to do something about the guilt that is eating me alive with these two boys. She hasn't been mean to me or avoided me, but she isn't being her usual chipper self and I feel partially to blame for that. I just don't know what I'm doing. Not only have I never dated a boy, but I have definitely never dated, or wanted to date, the same boy as one of my friends.

"Hey. Attie. Can I talk to you a minute?" I ask as I catch up to her in the hallway to the elevator.

"Sure. Let's go to the lounge on my floor," she says with a smile, "My feet are killing me."

As we ride the elevator, we make small talk about the dinner and amazing food we are always fed at Mile High. On her floor, we quickly take a seat on the couches, her on one and me on the one next to it. We are the only ones in the lounge on her floor.

"Look. I just wanted to clear the air about Henry. Before the dance, I know you really had your sights set on him. And now I'm talking to him a lot and I know that must bug you," I blurt out, straight to the point.

"Reagan," she starts but I cut her off.

"Attie, I never planned on it. I didn't mean to 'take him' or whatever. It just happened. I am really, really sorry," I say and shamefully look at my hands. "I don't want to lose you as a friend."

"It's really okay, Reagan." She shrugs.

"Are you sure you aren't just saying that?" I ask concerned.

She sighs. "It took Henry all of the first hour to see in you what we have all been seeing in you. Am I disappointed? Yes. But if it wasn't me he took a hankering to, I'm glad it's you. Plus, he and I didn't have the connection you two do. It happens! I just hope that maybe, just maybe, there is someone else here that I do have that connection with. I'm just bummed it isn't happening for me yet like it is for you. I wanted for it to be easy and not forced."

She's so nice it makes me almost want to cry. "They would be stupid not to see what an awesome woman you are," I tell her then I laugh and add, "Henry should realize it too."

"Thanks, Reagan. I was never mad at you. I was disappointed that first night, definitely. I was in my head and let my nerves get to me a little. That isn't your fault. It's also just weird that you have all these eligible suitors and then you see them date all your friends too. Don't worry though, I'm not pursuing Henry anymore." She reaches over to give me a supportive hug. "He is all yours. And I'm kind of glad too because all those girls just line up for him. I don't want to get in trouble for smacking one."

This makes me laugh. Smacking someone is the last thing Attie would do. Marcia maybe would, but not Attie. I sigh a big breath of relief. "Wow. I feel so much better clearing this up with you."

She laughs, "Had I known you thought I was mad at you, I would have approached you before now. I'm bummed…stressing myself out a little…but not mad. And definitely not mad at you."

"Thanks, Attie. I'm sure you will find someone, whoever it is. I'm sure." I give her a quick hug.

I hope she does find someone because not only does she deserve it, but she is one of my close friends here and I'm not ready to say goodbye to anyone else yet.

****

Two days later, we are finishing up all areas of our project in the morning as presentations will be that afternoon. I'm still giddy thinking about Henry and his kiss on my hand. I have played it over in my head at least a hundred times and I keep looking for something wrong with him. He just seems too good to be true. I watch him talk to other girls, like yesterday at lunch, and he is nice to them, but not overly flirty like with me. I think about the "connection" Attie says we have. I don't think he is kissing any other hands or even calling them beautiful. I can't think about anything past this presentation though because if I allow myself to think about what it would be like to be the Presidential Couple with him, I might just pass out from disbelief.

We are discussing our plans for the presentation we all have to take a part of and I'm barely paying attention until my name is said. "Reagan needs to have a large speaking portion," Joshua nods his head in my direction.

"I agree. You should hear what those other girls are saying about her. At least if she gets credit where credit is due, maybe they will shut their traps," Oliver offers while humorously slapping the air like he is slapping someone, making me laugh.

"I really don't care. I don't think whether or not I have a big speaking part will affect their animosity," I say looking at Henry's green eyes briefly and blushing. We are back to wearing our business wear during the week and he looks entirely too good in a tie. I feel like I should always be wearing formal wear in order to keep up with his good looks. Good thing I have Frank and Gertie to dress me.

"How about you start us off?" Lyncoln asks me. This is the nicest thing he has really said to me in days. No wait…that is the only thing he has said to me in days. I see his jaw clenched like he is mad about something, but I don't understand what.

I shrug, trying to be nice. "If that's what you want. Or you can, chief."

"It's what I want." He says it so bossily that I know he isn't just saying it to be nice. He looks at me a beat longer than necessary and then immediately starts discussing with Henry which portion of the presentation he will take.

That dude is intense for sure.

****

At lunch, I find Henry sitting surrounded by girls again. No matter how fast I enter the cafeteria, there are never any spots open by him. Yesterday, it was Katie and Isabella. Today it is Attie and Renae again, though I'm not worried about Attie, or even Renae really. I even wave at them with a smile. I find myself trying hard not to be a constant jealous mess though I do trust Henry. At least today he is still in the general vicinity of me.

I'm selfishly sad our project is coming to an end today. Although we haven't gotten much time together the last few days, at least for our project I get Henry all to myself without having to watch girls throw themselves at him. Pouting, I find a small opening by Vanessa and plop myself down not even noticing that Lyncoln is on the other side. He doesn't bother to scoot down to give me more room, so we are sitting super close. Figures.

"How is your day?" I ask Vanessa who seems quiet.

"It's going," she replies glumly and I look to where she is looking. Maverick and Elizabeth are blatantly flirting. They seem to be getting along very, very well. Although they are at our table, they seem to be in their own little world.

"I'm so sorry," I whisper.

"Don't be. I should have expected it by this point." She shrugs and gives me a smile to confirm that she is okay.

Our conversation is then interrupted when none other than Marisol and her sidekick Sapphire sit down across from us.

"Reagan. Vanessa. How are you guys today?" Marisol asks sweetly. Far too sweetly.

"Peachy," Vanessa says sarcastically as we exchange a glance wondering what she's up to.

"You ready for the presentations today?" she asks, taking a bite out of an apple in her hands that I only wish was poisonous.

"Sure," I respond with a smile. "And you?"

"I think so, but I'm a little worried. Some of us just haven't had to work as hard as others." She looks me dead in the eyes. I hear the accusation in her voice.

"Sounds like a personal problem to me," Vanessa defends me. I know Marisol is just trying to get under my skin before our presentations, but I'll be darned if it isn't working.

"October is your group leader and the smartest person I've ever met, so you'll probably win. You should have nothing to worry about," I say nodding in the direction of October. I'm trying to keep my cool while getting the attention off of me.

"I'm surprised you noticed." Marisol smiles an evil smile. "You seem to be a little too busy getting to know the boys in your own group." She looks briefly at Lyncoln while she and Sapphire laugh their evil little laughs.

My blood starts to boil as my temper flares. I'm about to stand up and leave before I say or do anything stupid, but Lyncoln softly squeezes my knee under the table and leaves his hand there.

He glares at her. "If she was, Marisol, I could tell her a thing or two about you that could make her life easier. Like, oh, say the time you were caught with Christopher? When you were 16?" He spits the words with obvious hatred towards her and I have never seen anyone so intimidating in my life.

They are definitely not in cahoots like I thought they might be that first night of the ball. He does not like her at all. At allllll. And I had better not get on his bad side. If he wants to be, he can be just as mean as she is. When he turns the evil switch on, I want to run for dear life.

The coldness in his eyes is downright unnerving. I hope he never turns those things on me. *Yikes.*

The color starts to drain from her face and Marisol looks mad. Sapphire hasn't said a word the entire time and now looks like she wants to run away.

"You just have daddy issues," Marisol says through clenched teeth.

I wonder what the deal is with Lyncoln's dad. He flexes his jaw and every inch of him tenses up. That was apparently not the thing to say. I make a mental note to ask Vanessa later what Marisol means.

Lyncoln squeezes my knee under the table again, this time I think for his sake and not mine. "Marisol, what exactly is your end goal here? You won't get Henry. No one from Denver wants you either, those who haven't already had you that is. So what are you trying to accomplish here other than intimidating your competition? In what world will you beat either one of these girls? Do you even have any guys chasing you?" He pauses as he knows he has struck a chord. "Didn't think so. While we are on the topic of daddy issues, you wouldn't still be here without yours pulling some serious strings, so why don't you just can it?"

She almost looks like she wants to cry as she plays with her apple and I would feel sorry for her if she hadn't just verbally attacked me. "I'm just not hungry anymore. Come on, let's go get ready for presentations," she says to Sapphire and they get up and leave with their long blonde hair bouncing as they sashay away.

Lyncoln leaves his hand on my knee for a while and I let him. I'm not sure who is comforting who but both of us are sufficiently pissed off.

****

"So we decided to demolish half of the town and then completely refurbish the other half, leaving a smaller town, but a usable one. We can do all of this on our budget without finding anything of value although there, of course, will be valuables found along the way, as there are in any city left untouched. So anything we do find will actually be pure profit. It will take more time, but will be worth it in the end," I finish explaining my portion of the presentation. I'm very nervous and the girls snickering when I began aren't helping anything. Lord knows what Marisol was back there saying under her breath.

"Smart," Professor Zax nods while taking notes. We are the third group to go so hopefully we nail our presentation.

"So we took Reagan's idea one step further," Lyncoln says, stepping forward to take over and purposefully name dropping me. As he begins his portion of the presentation, you can tell he works in tactical forces not just by his muscly body, but because he is very methodical and straight to the point in his delivery. He talks about the game plan, which direction things will go, and the fact that our city can be used as a backup township if ever the need arises.

Henry talks about safety precautions and budgeting while Joshua and Oliver discuss the demolition and refurbishing. Our presentation goes pretty fast, but goes fairly well.

October's group is next and will be the only group that might possibly beat us. They decide to use their budget to not only refurbish but also expand the energy plant within the city, thus creating a product immediately useful for the townships. Our idea is different, but I'm not sure it beats October's group. They nailed it. Which sucks because Marisol is in that group.

At the end, Professor Zax dismisses us for dinner telling us we will soon know who won the contest. I hope more than anything we are able to beat the group Marisol is in, but am not sure we got the job done. I don't even care if another team besides us wins, as long as it isn't Marisol's group that does. I head to dinner feeling exhausted and a little like I am starting to come down with something. I feel congestion coming on in my head giving me a killer headache and just feel a little achy all around.

"Can I get you anything?" Jamie asks, seeing me in my weary state.

"Would you please get me some cold medicine?" I ask.

"Yep. And I'll grab an electric blanket for your bed. What a crappy time to get sick," he says sympathetically.

"Tell me about it." I shake my head in agreement as I loop my arm through his as we head on down.

I manage to get through dinner. Henry is busy with Katie again, who can't seem to leave him alone. I try not to be a total stalker, but I do glance over often to watch him with her. Although he is nice, he doesn't seem to be putting any moves on her. Lyncoln is nowhere to be found all throughout dinner so I take the opportunity to leave early and ask Vanessa a few questions as we go back to our rooms.

"Hey, where did Lyncoln go?" I am confused why any of us can leave unless we are going home. We aren't due for any cuts, and even if we were, I don't think he'll be the next to go home.

"Uhhh. His military rank sometimes calls for him to be needed at weird times," she says vaguely with a shrug. She looks torn. Like she wants to say more, but isn't sure if she should.

"So he's a big deal?" I ask confused. "That's why his guards don't always have to be with him?"

"You could say that." She smiles and laughs a little nervously. "Let's just say that what he does is important. And he is kind of his own guard. I don't think I'm supposed to say more than that because of who my dad is. Sorry."

"Oh," I say even more confused than before but respect why she can't give me all the deets I'm wanting. "What about that thing Marisol said about his dad?"

"She shouldn't have." Vanessa clenches her teeth.

"Why?" I pause. "Can you tell me?"

"I'm not sure I should, but I will." She pauses and then almost whispers, "His dad was murdered. In front of him."

I can't find my breath. "No way!"

I'm slowly starting to put together the pieces of who Lyncoln really is. At first I thought maybe he was an enemy. I don't see him as an enemy or a friend. Lyncoln is just something entirely different. A puzzle I can't seem to figure out. And one with an entirely good reason for being dark and mysterious it turns out.

"Yeah. Since murders don't really happen anymore, it was a big deal in Denver." She shrugs. "It shook us all up. But he was definitely never the same."

"When?" I myself feel shaken by what he had to see. I can't even wrap my head around it.

"Would have been about eight years ago. So he would have been about thirteen." She shakes her head sadly.

"Oh my word. Thirteen? No wonder he seems so dark," I think out loud.

Vanessa laughs at that. "He is dark. He's definitely dangerous since he has done and seen stuff no one at our age should, and he definitely had his bad boy stage after his dad died, but he really is a good man underneath it all," she tells me. Before I can wonder if she's into him, she adds, "And no I don't want him in that way, I just really respect him. We kind of grew up together. And for the record, I have seen girls follow him around for his looks or bad boy image his whole life, but I haven't seen him follow anyone around until you."

"Thanks. I think." I think about what she is telling me. Other than the showdown with Marisol earlier, he hasn't given me much attention at all. I don't get it. "He's backed off a lot though."

"Yeah, probably because he and Henry are good friends," she says shaking her head and chuckles. "You really aren't good at this boy thing are you?"

I blush. "Ah, no. I am not. I told you I have no idea what I am doing, and I meant it!" I laugh and then add quietly, "You think both of them are really interested in me?"

"Yes," she says smiling without hesitating. "So what are you going to do about it?"

"I have no idea," I say totally flabbergasted. I would rather answer more tests than have to sort out my feelings about those two boys. "And hopefully I don't have to be the one to decide. The Culling is hard enough as it is. I just want to make another cut, not worry about my hormones wrapped up in those two boys."

"I hear ya," she nods and gives my shoulder a squeeze in support.

Despite feeling horrible, I toss and turn all night wondering what Lyncoln's job is that he gets to leave when no one else does, including Henry, and what I am going to do about the both of them. I don't want to give them the wrong idea or lead them both on, but I like parts of both of them. After a few hours of tossing and turning, I rationally decide that I don't really know either of them well enough to do anything about it. I need to get to know both of them better.

This whole process is straight up crazy! I can't decide who I want to spend the rest of my life with, or if we will even have a long lasting attraction, based off of only a few times in seeing one another. Asking me to do so, is unreasonable. And then there's always the possibility that I am dismissed and never see either of them again. I hope for my sake that the Culling lasts a whole lot longer and I stick around so I can figure this out.

Chapter 10

The next morning, I wake tired. Normally I can just turn the switch off and sleep, but these boys and this whole situation are making that darned difficult. I'm sure I look even worse than I feel and my voice sounds groggy. Gertie and Frank notice but don't say much and get me hot tea right away.

They are becoming the highlight of my day. I typically don't like mornings, but when I wake up to the two of them getting me prepared for the day, I am much less crabby about having to get my butt out of bed. I have my hair curled and half-way up. I'm wearing a navy pencil skirt, beige heels, a burgundy tank top with ruffles down the sides that I'm not sure about, and a cream blazer over the top. When it comes to putting outfits together, these two seem to have a knack. Ready for the day and the results for our group project, Jamie takes me downstairs.

"Ready to find out?" he asks in a good mood.

"Maybe if I wasn't scared to get murdered in my sleep," I respond, wishing I had had another cup of tea before class.

He laughs as he hits the button on the elevator. "We won't let that happen." He wishes me good luck, sensing that I am dreading these results.

If we happen to win, I will have a bigger target on my back. If we lose, Marisol and Sapphire will never let us live it down. So the only thing worse than winning, is losing. I kind of almost wish one of the other groups will win, just so I don't have to deal with either of those possibilities. How I haven't punched Marisol in the nose by now is beyond me. Miracles do happen, I suppose. Her schnoz is perfectly attached. Momentarily.

At our classroom, I see my group all already present and sitting around our table. I sit down and say a pleasant but not really heartfelt hello. Naturally, the only spot open is between Lyncoln and Henry and their cologne smells colliding are doing weird things to me again.

"Brought you this. Hope you're feeling better," Henry says, placing a tea before me. I smile a thank you and take a sip. He notices the little things about me.

Just then Jade walks by and smiles at me. "I can't wait for the next group project when I get to work with a bunch of gorgeous men and have them do all the work for *me*."

I'm already on edge and she threatens to send me over it. I'm about to open my mouth when I feel Lyncoln's hand squeeze my knee from underneath the table. How does he always know when I'm about to lose it? And why my knee? I glance up at him to see him glaring at her, jaw clenched. He's mad too.

"And that attitude is exactly why we didn't pick you," Joshua says coolly before Lyncoln can verbally destroy her like he did Marisol.

Oliver also looks mad but adds sarcastically, "But thanks for calling me gorgeous."

I'm surprised they have no reservations whatsoever in defending me. As she storms off I say, "Thanks, Joshua."

"Being a girl must suck. Heels and draaa-maaa!" Oliver says and I laugh. I avoid looking at the other girls in the room as I know I won't like what I see.

Soon Professor Zax breezes through the room and greets us excitedly. "Today, I get to inform the winners of their prize." He pauses and I can just feel glares bouncing off of me. "And then we will move on to our next project. Leaving immediately to skip the rest of the day of classes, our winners will be taking a helicopter ride to an un-refurbished area of an old city close to Denver. They will go for a tour of the area, then come back this evening for a special dinner with the President and myself. These people are dismissed immediately. There is special gear for you to wear in your rooms. Your guards will take you where you need to go. And last but not least, you are safe from the next cut."

He pauses for dramatic effect.

Please, let it be us! I want to get out of this room. And I want to be safe from the cuts.

"Please help me congratulate…" Professor Zax pauses some more for effect, "Lyncoln's team." He starts clapping with the others joining in, some in an almost murderous way.

We smile and high five or hug each other. I try not to be too feely with any of them since all the other girls' eyes are on me. As I am the only girl, I take this opportunity to be the first to leave to go get ready for our field trip like Professor Zax instructed. I might as well get out of here as quickly as possible so they quit with all the emotional hate I feel rolling towards me. The target on my back grows with every step in the direction of the door.

"See, not so bad, right?" Jamie smiles.

"You totally knew, didn't you?" I smile back. "That's why you were so chipper this morning."

"Yeah. They've been prepping us since dawn on the trip." He nods guilty.

"Well, I have never been happier to see you in my life, although I'm not sure how I feel about this helicopter business," I laugh.

I'm in such a hurry to leave that I don't have to share the elevator, which is probably a good thing. I'm in a funky mood *and* I still don't feel well. This is not a good combination. And it sounds like I'll be spending the whole day with my group. Which means a whole day with Henry and Lyncoln. Both.

We arrive at my room shortly and I don't hesitate to enter as I wonder what I get to change into. I'm more than glad to kick off my heels. I find black pants, black boots, a black tank top, and a black jacket. All are a sleek and smooth material I'm not familiar with. So basically the stuff Lyncoln is always wearing. I quickly change into them.

I take a look in the mirror. I look different. I'm not feeling feminine at all for the first day since arriving in Denver. I pull my hair up into a ponytail even though I know Frank wouldn't like it. I smile. This feels good.

No boys.

No Presidency.

This is me.

For the first time in a long time, I feel like me.

****

The helicopter is new and scary, but I find I actually love looking out the window as we fly. We are sitting on two long benches facing each other in the back part of the helicopter. Being the woman and getting first choice, I sit by the window. My subconscious also points out that this means I can't be sitting in the middle of Henry and Lyncoln again. Once is definitely enough for the day.

Henry sits beside me and Lyncoln across from me with Oliver and Joshua on the other sides of them. We also have guards on board with us. Half are sitting on the bench seats and half are standing holding onto a handle attached to the ceiling.

"You are crazy," Henry says over the headset to me.

"Why?" I ask confused as to which reason he is calling me crazy for.

He nods to the window where I am admiring the mountain-view. From up here, I think it may be the most beautiful thing I have ever seen.

"Are you afraid of heights?" I ask, wondering why he was on the roof the night I waved at him if he is afraid of heights.

"Yes, but I'm trying to get over it. I'm fine with planes and copters, just don't want to look straight down from the window," he says with a shrug. It must take a confident man to admit to something that he is afraid of so freely.

Looking out the window, I get completely lost in what I see. We fly over an area that is obviously maintained and inhabited, another area that looks desolate but still cleaned up, and then just a short half an hour or so later, there is total destruction. I see cars parked on the side of the road with weeds growing out of them where they were abandoned so many years ago. I see all sorts of wildlife, deer and antelope especially, as they run rampant and are becoming quite the problem, even in Denver. I see broken buildings and old houses. Some houses are just piles of crumbled brick it seems.

I get caught up in how disorganized everything is. The weeds are out of control growing on top of buildings, around the buildings, on cars, and just everywhere. In fact, in some places the weeds and grass are so tall I'm sure you wouldn't even see some buildings if you weren't above them looking down. The roads look cracked, faded, and deserted. Things are just left in the middle of nowhere and there is debris strewn about. Stuff is just everywhere, right where people left it in their haste to escape Trident. It's crazy to think that we aren't even that far from Denver and there are still areas that look like this. No wonder Professor Zax made us do this project. There is still so much that needs cleaned up.

A half an hour later, after flying around that area and beyond, I am told we are about to land in one of the deserted suburbs of an old neighboring city to the south of Denver. We have a half an hour to look around but are not to go into any of the buildings. We land and the helicopter with its huge blades shuts off and powers down. I'm about to jump down and just take off, but am instead given a hand gun, much to my own surprise.

"Just in case you need it. You never know with the wildlife. Keep the safety on at all times. That is the little red button here." The guard shrugs and places it in my hands seeming rather annoyed and then proceeds to give me a lesson on how to shoot the thing. Jamie is talking to the pilot unfortunately, so I just have to stand there and listen to the guy.

"Oh, like she knows how to use that," Oliver says with a huff. "Don't worry Reagan, I will protect you." He bows to me and gives me an overdone wink before turning towards the guy. "Is it necessary she even have one?"

I'm standing there somewhat annoyed while holding the gun, but not saying anything either because I just want the guard guy to shut up, when Lyncoln pipes up for the first time today sounding impressed. "She's shot a gun before. She knows how to hold it." He shakes his head. "Even Better."

I'm about to ask what that means before I see Henry's surprised look. "You have?" He grins at me with those amazing dimples.

Joshua whistles. "You have? That's crazy. Ha. You would. And I bet you are a better shot than Oliver here. Those other girls better look out!"

I'm ready to get moving, but they are all just standing there looking at me, waiting for me to explain. Even the guard guy who was giving me my gun lesson stops and looks confused.

"We have a huge problem with wildlife where I'm from." I shrug. I know exactly how to fire this weapon. Now aiming it is an issue. I have never had to defend myself from a wild animal with a weapon, but when packs of coyotes stray too close to our farm, a couple of shots in the air chase them off pretty quickly. Dad and Ashton sometimes even have to go coyote hunting to keep them away from the cattle. Coyotes and the occasional mountain lion are all we really have to worry about fortunately. Some people from other subdivisions have told stories about other predators, so we know it could be much worse.

One time I killed a wild turkey on a dare from Ashton. The thing is, I didn't kill the turkey I was aiming for. There were just so many of them that I managed to hit one about two feet from where I aimed, not that I ever admitted that to Ashton or anything. Smiling thinking of it, and wanting the attention off of me, I tell the boys that story as we start out and they get a big kick out of it. The stressed out guard even almost cracks a smile.

We walk around talking while holding our guns aimed at the ground. Oliver and Joshua go to check out an old gas station while Henry, Lyncoln, and I wander aimlessly. I should be annoyed by both of them feeling the need to be my bodyguards, but the fresh air feels so good and is distracting me from my head cold, that I try not to dwell on it. Plus, Oliver and Joshua were talking a hundred miles a minute. So it's nice to have some peace and quiet. Our guards let us meander, though they are always following at a distance.

We walk by an old grocery store and I wonder about the simplicity of what life used to be like. No more growing food on a large scale, just swing into the store and pick it up. They even had places that you could drive up to and get food without ever having to get out of your car. I just can't even wrap my head around the technology and busyness of pre-Trident. In some ways I'm glad that things are a bit simpler now. Their way of life seems intimidating and busy, but yet somehow lacking real purpose. Everything we do post-Trident is done purposefully and for the ultimate goal of rebuilding. Every little thing has a purpose.

"Can you imagine all these houses being plum full of people?" I say as we turn the corner and find a bunch of run down houses. Some have holes in the roofs. Some don't have roofs as they have completely collapsed. And some look like you could still live in them. Some even still have run-down cars in the driveway, and I shudder wondering if there are carcasses of the people inside the homes. After 150 years, probably just skeletal remains. I shiver as a breeze blows random plastic trash across our pathway.

"Crazy." Henry shakes his head in agreement with me.

As we round another corner and head down an old alleyway, I'm just thinking to myself that the other two are oddly quiet, when I am all of a sudden roughly thrown up against the old decaying brick of one of the houses. I drop my gun in the process and it skids across the ground. Lyncoln has his hand over my mouth and his dark eyes are inches from mine, just looking at me. I can't make a sound. Or breathe for that matter. Henry is standing in front of us, but not facing us. With his gun drawn, he walks a few steps down and listens, pointing his gun at different angles. Hearing nothing, he comes back shaking his head.

"I thought they cleared it since we were coming," Henry whispers, sounding mad for the first time since I met him.

Lyncoln is still inches from my face with his hand around my mouth though he loosens it a bit. The other hand is gripping his gun like he's held one thousands of times. "They did," he says defensively but quietly in Henry's direction, "Yesterday AND this morning. You think they would have let you out of the castle otherwise?"

"Then what the heck is on our tail?" he asks while listening again, never dropping his gun for a second.

Just then a black cat goes scurrying across the alley where we are hiding, carrying a large and dead mouse in its mouth.

Lyncoln starts laughing, then laughing harder, releasing me because he's laughing so hard. He rests his hand beside me on the brick like he will fall to the ground in laughter if he doesn't. I have never seen him laugh at all, let alone like this.

Henry joins in and shakes his head. "We need to get out more often. We thought a flipping cat was a drifter."

They banter back and forth for the next few minutes laughing together and paying me no attention.

"Ummm. Still here," I say confused but smiling at their good spirits. Lyncoln's smile is a work of art, but his laughter is pure magic.

"Hey," Lyncoln turns his attention back to me with the first real and genuine smile I think I have ever seen.

"What is a drifter and why would you think we were being followed here of all places?" I ask very much confused.

They look at one another. Lyncoln shakes his head back and forth. "Probably best you don't know, yet anyway." He then reaches behind my back and gently pulls me away from the wall and towards him. "Sorry if I hurt you at all. I tried to be gentle."

He picks my gun off the ground, dusts it off, and hands it to me, adding quietly, "Love the ponytail by the way."

I ignore that. "Well if I am going to have to actually use this," I say gripping my gun, "I would like to know why."

"I would love to tell you, but you don't have clearance, yet." Lyncoln shrugs and looks me in the eyes as if apologizing. "I promise I'll tell you as soon as I can."

"We both know she eventually will, so you might as well just tell her now," Henry says with a hand in the air as if to say "screw it".

"Yeah, but if for some stupid reason you decide you are done with her, I would like her protected, pretty boy. Rules are rules," Lyncoln says, squinting his eyes coolly. Goodbye fun Lyncoln, hello dangerous Lyncoln. It took all of three seconds for one to leave and the other to settle on in.

"Oh, is that all you would like to do...protect her?" Henry smiles and cocks his head at him, but I'm not sure it's a playful smile this time. It seems like more of a sarcastic one.

Having enough of their alpha male argument, I take off down the alley back the way we came before I even hear how Lyncoln responds. I hear them follow but they keep their distance. I really want to know what a drifter is and why they thought we were in danger, but it sounds like they aren't going to tell me. Which is fine, because right now I am more disturbed with their little spat.

I will not be the reason two boys who seem to get along great come to hate each other. I won't be that girl. I don't even know how I got to be that girl. Before the Culling, I hadn't ever had a boy look at me that way.

"You okay?" Jamie asks as I round the corner back the way we came, "You look pissed."

I just nod at him and keep walking rather fast.

"Boy trouble?" he grins knowingly.

I don't answer.

"Annnd we are walking," Jamie laughs, trying to keep up.

****

The helicopter ride back ends up being a quiet one. Henry and Lyncoln seemed to have kissed and made up, but I was more reserved, partially from not feeling well, and partially from being freaked out over their spat. Oliver and Joshua talked about the gas station and other things they found fascinating. I was grateful for the opportunity to be quiet and listen while getting lost looking out the window again. I don't think I will ever forget what the destruction and damage looks like from up there.

Upon returning, I find my way back to my room and Jamie brings me a late lunch. Frank knocks on my door in the middle of my lunch to tell me that they are going to get my dress for dinner and will be back soon. Upon seeing me, he gives me some medicine and tells me to nap and not leave the bed until they return. I gladly do so. I'm exhausted both physically and emotionally.

When they come back, Gertie somehow manages to bring me a full pitcher of iced tea, having found out it was my favorite. After my first full glass, I'm already feeling better. Maybe it was the sleep? Or maybe it was because I got away from those confusing and infuriating boys?

"Would you like to see your gown?" Frank inquires.

"Sure," I respond, not looking forward to my evening with more tension and the President on top of all that.

He opens a dress bag and I find a lovely, bright pink dress. It's floor length. It has lace sleeves above the smooth pink bodice that fall off the shoulders. My entire front will be covered in either the smooth material or lace, no cleavage or anything. However, for as well covered as the front is, the back is entirely open. The front is pure elegance and the back is a party.

"Frank--you're a genius," I say, admiring the dress.

"Well, we knew you wouldn't want to feel sexy since you are the only girl. That dress can be worn at a later date." Gertie smiles.

"So we went with feminine, yet intriguing," Frank says with a wiggle of his eyebrows and I laugh.

"I'm so glad I have you two with me for the long haul." I mean my words more than they know.

"I have a feeling we will be around for a while." Gertie gives me a quick hug.

Everyone around me seems to always be saying that, yet I don't believe it. I won't allow myself to believe it. If Henry and Lyncoln were logical, they would each find someone else. I'd like to make it as far as I can for my family, but I need to be honest with myself too. And the honest truth is that the Culling is a mess.

****

The elevator doors open and I walk out with my arm in Sarge's. He unhooks my hand and gives it a squeeze as we enter the Presidential Quarters. I smile at him thanking him for the encouragement. I look around to find everyone present and looking at me, well, more like staring at me, as I have stopped their conversations. I don't let it go to my head; I am just the only girl in the room full of men. Henry grins his dazzling grin. Lyncoln, who was talking to the President, looks dangerous as ever but has a hard time not staring at me. Joshua lets out a whistle and gives me a thumbs up. Before I can choose what direction to go, Oliver steps up and takes my arm. Turning away from the others, I mouth thank you to him and he smiles and gives me an exaggerated wink.

We walk into the dining room to a huge, long table. It only needs to seat the seven of us, but this table looks like it could easily sit twice that. Oliver leads me to my spot and I'm pleased to see more iced tea already there, but this time in the fanciest glass I have ever seen. I take my seat and take a drink while he heads for his spot across and down from me. I try to put my hair behind my ear as I usually do when nervous, but then I remember that my hair is curled and on top of my head. Instead, I put my hands in my lap while trying to sit tall, just like Dougall taught us.

The rest of my company enters the dining area, sits, and the small talk starts as our salads are served. From etiquette class, I know that they wouldn't have sat until I did. I think of home and how who sits first or where is never an issue. How my life has changed!

The President is sitting to my right at one end of the table. Professor Zax sits at the other end. Lyncoln is to my left, but far enough away that his amazing smell all freshly showered isn't quite so enrapturing. Joshua is on the other side of him. Henry is straight across from me, and Oliver is on the other side of Henry.

"You should have seen it, Mr. President," Lyncoln says with a rare genuine smile. I realize as I have been quiet, they are telling the story about the cat.

"Yeah, I about had to shoot a poor cat!" Henry pitches in as the others laugh. I notice no mention of the word "drifter" has been made again this time.

"Better you than Reagan," Joshua offers, "She can't even hit a turkey at 20 yards."

"I bet you can't either," Oliver says with a wink at me before turning to Joshua, "Mr. Demolition man. You aren't into aiming, just explosions."

"Saves time," Joshua says nonchalantly with a shrug and I can't help but snicker.

"I can see why this group won." The President nods at Professor Zax, "They seem to get along swimmingly. And are quite the characters, too."

If he only knew.

"Reagan, what did you think of your field trip today?" the President asks, nicely trying to include me.

"It was enlightening," I begin and slightly tense up thinking about the two boys and their showdown in the alley. "Kind of hard to see. With Trident there was just so much…loss. And destruction. All those people." I shake my head. "And not only that but art, engineering, technology…even music. It all just abruptly stopped. Everything stopped."

He nods, "I agree. I have been president for 30 years, and it still affects me. As much as things have changed in the last 150 years as we find our way back, things are still very much the same. We will be feeling the shockwaves from Trident for at least another 150 years. Sometimes it's just easier to live within the bubbles of our townships and not think about it too much. Ignorance is bliss, as they say."

Our entrée of steak is served along with cheesy potatoes. I smile at the President and he winks at me.

"What?" Henry asks, picking up on it and looking from one of us to the other.

"It seems all my favorites are showing up." I smile.

"Now how would I know that?" the President jokes.

"Well, you could have done someone else's favorite something," I offer with a blush.

"Lyncoln's favorite is steak also. Oliver loves chocolate as well. Don't worry, they aren't hurting any. Plus, it isn't often I have a good-looking lady over for dinner. I thought you might like the spoiling," he says with smile and a nod towards me.

"Well, thank you. It is appreciated, but wasn't needed. And now I can't wait for dessert!" I say enthusiastically and hear a "me too" from Oliver's direction.

I want to keep talking to just the President all evening. There is much less tension that way. He is a very intelligent man. Very tired and very intelligent. I suppose that's what happens after forty-some years of stress from running a country. And I can see that Henry gets his charm from his father too.

As we eat our steak, Joshua, Oliver, and I take turns discussing our townships. Professor Zax lets it out of the bag that he was from Detroit having also been in the same Culling as the President, and he and Joshua have quite the discussion on the place. I know Henry and Lyncoln have both been looking in my direction often, but I'm very purposeful in not looking at either of them after today. I stay focused on my food and drink and the President only.

Before I know it, dessert arrives and is a chocolate cheesecake with chocolate chips and chocolate drizzle on top. I take a bite and close my eyes trying to remember what it tastes like for forever.

"That good?" Henry smiles with a laugh.

"That good." I open my eyes smiling at him. "I could eat the whole thing."

"Reagan, what made you think of the idea for the project anyway?" Professor Zax asks, interrupting my love affair with my cheesecake. I actually feel disappointed I have to put down my fork to answer.

"I'm not really sure. I just knew that if we were going to do it, I wanted something fixable and livable. I realize we don't need another township because six is plenty for our current population, but somehow destroying everything seemed wasteful and a bit disrespectful. Fixing just a few buildings while the others rotted around it didn't feel right either, so that's when I thought of it." I shrug shyly.

"Well, it was an amazing idea, dear." He smiles at me and I blush again.

"I had a lot of help. Lyncoln is very determined and strategic; he's a great leader. Henry knew the little stuff mattered and took the jobs that weren't fun and did them anyway just because he knew they needed done. Joshua's knowledge saved us, as none of us knew anything about demolition before at all. And Oliver was the motivator, keeping us laughing and moving the whole time," I explain, meaning every word as I brag on our group.

"I wasn't the leader." Lyncoln looks at me as if suggesting that I was and takes a long drink while maintaining eye contact and giving me the "I know you" look.

"Didn't you just hear her?" Oliver butts in. "I was practically the leader."

We all laugh. Oliver is really starting to come out of his shell. When I am stuck between these two boys with all this tension, I gladly take his company and comic relief.

After we finish dessert, Henry and Lyncoln talk and laugh about some training drill while Joshua, Oliver, and Professor Zax discuss in-depth ways to fix the water dams across the nation that need fixing. I'm content just listening in.

"Walk with me for a minute?" the President leans over and offers me his hand.

"I would love to." I smile, knowing I really do like this man. He may have given me a watch that was bugged, but I still like him despite the fact that I feel like he's the sole owner of a thousand secrets.

"How is this process for you, my dear? I have heard the girls haven't been all that nice," he asks genuinely concerned as he guides me down a hallway.

"It isn't always easy, but I'm making it through." I shrug.

"You remind me so much of my Esther sometimes," he says, his eyes immediately going teary at the mention of his wife and I realize the magnitude with which he loved her.

"I'm sorry."

"Don't be. It's a very good thing. She was…" he stops and gestures, "my everything. I knew within two weeks of meeting her that I would throw away my hopes for the presidency if I had to just to be with her. It took me another two weeks for her to even give me the time of day though." He laughs. "She was stubborn and bull-headed, but with her by my side I could accomplish anything. Can I tell you a little secret?"

"What's that?" I smile.

"She ran the country just as much if not more than I did, even though I get all the credit because I'm the man. She took care of things. She talked me through decisions. She was the one I went to when the decisions became a burden. She was there with me every step of the way. She was in every meeting until the kids came, and even then she made it when she could. There wasn't a single thing I kept from her or didn't get her opinion on. That's why this process is so important, and that is why I believe a good relationship in the Presidential Couple is so important. Chemistry and trust between the two leaders is vital. You'll need each other more than you know. And having a partner in all the responsibilities gives you a distinct advantage."

Hearing about the love he had for his wife almost brings me to tears. I try to imagine what it would be like, putting myself in those situations. Then I start to wonder who I would be there with.

"I need you to know something," he says snapping me out of my daydreaming.

"Yes, President Maxwell?" I'm glad he doesn't seem to notice my blush, or at least say anything about it.

"Both of those boys seem to be completely enamored with you." I start to tense up but he puts an arm on my shoulder and smiles. "And I can't blame them, dear. Lyncoln is like a second son to me. He and Henry have similarities and high standards so I'm not at all surprised they have picked the same girl. You, of all the girls, will make an exceptional Madam President if you choose it. It's likely you will get to at least the final eight or better, but it's up to you if you truly want it. You are one of maybe five of the current girls I would say this to. My only worry is that when you truly see what you are up against, you will run.

"It won't be a matter of which of these young men you will pair up with as both of them are quite capable, but the question here is if you will choose the presidency itself. Trust me, running this country isn't easy. You will have to do things you will hate yourself for." With that he looks off in the distance as if searching for his mistakes.

I stand there speechless. Before I have a chance to say anything, he picks up a box off of the kitchen counter we walked to and hands it to me with a smile. "The rest of your beloved cheesecake."

"Thank you." I smile a confused and hesitant smile. What does he mean? What will I have to do that I will hate myself for? What mistakes has he made or thinks he has made?

"Think about what I said. The farther the Culling goes, the more you will understand what I am saying." Then as an afterthought he adds, "And don't you worry about those two boys. They'll be just fine."

Seeing it is now time to go as I have my cheesecake in hand, I return to the dining room to find the boys and Professor Zax to say goodnight. I find them standing around laughing with Professor Zax, probably discussing more crazy ideas about what still needs fixed post-Trident.

"Well, gentlemen, it has been a lovely evening. Thank you for letting me join you," I say properly and smile at them. I turn toward the foyer where Sarge is standing with the other guards. Well except for the

President's, who are right behind him and never leave his side, of course.

"Let me walk you to the elevator?" Henry smiles and takes my hand, looping it in his arm like I normally walk with Sarge or Jamie. Professor Dougall would be so proud.

Our guards, as usual, are about five yards behind us but definitely still there. I am unusually quiet, even more so than earlier in the evening as I think about what the President just said to me. That and with still fighting this cold, I am feeling worn out with all the day's events. I just want to go curl up in the electric blanket Jamie got me and sleep.

"I really like your gown," Henry says quietly.

"Thank you."

He smiles. "But not as much as I like the wearer, if you don't mind me saying so."

Those dimples when he flirts. Lord have mercy!

"I don't mind." I smile back and feel the heat rise in my cheeks as we walk down the hall. He's so straightforward. Unlike with Lyncoln, he never leaves me guessing. I always know where he stands.

"I mean, you don't strike me as a wearing pink type of gal, slippers or otherwise, but you sure can pull it off." Out of the corner of my eye, I can see him smiling mischievously. Reaching the elevator doors, he stops and turns to me, holding one of my hands and putting his other on my bare back making it harder to think as he brings me in closer towards him.

"Look, I know Lyncoln and my messing around earlier today got to you. I don't want you to worry about it." His green eyes are looking intense. I stand there silent as I stare into them allowing him to explain. "I know Lyncoln has feelings for you. I respect him. It won't ruin our friendship if we both care for you. I want you to know that you are the only girl I am interested in at this point, and I won't just brush you aside like he implied. We fight like brothers. Always have. Always will." He pauses and searches my eyes as if trying to read me like a book.

"That being said, if it can't be me with you, presidency or not, then I hope it's him. When his dad--" He stops for a second as if knowing what happened with Lyncoln's dad isn't his secret to tell. "Let's just say we've been like brothers for a while now. We fight like brothers, but we love one another like brothers. What you saw earlier today was just brothers being brothers."

My heart almost breaks with how perfect Henry is. Is there anything at all wrong with this man?

"Thank you," I say breathlessly.

"For what?" he asks confused.

"For being honest and kind. You are the epitome of chivalry," I smile and use the hand he isn't holding to reach out and pat his pec, which is a terrible idea because those things are huge and warm beneath my hand. I feel my cheeks blush knowing that I enjoy it entirely too much. I thought his chest was a place where I could touch him that wouldn't seem inappropriate. *Wrongo!*

He leans in to whisper in my ear, "I really would like to kiss you right about now, but I want it to be done right, and not after we were just talking about another man."

I close my eyes briefly wishing he would just do it already, as I am so very nervous about my first kiss, but then I feel him softly brush his lips across my cheek. It leaves my skin tingling for more.

"Goodnight, beautiful," he whispers and I can smell his minty breath again.

Then he pulls away and removes his hand from my back. He hits the elevator button for me, squeezes my hand, and leaves back down the hallway we came as soon as Sarge and I board the elevator. I feel cold replace the heat I was just feeling. I'm getting too used to having him near me. I'm not sure if that is a good thing or a bad thing.

Sarge takes his place at my side and since I know him well by now, I know he is trying hard to stifle a smile.

"Not a word," I say sternly, trying to hide my own giddy smile.

Chapter 11

T he next day, I don't have to worry about the tension between Henry, Lyncoln, and I. It turns out Lyncoln has found my replacement. I'm not sure why it hurts, but it does a little. He sits by Attie, smiling and talking with her like he never has to me. I'm kind of shocked, and if I'm honest with myself, I'm a bit jealous about how much he is talking to her, the man of few words I dubbed him to be. But, I guess I don't have to worry about that decision anymore. I know the President said both of them were "enamored" with me. But if that were the case, why is Lyncoln showing her a kindness that he never extended to me? We have never sat there talking like that.

Henry is stuck down and to my right by Katie again. He smiles at me and gives me a wink letting me know he isn't too happy about it either. I blush thinking about our almost kiss last night and then a tray loudly clamors as it lands next to mine. October has been hanging out at Marisol's table since the group project but has apparently decided to come back to ours.

"Well, look what the cat drug in." Vanessa smiles from the other side of me. Much to her chagrin, Elizabeth and Maverick seem to be a thing. And Renae seems to be having more than one thing at a time with William, Adam, and Pierce around her, down to our left. I would judge her for that, but I don't really have room to say anything. For those reasons, this is why Vanessa and Bronson are my go to people at meal times. Sometimes it feels like the cafeteria is the loneliest place for me, despite being full of people.

"Hey," October smiles nicely.

"Hey," I say somewhat harshly. It isn't a secret that Marisol wants me out of this competition. So why on earth would she pick her over anyone else for the group project? Why did she ditch us for her of all people? October is easily the smartest girl here. I would've thought she would have known better.

"So anyway," Vanessa says, turning to me and rolling her eyes in regard to October, "we get to start doing more physical stuff, and some sort of game or competition outdoors." She continues to fill me in on what I missed yesterday. "But, of course, everything will be graded."

"Sweet!" I respond immediately, feeling my spirits lifted. Anything that gets me outside is good news.

We continue eating our lunch of grilled chicken with rice and vegetables. I think of the amazing chocolate cheesecake waiting for me this evening in my fridge and my mouth waters. Last night was good in more than one way. I have a hard time not staring at Henry our entire lunch. I wanted that first kiss pretty bad. And I think maybe he did too.

After Vanessa gets up to go back to her room before our afternoon classes, October leans in close to me. "I need to talk to you tonight. May I come to your room?"

"About what? What's wrong?" Though annoyed with her actions recently, I'm still concerned with her serious expression. Something is up.

"Just please talk to me, I'll come at about 9:30," she says and then more loudly says, "See you upstairs."

And then she's gone. I have never seen her act so...*weird*.

****

"Paintball, my ladies and gentlemen! Paintball!" Professor Bennett says excitedly while slapping his hands together at the front of the room with Professors Zax and Dougall. The other two shake their heads in amusement at his excitement while he continues.

"Also, we will be starting to test your skills at getting to know one another, so we are going to be giving you more time in the evenings together. You will have a half hour appointed time, or 'social', with each person until you have been through them all. At that point, you will be given a test to see if you know each other well. The best leaders surround themselves with the best people and know the integrity of those which they are around. Your schedule of who you meet with and when will be delivered to your rooms this evening and begin after tomorrow evening's paintball exercise."

Professor Dougall chips in with her air of propriety, "So from this point on, you are allowed in the opposite sex's rooms. Mainly because we just don't have enough room or time to set up meeting areas. If you are with the opposite sex, the door must remain open at all times. Your guards will be posted at the door. I understand some of you are hormonal teenagers, but if you cross a line and take it too far, you will be dismissed immediately. I'm sure you all know what I am referring to."

The whole room seems to take a giant gulp, well except for Professor Bennett who is still bouncing on his heels excited about paintball. I can't believe they'd even have to keep reminding us, but I guess some of the girls are much more…*experienced*…than I am.

Professor Zax continues, "These are all exciting developments; however, I should warn you that cuts will be happening shortly. Some of you might not make it through all that Professor Bennett is telling you about. But, if you do, you will also start taking trips during the day to DIA to see how the President runs the country. You will be given real life situations and even go through a number of different simulations. Don't think of all of this as just a test, because it isn't. Your decisions will actually affect people's lives. You will become a real diplomat of sorts."

I sit there listening to the three close out our afternoon class and feel excited. Not just for the paintball exercise taking place outside of DIA tomorrow, but also because if I have more influence, maybe I can help projects like Marcia's go through. I'm sure that won't happen for a while, but one can hope.

Professor Dougall takes back over. "Now, I know we don't typically have a timetable, but know that if things work how we want them to, there will be half as many of you in this room in the next two to three weeks. Then things will slow down a bit as we really start to see what decisions you make with the increase in power given to you."

The excited feeling I have is all exhaled out of me with that and the end of class. Even though the President basically told me I was a frontrunner, I can't help but feel dread. What if I went home and Henry stayed? Henry obviously isn't going anywhere, but what if I did? Would I be able to go back to Omaha and live life working all day, every day knowing that he is somewhere here with a different girl? I should be safe, but what if I do something wrong and make the wrong people mad like Julia did? What if I get sent home before we even get to the voting portion of this whole thing? And when we do get to the voting, will they really want to vote me to be at Henry's side? The nobody from Omaha?

Who am I kidding? If they could, they would vote Elizabeth at his side and I would go home with my heart in a million pieces with no goodbyes and no second chance. I have no faith in this process. Zero. This is madness!

Henry seems to be picking up on my nervousness and walks out of the classroom and down the hallway with me, taking my hand and pulling me aside close to the elevators. I feel like I'm about ready to implode. Everyone is chatting about the upcoming cuts and paintball event, so we can talk without worrying about being overheard off to the side while everyone files into the elevators and heads down to the cafeteria.

"Reagan, don't even worry about it. You really don't have a thing to worry about. Besides, we are safe from the first cuts anyway, remember." He squeezes my hand.

"I just have so many questions and am still tired from when I wasn't feeling well. I feel insecure about this process, I guess," I admit as we start slowly walking towards the now empty elevators.

"You have no reason to be." He gazes his to-die-for emerald green eyes at mine.

The elevator door opens and we board. With Jamie and Henry's two guards and the two of us, it's a full house and not at all a private occasion. Since the guards stay out of our conversations though, it is the closest thing to privacy we have.

"Do you trust me?" he almost pleads.

"Of course I do." I don't even hesitate.

"Then please, don't worry about it. Don't lose any sleep over it. We'll take each day one at a time and head on," he reasons.

The door quickly rings again and I step out thinking that is the end of our conversation, but he keeps my hand in his and walks me down the hallway toward the cafeteria. This time, he never leaves my side and sits right beside me. It's nice not having to feel lonely during a meal. We talk with Vanessa and Bronson and I find myself feeling a bit reassured.

Afterwards, Henry goes as far as to walk me back to my room for the evening. I know he won't go in, but dropping me off at my door is a kind gesture, especially in my state. It means a lot that he recognized I was stressing out and took the time to help work me out of my funk.

At my door, he turns me to look at him and gives me a hug. He whispers in my ear, "Talk to me. Please." His arms feel familiar, which makes me feel worse. How will I ever go back home from this place after having met him?

Still in his hug and unable to look him in the eyes I say, "What if I don't make it? What if they don't vote me to be with you? How will I ever go home after this? Watching you win the Presidency with someone else would tear me to shreds."

He pulls me back to look at my teary eyes, resting his hands on my face, thumbs ready to wipe away any tears that may fall. "Don't even think like that. You will make it. We will make it. We will make sure of it. As more people leave, it will get easier. Besides, we will make it clear we are a couple before the voting, so they don't have a choice but to vote for us together."

He holds me for a while longer and rubs my arms up and down a few times before telling me goodnight, giving me another kiss on the cheek, assuring me I have nothing to worry about, and then leaving me at my room. I have the worst feeling in my gut that he is wrong. The farther this goes, it will become harder instead of easier. It's hard to believe I've already been here four whole weeks, an entire month. In a month more, it will be impossible to say goodbye to Henry.

If I even get to say goodbye at all.

****

At exactly 9:30, there is a knock on my door. Knowing October was going to come to see me, I am anxious to see what she has to say.

"Hey," I greet her as I open the door. I barely have the door open before she quickly enters the room.

"Hey. I have to be fast. Marisol's room isn't on your floor, but one of her minions could be," she says hurried.

"Okay? What is up with you and Marisol anyway?" I ask, cutting to the chase.

"Have you ever heard of the saying 'keep your friends close and your enemies closer'?" she asks, looking determined and brilliant as usual.

"Yes," I say taken aback. That same exact phrase keeps popping up, starting with when I heard it first from Lyncoln the night of the ball.

"Well I have officially infiltrated her circle. I'm supposed to be spying on you and Elizabeth, who she sees as her biggest threats," she says quickly.

"Okay?"

"I made up a lie about how you are just here for the boys," she says quickly again and winces as if knowing her words will hurt me.

It does sting a little. "Uh. Thanks."

She reaches out and squeezes my shoulder, "Of course I don't really think that, and it isn't really true, but I had to make it believable. I made up some stuff you supposedly said too."

"Okay…"

"So anyway, I will be spending more time with you and Elizabeth and then reporting back to her. But really, I'm going to be spying on her and reporting to you," she says with a shrug like that explains everything.

"Wait? What?" I say, sitting down on a chair in my room. "And why?"

"Marisol is evil. A woman like her at the helm of our country would be a disaster," she says matter-of-factly. "I'm a double agent of sorts."

"But what about you? In hanging out with her and playing a double spy, you will hurt your own chances of the presidency," I ask, still uncertain with what I am hearing.

"I never wanted it," she says simply while looking down at her shoes.

"What?" I feel confused for the hundredth time since she got here just a few seconds ago.

"I never wanted the presidency." She pauses. "You know the questions they ask, like 'Did you have a boyfriend before coming here?' Well. I did. I do. I don't want this, and I never did. I want to teach. I want to marry my boyfriend. I know I wouldn't be happy with this life.

"At first, they told me I had to try my hardest and if I didn't I would be relocated to a different township, unable to marry Lucas," she pauses again. "When they figured out I am more of a nerd and not so much a social girl, they knew I wouldn't ever win anyway, but they also know I'm smart. So they asked me to stay and help the next Madam President solidify her spot in the Culling. Like a support system. I knew I had to say yes. I couldn't go home and marry Lucas and be happy if someone like Marisol actually won."

"Okay?" I remember what the President told me about choosing to be the President.

October never would have chosen it, and in being forced to do something she ultimately didn't want to do, she would have hated it and became cold-hearted over time. She never would have forgiven them for not letting her marry the person she chose and she wouldn't have been a good leader because of it. For the Culling seeming so cutthroat in process, they do at least seem to understand that making someone do something against their will is detrimental to their cause. Our government may be messed up at times, but it isn't outright evil.

"So that brings me to you. I started looking for who should be the next Madam President. I looked hard, I paid attention to little things, I almost never read my book, and I just sat there at lunch listening in on different conversations. I also was given some inside information to help me with my decisions. I have been telling them for weeks now that Marisol is bad news, but for some reason, they aren't listening to me. I'm not sure what power she holds here in Denver, but she has it. Right before the ball, I knew you were one of my final four. Then when I saw how quickly Lyncoln and Henry saw what I saw, it only confirmed it. I have it down to three. You, Elizabeth, and Vanessa. But you are who I would personally vote for," she says smiling this time.

"Excuse me?" I say totally shocked. She finally sits down on the couch next to me.

"I will do everything in my power to help you and the others until they send me home, which could be soon. I want to go home, but I feel it's my duty to help you guys first. I don't know what's up with Marisol.

They monitor her, and they know how she is, but for some reason, she is very high on the rankings. She won't be going home for a very long time."

"Oh great," I say feeling dread. What won't that girl do to become Madam President? Or what has she already done to get this far?

"But neither will you. It's going to get crazy. The only reason I am telling you this and not the others is because at some point I may have to be mean to your face in order to get her to really believe me. We are going to have to fake a fight or something. I just couldn't start a fight with you or let you feel like I chose Marisol over you when you are kind of our group's leader. You're the one that got us all together and I couldn't do that to you. And if I did it to Elizabeth, she would just cry, even if she knew it was fake. And Vanessa would punch me. And I don't want punched. So that leaves you and means I needed to bring you in on the secret."

"This is crazy!" I say shaking my head. "So it isn't because of Henry?" I can't believe that she would have just picked me out of the bunch. But maybe she would because I have sort of paired up with Henry and he has been the favorite from day one. That would make more sense.

"No. I saw your lie detector test. I don't care who you pick. But just for the record, both Lyncoln and Henry would make fine presidents. Tough choice. I don't envy you." She smiles and gets up to leave.

"October?" I ask weakly as she heads towards the door.

She stops and looks back at me.

"These words seem inadequate, but thank you," I say emotionally. I feel disbelief. I feel grateful. I feel excited. I feel dread.

"Don't thank me yet. We still have our work cut out for us. Then there is the voting. This is only the beginning. Marisol cannot win."

And with that, she gives me a tight smile and leaves just as quickly as she came.

Chapter 12

I t takes about a half-hour ride to get to the location of the paintball
competition. It's late afternoon by the time we arrive in black
SUVs, two contestants per vehicle. I'm not sure the point of that
since we very easily could have done four or five to a car, but I remember
that somewhere out there, someone or something is a threat to the
presidency. I wonder how safe the paintball match will really be, but I
realize that they will have done every precaution possible. I'm feeling
nervous to know what it feels like to get shot with a paintball too. It
sounds painful. And just...bizarre.

We are taken to an open field next to a thicket. Off in the distance,
I can see DIA. Beyond the open field where we will be meeting for this
paintball match, there are logs and trees of every shape to hide behind.
It smells woodsy and abandoned. Guards, of course, are everywhere
though, some on the hills around us and others down on the open field
with us. With so many extra guards, I wonder how long it took to
organize all this.

Once it gets dark, this will become interesting. A bunch of tall
floodlights are set up around the field to help us see once it does get
dark, but they won't do as good of a job in the trees.

As the sun starts to drop beginning to paint the sky with its setting,
I am thankful for the fresh air and beauty both. Again, I am nervous to
get shot with a paintball, but feeling excited overall nonetheless. I'm also

a bit worried about tripping over a stick in the dark and getting injured. Shooting in the dark is dangerous enough without being a klutz. I just don't want to make a fool of myself and fall on my face in front of everyone...*again.*

We are all wearing the black gear given to us as well as glow in the dark bands around our wrists, ankles, and around our waists. We segregate into a large boy group and girl group and are then given guns, quickly taught how to shoot them, and are given a bag of glow in the dark ammo. I shoot a couple of rounds at a tree for practice and find myself quite entertained with the splatters of paint. This might be fun. I imagine shooting Marisol in the face. We have protective gear and masks we have to wear, but still. It sure would make me feel better.

We meet back together and Professor Bennett announces the five teams, which have two team leaders a piece. I'm a bit bummed to find out I'm not on Henry's team and Katie is. I'm sure she will follow him around like a lovesick puppy dog. I selfishly hope she goes home soon. I then find out that I am on Lyncoln and Trent's team along with Elizabeth, Renae, and Oliver. So that brightens my mood. Others on my team that I don't know as well include Isabella, Grady, and Christopher.

This will be the first time in the last two days Lyncoln won't be with Attie. I haven't talked to him since I don't remember when. He's been keeping his distance, but probably won't be able to ignore me for this. I'm not sure how I feel about that.

I'm also not sure how I feel about the fact that Elizabeth makes our paintball gear look far too good. Normally I wouldn't like being in her group, but since she and Maverick are a thing, I have felt less threatened and have been enjoying her friendship more and more. It's not her fault she is by far the most beautiful girl here. I head over to stand by and chat with her when we break into our groups to get the rundown on how this will work.

Each team has a flag we have to protect and we also have to try to steal other team's flags. You may make an alliance with another team or teams, or you can choose not to. The goal is to not lose your flag and gain as many other flags as you can. Once your flag is in an opponent's assigned area, you are out. If you are shot three times, you are out. Above all else, you cannot lose your flag. You must leave the trees for the opening once your team has lost your flag or once you have been shot three times. The game will continue until one team has in their possession at least three flags.

Professor Bennett is practically bouncing as he explains all the rules and dismisses us to our different areas to strategize amongst our teams. He is just wayyy too excited for this.

"I vote Lyncoln tells us what to do," Trent slaps him on the back as soon as we are to our assigned area and gathered around.

"Me too," Elizabeth adds and Renae and I nod in agreement. Renae tells me all the time that she is afraid of and intimidated by Lyncoln. He is definitely intense, but I'm not afraid of him. Intimidated maybe, but not afraid.

Lyncoln starts in all business as we crowd around closer listening to him strategize, "Okay, we will need to split up, obviously. We will make an alliance with one team and one team only. Half of us will be on the offense with that team and work on getting the other team's flags. The others will work defense in protecting our own flag. Once the first flag is taken, and make dang sure one of us has it in our possession, we'll then need to break our alliance and take our alliance's flag. We will need a covert group to do that, already in place having found our ally's flag, ready to ambush them by the time that first flag is taken. There can probably only be one or two people since the rest will be needed to protect our flag. So with our flag and two others, we will win, and win quickly.

"That means our offense, with the help of our ally, needs to pinpoint only one other flag. Don't make it too easy or too obvious. With the help of an alliance, it should be easy enough to take another team's flag. Go as fast as possible. Get the first one and act like you are helping for the second one, but stay back and then make your exit as clean and quick as possible. This will be the hardest part. Cover that flag bearer like our lives depend on it and make sure they get out with the flag, without getting shot, or we are screwed. Then the group waiting in ambush gets the third from our ally, and counting our own, that's the end of the game, we win."

I'm impressed with how quickly he thought of that and shake my head along with a few of the others who obviously feel the same way. Christopher smiles like he expected nothing less from Lyncoln.

"Cutthroat. I love it," Isabella offers.

"Me too," Oliver agrees and salutes Lyncoln.

Having our plan in place, now the only question that remains is who is going to do what. I kind of stay back and let them duke it out. I have no idea what I would be good at. This is completely out of my comfort zone. Trent and Lyncoln are our team leaders, so they can just put me wherever.

"Lyncoln, dude, you are ruthless. You need to be the one to steal the flag from our alliance." Oliver salutes again. "I nominate you to the ambush team."

"Grady and I will lead the offense then. We can take Renae?" Trent offers.

"I would feel better with Grady and Oliver both protecting our flag. I've seen Grady shoot. He's one of the best." Lyncoln smirks at Oliver as if knowing he isn't a good shot but not wanting to say it. "Take Christopher instead. He's who I would want holding onto that first flag we steal. The guy is crazy fast."

"You good with that Grady?" Trent asks.

"Heck yeah," Grady nods.

Lyncoln then turns to Christopher, "You will be the key in all this. Be aggressive. Take a risk and make sure that you personally get the other team's flag while still with our ally. Hold on to it and get the hell out of there. If you fail us, we lose. Just hold on to the dang flag."

"Got it, boss," he nods excitedly. He and Lyncoln seem to be cut from the same aggressive mold, so I have no doubt he will succeed for us.

Trent nods his agreement then turns to Renae, "Renae, are you cool being the only chick on offense?"

"Yeah, I would prefer offense." She seems to be beaming. I smile at her. Since the boys have been in the mix, she has been much less annoying and rude. I think Trent is on her list of boys to woo as well, so she will enjoy the extra time with him.

"So that leaves me, Elizabeth, Grady, Isabella, and Reagan at the flag. Why don't you take Reagan with you for the third flag and team ambush?" Oliver asks and grins right at me.

"Works for me." He shrugs looking none too happy about it.

Great. Thank you, Oliver! I give Oliver a look that tells him I know he's being a giant turd.

I turn to Lyncoln, trying my best to be nice and respect his wanting to distance himself from me. "Are you sure? I can help defend the flag if you'd rather?"

This makes him smirk. "With your aim?"

I realize he's referring to the turkey story and I squint at him like I'm insulted.

"I'm taking Reagan," he nods at me definitively, trying not to smile, "I trust the rest of you to protect our flag. Everyone good?"

Everyone nods and seems content with their jobs...everyone but me. I don't know if Lyncoln hates me or likes me. I just can't keep up.

And wouldn't you know it that our alliance ends up being with Henry's team? I have to steal Henry's team's flag with Lyncoln of all people.

The irony is real.

****

We have five minutes to go into the trees and hide our flag somewhere in our team's allotted area. We know the general vicinity of Henry's team since they are our ally. Now it comes down to the best place to put our own flag because once we place it somewhere, we cannot move it. Isabella finds a huge stump fallen over on its side and we place our flag inside of it. So if someone walks by, they would have to turn around and be looking for it in order to find it. If they do turn around though, its glow definitely gives it away. We are just banking on that if someone gets that close, we will shoot them the required three times before they turn around and take it.

After hiding our own flag, we set off on our assigned duties, spreading out and heading in the direction we each need to. The only sound heard is the leaves crunching beneath our boots. We don't want to give away our position although the glow sticks on our gear will do that if someone gets close enough. It is almost completely dark out. Surprisingly, we can still see quite a bit from the moonlight and floodlights.

Lyncoln and I stand on the east side of our territory, ready to go around the back way to our ally's area. He hasn't said much to me, or I to him. He seems in "the zone" and I don't want to mess with his master plan by complicating it with small talk. What he hasn't communicated to me that I do understand is that we have to be stealthy. Our allies need to not see us coming. Taking the long way around to the back of their territory will only give us an advantage if they don't see or hear us coming.

As soon as the bell rings, we're going to use what little light there is and hide somewhere in our ally's territory, wherever Lyncoln thinks will be best to lay ambush. My only hope is that Henry is with the team going to take out the other team's flags so he isn't around when we turn on his team.

We wait and wait in awkward silence. I try my hardest not to fidget, practicing stealth mode.

Finally, we hear the bell ring. It's game time and we don't hesitate to take off. The quicker we are, the less likely they are to notice that we are in their territory. I'm trying to walk as quietly as I can but every time I hear a leaf under my boot or a twig snap, I see Lyncoln tense up. He's obviously better at this covert stuff than I am. He steps with ease and confidence, his broad shoulders ready to pummel anything that stands in his way. If there was one word to describe him right now, it would be *predator*. He is definitely in his comfort zone right now.

And here I am just trying my dandiest to not make my mask fog up. Because of my nervousness, or Lyncoln in the vicinity, or the craziness of this exercise, or all of the above, I'm breathing heavy and it feels a hundred degrees in my mask. Outside of the mask, I'm glad my gloves are covering my hands or I would feel quite chilled. Even with the woodsy outdoor smell and the stupid foggy mask, I can still smell that distinctive Lyncoln smell every now and then on the breeze, and it makes it hard to concentrate.

We quickly make our way. About halfway there, I'm following his lead when a branch somehow manages to get lodged in the side of my mask. I stop right away to take it off and try to fix it on my own. Hearing me behind him, Lyncoln spins around and looks at me. He lifts up his mask to the top of his head and glares at me. I sheepishly point to the branch and shrug, which causes him to shake his head and grin. He should grin more often.

Two things happen simultaneously from there. I hear the crunch of leaves off to my right and I feel Lyncoln pick me up and pin me against something cold and rough. Probably a tree. I don't say a word and neither does he. He just listens and watches and listens and watches, all the while keeping his paintball gun aimed and ready. We are almost on top of one another and he doesn't even seem to notice. He just keeps his eyes on the prize, so to speak. I find it odd that in the short amount of time I have known Lyncoln, this is the second time he has thrown me up against something. Both times he was trying to protect me, and he tried to do it softly, but still.

Minutes pass and we don't hear or see anything. It could have just as easily been a mouse or some sort of wild animal out here. Or it could be one of our allies finding us before we find their flag.

I'm inches from him while we wait it out. I'm about to think that Lyncoln's feelings for me were all a figment of my imagination because I seem to have no effect on him whatsoever, when he turns his eyes to my gaze and his breathing falters just a touch while he gives me that intense "I know you" look. The air seems to sizzle around us.

There it is. Maybe I do have an effect on him after all? He is so confusing; it is absolutely frustrating.

I push off from the tree and try to move away from him and get two steps before I hear him whisper, "Screw it."

I'm about to turn around and rudely shush him, but before my brain and mouth can communicate, I am gently shoved back up against the tree, dropping my gun and mask in surprise. Before I even have time to prepare, I feel his lips crash into mine as his arms pull me in closer.

I don't have time to think. It just happens.

My pulse increases, and I feel warm--very warm. He kisses me hard. I feel what little facial hair he has brush against my skin; it feels…tingly. Actually, all of me feels tingly.

My now empty hands find themselves holding on to him for dear life. The kiss goes from absolutely aggressive to begin with, to soft and tender. By the time he pulls away, I am breathless and disappointed it stopped.

Holy crap.

He rests his forehead on mine for a moment and just smiles his killer smile. Then he kisses me on the forehead and retrieves my mask and gun. He takes my mask and gives me one more quick kiss on the corner of my mouth, almost my cheek but not quite, before putting it back in place. Then he gives me my gun, pulls his own mask back down, and continues walking and searching like nothing happened.

What did happen?

What. Just. Happened.

I think of Henry and feel all sorts of guilt. That was my first kiss. And it was from Lyncoln. And it was a heck of a kiss, if I do say so myself.

Ho-ly crap. Holy cow. Holy crapping cow.

All of a sudden getting shot with a paintball is the least of my worries.

After walking only about 50 more yards, Lyncoln points and I see in the distance the glow of our ally's flag. The sun is long gone, but I can barely make out four people and the glow sticks on their persons as they guard it. From what I can tell, they've simply stuck it in the crook of the tree and spread out to surround the tree so that their flag is protected from all sides.

Because of that, unfortunately, the only completely hidden spot for us to hide is behind a wide tree. There isn't enough room for us to stand side by side, so we kind of have to recreate the position we just kissed in, except sitting this time. I sit with my back to the tree. Lyncoln is crouched in front of me, facing me with his gun ready and watching. Even low to the ground he still tries to protect me as he positions himself so that I'm sitting with his legs on either side of mine. I'm just glad our masks are back on at this point, providing more of a barrier. I don't know what happened back there at that other tree, but I don't think I'd be opposed to experiencing it again.

I rest my head against the tree and try my hardest not to move, which isn't easy for me. Lyncoln's body is very close to mine, but not touching. He has one arm on one of his legs propping himself up and holding his gun steady. I have my gun resting across my arm pointed away from him. My fingers are starting to feel cold through the thin gloves as the clock ticks on. The longer we wait, the longer the sun has been gone and the temperature drops. I'm sure if I wasn't wearing this stupid mask I could see my breath. I feel chilled already so I hope we don't have to wait long.

I think of Henry and what he is doing. I bet he didn't randomly kiss someone against a tree. I look at Lyncoln. How can he act like nothing happened? Just back to the game, focused, and on task. He is the most infuriating creature I have ever met. I thought he was moving on to Attie now anyway?

Why on earth did he kiss me? And he didn't even ask or let me know it was coming. He just went for it.

As I rub my fingers together, Lyncoln grabs them and scoots even closer. He keeps holding them and I don't mind. He is warm and I'm starting to feel so cold I'm afraid my teeth will start to chatter and give us away. I take a deep breath and smell the Lyncoln and outdoor mixture. If I could somehow create a candle that smelled like those two things combined, I think my life would be more complete. I smile but then scold myself. We are playing a game. I might get shot by a paintball. It's time to focus!

We stay like that for about five excruciatingly long minutes and then hear the *pop, pop-pop, pop* that Trent and Christopher know to use to signal to us that the first flag has been taken. Then we wait some more. It's almost our turn in this crazy game. I tense up. I'm worried about what it feels like to get shot, but not terribly so because Lyncoln is right here. I have a feeling he could take out all four of the people guarding the flag before I even have time to aim properly or turn the safety off.

He turns to me and very closely whispers, "Two minutes and then we go."

My pulse accelerates. Holy crap. It's go time. And holy crap. He's impressive. And intense. And is wayyy too good at this. And my mask is fogging up again. Freak!

After the two minutes are up, he tells me to stay put and makes his way to the person closest to us. I'm not sure who it is, but he moves freakishly fast and shoots them at about five feet away, three shots to the back of the calves. Then he uses that person as a shield as he makes his way to hide behind another smaller tree closer to the others.

I see Vanessa turn to try to find the intruder, but he shoots her three times across the stomach before she can find where it's coming from. When she does figure it out, she's pissed.

"Dang it, Lyncoln. You jerk!" She says a swear word and storms off, hands in the air in signal that she's done.

In mere seconds, the other two are down also. I have yet to fire my gun or move from the tree. I just stand there stunned and irrevocably impressed. Seeing his small window of opportunity, Lyncoln sprints the ten yards for the glowing flag. He has it and has just turned around when I hear twigs snapping and footsteps pounding. Someone is coming and coming fast. Not knowing who it is, he tries to outrun them. They are gaining fast but he is fast too. As the intruder comes through an opening and although it is dark, I recognize the body shape of our enemy. I would recognize that body anywhere.

"I knew something was wrong when you weren't on the offensive helping us get flags," Henry pants after him, slowing down only so he can shoot along the way. He hits Lyncoln once in the back. Then misses. He keeps firing and this seems hopeless. Henry is about to ruin our chances at this.

I then remember the gun in my hand. I'm not useless. I can do this. I can do this. *I can do this.*

I turn off my gun's safety and jump out from behind the trees and start shooting at Henry. I thought that it would be impossible to aim in the dark, but the glow stick from my wrists provides just enough light that I can see the viewfinder and aim. I pull the trigger and shoot.

Then I hesitate for a second. *I'm shooting Henry!?* He hesitates too and slows down only for a second in confusion as he searches for where the shots are coming from. I start shooting again and keep shooting. I manage to shoot him once square in the chest. Ha! Guess my aim is getting better since my last run in with a turkey.

"Reagan!?" he asks confused as he gets back to full speed, this time is coming for the both of us, shooting all the way.

I keep shooting as Lyncoln is almost back to the tree where I am standing. He is coming in hot, zig-zagging a bit as he runs to make Henry's job harder. I just keep shooting, knowing there is nothing else I can do. Henry hits Lyncoln again. I hit Henry again. This time in the knee. Just one more and we are home free.

As Lyncoln gets near, the bullets are exploding everywhere. One ricochet hits me in the shin and really stings since it doesn't explode. Another one hits my shoulder and splatters at the bottom of my mask. As Lyncoln gets closer, I try to focus on the target I can barely see, so I aim for the glowing paint splatter on Henry's chest. I do the double tap we were taught, and hear Henry stop and yell out in frustration. Lyncoln chuckles as he grabs my free hand and leads the way back to our team's base.

"Nice shooting, babe," he whispers under his mask proudly. Instead of saying the term of endearment sarcastically, he says it like he means it this time.

He slows down to my speed and we make our way back to our base, which I assumed would be difficult in the dark. Surprisingly though, as we keep moving, the light from the clear moon illuminates enough to allow us to move quickly without tripping or running face first into a tree. With no more worrying about the crinkle of leaves under our boots, I am quite impressed with the speed in which I am able to go without falling on my face.

We hear people on our tail as we go down and back up a ditch. I almost fall, but Lyncoln catches me by the upper part of my hamstring and gives me a shove back up. Even with one arm, he can throw my entire body.

We don't have very far left, but I hear the pursuers closing in on us. And more shots are being fired coming from in front of us. The other group must be returning with the flag we stole, probably fighting off the rest of our allies. We can barely make out the spot where our flag hides off in the distance as we speed ahead and get closer to the gunfire. With the flag we have in tow, we are almost home free. We can't get shot now. We are so close to winning! So close.

"Go, Regs. Run like hell," Lyncoln says, stopping me to take my gun and giving me the flag.

I feel shocked he just handed me the flag over and left this in my hands. But before I can say anything or react, Trent and Oliver see us and run out to cover me. I run as fast as I possibly can for our flag knowing I can only get shot two more times. As I reach out to put the flag with the two others, someone shoots me in the arm. But it's too late. I drop the flag next to the other two. We now officially have three flags in our possession.

We won!

I'm shot one more time in the calf, but it doesn't matter because it's over. I'm sure that person knew it too. Cheap shot, but whatever. We won. That's all that matters.

The large lights on the outskirts of the field are turned on and off repeatedly in a signal for the end of the game and our team cheers. Trent lifts me up in a bear hug while the group from Henry's team chasing us grunts and curses in frustration. There are high fives and hugs all around for my team.

Henry soon comes up to congratulate me, giving me a hug. "Good job, beautiful."

"You shot me," I accuse.

"Well it's just not in my nature to go down without a fight." He shrugs.

"Nor mine," I laugh.

"Girl, you were flying. I can't run that fast." Isabella smiles, interrupting our moment.

"Thanks. I just didn't want to get hit," I laugh again. "Those little buggers can sting."

Christopher reaches out to shake my hand, "Good job getting flag three, Reagan."

"Good job making sure you had flag two," I nod at him smiling. He's smiling ear to ear and seems beyond happy we won. He, Trent, and

Oliver are acting like school girls they are so happy, jumping on one another and yelling like fools. *Men.*

Calmed down a bit, our team then swaps stories about how each part of our group did. Oliver informs me that a group of only three people made it to our flag and only one managed to turn around and see it before Elizabeth shot them. His saying her name reminds me that she was on my team. Where is she? We have been done for almost five minutes now and I still haven't seen her.

"Hold on," I say holding a finger up to pause Oliver and look around.

"What is it?" he asks concerned.

I don't answer.

Fifteen or so of us are standing around where our flag was hiding and we are slowly starting to leave to go back to the main open field. I look around at my teammates. All of us are here except I can't find Elizabeth or that sleaze ball Grady. Grabby Grady. I know in my gut something is wrong here.

Where are they?

"Reagan?" Oliver asks concerned as I start walking away.

"Elizabeth. Where is she?" I ask as I hurry over to where Oliver and the others were posted. I hope more than anything I'm wrong about this, but if Grady is missing too, this is not good.

I'm searching and looking around trees as I walk our team's area, but it is so hard to see. I am about to turn around and quit looking when all of a sudden I see an ankle band frantically waving around. Elizabeth is about twenty yards away and from what I can tell is pinned against a tree. The closer I get, the more utterly terrified she looks. I am running before I can even think of yelling for help.

Grady has his back to me and is pinning her there against her will trying to kiss her. She is trying to fight and get free, but he has both arms pinning her to the tree so she can't move. He isn't kissing her yet, but I think it's pretty clear he is going to and that she doesn't want him to. I'm definitely not interrupting a lover's moment.

I move towards them as fast as I can. She sees me come up behind him and I see relief flood her beautiful eyes.

"Hey. Get off her!" I yell loudly and pull him by his shoulder. I hope I yelled loud enough to get the attention of some of the others too.

He spins, throwing me off, and glares at me. He keeps a grip on one of Elizabeth's wrists so she can't get away.

"Stay out of it, Reagan." He spits the words at me and turns back to Elizabeth.

"Get off her," I repeat while throwing myself at him and climbing onto his back. The force of my jumping on his back loosens his grip on Elizabeth and she is able to pull free.

"Run!" I yell to her, still on Grady's back while he tries to dump me off.

She hesitates a moment, not wanting to leave me with Grady.

"Go, Elizabeth!" I yell again. She takes off fast, I hope for help.

Grady swings around and I lose the grip my legs have on his back. I try to keep my hands gripped around his neck though my feet are back on the ground. I have no idea what I'm going to do, but I'm hoping to just stall. I sink my fingernails into his neck and hold on for dear life. Hopefully all that wrestling with Ashton when we were kids is about to pay off; I know how to fight dirty, and I know how to fight like a girl...so in other words, claws and shots to sensitive areas.

"Fine. It can be you instead, I guess," he says as he abruptly pulls away and spins around, elbowing me in the face as he does so.

I feel pain from where his elbow hit me, but I move to run.

He lunges for me, easily catching me, and we both fall as he tackles me forcefully to the ground. I feel the back of my head hit the ground really hard as he moves to pin down my arms. I lift up my knee trying to go for his groin but feel dizzy. I'm about to lose consciousness but before I do, I see Lyncoln come flying in out of nowhere. He grabs Grady by the shoulders and chucks him at least five yards and then pins him to the ground. He punches him hard.

"You shouldn't have done that," he says with hatred boiling off of him. He punches Grady a few more times before more people show up.

"Reagan, Reagan can you hear me?"

I briefly see Henry's face above me. I try to focus on it, but everything is a little hazy and fuzzy. Then everything fades to black.

Chapter 13

As I come to, I'm lying down in what I assume is a hospital of sorts. I've never been to one before, so I wouldn't really know. I feel a warm hand in mine and smell Lyncoln's cologne so I know that he is here. Wherever here is. As I move my head side to side, I feel a dull throbbing. It makes me want to squint my eyes. Or turn off the lights.

As I sit up, I see Jamie standing at the foot of my bed looking worried. "You okay?" he asks as I sit up.

"Ouch," I say groggily.

"Can I get you anything?"

"Tylenol." I slowly finish sitting up and wince in pain. The dull throbbing is escalating.

"And bring some ice too," Lyncoln adds with a nod, standing up beside me.

Jamie quickly leaves and it's just Lyncoln and I.

"What happened?" I ask confused. "Where am I?"

I try to remember what happened...we were out in the field for paintball...and we won! Then I found Elizabeth and Grady.

Oh crap. *That.*

As I remember Grady tackling me and hitting my head hard on the ground, I can't help but shiver. I wasn't that scared when it was happening because I was focused in on one thing, fighting him off. Now that it's over, I realize how terrifying it all was. Then I remember the look on Lyncoln's face as he was punching Grady unconscious. He looked...*ready to kill*. He is still wearing the black paintball gear, minus the jacket and is now in a v-neck t-shirt that is entirely too tight on his pecs.

"We're at DIA for now. We'll be heading back to Mile High shortly," he informs me.

"Does Grady need a new face?" I ask softly while trying to take a peek at Lyncoln's knuckles.

He half-smiles as he picks up a bag of ice and sits on the bed next to me. He places the bag of ice at the corner of my eye. I have to suck in my breath at how cold it is. He doesn't respond to my question so we just sit there a moment.

"Before you start wondering, Henry just left for an emergency meeting with his Dad back at Mile High so he asked me to stay. Grady has been dismissed effective immediately, and they are in the process of determining proper punishment. Henry is personally making sure of that so he had to go back right away. We weren't sure how long you'd be out for, but it wasn't long, not even five minutes." He takes the ice away and ever so lightly presses on the skin around my eye.

I don't want to see it because I'm sure it's ugly. I will more than likely have a big bruise where Grady elbowed me. Great. I got my first black eye and my first kiss all in one evening. How about that?

I think back to that kiss. It was...intense? I remember thinking at the time that it was borderline violently aggressive, and that is exactly how I still feel about it. He acted like he was drowning and I was the air he needed to breathe. He went from almost ignoring me to consuming me in two whole seconds.

All of a sudden I feel slightly annoyed and then just downright pissed. That was my first kiss? How dare Lyncoln ignore me all week, hang out with Attie, throw me up against a tree and kiss me senseless, and then take care of me after Grady knocked me out, but bring up Henry all nonchalantly.

Who does that? Has he lost his ever-loving mind?

"What are you doing?" I demand annoyed and feeling brave.

He seems somewhat confused at my sudden mood turn but looks at me and simply says, "Putting ice on your eye."

His dark blue and brown eyes seem to be a door into my soul. Is there anything he can't see through those? And why does he look at me like he knows me and has me all figured out, but I am still completely clueless about him?

"I meant earlier. Kissing me…like that…after ignoring me all week. Now you are taking care of me yet talking about Henry. Maybe you should be with Attie," I say quickly and then wince as he puts the ice back on. I didn't want to sound jealous. I utterly and completely failed.

"Do you want me to be?" he asks without emotion but his eyes show a hint of amusement.

"Don't you want to be?" I ask sarcastically, zero amusement.

"No," he says honestly and continues to hold the ice in place.

A minute passes and he doesn't say another word.

"You are the most frustrating person I have ever met!" I try to move my head but regret it and wince again, this time from the pain and not from the ice. "Why would you kiss me if you are with her? She's one of my best friends, if not my best friend."

"I'm not with her," he half-smiles, looking me in the eyes again. I believe him for some odd reason.

"Then what is going on?" I ask confused.

"You have a smart head above those lovely shoulders, think about it." He shrugs.

"No. You tell me. Get to talking. I let you carry on doing your dark and dangerous thing being hot one minute and cold the next. After all that," I gesture to mean the paintball events of kissing and what happened with Grady both, "I deserve an explanation. You chitchat all day with Attie, and yet you can't even give me a straight answer to any questions."

He starts explaining in short sentences. "Henry is my best friend. He wants you. He's the better man of the two of us. You will become the Presidential Couple with him if you choose it. If you don't, the country needs a backup." He is not a man of many words, but the words he uses count.

"And Attie is the best one of us all," I interject, making him smile.

"No interrupting," he bosses me as he leans in closer causing me to immediately shut up. "I'm not interested in her. I approached her and told her I would help her find a partner. In a sense, she is using me. If you don't want this, we need to have a plan in place. We need a backup and a backup to the backup. The wrong person will not win this," he says determined and then softens a bit as he looks at me. "I want to help her as she is a backup plan, but I had to make sure with you that it wasn't in my head. I had to make sure you felt about me a fraction of how I feel about you."

"But what about you? You need a partner. Why are you doing all this?" I ask breathless, his eyes inches from mine.

"I want you, but it has nothing to do with the presidency or the Culling. I've tried to find someone else but I just can't make myself do it. Out of respect for Henry, I'm trying to stay away from you, but you are just so…" he closes his eyes for a moment, taking a deep breath, "intoxicating. I don't want the presidency. I just want you. You, however, would be the perfect Madam President. We need someone like you."

"Why are you deciding what I want for me? And why don't you want the Presidency?" I ask confused. This is the second person in 24 hours telling me they don't want the presidency, the whole reason why we are all here. Are there more of us still here that would rather not have all that responsibility? And what do these people know that I don't?

"Because my skill set makes me a bit...cold, you could say." He shrugs. "I wouldn't do the honor justice."

"You aren't cold, Lync," I respond, using my nickname for him and wholeheartedly meaning what I say. He almost killed Grady in protecting me. There is nothing cold about that. If anything, it makes me proud.

"Well, I only want you, so the only way I'd do it is with you. Otherwise, I'm good with my military career as is," he leans in to steal a quick kiss, half on my cheek and half on the corner of my mouth again. "And when you want me to do that again, just ask. I am here whenever, wherever, however."

"Maybe I should quit before I come between the both of you and go home." I look down at my hands. Maybe it's best to leave with my dignity intact before I fall for one of these two men and have my heart ripped to smithereens.

"Don't you dare," he scolds me and brings my chin up with his fingers, forcing me to look at him. "This isn't about us or Henry and me. It's about our country, and it really needs you. I wish I could tell you everything I know because, yes, I think it needs you specifically. You'll be happy with Henry." He gently massages my shoulder causing my pulse to accelerate before adding, "I will try to behave."

"Okay," I say feeling disappointed. Then I feel guilty for being disappointed.

"How's your head?" He reaches out to gently feel the spot where I bumped the back of my head.

"Excruciatingly...," I start sarcastically, but as he leans in and is just by my lips, I lose all train of thought, "...excruciating."

What happened to that whole him behaving gambit from not five seconds ago?

"Excruciatingly excruciating, huh?" He grins the real grin that I rarely see but already love.

"Yep." Neither of us moves.

"Do you want me to move?" he asks and I see a rare break in his confidence. Who would think that this confident and intense man could be vulnerable in any sort of way?

"Nope," I say honestly and then feel bad when I think about Henry. "Lync..." I look down, feeling like the lowliest human being left on this planet.

"Yeah, babe?" He says "babe" affectionately again and I can feel his breath on my face. I hated his terms of endearment for me at first, but now that it isn't in a sarcastic way, it makes me feel...alive. Turns out, I don't hate it at all. Not even a little.

"I really do like Henry, but I would be lying if I said I felt nothing for you." I search his eyes for answers that I don't even know the questions to.

Why can't I stop myself? I should just tell him I'm with Henry and be done. But after that kiss and seeing him take out Grady out of loyalty to me, I feel like he deserves the truth. Plus, I don't think I could lie to him anyway. I don't hold anything back with him and although he has this tough bad boy persona, I don't want to hurt him either. I know he has been through enough hurt in his life.

"I know," he half-smiles and massages my shoulder again. "You seemed to enjoy that kiss. I had to be the one to stop it."

I roll my eyes and can't help but smile. "Mostly you're a huge pain in the butt, but sometimes not." I like him like this, but there are times I just want to punch his face right off.

He lets out a laugh, "I think it's time you get to know me better. More than likely you will not like what you find and run far, far away. But on the very, very small chance I still have a shot with you, I'll take it."

If only it were that simple.

****

"So other than being bruised," the doctor man explains back at Mile High, "you just have a minor concussion. Just to be safe, we will monitor you here throughout the night, waking you every couple of hours, and you should be up and at 'em and released tomorrow."

I run my fingers along the red marks on my right arm where I can already tell Grady's fingertips will bruise me. "Thanks, doc."

"Also. I have tried to get rid of your suitors for you, but it looks like they will be taking shifts with you through the night. Just a heads up." He smiles knowingly.

I let out a groan and blush seven shades of red making him laugh.

I rode with Lyncoln back to Mile High once I got cleared by the medic there. Lyncoln insisted on carrying me and holding me the entire time. I would be lying if I said I didn't like it.

"One last thing, I know you won't feel like it, but try to eat something," the doctor nods kindly.

"I'll try," I promise though I'm not feeling even a little bit hungry.

We are then interrupted by Henry barging in looking worried. He doesn't even see the doctor standing beside me as he hurries over to me giving me a huge hug. The doctor smiles and slips out to give us some privacy.

"I'm sorry I wasn't here sooner," he whispers, tickling my ear.

"It's okay. I'm fine," I whisper back. He smells good. He is still wearing the paintball gear too, with the splatter across his chest from where I shot him.

"It's not fine. What Grady did was *not* fine," he pulls back and sits on the side of the bed at my feet while wrapping his fingers around mine. "I didn't want to leave you at all, but I also wanted him dealt with right away."

"Well, at least he won't become the next president then." I'm trying to find the positive in this whole debacle.

"Yeah. Over my dead body," he says protectively as he looks me in the eyes.

Those eyes! How can someone have such smooth green eyes? When he is happy, the green in them almost bounces. When he is angry, like now, it's as if the green freezes solid. I have never seen eyes so fluid. He lightly touches the skin around my eye where Lyncoln was icing. It must look really bad because I can see that it literally pains him to look at it.

"Are you okay?" I ask, having never seen him like this.

"I should be asking you that, but yeah." He shakes his head. "When I saw you lying there crumpled on the ground...I just haven't been that scared in a long time."

Trying to find a lighter subject, I think on the rest of the paintball experience, which was a lot of fun up until the whole Grady thing. "I know I said it before, but I can't get over the fact that you shot me tonight!" I say pretending to be shocked, trying to lighten the mood. It works.

He rolls his eyes and smiles. "I can't believe I didn't know what you two were up to. I know Lyncoln. I should have known he would plan something as cutthroat as that. And, of course, you would be in on it."

If only he knew exactly what we were really up to. *Yikes.*

Not wanting to think more about that subject, I ask, "Can you believe I'm stuck down here until morning?"

"Reagan, I saw how hard you hit your head. I would demand it if they didn't. Throw my dad's name around if I had to." He says it like he's scolding me but looks at me protectively. It warms me all the way down to my toes that he is trying to take care of me. He's a true gentleman. I wasn't sure those even still existed.

"I feel fine. I just want my soft bed in my room," I argue.

"Yes, but then I couldn't stay with you now could I?" He bounces his eyebrows flirtatiously.

I blush. "You don't really need to stay with me anyway. What if I am an ugly sleeper? What if I snore…or drool…or wet the bed even?"

"Then you will be all the more adorable, well minus the bed wetting, which I'm sure you don't." He pauses to give me a slow smile then adds, "Besides, it will be good for me."

"How so?" I see a dark cloud briefly pass across his facial features as I ask.

"I've avoided this place since mom passed. I spent way too much time down here when she had treatments so I haven't been back since. I've just avoided the whole hospital. Even when they need my blood drawn or if I get sick, I make them come to me. So it's time I grow a pair and get over it."

Wow. That wasn't what I expected and it's totally heartbreaking to hear him voice it that way.

"I'm sorry about your mom."

Word is that she died from some type of cancer. It was a slow killer, and unlike Trident, wasn't over within just a few days. It has been two years, but in seeing the pain in Henry's eyes, I can tell he feels like it was yesterday.

"Me too. She would have loved to meet you," he smiles, squeezing my hand.

He then picks up the soup bowl and crackers on a tray a few feet away and forces me to start eating. Since I know he hates hospitals but is here for me anyway, I decide not to fight him and eat as much as I can in cooperation. I also try my hardest not to dribble soup down my chin. He makes me so nervous.

"So what happened while I was out cold?" I ask as I finish up my now cold soup.

"I was with you for most of it, getting you to DIA before I hopped on a copter to get here faster, but what I have been told is that four guards immediately took Grady away. More so for his safety from Lyncoln I think. Lyncoln took it pretty personally. Then Bennett said the winning team's award would be announced at a later date due to the unfortunate turn of events. He informed everyone that Grady was kicked out. He gave a good long lecture on Grady's actions and if anything of the sort were to happen again. Then everyone got loaded up and returned back. You should know Elizabeth is fine. More worried about you than anything, and extremely grateful. If you hadn't noticed her in time, it could have been really bad." He shakes his head and I remember Grady's hands all over her and shiver.

"I just don't get it. Why would he do it? He isn't an ugly man by any means and there are a lot of girls here. Surely he could have wooed someone. He knew Maverick and her are a thing so why would he do that with Elizabeth specifically? I don't think he ever sought her out to begin with. I just don't understand." I can't put my finger on it, but something smells fishy about this whole thing.

"Me neither. Lyncoln neither and that's why he was so furious. Grady went through basic training with us. We not only know him, but he's in Lyncoln's unit. Yeah, he can be a jerk around girls and test his limits, but we have never ever seen him lay a hand on one like that before." His eyebrows come together confused. "It just doesn't make sense. He's seen Elizabeth before too. They are both from here. So why now?"

Something in my gut tells me there's more to this story, but I don't want to tell Henry that right now. If it were up to Henry and Lyncoln, they would have the head of Grady on a post by now.

****

I'm woke up in the middle of the night and immediately can tell from the smell and the dangerous tension in the room that Lyncoln is back. It's weird I know who is here based on their smells. They are different but equally enticing. One is more outdoorsy and one is fresher and almost minty.

"Regs. Regs, you need to wake up for a minute." He nicely tries to wake me up by squeezing my hand and tracing his fingers on my palm.

"Mmmm," I roll my head and try to flip over to my side to get comfortable. Hopefully, that is as awake as he needs me to be. I'm getting really sick of this waking up every few hours business.

"Regs, you need to say something other than grunts and groans so I know you're okay," he says and although it's dark, I'm certain he's at least half-smiling.

"You really know how to make a girl feel special," I groan as I sit up and glare in his direction.

"Mission accomplished. Thank you." He keeps my hand in his and sits down in the chair he and Henry have set up beside my bed. Their whole taking shifts thing is freaking me out and making me feel despicable. I hope the rest of the candidates don't know they are here doing this. It would make me some enemies I'm sure. Marisol would have a heyday.

"Don't you have something more important to be doing, macho man?" I ask, sounding annoyed.

"Macho man, huh?" He seems amused.

"What's your military rank, anyway?" I ask, feeling more awake now. He bosses most people around, even men older than he, so I'm assuming it must be high.

"Does it matter?" he deflects. Knowing him, the little that I do know him, I understand that he doesn't like to brag about himself. He doesn't need to; he just has that air of importance about him.

"Yes. You said I should get to know you. This is me getting to know you." I'm rather impressed with how strong willed I sound coming out of a deep sleep. It helps that it's dark and I can barely see him.

"Lieutenant Commander." I can almost see him shrug.

"Wow." I pause. "You're only 21. Sarge is a Sergeant, and you're a Lieutenant Commander? Impressive."

"Well let's just say I have a certain skill set that makes me valuable."

Like his broad shoulders and dangerous eyes? Or the way he is a natural predator?

"Sarge would be higher than a Sergeant too, but he has a family and chose to stop climbing the ranks a while ago," he explains.

I don't even hesitate to ask, "What is your valuable skill set?"

"Tactical Special Forces." He uses the politically correct term, the same one that is in the packet of information we receive on the candidates. So really, he isn't telling me much.

"Which means?"

"Which means I'm good in combat. Some would say ruthless. I started out as a sniper, but am more useful in hand-to-hand combat. I'm too aggressive to be a sniper. I want to be up front instead of sitting in wait."

This is a bit confusing. What is there to combat against anymore? Most of the population was wiped out with Trident. What exactly is he defending us from? Or who?

"Have you ever had to kill a person?" I can't help but be curious. *Annnd now we are getting into the serious stuff.*

"Yes."

"Okay." I yawn. Worst possible time to yawn but whatever. It's honestly not that surprising.

And at least he was honest. I picture him punching Grady in the face. I know he is dangerous and a bit aggressive, but I don't really think he would hurt someone unless they deserved it. That look he had in his eye while doing it made me think it wasn't his first time either.

"Okay?" he asks, concerned about my reaction to that news.

"I just wanted to know is all. I trust your judgment," I offer.

"Okay."

"Tell me the story sometime?" I ask sleepily, knowing that this is not the time or place.

"Another day. You seem a little tired, sweetheart." He gets up to give me a kiss on the forehead then sits back down.

"Nonsense," I say sleepily, but as he rubs circles with his thumb on my palm, I start nodding off.

"Just sleep, Regs," he commands me. His bossiness should irritate me and normally would, but I can hear the clear concern in his voice so it has the opposite effect.

I close my eyes. I'm exhausted and sore, but knowing he is here just watching me with those intense eyes makes it hard to give in to the sleep.

"It's hard to sleep when you smell so dang good," I mumble.

When he laughs I'm horrified to find out I said it out loud and not in my head.

****

Hours later, I feel a warm hand brush across my cheek. I move my head away from it. I just want sleep. More sleep! What is with these two and waking me up so often? Wouldn't I have had other symptoms by now if it was a severe concussion? And why are the powers to be even allowing this whole thing to happen? Isn't it improper for not only one boy, but two boys, to be in my hospital room all night? I take a deep breath and know from the fresh manly smell that it is Henry. Last time he was here, he woke me up but shushed me and told me to go right back to sleep when I tried talking to him. At least he's trying to let me sleep.

"Hey, beautiful," he says, sitting on the bed beside me and leaning in to give me a kiss on the cheek.

"Hey," I respond groggily, "Whatsittake toget somegoodsleep roundhere?" I hope he understood me because I mumbled it all together.

"Doctor's orders. Don't kill the messenger." He squeezes my hand.

"Fine," I say annoyed.

"At least I get to see you more often," he offers affectionately but it infuriates me instead of pleasing me. He knows Lyncoln is here when he isn't. Doesn't that irritate him? That his "girlfriend" has another "boyfriend"? I know we are all encouraged to date around, but this is just weird.

"Yeah. And now I get to feel like a horrible person every time you two switch shifts," I snap, definitely feeling awake.

I immediately feel guilty about it though. He has never snapped at me or treated me like I am treating him. Lyncoln and I spend half of the time arguing and fighting with one another, but not Henry. He's like the male version of Attie. He's the best of us.

"Reagan," he says softly in a disagreeing tone.

"What?" I fire back, still crabby but not as angry.

"Reagan, this situation is anything but normal. If it were, I would be punching Lyncoln in the face for so much as laying a hand on you or looking at you in that way. Don't take my indifference to mean I'm happy about it. I am anything but. I'm jealous. But I also know that we aren't here to just find our wives. We're here to find the next presidential couple and our country needs it now more than ever. Lyncoln and I both see that it should be you. Not only that, but in getting to know you and how you react in certain situations, we both became drawn to you.

"How am I supposed to be mad at him for something that I did too? How am I supposed to tell you to not talk to him when he is one of the best men I know? The situation is messed up. I have faith that you'll do the right thing, whatever it is, even if it isn't me. Right now, I just want to enjoy the time that I do have with you. Since we have to spend time with other people, be it projects or what-not, I'm glad it's Lyncoln who is also with you a lot. I trust him with my life," he gently rubs my cheek with the hand that isn't holding mine as he finishes his diatribe. I'm glad it's dark enough that he can't see the tears in my eyes, just the outline of my face.

"I don't like feeling like this," I whisper. His kind words were a knife stabbing into my heart. "I don't know what I'm doing."

"Well, I don't like having to talk to Katie instead of you all the time, but I do it anyway," he shakes his head for emphasis.

"That's different," I respond, thinking of my first kiss. I don't think Henry is kissing her. And I would be pissed if he was. Especially like that.

"No. It isn't. Do you like it when I talk to Katie as much as I do?"

"No," I respond honestly.

"But you allow it to happen anyway?" he asks, already knowing my answer.

"Yeah, but--"

"No buts." He puts a finger to my lips stopping me from arguing. "It's the same thing. Even if we win this thing and are the next presidential couple, we owe it to the others to get to know them and give them a shot. It is what we have to do. It's how this works. Like I said, it's just a messed up situation, especially since we can't even officially couple up yet."

I sigh. I haven't even really gotten to know Lyncoln that well, and we have already kissed. Guilt eats at me for that. I think of my mom and what she would say or do about this situation I find myself in. She would be livid! But the only thing worse than feeling like a bad person over all this is thinking of what it would be like to say goodbye to Lyncoln. I just can't do that yet. I have to figure him out. He is full of so much pain, but he hides it behind a mask of macho confidence. He is a puzzle that I have to finish. I hope that once I do, once I figure him out, I can say goodbye and move on fully with Henry.

"You are better than I deserve." I squeeze Henry's hand and try to go back to sleep.

****

I wake up to a light on in the bathroom of my hospital room and sounds of a toothbrush. I am sleepily trying to figure out which of my two men is in the room with me now and why they would be brushing their teeth of all things when Lyncoln comes confidently strolling out of the bathroom...without a shirt on. It must be dawn already because there is enough light in the room and coming from the bathroom that I can see every last muscle of his chest and abdominals.

Holy crap.

My breath catches and stops altogether. Other than Ashton, I've never seen another man shirtless before. Although I have fantasized about what Lyncoln's muscles would be like, it is *sooo* much better in real life. I notice a scar runs about six inches from beneath his right pec down across his six-pack of abs. It just makes him look all the more amazing and adds to his dark and mysterious persona. I'm not sure how he got it or if I even want to know, but he doesn't even seem to notice or care that it's there. He has a body that is perfection with his shoulders, neck, and chest bulging in all the right places. What sort of workout does he do to maintain all this?

"Careful, sweetheart. If you keep looking at me like that, you'll find out how dangerous I really can be." He half-smiles and grabs a black v-neck shirt off the chair and pulls it over his head.

Did he really just say that? He was kidding, wasn't he? And why is he half-naked in my hospital room anyway? Did he just threaten me and flirt with me at the same time? Was that a threatening flirt or a flirtful threat?

"Feeling ok?" he asks, slowly rubbing my arm upwards and stopping at my shoulder to massage it. It feels so darn good on my achy body. He sits down on the bed beside my feet and plops one of his legs up, resting his elbow on his jeans.

"Ummm...yeah." I am such a big fat liar. No, I am not feeling okay. He was just half naked in my room and then made that threat, empty or not. My pulse is going crazy and I'm feeling sweaty. I am anything but feeling okay! I am vexed. Hormonally vexed. Hormonally hormonal.

"Glad to hear it, babe," he half-smiles again.

It's way too early in the morning for this much blatant flirting. Can't a girl get some breakfast first?

"Sorry about all that," he explains to me, "I had a meeting before coming to check on you and have to go to another quick meeting before breakfast so I just brought my stuff down and changed here."

Before I have time to think of anything clever to respond with, a man, obviously military, walks in with a clipboard.

"Sir, the morning report is ready," he says all-business.

"Bring it on over, Langly," Lyncoln commands.

Does this man ever ask? For anything? Knowing the way he kissed me, I'm pretty sure not. I wonder how etiquette class is going for him. The thought makes me smile.

"Sir," the man says, looking to me and hesitating.

"What?" he fires back while squinting his eyes at him.

"With all due respect, sir, Ms. Scott does not have clearance," he switches his weight from one foot to the other, obviously uncomfortable.

"Langly. Just bring me the dang report," Lyncoln snaps at him and squints his eyes again in disapproval.

"Yes, sir. Sorry, sir." He hands it over and tries to leave the room as quickly as possible.

"Langly," Lyncoln barks as the other man gets almost to the door.

"Yes, sir?" he turns nervously, awaiting what Lyncoln has to say.

"It doesn't piss me off you were trying to protect this information. What does piss me off is that you assume I am so feeble-minded that I would share its contents with Ms. Scott. She may be remarkably attractive, but I won't risk our national security because of that. You don't know her so I understand your hesitation, but you do know me. You should know me better than that." He is scolding him, but somewhere in there, I get the feeling that Lyncoln genuinely cares about this man too.

"Yes, sir. You're right, sir. My apologies." He looks truly sorry for disappointing Lyncoln before he turns back around and exits.

Lyncoln sits reading the report, flipping through pages. Whatever this report I don't have clearance for says, it isn't good news. He runs a hand through his short hair and sighs.

"I don't mean to pry since I don't have clearance, but rough day?" I try to comfort him without making him feel obligated to tell me. Of course I'm curious and want to know what is in the stupid report, but since he made it clear earlier that he won't tell me, I don't want to beg or even ask. He did call me remarkably attractive though, so I guess that will make up for the fact that he keeps telling me I don't have clearance for things.

"Not good news, that's for sure," he sighs then brings my hand to his lips and kisses the palm of my hand before looking at me in the eyes. "I want this to be over quickly. We need new leadership in place in a hurry, but at the same time, I want it to last awhile." He doesn't release my hand and rubs circles with his thumb across it.

"Why? Wouldn't the Culling getting over quickly actually be detrimental to finding the right people?"

"This Culling will more than likely go faster than all the rest have due to necessity. I wish I could tell you more today, but you'll soon find out what I'm talking about." He shrugs. "Plus, there has been far more monitoring this Culling than any of the past Cullings."

"Why would you tell me that if I don't have clearance?" I'm confused by his statement. I'm also doing some quick math with what I now know about the Cullings. If this one is less than three months, which is the shortest Culling length, that means we are a very short time away from being done with this whole thing. And I feel like we just began. We are only a month in.

"I know you already figured out we were monitored. One of the first girls to do so I might add." He winks at me.

I ignore the heat my body feels from just a stupid wink and try to gather my thoughts. "How do you know that? Is it because of your rank?" I feel like he has such an advantage with what he knows. Is it just him or is it everyone? When will I quit feeling like the last to know things?

"Uh..." He never hesitates about anything so this is interesting to see. He doesn't want to answer this question.

"Am I not cleared for it?" I demand.

"Not exactly." He shrugs.

"Then spill it. How do you know?" I use the same tone he used with Langly. Demanding but caring.

"Easy, Regs." He puts his hands in the air in surrender and then picks up my hand again to continue rubbing the invisible circles on my palm. He sighs before beginning. "I know because the guys were shown highlights of the girls. They wanted us to have an advantage before we met you so that instead of just getting to know you, we would already know the ones we wanted to approach. That way, all that was left to do was test compatibility with one another. It saved a huge chunk of time. We were given much more about you than all of you were given about us." His explanation is the longest I have ever heard him talk, but it doesn't help the immediate rage I feel.

"What?!" I am furious. *FUR-I-OUS.* I try to yank my hand away from him but he holds it in place, his eyes drilling into mine. It may have saved time for the men, but not for us. They know our true colors while we still do not know theirs. I would have loved to see what Henry, Lyncoln, and the others were up to before the ball. To say this is not fair is an understatement.

"It really isn't that big of a deal. It's not even the first time in a Culling they have pulled that move." He tries to make it better, but I am instead angrier at even more information he has that I don't.

"If it isn't that big of a deal, then why weren't we shown the guys' highlights?" I say haughtily.

"Because." He looks uncomfortable but doesn't look away from me, just takes one long blink.

"Because we are women?" I ask, dangerously close to punching him in his beautiful face.

"Pretty much." He looks at me like I'm a bomb about to explode and I'm not sure he's wrong. "Look at the bright side though, all of us saw what Marisol has been up to this entire time. We didn't know ranks, but we knew enough about some of you to know who you were and what kind of leader you would make."

"How can you know that much about us from just some highlights?" None of this is making any sense.

"Because we were shown highlights of each day." His words make me even madder if that were possible. I push my head against my propped up bed and close my eyes. I try to tell myself that it wasn't Lyncoln's fault.

"I feel lied to. When we met wasn't really when we met. Or not when you met me, anyway." I think back to my fall at the Canidatorial Ball. He already knew a lot about me at that point. And he knew Marisol was conspiring against me, which is why he said what he did about keeping enemies close. I always think that he looks at me like he knows me. Well, turns out, he actually kind of does. And I still don't really know him!

"No it wasn't," he admits.

"When then? When did you know you wanted to get to know me better? What was it about me that had me on your list, or whatever?" Do I even want to know the answer to my own question? This is probably going to make it worse, but I just feel like I've got to know at this point.

"Honestly? When you were working outside with your brother right up until the results were announced. Most girls were all giddy and acting like fools, but you kept your head down and worked. It made me respect you. Plus, the banter between your brother and you intrigued me. I don't have any siblings, but if I did, I would like to think I would be with them like you and Ashton are. So right away you had my attention. From the start."

WHAT!?

How would he know about the results? I was at home. *AT HOME.* We were being monitored at home? For how long? How long were they watching my family's every move? Are they still?

"Before you get all crazy mad again, yes, we were all monitored from the minute we took the first test on the first day. I didn't know for a while either if it makes you feel any better. I was mad too, but it was needed in order to monitor the integrity and character of the candidates. Our 'tests' began long before we got here." He pauses a moment. "As for when you got here, that first day when I saw you stare down Marisol in the cafeteria with Marcia and refuse to back down, I knew you would be the only girl I would even remotely consider. That in combination with the one tear you cried watching the Trident slideshow. Those two things told me all I needed to know." His gaze heats my entire body despite my still being borderline livid.

I'm still upset we weren't told we were being monitored. I'm also super confused about how they were able to have monitors in our home townships. But hearing Lyncoln talk about how impressed he was with me eases the anger. With him anyway.

"Why are you telling me this?" I ask.

He shrugs. "Because this is something I *can* tell you."

I sigh and put my hair behind my ear. "Why don't you have any siblings?" I try to change the topic. I don't even want to think about this new information right now. All it does is makes me angry.

"My mom had three miscarriages after me before they allowed her to quit trying. Each one killed her just a little bit more. My dad hated it too. Then not long after, he died. So it has just been my mom and me for a while now." As he talks, I recognize the quick expression of pain that he shows only for a brief moment before he masks it just like he does everything else.

"I'm so sorry," I offer, feeling some tears sting my eyes. Three miscarriages and then losing your husband, and because he was murdered? I cannot imagine.

"Don't be." He shrugs but I can tell his family is a painful subject for him.

"I bet your mom is a strong woman." I try to picture her in my head. To live through what she's had to live through? And raise this man before me? She's got to be amazing.

"That she is." He smirks and adds, "So are you. I've never seen a woman with a bruised face be so demanding or angry."

"Ugh. Thanks for reminding me," I say, touching my face where it's tender.

"You are still irresistible, black eye or not." He takes over for me and lightly presses around my eye adding, "But every time I look at your face, I want to go pound on Grady some more."

"I'm sorry. I know he was in your unit," I offer.

"You have *nothing* to apologize for. I don't know who or what got to him, but I'll get to the bottom of it." He stares into the depths of my soul and I have no doubt he will do just that.

"Thank you for defending me," I say quietly.

He leans in, gives me a kiss on the forehead, and whispers, "I will always protect you, sweetheart."

Chapter 14

"Iff I could get my hands on that man!" Frank fusses over my bruised face back in my room after finally getting doctor's orders to be released.

Now that I've seen my reflection, I know they have a lot of work to do in making me look presentable. My bruise around my eye is red and ugly and will only be getting worse I'm sure. More bruises trail up my arms too, but they are already starting to feel better. My neck and shoulders are still a bit stiff from the impact of the fall, but overall I think I feel better than I look.

"I think that has already been taken care of." I smile amused at my attendants and their loyalty.

"Who got to him first?" Gertie asks while handing me an iced tea.

"Lyncoln."

"Ha! I knew it." Gertie claps and reaches out a hand to Frank as if telling him to pay up.

He rolls his eyes and ignores her, "Well, here's what we are going to do about this eye. I will make you look drop dead gorgeous but we are going to minimally cover your eye with makeup. I want the other girls to see it. And I want you to act like it isn't even there. They will see it and watch you and know that no one will be messing with you again.

We are going to dress you in something bold and sexy. You will be the most exquisite woman to ever have a black eye."

"Deal," I say with a snort not really believing him but still wanting to do as he wishes.

He holds up leather looking pants and bounces his eyebrows. "Do you trust me?"

I immediately don't want to wear those things, but Frank has never steered me wrong before. "I think so…" I say hesitantly.

"Good! Then let's get to work," he nods.

"First let's get your skin all nice and soft," Gertie steers me towards a buttery full tub.

****

An hour later, I'm quite impressed. It's still the weekend, so we get to dress more casual. I have on the tight leathery leggings, black heels, a white blouse that has a zipper at my chest, and a bulky cardigan. My hair is halfway down and unusually straight. I have a full set of makeup on except around my black eye where it is a lighter layer of makeup, which is good because it didn't feel very good for them to put on what little they did. I am dressed up, but yet dressed down all the same.

Frank and Gertie did amazing and although I'm not sure I can pull off the black leather leggings, I'm doing my best. I just have to trust them. They haven't ever let me down before. I'm not sure I'd call it "sexy", but I am trying. If anyone tries to laugh at me, my black eye should at least shut them up. So there's that.

I open the door and Jamie turns to me and smiles. "Wow."

I punch him on the arm. "Not helpful."

"You look great, Reagan. The girls are going to hate you," he says with a laugh.

"I have a black eye," I scold him.

"And look like you could kill any of them," he says as I take his arm. "I would bet money on you any day, by the way."

"Thanks." I smile shyly and feel glad for his continued friendship. If I didn't have the support of my guards and my attendants, I'm not sure how I would be holding up by this point.

As we make it almost to the elevators, the doors slide open and Elizabeth and her guard step out. She is wearing a dress with a sweater and looks amazing as usual with her long dark hair in curls down her back.

"Oh my god," she says in horror, seeing my eye. She hurries over and embraces me. She starts sobbing before she even finishes hugging me. "I mean, you look fantastic. Love those leggings. I am just so sorry. So sorry! But thank you. Thank you, thank you, thank you."

"You're welcome."

"That's twice you have come to my rescue, Reagan. Most girls see the way I look and just leave me to my own defenses like I brought it on myself, but not you. Thank you," she says, wiping her tears away.

"How are you doing?" I ask, looking her over for bruises. Grady's hold on her was tight. I'm just glad I got there when I did.

"I'm fine. Had a hard time sleeping last night, but fine otherwise." She shrugs. "I came to see if you wanted to go to breakfast together. I thought you might not want to show up alone."

"That was thoughtful of you and yes, I would love that." I feel relieved with her offer. It's bad enough to walk in there with a black eye. It's a whole other thing to walk in there in these dang pants.

As soon as we walk in the door, the entire room is silent and all eyes are on us. I find Vanessa who gives me a thumbs up. Trent whistles and Oliver claps. Not wanting to draw any more attention, we quickly grab our trays and go through the line chatting about the day's unknown events.

Much to my dismay, as I walk toward our table I see there is only one spot open and more than likely was saved between Henry and Lyncoln. I'm not sure what they are up to, or what message they are trying to send, but it seems weird. It's almost as if they want everyone to know that both of them are interested in me. Though I'm not the only one with more than one suitor, I do seem to be the only one with more than one suitor at the same exact time. And that will not help with the group of girls that hate me.

I sit down and Attie, who is sitting across from Lyncoln, grabs my hand and squeezes it. "I'm glad you are okay," she smiles at me almost teary eyed. After our discussion about Henry, all hostilities between us are gone, especially now I know that she and Lyncoln aren't a thing either.

"Thank you." I smile and give her hand a squeeze back.

"Good morning, beautiful." Henry leans in and kisses my forehead above my bruise. "That looks horrible. I hope your nurses treated you well last night." He winks at me. Apparently, it isn't common knowledge that my so called "nurses" were, in fact, the two men on either side of me.

"Did they ever," I say sarcastically and both boys try to stifle their laughter. Once again, I find myself in this situation between the two of them with neither seeming to care. Henry says he cares, and Lyncoln's personality definitely fits the jealous type, but they wanted me here in-between them. How weird is this?

I try to listen in on the group's conversation as hard as it is being between both boys I am drawn to. While I'm listening to Attie, Trent, and Vanessa, Henry has his arm sort of around me with his hand on the bench behind me. While his arm is still there, Lyncoln at one point gives my knee a quick squeeze of support.

Is this real life? Are they both putting moves on me at the same time? What the heck? Why am I the only one bothered by this?

"No word on what today's activities will be, other than we have to start our one-on-one sessions tonight since last night they were rescheduled," Vanessa shrugs.

"Fantastic," I mumble.

Attie smiles warmly, "Not to worry, I'm with you today."

"Thank goodness," I say relieved. "Who else am I with?" I obviously missed the schedule or the announcement with all the hoopla from yesterday.

"I think Ben," Renae chirps in.

"Thanks," I respond and try not to act disappointed in that piece of information as I know Renae has been spending more time with him recently. I'll let her make her own conclusions about Benjamin.

I pick at my breakfast even though Lyncoln is glaring at me as if telling me to eat more. At one point, I just glare back at him in challenge and he seems to get a kick out of that. Everyone else seems to treat me like nothing happened yesterday, and I'm grateful for that.

As I continue to listen in, I'm surprised to learn that four people, in addition to Grady, are missing from breakfast. We are down two girls and three boys counting Grady. I knew cuts were coming, but I have grown to really like my group of friends and am not looking forward to having to say goodbye to anyone. Or rather anyone going missing I guess, since goodbyes aren't a privilege we're extended.

Half an hour later, I'm sitting with my paintball group in Professor Bennett's classroom. I still feel awkward in these pants. The good news is, my attention is so focused on the leathery leggings I am wearing, that I kind of forget about my black eye. Mission accomplished, Frank.

I sit in the back corner of the room by Lyncoln and Elizabeth while Trent, Renae, Isabella, Christopher, and Oliver sit in front of us. It's weird to think that 24 hours ago I didn't have a black eye and Grady wasn't acting like a crazy man.

What was it that made him go off? Was the pressure of this thing just too much?

"Today we will be leaving Mile High for DIA. You will be prepped for next week's events while there and go through all the proper security measures." Professor Bennett winces. "It will be a long and boring day but is needed in preparation for the days to come."

"Now. Before we get to the groups and times they will be heading out, I want to make two announcements. The first of which is that Friday another ball will be held in honor of those of you remaining. As you know, we typically have three in addition to the Inaugural Ball. As for the other announcement, it is in regard to the prize for the winners of the paintball competition," he smiles and pauses as we all wonder. "Tomorrow afternoon while the rest of you take a geographical test with Professor Zax, the winners are excused and get to spend two hours with their families at DIA, all eight of which will be flown in, or brought in, in the case that they reside here in Denver."

I hear the jealous groans from others.

What?! Tears spring to my eyes. My family? All of my family or just Ashton again? I don't even care. I feel like it has been years since I've seen them instead of only just a month. Before I can help it, I am sniffling and trying super hard not to start all out bawling. I'm tired and after what happened yesterday if I started crying, I'm not sure I would be able to stop.

Lyncoln reaches over and protectively grabs my knee. What is it with him and my knee and his weird sense of when I'm about to lose it?

"Now, to the groups. We will go in three large groups." He continues talking about the groups and times we are to leave, but all I can think about is my family. Are they really coming? I can't wait. This will be the best prize ever.

****

A few hours later, I'm getting changed into my black gear and waiting for my group's time to head to DIA. I'm somewhat relieved to find out neither Henry nor Lyncoln are in my group. Elizabeth and Vanessa are and I couldn't be more excited for some time without the two confusing men in my life. Last night and breakfast were about enough to do me in.

Hearing a knock on the door and assuming it's Jamie bringing me lunch, I answer in my black tank top. Much to my dismay and excitement both, it's instead Lyncoln, already changed into his black gear and holding a box of some sort.

"Hey," he says and pushes open the door to walk in, looking me over as he does and adding, "Cute."

"Hey." I'm puzzled as to why he is here and in my room. "I didn't even ask you in."

He smirks at me. "Okay."

"Okay," I say annoyed and gesture him in the room.

"This is for you," he sets the box on the coffee table, opens it, and then plops down in a chair, putting one leg over the other in a signature relaxed look of his.

I look in the box to find steak with sweet potato fries and broccoli, and last but not least, a piece of chocolate cheesecake. It's all my favorites, well, minus the broccoli.

"How'd you know?" I stay where I'm standing and try to rein in my smile.

"I pay attention." He shrugs. "Now eat."

When he's bossy it reminds me of Ashton and it makes me so, so mad. I don't like being bossed around. Never have, never will.

"Make me." I challenge him just like I would Ashton without really thinking about it much.

Before I know it, he's rapidly walking towards me like a lion after its prey. He is a predator. There is no doubt about it. And I definitely want to run far, far, far away. He gets to where I'm standing and I back up until my back hits the wall. He puts his arms on either side of me trapping me. I might just try to make a run for it if it weren't for how good he looks in his black gear. My heart, on the other hand, is definitely making a run for it.

He doesn't say anything, he just stares me down. Somehow that makes my skin start to tingle. Does he have this affect on every woman? Or just me? How does he know how to make me feel this way? It's like some sort of manly superpower. Add that to his "skill set".

"What are you doing?" I ask, barely finding my voice and getting nervous he is going to kiss me again.

Reading my mind, he says softly with his velvety voice, "Don't worry. I'm not going to kiss you, but you hardly ate breakfast. Believe me, coming off of a concussion, you need to eat. So. We can do this the easy way or the hard way."

Not being able to take his intense stare a second longer, I duck under his arm and move toward the food. I'm pretty sure he was bluffing, but I'm a little too scared to find out for sure. I sit down in a chair and begin to cut the steak. In Lyncoln's own crazy way, he was really just worried about me. He's bossy in everything that he does, but he still has a kind side. He took the time to know my favorite foods for goodness sake.

"Try asking me next time. I don't like being bossed around," I mumble, feeling weird that I am the only one eating. I find the steak and fries are absolutely heaven with my first two bites though. "Where's yours?"

"I already ate. I have to leave in five minutes for DIA, anyway," he says glancing at his watch.

"Haven't you already been through everything there?" I ask with a laugh. He, Henry, and Christopher have extra meetings all the time. I venture to say they know more than most of the guards here.

"Yes. And then some. I practically grew up there." He rolls his eyes. "Just another silly part in this whole thing."

"So do you have to go through everything with the group or do you get special privileges?" I ask as I continue to eat. I find I'm quite hungry but still try to eat slowly to not spill food on myself.

"I wish. Nope. I'll be stuck with everyone else." He sighs. "Excited about your family?"

I keep eating and don't look at him because if I do, I might start crying. "Yes."

"Good."

I take a deep breath, look back up at him, and ask, "Will you get to see your mom?"

"Yeah. She works at DIA and serves on the President's cabinet so I was bound to run into her anyway." He shrugs.

"Oh, wow."

In my head, this woman is nothing short of superwoman. I wonder if I will meet her when we are there. I've met Henry's dad, who is the most powerful man in the nation, if not world, so I shouldn't be as nervous about meeting Lyncoln's mom as I am.

"I'm glad you are eating better," he says. He looks at me affectionately and it warms me. "You didn't eat much at breakfast."

"Yeah. Well it was a long night and I was distracted this morning." I roll my eyes. I was just a ball of nerves in-between those two boys this morning. I couldn't form a sentence let alone hold a fork. I was nervous about my eye and even my pants too.

He smirks. "Oh yeah?"

"Yeah," I respond, looking him dead in the eyes.

"Is it because you saw me half naked?" he flirts with raised eyebrows.

Remembering early this morning, I blush multiple shades of red. He just laughs and I can't help but laugh too.

"You are incorrigible." I take a bite of oh-so-delicious cheesecake.

He stands and walks over to me, leaning down with both hands on the armrests of the chair I'm sitting in. "I have to go now. I'll see you later, sweetheart." He leans down and kisses the top of my head and leaves just as swiftly as he came.

How can one man be so bossy and so compassionate at the same time?

****

My group is the last to get to DIA. I remember all the terminals from when we got here just weeks ago. I'm wondering what sort of "preparation" work we will be doing today. I would rather be catching up on sleep as I feel tired from the night before and all the interruptions, but am glad for the distraction too. I get to see my family tomorrow! I could not be more excited and anything to help the time pass more quickly is welcomed.

After all of us finally arrive, we go up a few escalators to a big room with about 15 chairs around a huge oval table. Everything is black, the table, the chairs, the walls, the ceiling, and even our gear. I take a seat beside Oliver and Vanessa.

"First we will be doing blood tests and getting you fitted for proper equipment. Then we will give you key cards for the floors you are cleared for. You will be taught how to do the retina and fingerprint scans. Both are needed at the beginning of every drill. There is only one rule here. Don't go where you aren't cleared to go." A man is telling us what we are to do. He doesn't exactly look inherently nice either.

Afterward, we don't hesitate to do as we are told. Two stations are set up and half of us go to the gear fitting station and half of us get our blood drawn. I sit by Vanessa as we get our blood taken at the same time.

"I hate needles," she shakes her head and I laugh. You would think she would be used to them by now. And Vanessa doesn't strike me as the type to be afraid of anything, much less a needle.

We then head over to get fitted for gear. I was thinking "gear" as in more black outfits, but this is more weaponry and less "gear". I get my arm lengths measured and hold different objects that look like shields. I am measured for a bow. I hold three different guns and have to tell them which I prefer. My waist is sized for a belt which holds about a hundred different ways to kill someone. Boy am I glad Marisol isn't here. She would probably chuck a grenade or something at me.

When we finish with that, Mr. Grumpaluffagus takes us on a tour.

"Floors 3 and 4 are mainly where you will be. Floor 5 may be used on occasion. All simulations are on the third floor, which is also where your self-defense class will be." He walks us down a long hallway with no windows.

"This is the practice range where you may practice shooting, though not with real ammunition of course." We enter a huge room with tall ceilings. Targets are everywhere and some ranges look special as they are enclosed in glass and separated from others. I bet each of us could practice at the same time. I imagine practicing while he continues talking, "Some of you are women and may think that it doesn't matter, but even Madam Maxwell was a great shot. You need to be able to protect yourselves. Denver contestants have already learned the basics. The rest of you will need to catch up. Any of you may use your key cards to enter this room whenever you have time."

We leave through sliding doors and head down a floor via escalator to stand outside of more doors. It takes our tour guide a while to enter in all the proper codes in a keypad, and then huge metal doors open up to a room even bigger than the last one. The lighting is dark and the room looks like the room we were in for our lie detector tests but much, much bigger. Thick black foam or rubber lines all of the walls.

"Welcome to the simulator," he says, almost smiling. He likes this place, wherever we are. "This is a room you are about to spend a lot of time in." He hands out a pair of high-tech looking glasses to each of us adding, "We run you through different simulations here. You will use weapons the actual weight of real weapons and be given what feels like real life situations where you will have to think on your feet and defend yourself. For obvious reasons, we use the simulator mainly for military training. You will be graded on how efficiently you will carry out different exercises in the simulator. At first, it will be you alone. Then you will go with another or even a group."

He walks over to the touch keypad on the wall and hits a bunch of buttons. "Here is a demonstration for you to see how real the simulations seem. Please put on your glasses now."

The room completely transforms around us. We are outside. There is blue sky and even clouds for Pete's sake! I see trees and grass and I can even feel a slight breeze. People laugh. Oliver reaches out to touch a tree, but his finger goes straight through it. I walk around on the grass, trying to feel it with my shoes. It's there but it isn't there. I reach down to pick up a piece of grass. It's in my hand, but yet I know there is nothing there. It all looks *so* very real. Even three dimensional.

Vanessa smiles beside me but isn't as surprised as the rest of us. She must have been in this room before.

"And this is an example of what an enemy will look like," our tour guide adds, hitting a bunch more buttons.

In the middle of the room, a simulated person pops up. He is tall and well-built and looks real besides the fact that he is a bit see through and doesn't have any facial expressions. Still, he looks eerily real and it is a bit unnerving that we will have to shoot what seems like a person.

Abraham has also obviously been in here before because he isn't hesitant at all to approach the simulator dude. He walks over to touch him, but unlike with the tree, rather than his finger going through the man, it looks like he pokes him. That must mean that through the three-dimensional glasses, we can interact with the sim in different ways. Sometimes it is more like a projected object like the tree and sometimes it feels real. And yet nothing is really there in either instance.

After we explore the simulator and walk around for a bit, the grumpy man hits a few buttons to bring us back to the rubbery black room. "We have simulations for a variety of different situations, but mainly combat situations and testing you on your ability to think on your feet. These simulations can be scary, but all can be passed. The person with the least amount of kills at the end of this will be given a prize and own bragging rights until the next Culling. Also, we can use the simulator to test you with different people of the opposite sex to see who you work best with. Sometimes, we find the person who you work alongside best isn't who you think it is.

"Lastly, there is a locker room outside this room in which you will each have a locker to store your glasses and any other gear you may have on you. There is also a lounge area with a television screen set up in which you can watch others complete their sims should you have free time," he says nonchalantly as he finishes explaining and we head to the next area.

Who will I work alongside best? Henry? And kills?! Yikes.

I feel like I want to go back to the practice range and work on my aim. It looks like I'll need to be able to shoot more than a turkey after all. Then again, maybe I should be watching and studying other people's sims. Regardless, this just got a whole lot scarier and more serious.

****

I have learned my four-digit code and how to run the retina and fingerprint scans. I am given my key card that gets me into the practice range among other places. Other than floors 3 and 4, we aren't given a tour anywhere else. I'm anxious for the next week to begin. How will I do with the simulators? Won't Denver people, specifically those that have already been through it like Vanessa, have a severe advantage?

Other than the practice range and the simulator, I'm not sure why it was needed that we get a tour of just two floors. Floor four has a bunch of meeting rooms that we are allowed to wait in or grab a drink from. It also has a few observation rooms and, of course, the practice range. While others go through the simulator, it is apparent that we will be doing a lot of sitting around. Where everything feels inviting and homey at Mile High, it feels opposite at DIA; there is a very serious atmosphere.

I can't help but think of Henry and Lyncoln. I'm not at all a good partner for them. I can't really even aim a gun. If I want high enough scores to be able to stick around or look deserving at their side, I need to put in some serious work. I mentally promise myself to go to the practice range as much as I can.

Upon arriving back at Mile High, I'm reminded that we have two socials tonight with other candidates. Mine are Attie and Benjamin. In looking at the schedule in my room, I find I will be going to Attie's room and then Benjamin will be coming to mine. I only have time to grab a bite to eat and change before I have to be at Attie's room. I eat a sandwich then throw on jeans and a blouse with a matching cardigan and head with Sarge to her room.

I knock and the door opens right away. "Hey. DIA though, huh?" She smiles and greets me warmly. I'm so glad she seems to be over being mad or disappointed or whatever.

"Oh my gosh. The simulator. I have never seen anything like it." I shake my head as we sit down at her coffee table. She has a soda and has already gotten me a glass of tea. That's just how she is. I'm sure she ordered them earlier. She is always thinking of others and going the extra step, the step that most of us don't even think of. Attie would make an amazing Madam President. If I'm honest with myself, her and Henry as a pair would be perfect and make more sense than him and I. I have to shake that thought out of my head. "I could even feel a breeze," I add with a laugh.

"Oh me too," she pauses. "But kills? We can be killed and kill? Funnn." She shakes her head.

"You will do great, Attie." I smile supportively.

"No, you will. Now, if there were situations where I needed to respond to a medical emergency, that I am good with. Even with blood. I'm good with saving others. Just not so much at being the one to pull the trigger. I fix the bloody messes, not make them." She shakes her head nervously.

Again, this is why she would be perfect as Madam President. "Attie, I'm glad we fixed things between us. To be completely honest with you, it should be you with Henry. You were made for this. I sincerely feel that you'd be a great madam president," I say honestly, feeling emotional again. I want this, but standing next to someone like her, I feel completely inadequate. Will it ever really be Henry and me in the end? It seems unlikely when I take a good hard look at the facts.

"You'd be great too. And stop feeling bad about Henry. His feelings weren't there. I'm fine with that. Besides, I have my sights set on someone else now." She winks and shimmies twice.

I feel a jealous pang of anger thinking that she's talking about Lyncoln, but I remind myself that they have an agreement. "Oh?"

"You know me well. Guess." She gestures for me to go ahead.

I think of the boys remaining. Pierce, Douglas, and grabby Grady were sent home leaving 19 boys to pick from. I think of what I know about Attie's personality. She is kind. She is bubbly. She would do anything for someone else. Other than Henry, who would make a perfect fit for her?

"My money is on either Adam or Knox," I guess after thinking it through.

"Ahhh. See? You are very perceptive," she nods in approval.

"I was right?" I ask surprised.

"Yep. Knox. He's quiet though crazy smart and calculating. He's also kind and good-hearted too. Lyncoln took me under his wing and helped me get to know the other candidates, well the good ones anyway, and I saw how much I respected Knox. I didn't even really know Henry, I was just fascinated by him because he is the heir. With Knox, I think because he is laid back and doesn't have an overbearing personality, I thought he wasn't kind or wasn't interested. That couldn't be farther from the truth. He would make a great president. And the fact that he didn't train for it his entire life, makes him even more appealing to me. I can't wait for the ball Friday if I make it," she bounces her shoulders excitedly.

Listening to her, I feel relieved. They will make a great pair. With his brains and her heart, the country would thrive. I know from her comments she isn't meaning to knock down Henry or Lyncoln, she is just excited about Knox. As she should be.

"I am so happy for you," I say fully meaning it.

"Thanks. I don't envy you though." She laughs and adds, "You have gotten yourself stuck between two amazing men."

"Ugh. Don't I know it." I blush and look down embarrassed. "I don't even know how it happened."

"Reagan, at this point in this whole process, it doesn't matter. Don't feel bad for wanting to be with both. Like I just had to learn, you can't go on just their packet information; you have to get to know them." She squeezes my shoulder. "This is for the presidency, but should you win, you are stuck with that person for life. So take your time. No rush."

"That makes sense, but why do I feel like a tramp for just wanting to get to know them both?" I ask. It feels good to be honest with her. I'm tired of Henry and Lyncoln shrugging it off like it's no big deal. And it feels good to talk girl-talk about my situation, to talk with someone that would understand how I feel. Someone who knows what it feels like to not know anything about the boys.

"Because in what other world do you have the opportunity to date 20 guys at the same time? And are even encouraged to do so?"

I have to laugh at that. "True."

"At least it's just two men. It could be four or five. I think seven boys wanted Elizabeth that first night. Renae is starting to date Benjamin though she hasn't completely cut it off with the others. This is what? Her fourth? So it could be worse." She wiggles her eyebrows and I laugh.

"Now, getting to know one another. Tell me about your family. I know you have sisters. Two right?"

"Three, actually." She smiles and stands walking to the microwave to set a timer. "So we don't get distracted. You make me chatty," she stares me down like I'm in trouble and I laugh.

She sits back down and continues, "So three sisters. And we all get along surprisingly well. I am the oldest, which is probably why I have always liked taking care of people. I helped my mom with my sisters when they were little so it is something I have always done."

"You miss them, don't you?" I smile in understanding.

"Yes. I wish I would have been on your paintball team more than anything." She smiles teary eyed and then shakes her head.

Wanting to move things along without her looking sad, I keep asking questions. "If not Madam President, what would you want to do?"

Her face lights up. "I have been training in Neonatal Intensive Care. So basically, I will be a traveling nurse that will transfer to a township where a baby is born that needs help. We will go where we are needed and stay a short time with the child until he or she is better. We have a NICU much like pre-Trident in Vegas, but the other townships barely even have nurseries. And the level of premature babies after Trident has sky-rocketed. We are doing tons of studies in Vegas trying to figure out why, but nothing has been conclusive.

"So, until I have my own family that is what I would do. I realize traveling careers are few and far between. We have only six sets of traveling nurses for NICU for the entire country, so I know it's a longshot. But, I feel like with a wanted population growth, and the preemie rate as high as it is, too many babies are falling between the cracks. There has been too much death already. And dying babies because we can't get to them fast enough? That isn't acceptable. Especially when we have the technology to save them. It isn't like cancer, where sometimes there is nothing we can do. We know exactly what to do. So why aren't we? There should be a NICU in each township's hospitals."

"So why isn't there?" I ask, not even realizing that this is an issue. Why haven't we been told about this? Babies are dying? I think back to our hospital in Omaha. We have a nursery with a dozen or so beds for babies. What's the point of having those beds if we don't have all the technology available to help save those babies?

"Not enough resources, I guess. Each township gets a team of six doctors and fifteen nurses, except for Vegas. The doctors aren't really even specialized. Not to mention once they leave for another township, they never return for any training. Everything is done through email or online presentations. It isn't enough. I understand that we need to be separated, but we have the technology and knowledge to save a lot of people. Each township needs at least a cardiologist and a neurologist. Heck, even a chiropractor! And double the nurses for sure." She pauses. "How big is Omaha?"

"Roughly 100,000 people," I respond.

"The smallest township has 100,000 people. What if there was an outbreak of something? Not a pandemic, but just a viral outbreak? Like Influenza-A or whooping cough? Fifteen nurses would have to take care of an entire hospital of patients? And really it would be more like half of that because they would take shifts. So eight nurses? That is a disaster waiting to happen." She shakes her head.

Holy crap. Between Marcia and her water purifying and Attie and her philosophy on the hospitals in the townships, these women are making huge strides in helping our country. It makes my irrigation technique seem inadequate. No lives were saved or helped from my idea, just carrots.

"Why do you think they haven't fixed this yet? I'm sure it has been an issue for at least the last two presidencies?" I ask as I remember President Maxwell's comment about how it's sometimes easier to stay within the bubbles of our own townships. Knowing all this new information, I feel like it will be hard for me to return to that bubble.

"I don't know. All I know is the more we could travel between townships, the better our lives would be. The more lives would be saved! But the more it is suggested, the more it is dismissed. If there were a solid reason, I would maybe accept it. But telling me no and letting people die without justifying it isn't good enough for me," she adds a frustrated gesture, "And completely viable babies dying will never be acceptable to me."

"Ummm, helllllo, Madam President." I shake my head for emphasis. "This is why you need to be Madam President. You need to do this. Use this platform to fix it."

We talk about hospitals for a bit more and compare what Omaha has to what Vegas has. I am astonished to learn what sorts of medical emergencies Vegas can handle. The difference is like a candle to electricity.

The alarm from the timer soon goes off, startling Attie. "Holy cow. The time is already up. I'm sorry. We didn't even really talk about you. You just had me going."

"That's okay. What we talked about was way more interesting. I just water plants." I smile and stand, giving her a hug. "Have a good night."

"See you in the morning," she smiles.

I leave her room with Sarge on my arm and wait for the elevator. As we wait for the doors to open, he gets me talking about my family arriving tomorrow. I am so excited I can barely breathe. I'm super exhausted from the last 24 hours but am smiling and happy nonetheless.

The doors to the elevator open and Lyncoln is standing there, arms crossed, looking not at all happy. This is the version of Lyncoln that everyone is afraid of. Dark and mysterious…*and moody.*

"Hey." I smile at him, wondering what he is upset about. I decide to try the "kill with kindness" that Attie swears by.

"Hey, yourself," he says coolly and steps off the elevator.

Did I do something to make him mad?

"Going to see Attie for a social or for fun?" I ask, stepping in his path. I'm glad that there is zero jealousy in my tone. Although I am jealous that he can laugh and talk with her in a way he can't with me, I know that their friendship is just that, a friendship.

"Social."

One word answers again. My favorite.

"Cool. I have Benjamin next." I feel like I'm having a conversation with myself. He looked ticked off and I was making an effort to be nice since he brought me lunch.

"You're going to his room?" He stares daggers at me, clenching his jaw.

"No." I shake my head.

"He's coming to yours?" More glaring, but at least he formed a sentence this time. Goodness gracious, what have I done to make this beast mad?

"Yes?" I ask, wondering what the problem is.

"I'll check in after." More glaring.

"Why? What's the issue?" I snap, feeling annoyed. If he is mad at me, he could at least tell me why.

He steps closer to me, continuing to stare me down. "I don't like sharing."

Okayyy, if you can't kill them with kindness, the next move is to smack them up top the head, right?

"You already share me," I blurt out boldly, glaring back and refusing to back down.

This must amuse him because he smirks for the first time since our encounter. "With Henry. Who I trust. Impeccably."

"Well maybe you should try trusting me. Impeccably." I poke him in the chest while I say it, and try to keep glaring, but his pecs are distracting.

He half-smiles this time and backs down. "I will see you in a little bit, okay Reagan?"

He seems to be coming out of his funk. I get out of his way and turn to get on the elevator but stop before I get in.

"Lyncoln."

He stops and turns back around. "Yeah, Regs?"

"Please pull out the stick up your butt before then."

I don't wait to see the look on his face or how angry I made him, I just get on the elevator with Sarge and position myself so I can't see the look on his face. I bit his head off, but I did at least say please. So there's that.

When the doors close, I breathe out the breath I was holding. Sarge is trying hard not to laugh. I can tell by his cheeks and the creases in his eyes as he hits the buttons to go back to my room.

"Something you need to say, Sarge?" I ask, feeling like I could take on the world after my run in with Lyncoln. I mean, who treats someone so coldly like that for no apparent reason? One minute he is bringing me lunch and the next he is trying to brush me off. What the actual heck?

"Whoo-ie, girl. You have 'balls of steel', as they say." He is still trying to contain his laughter and failing miserably at it.

"No. I just constantly struggle with not strangling that man." I shake my head in frustration.

"When you aren't ogling him that is," Sarge reminds me.

I try to be mad at that but it makes me smile. He's absolutely right.

"I'm not sure which I do more of," I joke.

This makes him laugh harder. He puts a hand on my shoulder, "Welcome to dating."

****

I have Sarge get some drinks after seeing the example Attie set and tidy up my room nervously though there isn't much to tidy up. I just want to crawl in bed and go to sleep instead of talking with Benjamin, of all people, but I know it really isn't optional.

He knocks right on time.

"Hey," I say, gesturing him in and propping the door open.

"Hey, Reagan." He comes in, sits down, and grabs a soda. "Thanks for this. How are you doing really? I mean, you seem like you're fine, but how are you really?" he asks concerned as he looks at my bruised eye.

I look in his baby blues and realize he is very charismatic. He always asks the right questions at the right time. He's...calculated. I think he and Renae might just be perfect for one another. Calculated chameleons the both of them.

"A little sore, but really I'm okay. It looks worse than it feels." I am surprised with his sudden concern.

"Well if Lyncoln hadn't gotten to Grady, I sure as heck would have."

His statement annoys me. Benjamin was a bully on the playground during school. All of a sudden he is the all mighty protector?

"Ummm. Okay." I shake my head and take a deep breath.

"What?" he asks confused.

"Kolton McKinney," I say and watch his reaction. "I don't understand why you would protect me when you let a helpless kid like Kolton get bullied by your group of friends. But then again, the presidency wasn't on the line then, so you didn't have an image to uphold."

My words are a little harsher than I intend them to be, but I'm tired and it's been a long day. At least I got the point across.

He looks down in shame. "I can't really argue with you on that. It's true. I didn't help Kolton. I didn't instigate it either though." He shrugs.

"And you are just different now?" I blatantly ask and am surprised by how honest and rude I am being. My argument with Lyncoln earlier has my claws still out.

"School isn't easy. I was just doing what I had to in order to get by." He shrugs, still avoiding eye contact.

"No. You were doing what you needed to in order to stay popular," I correct him.

"You're right, as usual. But since I graduated, I haven't hung out with any of those people, nor do I want to." Then he looks at me and adds, "Will you continue to judge me on your perception of me and who I was in Omaha, or will you get to know who I am now?"

This takes me aback and I realize I haven't been fair to him. I just have a gut feeling about him that I can't shake. But is it fair to judge him for one wrong choice? He's right, he didn't do anything to Kolton, but he didn't do anything to help him either. I have just written him off as guilty by association.

"You have a point." I sigh and tuck my hair behind my ears. "I guess I don't even really know you that well, Benjamin." I shrug. "Sorry."

"Well, let me remedy that for you." He smiles. "You know I have three siblings. You know I work in the fields just like you do. Things you may not know about me include that I love reading anything and everything, I love little kids and their chatty honesty, I have a thing for fixing up cars, I like card games, and I am constantly and relentlessly worried about my mom, especially now that I'm here."

"Marianne?" I ask, confused with his last statement.

"Her cancer escalated to stage three right before I left. So my getting far in the Culling would really benefit her. Especially if I could somehow get her to Vegas for treatment. My dad is a mean jerk. Even meaner when he drinks, but my mom is the best person I know. I'd do anything for her," he says it sadly and I feel worse for being super judgmental of him.

I think of the conversation I just had with Attie about the hospitals in the townships. I'm from Omaha and had no idea. I feel bad for judging him on the little things when I had no idea about the big things he was going through. We all know his dad is mean, never abusive but right on that ledge, but his mom being sick is another thing. He has to be putting so much pressure on himself to do well in the Culling.

"I had no idea," I say sympathetically.

"Well, no one really does. I have very few friends here I trust with that information."

So why does he trust me with that information?

"May I ask my family about her tomorrow?" I ask, trying to be nice.

"Would you?" he asks, his face full of concern for his mom.

"Absolutely. It would suck not being able to talk to her knowing that she isn't well." I nod.

"That'd be awesome. Thanks," he shrugs, "What about you? How are you taking this whole crazy thing?"

We talk for a little bit about the other girls and the training and the tests. Although we take tests almost every day, neither one of us thinks that is the worst part of this. We also talk about the simulator and what is to come. He asks my opinion of the other girls, specifically Renae. I encourage him to keep getting to know her better. Then he starts asking about Lyncoln and Henry and I get uncomfortable. He is the last person I want to talk to about my love life.

"Both seem to be into you," he says with a laugh. "The rest of us never even had a chance if we wanted one."

I sigh for a response. I will talk about this with Attie and Vanessa maybe, but not Benjamin. I shake my head as if trying to get out of talking about this.

"Well, have either made a move yet?" He wiggles his eyebrows suggestively.

I blush which seems to answer the question for me. *Dang traitorous blush.* Why, oh why, can't we change the subject?

"No way! Which one?" He claps his hands together. "I bet it was Lyncoln. He's freaking scary aggressive. Was it Lyncoln?"

Again, I don't answer and try hard not to blush.

"Do you not trust me?"

I don't, but I don't want to tell him that.

"I just don't want to talk about it. It's my own personal business and even I don't want to deal with it right now. I've had a heck of a week and the last thing I want to do is talk about this. I was in the hospital all night for observation after hitting my head. I'm beat." I yawn and find that although I was faking it, it ends up being a real yawn by the end of it as I really am that beat.

"Crap, Reagan. I'm sorry. We've been talking for almost twenty minutes now. I'll leave you to get some sleep."

"Thanks, Benjamin." I smile nicely and stand.

"Have fun with your family tomorrow. I'm so jealous." He gives me a hug that lasts a few seconds longer than I want it to.

"I'll ask about your mom," I say as I move out of his embrace. I may not like him, but his mom is a sweetheart.

"Thanks."

I see him out and decide to change into pajamas. I have made a mental decision that I'm not going to open the door when Lyncoln comes to check in. I have had enough of his moodiness for one day.

Knock on it, he does.

He tries for almost a whole minute before getting impatient. Knowing that I have to be in there if Sarge is outside, he decides to threaten me.

"You do know that I have clearance to go into any room I want at any time?" he growls.

I didn't know that. But I still don't move.

"Hold on. I'll just go get Henry, too. That way we can all hash this out together," he says through the shut door.

This gets me. He might be bluffing, but the last thing I want to happen is to have both of my boy toys in my room while I'm wearing pjs, especially when I'm currently ticked off at one of them. It's not a gamble I am willing to take.

"Have you lost your ever-loving mind?" I say, swinging the door open angrily.

I find him standing there looking exhausted. His shoulders look heavier than usual. He's holding a tray with a plastic shaped thing I don't recognize and a small box.

"Yes, but no." He shrugs.

"Are you going to come in, or what?" I ask snappy, still somewhat annoyed.

"No. You need to sleep. I just brought you a heat pack for your eye and some more chocolate cheesecake. I thought you would probably want that eye less bruised for seeing your family tomorrow. That and you have a ball to go to on Friday, gorgeous."

I'm shocked. No bossiness? No smart comments about what I told him in the hallway? No more moodiness?

"Thank you," I say softly, stunned.

"I'll just set it on your counter." He comes in three feet, sets it by my small kitchen sink, and then returns to his previous spot, all while I haven't moved, partially because his smell is intoxicating and partially because I can't keep up with his moods.

He picks up my hand and kisses my palm. "I'm sorry I was out of line with you earlier. I had a rough day and took it out on you. Not my proudest moment. Sleep well, Regs."

And before I have a chance to pick my jaw up off the floor, he's gone.

Chapter 15

The next day drags on as I wait to see my family. It has only been a month since I've been gone. How much has changed since then! I'm not sure who I am more excited to see, my mom, my dad, or Ashton, if he will even be there. It's a Monday so maybe he will need to stay home and do the chores. Or maybe he won't come since he was here for the lie detector test. I don't even know, but I'll take whoever I can get.

Henry and Lyncoln corral me between them again at breakfast. I wonder if other people think our situation is as weird as I do. No one says anything, well, except for Vanessa teasing me whenever she gets a chance. I think people are used to it. I wish I was.

In the morning we have another verbal, which means a lot of waiting around. This one is a bit peculiar as there are all sorts of questions on what you would do in war-time situations, or how you would treat prisoners. I manage to make Mr. Winters smile at least once even though it's a very serious verbal. I answer honestly but have no idea if I give them the answers they want to hear.

I get to skip lunch since I will be getting a late lunch with my family. I go to my room to tidy up and make sure I look good enough that my mom won't bicker at me. My eye already looks a little better, but is still tender and is darker and more yellow than red looking now. Frank has been doing an amazing job concealing it. I straighten the cream colored blouse tucked into the long, navy pencil skirt I'm wearing and try to fix my hair. I slide on a pair of navy heels and am lotioning my now baby soft hands when I hear a knock at the door.

Assuming it's Lyncoln coming to boss me around some more, I open the door with an annoyed look on my face.

"Hey, beautiful," Henry smiles, showing off his to-die-for dimples while his green eyes dance.

"Oh, hey," I smile back, somewhat relieved to find Henry instead of Lyncoln. Lyncoln is just a roller coaster of emotions.

"Expecting someone else?" He winks at me as he comes in. I prop the door open as is the mandate when a boy is in your room.

"No." I shrug then realize what time it is. "Time-out, shouldn't you be at lunch?"

"Yes, but I ate quickly so I could come talk to you before you leave for DIA. Would you believe me if I told you I missed you? It's weird. Even when I know you aren't somewhere, I keep looking for you anyway." He shakes his head and smiles shyly. He stands half leaning against one of the chairs in my sitting area. He crosses his legs and puts his hands in his suit pockets. His honey colored hair is styled slightly to the side and adds to his look.

Why is he so darn perfect? Could he at least have a zit or something?

"Plus, I didn't get to talk to you much this morning." He cocks his head to the side. "Someone was a bit distracted."

I laugh. "I'm just excited. And the morning took forever."

"I'm glad for you. I wish my family was as excited to see one another as yours is."

"You'll have it someday, Henry. I just know it," I say affectionately.

"What do you mean?"

"I mean your family is still healing from the loss of your mom. I'm sure you'll get back to being a happy family eventually. Especially, after all this." I stop to gesture then move close enough to him to put my hand on his bicep that looks way too good in his suit jacket. This man just looks good in a suit! "And even if you don't, I know you well enough to know you'll have that with your future family. You will make a great husband and dad someday."

I blush and look at my feet knowing that a huge part of me wants me to be his future family someday. But even if it isn't me at the end of the day, I still know that he will be a great dad. The thought of a little Henry running around makes me feel gooey.

Rather than responding to what I said, he grabs me around the back and pulls me into him, wrapping both arms around me as I feel both of his hands on my back through my thin blouse. I look up at him as he does and before I can even form a thought about what is about to happen, I feel his lips on mine. He kisses me soundly. First aggressively, and it's passionate, but not quite violently so like when Lyncoln kissed me. Then, it slows and softens. He gives me one last soft kiss then pulls away.

My head is spinning and my pulse is out of this world. I am fairly certain that is how your first kiss should be. It was passionate enough, but in a tender way, just like Henry. I find myself wanting to repeat the experience.

"I need you in my life, Reagan." He sighs and I feel his minty warm breath on my face.

Just then Jamie calls from the hallway, "Ms. Scott, we need to leave for DIA now." His tone is all professional, but in getting to know my guards as they've been with me every day for the last month, I can hear a bit of humor he is holding back and I know he smiled while he said it. I'm sure he's imagining me getting into all sorts of trouble with Henry.

I jump at Jamie's voice and instantly want to separate myself from Henry. I blush, but Henry keeps holding me right where I am and smiles at my blush, brushing his hand over one of my cheeks.

"Let me get out of here so you can go. Have fun, beautiful. Tell me all about it later." He leans in and takes my face in one hand while the other is still on my back, and kisses me once more, this time just soft and perfect, but like the start of a kissing session, not the end.

He breaks away and takes a few steps towards the door. I stay where I am, breathless and wanting more, wanting him to finish the kiss he started. Then I realize that is exactly why he did it.

He smiles and I squint at him. "Hey. Get back here," I demand playfully.

"I'll talk to you later, beautiful." He grins as he leaves.

I manage to let out a weak and aggravated, "Bye, Henry."

I quickly run to the bathroom and check the mirror. My face is on fire. My hair still seems to be in one place. My lips look a little funny. Will mom know I've just been smooching someone? And Henry of all people!

Henry kissed me? Did that really just happen?

I don't even have time to process that kiss, or kisses I guess, before we are down the hallway and on the elevator.

****

A door to a conference room opens and I step into the room, my arm in Jamie's. I know I'm supposed to be proper and greet them using my newly worked on etiquette, but when I see Ashton stand and whistle at me, I immediately launch myself at him. I hear Jamie laughing as he turns to his post outside the door.

"Oh. My. Gosh." My mom starts squealing, "Look at you." But then she freezes where she stands and looks concerned. "What happened to your eye?"

I thought Frank did so good of a job that she might not notice, but then again, nothing gets past her. Good thing I practiced a story to tell, just in case.

"We were running a training exercise and I got bumped, elbow to the face." I shrug like it's no big deal. No need to worry them. I can tell them the whole story later when we have longer to talk. It's still kind of the truth, just a very, very watered down version of the truth.

"Oh," she says, continuing to look me over.

"Must have been some exercise." Ashton gives me that look that tells me he doesn't buy it, but fortunately doesn't push the issue.

"Oh my word, your hair is getting so long." Mom squeezes my hand. "And your hands are so soft. And look at this outfit." She looks over my navy pencil skirt and cream blouse nodding in approval.

"Quit critiquing her," my dad says, moving her aside as he gives me a strong hug.

"But she looks so...so like she was meant to be here," Mom says, trying not to cry.

"Moooooom," Ashton groans, "You said you wouldn't cry. It has been less than a minute."

"I know, I know! I'm sorry." She shakes her head and gathers herself.

Ashton rubs his hands together excitedly, "So what are we eating today, sis?"

As if right on cue, a waiter brings in a tray with salads. "Hello, Scotts. Would you like to be seated and I can place your salads for you?"

We all sit to the back of the room. Dad and Ashton sit on one side of the huge table, and then mom and I on the other. It's identical to how we sit at home. The waiter drops off the salads and drinks and leaves us to talk.

"Oh my, these are impressive. The salad and dressing look so fresh too!" Mom says in complimenting both the salad and the fancy plates it all sits on. Dad is more impressed with his glass of fresh lemonade.

They fill me in on harvest in Omaha and how the crops are yielding. I'm pleased to find out the wheat field using my irrigation technique had the highest yields. It seems insignificant compared to other things the girls have created or are working on, but it's still my pride and joy. I can't wait to find out the yields from our winter vegetable crop in the greenhouse. They should be better than they ever have been before. With any luck from the weather, Omaha might actually have a surplus of crops for the first time in years.

In thinking about life in Omaha, I remember to ask about Benjamin's mom. Mom tells me it's only a matter of time. They caught her cancer too late and it had spread too far. I feel bad for Benjamin. I'm sure it's hard for him to be here when she is dying. Even harder leaving her with his dad. I make a mental note to cut him some slack in the future.

Trying to move to a lighter topic, Ashton slaps the table. "So. Boys. Spill it."

I immediately blush. If only they knew Henry, Henry out of all the boys here, was just kissing me before coming here, they would freak out.

"What about them?" I ask, trying to get my blushing under control. Life would be much easier if I could control it so it wasn't a dead giveaway.

"What about them? Please. You get to date twenty-five of the best men in the country and all you can manage is, 'what about them'?" Ashton rolls his eyes. "Give me a break."

I hesitate. It's one thing to talk about my love life with my brother, it's another thing with my mom and dad both sitting in the room.

Especially when there is more than one boy involved. Awkward doesn't even begin to cover it.

"Well?" Mom gives me "the look".

Still feeling like a child when she does that, I don't hesitate to give in to her. "Well, there are actually only nineteen boys now. When I met them at the Canidatorial Ball there were twenty-two and we are down three since then. And more cuts are supposed to be happening at any moment. We have another ball on Friday though." I am quiet a moment thinking about that.

What if I don't make it to Friday? What if I go home and never experience kissing Henry again? That would be a crying shame. A shame indeed.

"And how many of these boys have you taken a fancy to?" my dad chuckles. Ashton rolls his eyes at Dad's usual embarrassing choice of words.

"Two, I guess," I respond shortly. I don't want to get into this with my family right now. Or ever, for that matter.

"Where are they from? What do they do? Names. Seriously, you're going to have to tell us sooner or later so it might as well be sooner." Ashton grins his signature grin knowing that he and I both know he's right.

"They are both from Denver. Lyncoln Reed and Henry Maxwell," I say then take a bite of a cucumber from my salad, trying to avoid their gazes. I know I'm blushing. I would be even more embarrassed if they knew that I have kissed each of them and liked it tremendously.

"Well, I'll be," Dad says with a chuckle again.

Mom says, "Henry?"

At the same exact time Ashton says, "Lyncoln?"

"What?"

"Henry? I mean the heir? I know that means he's not necessarily a shoo-in, but for real, he's got a decent shot. You always did aim high." Mom shakes her head and snorts a chuckle at me.

"Well someone always told me to settle for nothing less than the best." I roll my eyes then look to Ashton. "How do you know Lyncoln?" I knew they would freak out about Henry, but I didn't know they had ever heard of Lyncoln.

"Military training. He's a legend. Good Lord, Reagan, you can pick them." He shakes his head. "Lyncoln *AND* Henry?" He keeps shaking his head and I don't know what to do, so I just sit there awkwardly waiting for someone else to say something.

"So how does it work? Do you pick which one you want? Or does the country vote? And how do you court, I mean date, in the middle of all that?" Dad asks and I hear the genuine concern for his daughter in his voice.

"A little of both actually. Once we get down in numbers, candidates normally pair up with who they want to end up with before the voting so that the citizens vote for an already solid couple," I try to explain even though I hardly understand it myself. "And we can date and hang out leading up to that. Once we hit the final eight couples though, you are pretty well stuck with your partner."

"So you have a big decision to make," Mom says, reading between the lines.

"I suppose so." I sigh as the entrée plates are brought in.

"Sounds like you don't really want to choose," Ashton says in an oddly serious moment of his.

I decide to be completely honest with them. "Not really. I didn't expect to get attention from any boys, let alone two. I care about both of them and they are both really great people. I never even had a single boyfriend before coming here so this all seems overwhelming. What am I supposed to do? And this could very well be a decision for life. There's no turning back."

"Just listen to your heart, double check with your brain, and then go with your gut." Mom reaches over and squeezes my hand.

"If it were only that simple, Mom."

Pasta dishes are then brought in and Ashton gets completely distracted by the food. We talk more about the upcoming ball, how much longer the Culling should take, and their plane ride here. I wish they could stay longer. A few hours doesn't feel like nearly enough time with them.

I remind myself that the farther we go, the better influence my family has. My family already has more influence in Omaha as it is. Dad and Ashton have been promoted to help manage the farms in our subdivision and mom is now an assistant principal at the school. And even if I go home tomorrow, they got to make a trip to Denver for this moment right here and now. I've already given them something that they wouldn't have ever been able to do before. And for that, I feel proud of myself.

But, I can't help but think too, what if we actually moved to Denver?

Then again, what if I went home while Henry wins with a different Madam President?

****

An hour later, I say my goodbyes to my family. It's painful to say goodbye, but it's a pain I'm glad to have knowing I got to see them, even if only for a short time. In thinking of my schedule for the rest of the day, I'm dismayed to remember that my first social this evening is with Sapphire before dinner. I get to go from something that has been a favorite part of this whole experience, to that.

Ugh.

Back at Mile High, I get to her room right on time. Surprisingly, although I wouldn't say we are exactly cordial, we manage to get through it, sharing about each other's family. I'm beginning to wonder if Marisol just brings out the worst in people. Sapphire seems fine enough when she isn't around. I wouldn't say we are going to become besties now, but we were nice enough.

Down at dinner, people ask about my family. I gladly tell them as I feel refreshed having been able to see them. My family reminds me of why I am here. They remind me of the good in the world. They remind me that family is important. Hearing the others talk about their families also makes me feel good. This prize wasn't just for me.

I am again sitting in-between Lyncoln and Henry. Henry scoots entirely closer than necessary but I don't mind. I also wouldn't mind finishing that kiss he started, but now really isn't the time.

"My brother Ashton said he would be dreaming of the strawberry cheesecake for weeks," I finish telling Vanessa and she laughs. I'm the last of us to share about our families, and maybe the most excited except for Oliver, who matches my level of sheer joy.

Just then October sits down, clanging her tray in interruption as she does. She goes between Marisol's group and our group often. And often she is the last one to the cafeteria for meals.

"Well, look who it is!" Maverick teases her.

"Yeah, yeah." October rolls her eyes and sits down. "Did you hear that Katie, Dylan, and William are out?"

"William? A Vegas boy. Darn," Maverick says and nods at Attie who is also from Vegas. I understand what they mean. I would gladly like to have Agnes beside me and although I don't completely trust Benjamin, I don't necessarily want him to go home next either. The longer we make it, the better it makes our home township look.

I silently feel bad for thinking that I won't miss Katie too much since she was relentless in her pursuit of Henry.

"That's too bad," Elizabeth says sadly.

We all seem to remember that a bunch of cuts are supposed to be happening. I look to Henry and he gives me that "don't worry" look.

"I heard that our numbers will be well under 25 total by Friday," October offers and I know that's why she's here. She wanted to give us a heads up. Marisol must know things or know someone deep in the Culling. How much power does her source have? She should have gone home weeks ago.

I chat some more with the group. I look at Vanessa across from me and Attie down from me on the other side of Lyncoln. I really hope both of those women make it to Friday. I don't know what I would do without either of them.

"Well, I have a social with this fine young woman here." Trent grins as he walks over, interrupting the group conversation but not caring, as he reaches a hand out to me. "Shall we?"

"We shall." I smile and turn to take his hand to stand up, feeling glad that he is my other social for this evening. I got through the one with Sapphire in my good mood and now I'm looking forward to the one with Trent since he is so darn funny. Plus, he just got to see his family too, so we can swap stories.

We are about to make our exit when Lyncoln speaks up, stopping us with his words and using his fork for emphasis as he says, "Touch her, and I will kill you."

He also says it right in front of everyone, just staring Trent down and making it completely awkward.

"Sir, yes, sir!" Trent responds loudly and salutes, causing our table to erupt in giggles. Henry laughs hard and slaps Lyncoln on the back while even Lyncoln has a hard time not laughing. He gives me one quick half-smile as Trent and I leave.

****

"Girl, I never even had a chance with you," Trent jokes affectionately as we sit around my coffee table, with the door open of course.

"I wasn't aware you wanted one," I joke back.

He gets more serious, "Well I did. Not to worry, I found a replacement. You have more than enough testosterone in your life."

Did he seriously want to date me? Is that what he just said? I have to remind myself that they were shown highlights of us. So I may have been on his list of people of interest. That's all.

"Who's that?" I ask, thinking back to what I've seen in the cafeteria and ignoring his comment about testosterone.

"Morgan." He grins as he says her name. I wonder if I have that same dumb look on my face when someone mentions Henry.

"Nice choice." I nod my approval. "She has brains and looks."

"I know. Double trouble if you ask me," Trent says and we both laugh.

"How well do you know Knox?" I ask somewhat out of the blue, knowing they are both from Galveston.

"Pretty well. We aren't very similar, but we've worked on a bunch of projects together. He's the brains and I'm the mouth," he says with a shrug.

I smile. "Doesn't surprise me. But he's a good guy, right? I hear there might be something going on between Attie and him and wanted to make sure she's in good hands," I say protectively. She may not have gotten Henry, but she still deserves the best. And as far as I'm concerned, she should be the next madam president. So she needs to have a reliable partner.

"Ummm. Let's just say she couldn't have picked someone more intelligent." He gestures. "But, he's also a good guy too. Kind of quiet. Well, everyone is quiet compared to me anyway."

"And he likes her?"

"Yeah. I don't think I've ever seen him give a girl the time of day before Attie." He smiles suggestively and I laugh. "So now that you have that out of your system, tell me about your family. How was today?"

I tell him and then I ask him about his family. Trent has two brothers and is the youngest of the three of them. He says the only way he could avoid getting beat up by them was to make them laugh, so he became a jokester at a young age. Only his mom and dad came today since everyone else is older and has families of their own, but he was more than happy getting some time with just his parents.

I ask him basic questions about Galveston and he knowledgeably answers. He tells me about wind turbines, the electricity output they provide, and how they are trying to make them more efficient and cost effective. When he's done, I'm left feeling quite impressed not only with what he is telling me, but also in how intelligent he is. He downplays it, but he is very smart too.

As he leaves after getting me laughing again, I think that if this really is just a competition, Trent is so charismatic and smart he might just win the whole darn thing.

****

Tuesday morning, Joshua and two girls from Seattle, Sophina and Melissa, are gone. Unfortunately, I didn't get to know Sophina and Melissa that well, but I was always nice and polite to them since they came from the same township as Marcia. I do remember Joshua well though, Mr. Explosive. I remember his input on our group project and that he didn't hesitate to defend me. If I could have, I would've told him I wish him all the best.

Joshua leaving does make me a little skittish about who else is going to go next. If someone like him can go, who is really safe? I feel like everywhere we go, if anyone walks into a room even a little late, people are wondering if they are cut. We are all extremely excited for Friday, but at the same time, we are just ducks on water while we wait. Calm above the surface and anything but beneath it. Ten more people or so will be leaving before Friday after all.

"Two quick announcements, ladies." Professor Dougall begins class and snaps me out of my reprieve. "The first of which is somewhat important and you need to take seriously. President Maxwell and a dozen or so of the cabinet members along with their families will be in attendance at the ball Friday. I assume I don't need to remind you to use your manners. Remember that these people will be voting for you.

"The second, and more excitable matter at hand, is that in honor of the old holiday of Halloween, Friday's ball will be a masquerade ball. This means your attendants can make you custom made gowns with matching headpieces." She smiles.

Some girls get excited but most of us have no flipping idea what she is talking about. What was Halloween and what in the world is a masquerade? I've heard both words before, but I have no idea what she is trying to tell us. I can tell by her rare good mood and excitement that we are supposed to like this. This is good news, I guess.

"Oh, good heavens. Okay, backtrack." She laughs. "So Halloween used to be a holiday supposedly celebrating witchcraft and the like, but really little kids dressed up in costumes and went door to door trick-or-treating for candy. At the end of the night, they would have a bunch of candy that would last them for days. This holiday used to be the last day of October, and since we are about halfway through October, we have decided it would be a fun thing to incorporate into a theme for this ball."

I vaguely remember something like this when we learned about all the pre-Trident holidays in junior high. That must be where I've heard the word before.

"So a masquerade then is a kind of a dance with costumes, the key ingredient being masks." She pauses and hits some buttons on her computer pulling up some pictures on the big screen behind her. "Here are examples of masks. It isn't like you won't know who people are; it's just a fun way to have a theme for the ball. You may also choose to coordinate your attire and/or mask with your date if you wish."

Now fully understanding what she is talking about, we are now whispering amongst ourselves in excitement. They look a little silly, but with everyone doing it, it might be kind of cool. It's different nonetheless. It will be a nice, fun way to liven up the seriousness of having more cabinet members joining us.

"I can tell you are excited now that you understand." She laughs again. "Before I dismiss you to go discuss ideas with your attendants waiting in your rooms, I need to remind you that with more people, there comes more responsibility. This is the first chance you have to make an impression on the President's cabinet members. These are very important people. Don't mess it up."

That seems to knock the wind out of my sails a little, but I quickly leave along with the rest of the girls, wanting to figure out what Frank will have me wear and what this mask business is all about. I'm dreading the whole coordinating attire thing.

Who is my date again, anyway?

****

"So, my dear. Let's talk gowns, color first, and then we will go from there." Frank paces my room, tossing ideas out to Gertie, who is sitting on the chair with a huge book of pictures of gowns. He stops for a moment. "This is the most important dress you have worn yet," he says with emphasis and gestures wildly with his hands before continuing mumbling as he paces.

I take off my heels and rub my feet before setting them on the coffee table as I wait for his mumbling to stop. It always does and then what he has to say is usually profound. You just have to give the madman time to work it out.

"So I'm thinking forest or emerald." Frank stops pacing and turns to me. Gertie flips to a picture of a gorgeous gown and shows it to me.

I think of Henry's smooth emerald green eyes and falter just a second. The dress is the exact color of his eyes.

Never missing anything, Frank hesitates. "No? I guess you already did wear a form of emerald. My second choice is a deep blue. How about this?"

I look at the dress. Although it doesn't have brown undertones like Lyncoln's eyes, it's darn close to the main color of them. I lean my head against the couch and my head touches the wall behind me. I know that no one will understand that my dress and their eye color matches, but I will know and it will drive me bonkers. It will be like I have silently chosen one and slighted the other. I'm nowhere near ready to make a choice like that. And I must be off my rocker if I look at dress colors and immediately think of the colors of their eyes.

Who does that?

Someone not emotionally stable, that's who. *Dang hormones.*

"Reagan? Dear? What is it? Just tell us," Gertie shushes Frank who's mumbling on some more and flipping through the big book placed in her lap.

"Emerald is the color of Henry's eyes. Blue is Lyncoln's. I realize it may be silly and no one will know, but I can't pick one over the other yet. I'm just not ready." I sigh feeling exhausted. "Dougall mentioned we can match our dates, so I guess I'm just a bit panicked about matching either of them. Eye color or otherwise."

I haven't slept well lately as I've been having nightmares I'm told I have to leave and never get to say goodbye to either Henry or Lyncoln. Then when I do see them next, they are with Marisol and Sapphire and barely remember me. Silly dreams, but freakish.

"Ahhh. Not silly at all now that I know, my dear." Frank sits beside me and squeezes my shoulder. He looks at me for a moment then looks at Gertie. "Gertie! Get me my drawing pad from my bag. Quick!" he demands and then is back up walking and mumbling again.

When Gertie hands him his drawing pad and colored pencils, he sits down right away and gets to work. Gertie and I know to just be quiet and let him be. He is in his creative zone right now.

"My dear, you have just given me the best idea for a dress ever. It will be a custom job. The shop will kill me, but this is going to be one legendary dress. You will have your blue and you will have your emerald," he says excitedly, pencils flying across the paper while he speaks.

He shows me the picture a few short minutes later, and although it's in pencil, I'm pleasantly surprised. The top of the gown will hug my chest, and with the depth of Frank's shading I can tell there will be something eye-catching and sparkly. The dress starts in a deep blue at the top and fades into an emerald color by the time it brushes the floor. More sparkles trace one of my hips and cascade down to the floor next to the slit up the leg.

"This is amazing, Frank. I can't wait to see it," I say nodding then add, "Thank you for taking my feelings into consideration instead of chalking it up to my being a silly girl, even though that is exactly what I am being."

"You are many, many things, Ms. Scott, but silly is not one of them," Frank says softly and then slaps his hands together making me jump. "I'm heading to the shop right now to get to work on this tonight, before any other orders come in. I have an idea for your mask also, which will match the sequins in your dress instead of either color. Gertie, run her a bath. I want her to take a butter-bath twice a day all this week in preparation for the ball."

He is turning to leave as I joke, "So I guess you guys think I'll make it to Friday then?"

"Oh honey, you have it in the bag," Gertie laughs while Frank nods exaggeratedly.

****

Frank didn't return the next morning because he was "on gown duty" as Gertie put it. Gertie helped me get into a skirt and blouse combination that seems to be my go-to outfit. This time it's a hot pink skirt with a black v-neck blouse tucked in. Sometimes I am dressed totally elegantly, and sometimes it's a bit fun and out there. I love days like this where it's something different.

Jamie leads me down for breakfast and I'm a bit worried. Who will be missing today? Is today the day they destroy my hopes and dreams and send me packing? Jamie gives me a squeeze of encouragement around my shoulders as if understanding my unease.

I walk into the cafeteria to find everyone talking and conversing. I quickly grab some food and take my spot between Henry and Lyncoln, extremely happy to see them both though I knew they probably weren't going anywhere.

Lyncoln eyes my hot pink skirt and raises his eyebrows at me. I blush.

"What's all the chatter about?" I ask, feeling like I'm the last one here.

"Well, they sent home six people last night. SIX!" Attie says astounded.

"Anyone we know?" I ask, looking around. Obviously, Henry and Lyncoln are beside me so I can selfishly say that that was really all I was worried about. Attie is here. Elizabeth and Maverick are here. Vanessa is here. Who is missing? I look around to the spot where Benjamin is sitting. I spot him and let out a breath of relief. Even he is still here.

"Adam, Stephen, Emily, Savannah, Ellie, and Charlotte," Attie names off. I would venture to say Attie probably even knows everyone's middle names in addition to first and last names and townships. She just pays attention to details like that.

"Another bad day for Vegas." I shake my head. "Sorry, girl."

"That's okay. I will miss Savannah though. She's quiet but genius." She shrugs then adds, "But I'm glad we are all still here and avoided another cut." She looks to Knox and smiles, and I know she is even most glad he is still here.

He smiles at her from where he is sitting, in his new usual spot across from her, and in a rare moment of spontaneity he says, "They would have to drag me out of here kicking and screaming. Are you kidding me? If I left you before this ball, you would come all the way to Galveston just to kick my butt."

We all laugh, knowing that it sounds exactly like something Attie would do. She blushes but laughs too and I'm glad my friend has found someone who makes her feel special. Everyone seems to be coupling up in our group. Oliver is still a part of our group but sits farther down in pursuit of Isabella. They seem to have hit it off since paintball. Vanessa and Bronson aren't a couple but sit together often though sometimes he sits with Haley too. And, of course, Maverick and Elizabeth are a deliriously happy and perfect couple.

And then there is the trifecta of Henry, Lyncoln, and I. With cuts being made frequently and bigger ones at that, how much time do I have left with these boys? When will I have to say goodbye?

And even worse, what if I never do get to say goodbye?

Sensing my unease, Henry leans over and whispers in my ear, "You aren't going anywhere, trust me."

Instead of making me feel better, it makes me feel worse. What if it isn't up to him?

****

"So as you await Friday, I thought it best we do our heritage project in which you will track your lineage from the bunkers to current times. Obviously, if you were remotely related to any of your romantic prospects here, we would step in immediately. For example, Lyncoln and Elizabeth are distant cousins," Professor Zax starts in, telling us what we are to be doing for the morning. I look at Lyncoln and Elizabeth and notice their similarities. Flawless complexion, dark hair, high cheekbones. I can see that they could be related.

I hear groans from some people as he finishes instructions, but I'm honestly just glad for something to do. Six people were missing at breakfast. Six. With at least four more to go, I need to keep myself busy.

I work with Attie and Vanessa as we go through our charts filling in names. We giggle and laugh at the weird names, wondering how our ancestors met. Attie always has a romantic story with a happy ending for each of hers which makes us laugh. Vanessa always kills someone off in her stories just to make Attie mad. I find myself realizing I will very much miss them if I were to leave. They along with Marcia are the best friends I've ever had.

Not finding the name for a great-great-great uncle, I head to the front to ask Professor Zax about it.

"Professor Zax, I cannot find this ancestor's name," I say pointing to my chart. "It's missing from all the books. Am I mistaken or is there a reason?"

"There is a reason, my dear. When someone has undergone expulsion from the country, their name is removed." He smiles like it's no big deal.

"Are you serious?" I ask, wondering what this man did that was so awful he was banished.

"You aren't the only one dear, there are quite a few in that time period actually. I have a great aunt myself. Don't sweat it." He smiles kindly. "But the next time your temper gets the better of you, you can just blame it on that relative. I know I do."

I laugh and thank him for his help and finish up my project with Attie and Vanessa. Surprisingly, it does help to pass the time.

****

That night, as I'm dreaming a crazy dream about the banished relative of mine and how he murdered Lyncoln's dad, I hear a pounding on my door followed by a light being turned on. I immediately jolt awake thinking that they have come to dismiss me.

Seeing my panicked look, Elle smiles as she turns on my lamp. "No worries, we are only here for another verbal."

"Goodness. Well at least you got my heart pumping," I say as I prop myself up against the pillows.

Mr. Winters smirks.

We go through the typical questions before the annoying ones come about. More questions about how to handle traitors and if and when to use expulsion. Tons of hypotheticals that are kind of boring.

"You recently were assaulted by Grady. Would you consider that form of punishment for him?"

"No," I say without hesitating. I wish I could just go back to sleep, this time not dreaming stupid things. I have never felt so sleep deprived as I have throughout the Culling.

"Elaborate please. The man assaulted you. You are still bruised and battered. And yet you do not choose banishment? Why?" he asks. These questions are more complex and specific than any of the past verbals.

"Grady just up and attacks Elizabeth because she is beautiful and his hormones are raging? I don't think so. There was more going on in that situation." I shrug and make a mental note to ask Lyncoln if he found out anything.

"So how would you handle it? Torture him? How do you get him to talk?" Mr. Winters continues with one question right after the other.

"My position and opinion on torture is that if someone truly fears for their life, they will tell you whatever you want to hear regardless of its truth. So, with torture, you get a bunch of people that falsely admit to crimes. We know that from the pre-Trident wars." I pause a moment. "So with Grady, there needs to be a fine line. He needs to be scared, but not too scared. Threaten him with expulsion and let him talk to someone he knows and has a connection with, like Lyncoln, and see if that can get him to talk. Isolate him. Make him feel hopeless and despaired, but not pain. Sometimes emotional pain is more manipulating than physical pain," I finish, feeling proud of my answer though I'm not sure it was the correct one.

"So do you approve of any other forms of torture then?"

"What is with all the torture questions?" I snap, clearly annoyed. We have been at this for at least twenty minutes and I just want to go back to bed. Why is torture even an issue? Then it hits me.

"Wait, you wouldn't ask and spend so much time on it if it weren't a current issue, now would you? Who needs to be tortured? Why are there more guards than necessary whenever we go outside? What is everyone afraid of?" I blurt out.

Elle and Mr. Winters look at one another and exchange a glance and then he looks back at me.

"I'm sorry, but I don't know what you're talking about."

He's lying and we both know it.

I don't say anything so he tries to ask again, "So no forms of torture then?"

"I'll tell you when I know all the circumstances, like who we are torturing, why, and to what end," I say confidently.

Mr. Winters smirks. "A very intelligent answer." He turns to Elle, "I think we are done here."

They start to leave, but Mr. Winters hesitates and turns back for a moment. "I understand that you may be confused by this verbal, but you will soon know the answers to your own questions. I applaud you on your perceptiveness though. You continue to impress me. Good night."

I'm stunned by both what he says, and how many words the normally reticent Mr. Winters used. The light shuts off, I turn off my lamp, and I'm left to sleep again. It doesn't find me quickly. I always assumed being Madam President would be making decisions to better and help rebuild our country. Now there is some other outside threat? And torture, of all things, is a current issue?

What exactly did I get myself into here?

Chapter 16

The next morning, I'm tired as I plop down at my spot between Henry and Lyncoln. Henry scoots closer and Lyncoln immediately puts his hand on my knee, almost a protective reflex. They are consoling me. From what?

"What's wrong?" I look at Lyncoln's crazy blue and brown eyes and can physically feel that he cares about me.

As I look around, I figure out the answer to my own question.

"Maybe she just isn't here yet?" I ask in denial.

"Her guard wasn't at her room. Sorry, Reagan," Elizabeth sympathetically smiles at me.

"Vanessa is gone?" Now I turn to Henry.

"We think so. Her along with four other girls and four boys." He rubs a hand along my back.

I pinch my nose trying to digest this information. I hate mornings. For more than one reason.

"Please tell me then that Marisol and her following are gone," I say with my temper flaring. Why did Vanessa go when the worst person is still here?

"Well, Georgia and Jade are gone," Attie says with a shrug and shakes her head. Both of those girls were in Marisol's group at least. "I don't get it either," she adds.

They fill me in on the other missing people. Our numbers are now at 20 total, ten girls and ten boys. There is a lengthy discussion on if that was the last cut and we made it to the ball. I should be happy if that is the case, but I'm still angry Vanessa is gone. She is gone and Marisol is still here. In what world would Marisol make a better Madam President than Vanessa? I'm tired and my temper is really starting to flare.

As if sensing it, Lyncoln squeezes my knee and then rubs his thumb in circles on it. I have one boy with his arm around the back of me and the other with his hand on my knee under the table. I should be ashamed of myself, but at this exact moment, all I can think of is that I'm glad they're both there. They both know me well enough to know that it would bother me when Vanessa was gone. She was my closest friend here other than Attie. I know in my review my professors told me that I seem to care about others too much, but it wouldn't be respectful to Vanessa if I had the attitude of being glad she was gone so there were less standing in my way. What kind of a leader would I be if I did that? You might as well call me Marisol if that were the case.

Since Bronson and Haley have somewhat started dating or hanging out or whatever, I guess I should've been more skeptical about it and seen it coming. Everyone remaining is part of a solid couple except for October and Lyncoln who are the oddballs. I have a feeling neither one of them will be next to go either because they are too smart and too good at what they do.

I feel furious at this whole couple business though. What if the best girl for the job didn't like any of the boys here? Vanessa wasn't romantically involved so is that why she's out? Why do we have to be coupled up? I know by law we all have to be married, but why do the Presidential Couple have to be married to one another? Vanessa would have been a darn fine Madam President as far as I'm concerned.

"Ladies and gentlemen," Elle says walking into the cafeteria with such purpose that it interrupts all conversations and grabs all of our attention. "Two quick announcements I am happy to report. Today instead of your usual morning classes, we will be going in shifts to DIA and will begin your self-defense classes. You may also practice at the range. We will go for two hours this morning and two hours tomorrow. Unfortunately, I didn't get you guys out of etiquette class. Dougall was adamant that you have as much time with her as possible before the ball, although you do have tomorrow afternoon off for preparations." She stops for a moment as there are a few chuckles and groans at her comment about Professor Dougall. "Also, and more importantly, I'm pleased to announce those of you who remain have made it to the State of the Union's Culling Masquerade Ball and have passed another round of cuts. Congratulations."

I hear whoops and hollers but find I can't be very excited about this without thinking of Vanessa. I'm still here. For now. But I'm in a love triangle of sorts, and if you only get to stay if you are coupled up, my time with Henry and Lyncoln both is dwindling.

****

That evening after my rather pleasant socials with Bronson and Elizabeth, Frank and Gertie are flying around my room like crazy people. I'm exhausted from a long day. My arms are sore from holding the gun too tight as I practiced my aim earlier this morning, or maybe it was from our self-defense class, I'm not sure which. On top of that, we had to practice different dances and proper greetings of people for five long hours this afternoon. I just want to crawl into my bed and sleep for a minimum of 12 hours.

"I know you are tired, dear. But you will be the best-dressed woman at the ball, guarantee it!" Frank says excitedly.

"I don't doubt your abilities at all, Frank," I respond with a laugh that turns into a yawn.

"How about this, we will fit you for your dress tonight, to make sure it fits and no alterations are needed, get you a bath, and then you may get to bed, hopefully within the hour?" he asks.

"Sounds perfect," I say relieved. I love them dearly but am not in the mood for these shenanigans right now.

I go to the bathroom where my dress is hanging and unzip the bag to find the most gorgeous gown I have ever seen. The deep blue fades to emerald with sparkles on the chest and waist also fading into one another. It's exquisite. It is even better than I imagined it would be. I will be like a walking, sparkling jewel. I'm amazed Frank was able to concoct such a masterpiece in such a short amount of time and tell him so.

Gertie helps me zip in and step into heels as they both make observations. I can't help but feel more excited now. I have made it this far. I get to go to the ball tomorrow! I owe it to Vanessa to kick some butt, too. Preferably Marisol's.

"Now for your mask, which we are just finishing up with, do you want to have it on a stick to put on like so," he gestures with his hand, "or do you want it attached to your hair?"

"Well if you want me to wear it at all, it had better be attached," I laugh.

Gertie looks at Frank and says, "See? I told you so."

After more discussion on what needs to be adjusted, which is apparently just the length a half an inch, Gertie quickly ushers me to the butter bath. Before I know it, I am bathed, jammied, and alone in bed. Sleep finds me faster than it has for the past week.

I dream of a blue eyed boy and green eyed boy accompanying me to a ball.

****

The next morning, I'm surprised that my aim at the practice range is improving. Only about half of the boys are there, the rest have started some simulations. Oliver helps me practice and works with me on not being so tense when I shoot, mostly by cracking jokes since he isn't any better at aiming than I am. I find I'm hitting the target, but not the bullseye. My precision also stinks since bullet holes are all over the target. Attie joins us later and works on her shooting too. I'm glad I'm not the only girl who seems to struggle with this. Elizabeth, in all her beautiful glory, hasn't missed the target once. *Go figure.*

On the way back to Mile High, we are told they are having lunch sent to our rooms. Other than briefly at breakfast, I haven't even seen Henry or Lyncoln today. Many of the girls don't even mind the lack of boys as they are giddily talking about their dresses and dates.

As I get on the elevator at Mile High, a hand sticks in the door and October and her guard quickly come in, hitting the button for the doors to close.

"Reagan," she says out of breath, "she's planning something for tonight. She wants you to come unglued in front of cabinet members. She wants me to pick a fight with you there, too."

"What?" I ask angrily, wondering what Marisol has up her sleeve.

"Yeah," October shakes her head and takes another deep breath. "Her dad told her ranks. She isn't in the top five and you are. He's irate. He told her to step up her game."

"I thought we weren't supposed to talk to our families?" I ask bewildered.

"Well, apparently that rule doesn't apply when your dad is at DIA in a pretty powerful position and checks in frequently." She rolls her eyes as the door dings signaling our arrival. "Just be careful." She gives my shoulder a squeeze and goes on her way.

Other than her being present at our table at meals, October has been distant. I know she's being a double agent and trying to help, but I wish I could talk to her more. I feel like she has more information than I do and I wish she would share that information more often. And more than that, she's a cool person and fun to be around.

I reach my room and think about how lovely a quick nap would be, but upon turning the doorknob, I find Gertie and Frank already in my room and looking distraught.

"Darling! Someone tried to tamper with your gown. Fortunately, I'm not a fool so I put a fake, and less beautiful one in its place. Your real dress was with us last night," Frank stomps angrily, pacing in my room.

"Funny that, October was just telling me that Marisol was up to no good at this ball." I shake my head. "I don't think that's the last we have heard of her for tonight either."

"That girl…" Gertie begins, looking venomous. I think this is the first time I have ever seen her angry like this. She was concerned for me after the Grady incident, but not downright angry.

"She will get what she deserves," Frank says determinedly. "We will eat a quick lunch. Then we will make you so beautiful that she explodes mid-air."

I laugh but know he's only half joking. He knows he's good at what he does. Frank is truly an artist, he just expresses it through a different medium than most.

"Let's do this," I say affectionately and decide to be helpful adding, "What do you need me to do first?"

****

Hours later, I'm standing before the mirror in my room and barely recognize myself again. I have been poked, plucked, butter-bathed, and more. My gown hugs my body, drifting to the floor. This is my favorite dress so far. It's navy at the top around the sparkles. It is cut in a v-shape around my chest, highlighting it in a tasteful way. Then the dress fades to pure vibrant emerald at the floor after it swoops to more sparkles on my waist. The colors are spot on and shimmer when I move. The sequins are in just the right spots to help the transition between the two colors which normally don't blend into one another. Frank says it is somewhat of a double ombré, and though I don't really know what that means, I suspect it has to do with the dark colors both fading into the sparkly sections. The back is open and to the middle of my back. The slit up my leg gives an element of sexy to the otherwise completely elegant dress. When I stand in the mirror and move side to side, it looks like the dress rains sparkles to the floor. I love it.

The mask Frank made for me is half matte silver and half sparkly, the same sparkles and sequins as my dress. On the sparkle side, it flares out and sits in my hair adding sparkles there too. He has my hair curled and done up off my neck, except for a few tendrils that have already managed to escape. The mask attaches to my hair, but he shows me where the pins are. It settles over my smoky eyes done in silver tones. The mask is more amazing than I thought it would be. Thinking the whole mask business is a little silly anyway, I'm pleased to find I actually don't mind wearing it. It matches the dress perfectly, and the shoes too, which are solid sparkly silver heels.

Frank and Gertie do their finishing touches and then hurry off after gently hugging me and wishing me luck. Frank is just sure that I will be the "belle of the ball".

Knowing that we have to be downstairs in a half an hour and feeling nervous about arriving as one of the few uncoupled candidates, I decide there is no better time than the present. I feel elegant and beautiful, and for the first time ever, like I am able to keep up with the good looks of my counterparts.

I open the door and find Jamie, who loses his composure and whistles at me.

"Shut up," I say with a smile.

"You look great, Reagan, really." He gives my hand a squeeze of support as he loops it around his arm.

"Thanks, Jamie," I smile at him affectionately.

He gets me laughing about the masks and before I know it, the elevator opens and we walk down the hallway. We have arrived.

The room is decorated to perfection again. Huge pieces of fabric drape down to the dance floor in an artsy and dramatic manner. Everyone is wearing masks, even the waiters. There is an odd type of music playing in the background, giving it more of a mysterious feel. Some couples are already dancing while others are standing around greeting one another and helping themselves to the drinks or hors d'oeuvres. More people are still shuffling in and it is apparent that the President and his cabinet members have not yet arrived.

As I walk in, I see Lyncoln across the room in discussion with the only man not wearing a mask and instead in military uniform, the one named Langly from before. They are in a heated conversation, but Lyncoln stares as soon as he sees me. He is wearing a black suit with a thin, long black tie and a black vest with a square black and gray pattern adding life to the otherwise usual suit he wears. He also wears the mandatory mask, which is simple and matte black and very much the Lyncoln style. Although he is wearing a mask, I would know those eyes anywhere.

He continues staring at me while he starts talking to the anxious-looking military man. I try not to, but I'm pretty sure I'm grinning at him. It feels oddly empowering to be able to stop a force of nature like Lyncoln in his tracks.

"Here." I hear a familiar voice as I am handed a glass of champagne. "You look exquisite. With your two love prospects, you're going to need this."

I take the drink and turn to see Isabella and Oliver, Oliver handing me the champagne. Isabella is wearing a dark purple dress and Oliver is wearing a dark gray suit with a matching dark purple tie and vest. They both have the mask on the stick thing and are clearly matching.

"You guys look great. Love the matching," I compliment them.

"Ummm...that dress. It's a good thing I like you, or I would hate you," Isabella says and we all laugh.

"So you're saying I should steer clear of Marisol then," I joke.

"Way clear. Don't look, but she's already glaring," Oliver adds and does an impersonation making us laugh.

"May I interrupt to ask for a dance with this ravishing woman?" I hear and feel Henry at the same time as he comes up behind me and puts a hand on my bare back.

I turn to see him wearing a black suit with a black vest and bow tie. His mask rather than covering both eyes covers only one and looks to be made out of some sort of black metal material. The one eye thing looks really good on him and very much compliments those smooth emerald eyes. When seeing the pictures of masks, I wasn't sure they would look good on the men, or on anyone really, but his is very masculine and it definitely works for him. Henry has a way of making everything more manly, like those dimples for example.

"Go ahead," Oliver says to him with a grin, "We were on our way there too."

After putting my drink back down, I am swept up by Henry and danced around in circles. For the first few moments as he spins me around, I don't even have time to say anything. I'm just focusing on following his lead and not tripping in these heels. After a few minutes of his showing off, he slows us down for a bit.

"You look amazing," he whispers to me and I blush. "And you smell even better." He rests his head on my head as he pulls me in closer than is probably necessary.

"Hi. It's nice to see you too," I shyly laugh.

"Mmm. Can we just do this all night long? I don't want to talk to any cabinet members. I just want this right here," he whispers. His breath on my ear gives me chills.

"You look good tonight. Your mask is my favorite," I say honestly.

"Thank you. Just for the record, I guess both Lyncoln and my attendants tried talking to Frank to figure out what you were wearing so we could match. Not that you have to match because not everyone is, but whatever. He completely blew them off and acted like it was a big secret. I can see why. That gown is one in a million. Much like the wearer." He shakes his head amused.

My heart skips a beat at Henry's compliment and I'm secretly thankful for Frank's evasiveness. He knows I would've been uncomfortable matching one or both of them.

Henry then spins me around and dips me, causing me to laugh. As I am dipped, I see Elizabeth and Maverick. Elizabeth in a red dress and mask and Maverick in a black-on-black suit and looking uncomfortable in his silver mask. Whew. At least one other couple isn't matching.

"You look great!" I nod at Elizabeth.

"Likewise, girl!" She and Maverick smile at us and she whistles at my dress in approval.

"So don't look now. But my dad and the cabinet members are starting to arrive," Henry groans. "Here's the deal. We're going to dance and I'm going to show you off. You are going to look even more amazing than you already do as I sweep you across the dance floor. Then we are going to go talk to said cabinet members and I will introduce you to who you need to know. Then we are going to be back here dancing. Close." He moves closer in demonstration then adds, "I want to get the part of this night where I can't be this close to you over with. In and out with all the fancy business taken care of in, say, fifteen minutes?"

I smile. "Do I even have a choice in the matter?"

"Nope." Henry drills me with those emerald greens again. I love how playful and affectionate he can be. For someone who has had a very serious childhood being raised at Mile High, he can still kick back and have fun.

We dance across the floor until I am completely out of breath. A few people clap by the time we are done, but not Lyncoln, of course, who either wasn't watching or was busy talking to that Langly guy. I'm certain that Henry is a much better dancer than I am. Where did he learn to dance like that, anyway? *Wow.*

"Let's go check in with dad before he gets swarmed." He takes me by the hand and whisks me into the group of people introducing one another. He holds my hand rather tightly. I couldn't let go even if I wanted to.

"Dad." Mr. Winters and the President end their conversation about the time we arrive and Henry butts in before anyone else can.

"Son. Oh, my! Never mind you," he brushes Henry off and turns towards me, "Now this. This woman looks absolutely breathtaking." The President takes my hand and gives it a light gentlemanly kiss. "How are you this evening, Ms. Scott?"

"Well, I am feeling a bit blushed now," I say honestly and Mr. Winters smiles almost a full smile. "You gentlemen are looking handsome." The President looks flawless in his mask while Mr. Winters looks more uncomfortable. Now I know where Henry gets his ability to look amazing no matter what he wears or where he wears it.

"Why, thank you. Enjoy your night. And don't worry too much about meeting some of my cabinet. They are all just a bunch of spoiled babies. Right, Winters?" He laughs and claps the other man on the back.

"Some of us more than others, sir," Mr. Winters says as he looks pointedly at the President making us all laugh.

In a matter of thirty minutes, I have met most of the cabinet members present and their significant others. Most seem nice and genuinely interested in meeting me, just like the first two we met before we mixed with the boys. Or, I guess since I am standing next to Henry the whole time, most of them are genuinely interested in him. I'm surprised that there are a few younger cabinet members. Of course, most seem to be the age of Mr. Winters and the President, but there are some that look just a few years older than Ashton.

The one that seemed not at all pleased to meet me was Mr. Hadenfelt, Marisol's father. He seemed cold and disapproving, to say the least, but Henry kept me close and made it clear that we are a team. I sensed some tension between those two also. I'm not sure why he is still in a position of power if he and his daughter seem to be cut from the same shady character mold. Doesn't the President appoint the cabinet? If he does, why does he keep this man that no one seems to like in power? I know he has the power to replace him, so why doesn't he?

Out of the corner of my eye, I keep seeing Lyncoln in conversation with military men. They are going between Lyncoln, the President, and Admiral Taggert, who I learned serves on the cabinet as the Head of Defense. He looks like a bad boy version of Santa Claus with white hair and a bit of a belly. None of the three seem to relax and I'm worried there is something that needs attending to.

I think of how stressed out Lyncoln looked when he read the report that morning in the hospital and again when he came to my room after his social with Attie. What's going on? What has them so tense? At least the President and Admiral Taggert are pretending to be social and meet people. Lyncoln however, seems to be just working. And if he works in combat, why is he needed tonight of all nights?

As Henry and I finish up and head back over to dance, Lyncoln walks over in-between us, puts his hand on my back, and whispers something in Henry's ear which Henry doesn't seem happy to hear as his face goes stern.

"What do we need to do?" Henry asks, looking at Lyncoln, looking to me, and then back at Lyncoln.

"Nothing for now. Just a head's up," he shrugs and flexes his jaw determined.

Interrupting us, Marisol strolls over wearing her green dress with her arm through Christopher's arm. They are matching and coupled up though none of us really know why since Christopher doesn't even seem to like her that much.

"Oh, hey guys. I like your dress, Reagan," she says loudly. She apparently wants to appear nice. Never mind the fact that she was probably the one who tampered with my fake dress, or was behind it anyway.

"Hey," I respond back shortly. Lyncoln gives my back a rub with his thumb and turns to leave but Marisol stops him.

"Before you go," Marisol says more quietly but with that same fake, sweet voice. Through her green sparkly mask I can see the venom in her eyes. "I was just checking in to see if you both have finally kissed her or only just the one of you. Let me guess, Lyncoln was first, right? Just wanting to make sure it stays fair." She looks at me and winks. "So you *have* kissed both of them now, haven't you?"

I blush a deep red and feel heat and anger pulsing throughout my body. I guess now Lyncoln knows I kissed Henry and Henry knows I kissed Lyncoln. *Great.* What a disaster. I know I don't even have to say a word because my face will do all the talking she needs.

I'm going to kill her.

"I think I'll go dance now!" Marisol says with an evil laugh as she and Christopher leave. Christopher winces and looks remorseful, but Marisol pulls him away without an option otherwise.

"I can't even deal with that brat right now." Lyncoln shrugs and shakes his head even though all of us are clearly uncomfortable with this bit of information. I want to go after her, but I'm trying my best to stay cool. October warned me of this.

She wants me to make a scene. She wants me to make a scene. I keep saying it over and over in my head so that I don't walk over there and deck her.

"I don't even know how she gets off thinking she knows every--" I stop mid-sentence as I realize something. Only one person even knew that I had kissed either of them, and only from my blushing in admission, not my telling them in confidence.

"You okay?" Henry asks, taking my hand as he sees the color drain from my face.

"That jerk!" I whisper angrily but give his hand a squeeze. "Can you excuse me a minute, gentlemen?" I ask in the sweetest voice I can muster up, much like Marisol's fake tone earlier.

I turn to leave but Lyncoln grabs my arm spinning me back and pulls me in close to him, so close I can feel his breath on my face. "I know that look in those gorgeous eyes of yours. You're about to destroy someone. Just keep in mind where we are and who is watching. Marisol and Hadenfelt want nothing more than for you to lose your cool. Don't let them win."

"I'm fine." I stare him down to prove my words and finally turn away.

It takes me a moment to spot him, but I do and move in his direction stopping here and there to smile at someone or say something nice. I need to not be too obvious about this. Waiting for my chance and finally finding him alone getting another drink, I approach the traitorous Benjamin. He is in a navy suit to match his date Renae, who fortunately for me, must be having a potty break at the moment.

"Benji," I say with a fake voice using the nickname I hate.

"Reagan," he greets me suspiciously as if knowing that by using that name, I am up to no good. To an outsider, I look like I'm chatting with a friend from my home township, but on the inside, I am absolutely fuming.

"So tell me, old friend, did you use your mother's sickness to gain my trust so you could run back and tattle to your pal Marisol?" I stop to smile and laugh a little as fake as I possibly can. "I mean, you are the only one who knew I had even kissed one of them and mysteriously Marisol of all people finds out? Wow."

"Reagan," he starts as he tries to explain and begins shifting on his feet. He is obviously uncomfortable with this confrontation.

"Oh. Didn't think you'd get caught?" Again, I fake smile like we are friends while my eyes cut daggers at him. If he tries to deny this, I swear I am going to kick him right here, right now, right in the nuts.

This time I see his eyes change from suspicious to downright cold. "I did what I had to do."

"And betrayed me to do it? You wonder why I didn't trust you. It's because you aren't worthy of my trust, Benjamin." Struggling to compose myself, I turn to leave but stop myself and turn back to say one last thing, losing my smile as I do. "I understand more than you know wanting to win. What I don't understand is how you could turn into a jerk like your father in order to do it."

And with that, I walk away. I don't even think about looking back. Even Renae deserves better than Benjamin. Not wanting to go back to Henry or Lyncoln, I chat with Trent and Morgan briefly as I figure out where I'm going to next.

Trent and Morgan head off for the dance floor and I wander aimlessly, avoiding the men in my life who are both busy with military dudes anyway. I realize that both of them were going to make a move on me eventually, but somehow having someone else point out that I have been kissing both of them makes me feel about an inch tall and also completely relieved at the same time. Now everyone knows and it isn't like some big secret.

I see some chairs off in the corner and a comfy looking couch. There is an older child of maybe around ten years old sitting on one of the couches, playing with some cards while he itches at his mask. What on earth is a child doing here?

"Hi," I say and plop down on the other end of the couch he sits on.

"Hey," the kid greets me shyly. "I don't suppose you want to play 'Go Fish' with me, do you? My aunt says I need to sit over here while she talks to people so I don't get bored. I am her date!" he says excitedly.

"I would love to. My name is Reagan." I introduce myself, holding out my hand.

"I'm Wyatt," he says and shakes my hand quickly, then picks up the cards and shuffles them with expertise. He deals out the cards and we start playing.

"Don't let me win." He says it so seriously I almost laugh out loud, forgetting all about Benjamin and my boy troubles.

This little duffer in his mask is almost more cuteness than I can handle. His dark hair is already messed up even though he's trying to keep his mask on and his suit clean. He reminds me of someone, but I just can't put my finger on it. Probably Ashton, but Ashton was older than me so I wasn't ever the big sister.

We play for a little while. He asks me where I'm from and about Omaha and I ask him about his school and his favorite subjects.

"Do you play kickball?" I ask while I draw a card.

"Yes, I love it. Do you have any threes?" he asks.

"Just one." I hand it over. "Kickball was my favorite. We even played a version of it in Omaha with some movable bases made out of cardboard and we called it 'pinball'. Any time your base, or your pin, fell over, you were out."

"No way?" he asks excitedly, "Can you teach me sometime if you become Madam President?"

"Sure. I would love to," I nod and mean it. "Do you have any sevens?" I don't tell him that if I don't make it to at least the final four, I will be back in Omaha and he will never see me again.

He holds out two cards. "You would make a good Madam President. You're pretty, too. And I like your mask." He rambles on making me want to laugh again.

"Wyatt. Are you talking Ms. Scott's head off? What have I told you about that?"

A very beautiful woman in a gorgeous gown walks over to us smiling. Her eyes though. I have seen those eyes before.

I stand and reach out my hand and smile. "Hi. I'm Reagan Scott."

I know exactly who she is from her eyes, but I let her tell me anyway. "I'm Audra Reed. I have heard so much about you," she says with a kind smile.

I'm taken in with what an amazing figure she has. She has the same blue and brown eyes as Lyncoln, but her hair is light brown instead of dark. He must have gotten that from his dad. Wyatt has the same dark hair too.

"Hopefully all good things," I say bashfully.

"Yes, dear." She nods and smiles a real smile and her eyes almost dance. I wonder if Lyncoln's would ever do the same. Probably not, he is too dark and moody for that. She gestures, "Wyatt, I am about done here. Are you ready to go?"

"Can we finish, please? She's about to win. It should only take a minute. I want to see if she will or if I still have a chance."

"Okay. You may finish. As long as it doesn't take too long." She smiles nicely and we both sit down, Wyatt and I continuing our game.

I remember Lyncoln telling me about his mom's miscarriages. Her patience with her nephew and her affectionate way with him speaks volumes about who she is. She is a woman with a soft spot for children and would have probably loved to have had three or four herself. I can already tell she is a great mother. And I can't imagine the amount of pain and hurt this woman before me has endured. She seems so put together. But then again, sometimes the most put together people have been cut the deepest by life.

As we finish up playing, she asks me about the other girls and how it's going. I tell her how I am missing Vanessa and Marcia but looking forward to learning more and improving my aim. I tell her about the story of Ashton and I shooting turkeys and how my aim isn't very good. She laughs quite a bit at that.

"Mom," Lyncoln interrupts before I even know he's there. I can hear the affection oozing out of his velvety voice. "I see you found Reagan."

"I did. Wyatt found her first though." She shakes her head amused.

"Of course he did." Lyncoln smiles a rare real smile.

"Dang!" Wyatt announces. "She beat me. No one ever beats me. Remember the last time we played and you got mad and chased me around because you were trying your hardest to win and still couldn't beat me? Well, she just did! I actually lost."

Lyncoln laughs and I realize again how rarely it is that I hear his laughter. "Yeah, and then it turned into a water fight."

"And then we got in trouble," Wyatt adds, looking at his aunt mischievously.

"Alright troublemaker, it's time for us to go," she says standing.

"Yes, Aunt Audrey," he replies begrudgingly as we all stand.

I smile at him. "It was nice to meet you, Wyatt. I look forward to playing you again someday."

He turns to me, reaching out to shake my hand again, but instead surprises me by giving me a big hug, throwing his arms around my waist and whispering, "I like you. I hope you win."

"Thank you," I say, trying to be serious and not laugh at this little man.

Lyncoln gives his mom a quick but affectionate hug goodbye and does a secret handshake of sorts with Wyatt, and they leave the ballroom.

"Dance with me?" Lyncoln asks softly after we watch them go.

"Sure." When he looks at me like he's looking at me right now, it makes it pretty hard to deny him.

He leads me to the edge of the dance floor and the song changes to a slower one. He brings me in close and sighs as he rests his head down on my head for a moment. I feel his chin on the top of my head because he is just that much taller than I am. We are close enough I can tell from how tight all his muscles seem that he is exhausted and worried about something. Tense.

"Are you okay?" I ask quietly.

"I am now, though I promised myself not to dance with you." He rubs his thumb along my back. "This dress though," he adds in almost a whisper.

I'm not used to this soft-spoken Lyncoln. Where is the demanding and bossy man? There seem to be two different Lyncolns and I'm caught in a whirlwind between the two.

"Thank you," I say shyly.

"Interesting color choice though. Kind of dark and mysterious for you. Did you pick it?" He moves to look at my dress again and then back to my eyes, his eyes peering into the depths of my soul.

"I did. Yeah. I…uh…okay, so if I tell you the whole story, will you promise not to make fun of me?" I can feel myself blush. I don't know why I am about to tell him this, but I feel like distracting him from whatever has him so stressed out.

"No promises, but I will try," he says with a half-smile.

"Frank wanted me to wear emerald, but it reminded me of Henry's eyes, and I just couldn't. Then he said navy and it reminded me of yours and the same thing. I didn't want to subconsciously leave either of you out or make it seem like I had decided anything yet. Especially with all the matching business for tonight, which was obviously making me crazy. So, he made a dress using both colors, which just so happen to be my new favorite colors. I know no one would have known but me, and now you since I can't keep my mouth shut, but it still bothered me for some reason," I babble out quickly. "Silly, I know."

He almost stops moving and just looks at me a moment before he pulls me close so that his cheek is on mine and whispers in my ear, "You look good in both colors."

My heart rate goes through the roof and I feel heat radiating across my skin. I thought he would laugh or make fun of me, not whatever this response is.

"And oh, by the way, whatever you did to Benjamin got to him. He's getting plastered off champagne." He pulls away slightly and changes the topic but is still burning me with his hot stare.

"He is?" I ask, feeling only a pang of guilt for being so hard on him. He deserved everything he got and more. But then I think of his mom.

"I take it he is working with Marisol?"

"You are perceptive even while you've been working the whole night." I nod and look down. "And I didn't even disclose any information to him either, for the record. He asked and my dumb blush gave it away."

"I like your dumb blush." He smiles his half-smile.

"Because you can torment me with it?" I joke.

"Well yeah," he grins.

I laugh. "I love your mom and Wyatt. They're awesome." I change the topic before he has me blushing again, or talking about the information Marisol made public.

"I do too," he agrees.

The song ends and Langly is waiting to talk to Lyncoln, shifting from one foot to the other nervously.

"You don't get to have any fun tonight do you?" I ask.

"I just did." He smirks and trails his hand slowly across my back one last time as he turns to go talk to him.

I find Attie, Knox, Trent, and Morgan and talk to them for a solid twenty minutes while Henry, Lyncoln, and Christopher talk with the military dudes in the room. The President and Admiral Taggert have already left for the night, along with the other cabinet members. It seems to be only the Culling candidates left, and I find myself surprised that the President and cabinet members stayed for only about an hour. That seems hardly worth all the hoopla. Dougall made it sound like it was a much bigger deal.

Across the room, I can see Benjamin stumbling around while Renae seems ready to kill him. Lyncoln was right about that one. My bad.

Another twenty minutes passes while I continue to talk to our little group and I find I'm enjoying myself. I managed to meet the cabinet members here tonight and not mess up too badly. I handled Benjamin's betrayal right in the midst of it all too. Henry and Lyncoln found out I have kissed them both, but even that seems to make me feel relieved instead of uneasy. Despite being an emotional one, this night seems to be a success, other than I wish Vanessa or Marcia were here to make all the drama and masks more bearable.

A half hour later, all the candidates are standing in a group laughing and telling stories. None of us have left for the night and are sticking around to enjoy the party without all the seriousness of the President and the cabinet members from earlier. I, of course, have Lyncoln on one side and Henry on the other. We are all about to call it quits for the night when someone I don't recognize comes running over to Lyncoln looking panicked.

"Code black, sir," he says out of breath.

"*How*?" Lyncoln answers angrily.

I hear some popping noises in the distance and immediately recognize them as gunshots. This must be what they have been whispering about all night. I take from the panicked look on everyone's faces that this is very bad and not just a test either.

As people look around wondering what to do and where to go, or even why someone is shooting a gun, a guard opens a door in the back of the room and tells everyone to hurry and follow. Our personal guards are all immediately in the room and at our sides with guns drawn. They form a sort of barrier around all of us.

Before I even have time to mentally comprehend what is happening, Lyncoln scoops me up into his arms, kisses me on the forehead, and then places me in Henry's arms.

"Get her out of here," he demands. They exchange a glance and he nods.

As Henry starts moving me through the crowd of us going out the door I didn't even know existed, I look back and see Lyncoln rip off his mask and pull out a handgun from around his ankle and another from his back. He then takes off in the opposite direction we are all going with two uniformed men, not his guards, at his side.

Have those been there the whole night? Where the heck is he going?

He's a candidate too, dang it!

And who the heck is shooting at us?!

Chapter 17

Out the door, we go down what seems to be a hundred stairs, and then more stairs followed by a hallway that seems to go on for forever. I try to get Henry to let me walk at least a dozen times, but he refuses to put me down. I feel a bit better seeing a few other boys carrying girls in heels too. It can't be easy carrying someone down stairs, but it sure is faster than trying to run down them in heels.

Finally, we arrive in a dark room with metal looking walls, which I assume is underground. The guards lock all of us in. They perform extra security measures and then station themselves near the entrance of the massive room. It's dark so they light some lanterns and pass them out. Considering they just locked us in with retina scanners, it seems weird they would use something as old fashioned as lanterns.

"Doing okay?" Jamie asks me, in warrior mode, tense and looking around as he hands me one.

"I'm okay. Confused but okay."

"Don't worry, this room could survive a nuke," Jamie shrugs as he hands me a water bottle. I wonder where he got it. There must be some sort of food and water supply down here.

Henry and I find a corner of the large room and sit up against the wall. The light-hearted mood and camaraderie from earlier are now gone. We are coupled up and sitting separate from one another except for October, who is gladly sitting by herself and chatting softly with her guard. Henry takes off his mask and I do the same though mine takes more effort. He puts an arm around me and I lean the back of my head against his chest. I take a quick count as I look around to make sure we all made it…except for Lyncoln, of course. I can feel how hard Henry's heart is beating through his suit. I realize mine is beating hard too. My hands are shaking also. We were in real danger back there, whatever it was. Whoever it was.

"So I know you can't tell me much, but someone has been trying to attack Mile High haven't they?" I ask quietly.

"Yes," Henry responds honestly and moves to wrap his arm around my cold shoulders, rubbing them. I didn't even realize how cold the room and the wall we are leaning against are, but Henry did. He always notices the little things. He reaches his other hand around and takes my shaking hand. "If it were up to me, I would've told you everything a while ago."

"Thank you for telling me even that much. Lyncoln is up there doing his tactical forces thing?" I ask, not even bothering to disguise my concern.

"Yes. Don't worry. You should be more worried about them than you should be about him. And I would be right there with him if I weren't my father's son. I wish I could be." The way in which he says it makes me hear his torment. He has always had to struggle with being the son of a powerful man, essentially royalty, and trying to make his own way and be his own person. There are a lot of expectations weighing him down wherever he goes and whatever he does.

"I'm glad you're here," I say sincerely.

"Good." He rests the front of his head on the side of mine.

We sit there a moment in silence as we draw strength from one another. If it weren't for my adrenaline rush and fearing for our lives, I think I would probably fall asleep right here in Henry's arms. He's just so darn comfy. He's helping me to calm down and feel safe. Well…*safer*.

"So Marisol," Henry starts a conversation a few minutes later.

My eyes immediately go to her and try to stab her with my glare. She almost ruined my entire evening. And probably would have made me freak out if Lyncoln wouldn't have stopped me.

I sigh. "What about her?"

"I'm afraid she's going to be around awhile. I just wanted you to know. She's picking on you in particular. You should know that it's because you are her biggest threat. Just try not to let it get under your skin." I feel him shrug from behind me.

"She was trying to pit you and Lyncoln against one another. That's just cruel," I say angrily.

"Yeah, but it won't work. She won't." He says the words softly and sure.

"No. I will be the one to do that."

"Reagan," he whispers in my ear, scolding in his tone.

I turn to look at him. "Don't 'Reagan' me. You found out I've kissed both of you tonight. Don't you see how messed up that is? Instead of feeling guilty, I actually feel relieved that you both know. At what point will you start to hate each other? At what point do I become the girl that came between you and ruined not only a friendship, but your brother-like relationship?" I speak quietly but still fiercely. This isn't the time or place for this conversation, but it keeps my mind off of whatever is going on upstairs.

He looks me in the eyes, never looking away. "What you said right there? That guilt and care and concern for both of us? That's the reason why you won't ruin our friendship." I hear the truth and confidence in his voice. "Does it bother me he kissed you? Heck yes, it bothers me. But, I have also relived our own kiss at least a dozen times. I know you wanted it just as bad as I did. So I hold onto that instead of my jealousy. I'm going to focus on us, and hope that the rest will work out in the end."

How is this man that perfect?

"You are ridiculous." I look to the ceiling and let out a frustrated sigh.

"Ridiculous?" he asks taken aback, thinking I'm mad at him instead of hearing the admiration in my tone.

"You are ridiculously perfect. You always have the right attitude and say the right things. I don't know how you do it," I say honestly. "I would be livid if you had kissed another girl."

"My mom was that way so I try to emulate her. I don't always succeed, but I try." He shrugs and ignores my other comment.

"I know you miss her." I squeeze his hand.

"It has almost been two years. I miss her more now that I've met you. I want her to meet you. I want her to joke around with you. I also want her to be here for this crazy process. I want her advice." He shakes his head. "Sometimes I don't even know if the presidency is worth it, with all this going on. If it weren't for you, I think I would somehow sabotage myself."

His self-doubt is heartbreaking. He is, hands down, the best person I've ever met.

"Henry, you'll be amazing if you're the next president." I pause, making sure he is looking at me while I speak. "You will be kind and compassionate and work harder than anyone else. I don't even know what is going on with this attack, but I'm sure you will handle that too. You aren't the man for the job because your dad did it and you are the so called heir, you are the man for the job because you are you. You are more capable than you know. People want it to be you because of your dad and they have high expectations. If they actually knew you, you would blow those expectations out of the water. It really should be you. Not because you are the heir, but because of the man *you* are."

He briefly looks around the room and then puts his hand on my cheek, leaning in to kiss me. It's quick but emotional. In one kiss he makes me feel wanted. He makes me feel cherished. He makes me feel needed. And every single time it makes me want to continue kissing him.

He pulls away and sets me back in his arms. I can feel his breath on my back.

"By the way, I kind of have a thing for your neck." I can hear from his voice he is smiling.

"What?" I was not expecting him to say that.

He is talking so quietly it's almost a whisper, "Your hair is magnificent and always down, but I kind of like seeing your neck and back too."

"Oh." Oh is all I can manage to say.

We continue to sit there for what seems like hours. Henry at some point gives me his suit jacket and takes off his bowtie. I continue to sit in his arms as we ask each other random questions to get to know one another even better. I'm feeling safer the more time passes, but am still worried about Lyncoln. I can't get over the look on his face when I saw him grab his guns and run in the direction of danger. He had no fear, just raw determination. He didn't even hesitate. That was predator Lyncoln in all of his hot, majestic glory.

"Shouldn't Lyncoln be exempt from combat type situations while the Culling is going on?" I ask after a while. I see Attie and Elizabeth have both fallen asleep, heads on the shoulders of their dates.

"Yeah. They tried. You know him. He's the best we have right now and he knows it. So when something happens, he gladly volunteers." He shrugs. "He can be a total jerk sometimes, but above all, he is protective. I've seen him in action. His instincts are unlike anything I have ever seen before. He's an animal. He just doesn't want to risk anyone else's life if he knows he can handle the situation himself."

"Makes sense. Sucks…but makes sense," I say quietly.

"Yeah. Welcome to the curse of loving Lyncoln. You never know if he's going to come back in one piece, but you love him enough to let him go." He shakes his head sadly.

His words make me realize that I do love Lyncoln and Henry both. I'm not sure I'm romantically in love with either of them yet, but I love them like family. Like I love Attie, Vanessa, or Marcia. I can't imagine going back home and living life without either of them. Or Attie or Vanessa or Marcia for that matter.

"How long do you think this is going to take?" I ask, wondering when we will see Lyncoln next. I just want to make sure he's okay.

"Since the guards at the doors aren't quite as tense as when we walked in, I'm sure everything is already taken care of. They'll go room by room and clear all the floors though, so it takes a while. That's probably what they're doing now. Could take a few more hours though," he explains with a sigh but then adds, "Not that I don't like sitting here with you, I just wish we were somewhere more comfortable or alone. I would much, much, much rather it be we were alone."

My pulse jumps as I think of the last time I was alone with Henry. I wouldn't mind a repeat of the experience.

We continue to sit there for probably another hour. I hear Henry's breathing slow as he must have fallen asleep. I look around and see that most people have, with the exception of Bronson, Marisol, Renae, and Oliver. To Marisol's credit, she looks genuinely horrified. I think it's the first real emotion I have seen on her face. I give Renae a tight smile and she returns it. I almost feel bad that Benjamin is sleeping off his drunkenness next to her and that I ruined her date, but he deserved it.

Much later, as I am beginning to think we will never get to leave and that I would like to be able to empty my bladder, the guards get word that it's all clear and we can return to our rooms. Our personal guards come to us and tell us we are good to go.

I gently wake Henry as Jamie sees that I'm still awake. Henry seems surprised that he fell asleep. He stands and pulls me up with him.

"I'm still double checking your room." He says it not really to me, but more to Jamie and his guards.

"Yes, sir," one of his guards respond.

The trip back up from wherever we are is quicker as we can use an elevator. It takes close to ten loads of us before the candidates plus guards are all out of there. Henry and I opt for the last elevator and I'm glad. I'm not ready to go to my room and try to sleep knowing that there was an attack here tonight. There are so many unanswered questions for what went on here.

What were they attacking? Us, the Culling candidates? Or were they after something else? Why so late? Why not when the President was there?

When we make it to my doorway, Henry has me stand outside while he checks everything through. Then he opens and props open the door, asking the guards a few questions before he leads me in.

"Do you want me to stay for a while?" he asks politely.

He seems exhausted, and not just from this evening. "No. I mean yes, but no. I'm beat. And you need to get some sleep, too."

"I wish I could just sleep with you," he says softly.

He must see the panicked look on my face because he laughs and puts his hands in the air in surrender, "Don't worry, nothing more than sleep. That hour of sleep I just got with you was the best sleep I've had in a while, that's all."

I laugh and blush, embarrassed that my mind was in the gutter.

"One more thing though," Henry says as he walks purposely for me. I haven't looked in the mirror, but I know by now I look like crap. He, however, looks exactly like he did when I first saw him this evening. In fact, without his jacket and bowtie, in just his dress shirt unbuttoned, his dress pants, and vest, he might look even better. He looks tired, but still put together. Not fair at all if you ask me.

He reaches me and grabs his suit jacket by the lapels. I move my arms so he can pull it off, assuming he wants it back. He just pulls me in close using the lapels and then wraps his arms around me trapping me. He has one hand around my back and one hand on my cheek and kisses me.

This kiss is soft and affectionate. For some reason, these kisses melt me. I remember thinking Henry's lips looked soft like little pillows when we first met; I was right, they are very soft and very kissable. He breaks our kiss shortly after, keeping it appropriate, and kisses my cheek.

"Good night, beautiful," he whispers.

"Good night, Henry," I smile at him and he turns to leave, shutting my door behind him as he does.

I turn and sit on the edge of my bed with Henry's jacket still on. I'm still worried about Lyncoln but decide he must be okay. Wouldn't they tell me if he wasn't?

I slowly take off my shoes which murdered my feet and then slip out of my dress, trying not to process everything that happened this evening. So much happened. So very much. I feel emotionally numb from it all. I slip into a big cotton t-shirt and some pajama shorts. I take down my hair, which takes me awhile since all the pins are in it. I half-heartedly brush my teeth before giving up and calling it good enough. I feel too tired to take off my makeup so I don't even bother.

I lay down in my big, comfy bed and try to sleep. Despite being overly exhausted, I can't. I think of about a hundred different scenarios in which Lyncoln gets hurt or injured and the fact that when I saw him turn and run into danger, it could have been the last time I ever saw him. After trying for over an hour, I finally punch my pillow in frustration and get back out of bed.

I open the door to find Sarge and Jamie in an informative discussion, as they must be switching shifts.

"Ms. Scott. Are you okay? Do you want some sleeping medication? Want to leave the door open so we are right here?" Jamie asks, looking concerned. It warms my heart a little since I have seen that same look from Ashton a hundred times.

"Do either of you know if Lyncoln is back in his room yet?" I ask. "I can't sleep because I don't know that he's safe yet. I keep imagining a hundred ways he has died."

They look at one another and don't say anything so I take that as a no. I reach back in my room and grab my slippers and a cardigan and head down the hallway. They know something or they would have just told me right away.

"Don't you think you should wait until morning?" Jamie asks.

"Until I know for sure he isn't bleeding or worse, I won't be sleeping. Let's go," I say determined.

Sarge catches up to me at almost the elevator, looking amused. I know nothing horrible has happened or they would both be acting different, but they aren't telling me anything either. So is Lyncoln hurt or something? Or is this one of those weird times where they aren't supposed to be sharing certain information?

When we get to the door to Lyncoln's room, Sarge tells me to wait a moment. He talks back and forth on his radio device.

"They aren't quite back yet. Do you want to wait out here or in his room on a chair?" Sarge asks kindly. "I'm sure he won't mind."

"I guess I'll take the chair option. My feet are killing me," I say honestly. I don't think I will be able to wear heels ever again, let alone on Monday morning for class. "If whatever happened tonight doesn't kill me, I think heels will."

He opens the door for me with a chuckle and says, "Let me know if you need anything. I don't think it should be too long."

I turn on a lamp and walk around Lyncoln's room. I feel like a spy or something. I have a hard time not curling up in his bed while I wait. I'm sure his pillows smell exactly like him too.

He doesn't have many things out in his room. His counters are clean. I grab a bottle of water out of the fridge and see it's almost empty too. Either he doesn't spend much time here, or he's a neat freak. There is only one personal possession in the whole room, a picture of his mom, Wyatt, and I assume Wyatt's mom--his cousin, on the dresser. Other than the smell of his cologne, it's the only thing that lets me know I am in the right room.

I try to sit in a chair but soon realize that his are just as uncomfortable as mine. Feeling exhausted but still worried, and seeing that it is now three in the morning, I grab a pillow and curl up at the bottom of his bed. Getting in his sheets seems like crossing the line and may send a way wrong message when he returns, but the bottom of his bed seems like a safer zone.

The pillow smelling like him is oddly comforting and I drift off, waiting and hoping he is coming back in one piece.

****

Hearing a noise and what sounds like my name being said faintly, I wake up and remember where I am. I look at the clock to see that it has only been twenty minutes. I sit up and hear the door open and close. It must be Lyncoln coming back. He is moving quietly, doing something and trying not to wake me though he must obviously know I am here. His back is to me as he faces his closet. He takes off his jacket and with only the lamp as light, I can see some small red splatters on the collar of his white dress shirt.

As he finishes hanging up his jacket and begins loosening his tie, he turns and we lock eyes. I see his deep blue-brown eyes full of concern for me even though I was the one safe and sound. Time stands still as we just stare at each other for a moment, taking each other in, and then before I know it, I am flying across the room at him.

He catches me in his arms and our mouths find one another before our bodies even do. He kisses me roughly. My feet not touching the ground, he continues kissing me and backs me up until my back hits the wall. He puts me down carefully and then wraps one arm around me and rests the other on the wall beside me as he deepens the kiss. By the time he pulls away, I am completely out of breath.

"Hey," his velvety voice whispers, seconds later.

I feel tears spring to my eyes. This man is exasperating. He is cold and quiet and moody, yet I know he wouldn't hesitate to take a bullet for me.

Seeing my tears, he asks, "Regs? What's wrong, sweetheart?"

Not being able to answer, I just put my head on his chest and cry. He runs one hand through my hair and the other back and forth on my back. He just lets me cry there for a moment. I hate myself for losing it. I'm not at all a pretty crier. And we went from making out to me bawling my eyes out in approximately 2.4 seconds. *How attractive.*

When I have calmed down a bit, he says, "It's going to be okay. You're safe. I've got you."

Sniffling big ugly tears and snot, I finally find my voice, though it sounds higher pitched and a bit shaky. "I know I'm safe, you jerk. I was worried about you. Are you okay? What were you thinking?"

I see the blood splatters again and my face pales.

"It's okay, Regs. It's not my blood." He runs his hands up and down my arms as if trying to warm me. "Promise, not mine."

"What were you thinking? You can't just take off like that. You could have gotten killed," I sniffle through my tears.

He leans in closer to me, evaporating my anger as he does, and whispers, "I was thinking that if anything happened to you, I wouldn't be able to handle it."

He kisses me again, this time softer and quicker. I move one of my hands to his shoulder and he flinches.

"Are you hurt?"

"I'm fine." He shrugs knowing that I caught him flinching. "Promise."

"Don't you dare run out on me like that and then lie straight to my face," I demand, staring him down unwaveringly.

He half-smiles. "It's just a graze, babe. Not even a full graze even. Maybe more like a graze of a ricochet." He nods to his shirt where I see a small tear.

"From a bullet?!" I ask, my voice going up an octave.

He just shrugs.

"Sit," I say and point to a chair.

He does so but is holding back a smile and mumbles something about me being bossy.

I lean over him, take off his tie and vest, and unbutton his shirt so I can get to his shoulder. Why didn't he tell someone so they could bandage it up for him? It may not have needed stitches, but at least some antiseptic so it doesn't get infected. Between our animals and ourselves and having to take care of small injuries, we all become first-aid handy in Omaha. And I've learned from experience that sometimes it's easier to treat it right away than to ignore it and wait for it to get worse.

Three buttons down his dress shirt, he puts a hand just above my knee on the back side of my leg and I realize I am undressing him. In his room. In my pajamas. At four in the morning. If anyone saw us, this would look bad. Very bad.

"Well this isn't exactly how I envisioned it, but I'll take it." He grins as if reading my mind. "And I like these," he adds, feeling the fleece on my shorts by my upper thigh then moves his hand down my bare leg back to an appropriate spot around the back of my knee.

I glare at him though my body goes tingly and finish unbuttoning his shirt. As I go to pull it over his left bulging shoulder, he winces slightly.

"Sorry," I whisper apologetically, gently pulling it down the rest of the way.

He's actually right. I see a spot maybe a half inch thick of pink skin where the bullet grazed. Other than looking like it's tender, it really isn't that bad. Not even bleeding. Almost kind of looks like it could've been from a burn, not a bullet. If that bullet would have been six inches lower, however, it could have hit his heart and he probably wouldn't be here.

Now that he is shirtless before me, I'm having trouble focusing. His muscles are perfection. I can't help but run my hand down his bulging neck muscles to where his wound is. I shake my head and remember I was going to get a first-aid kit. He smiles with eyebrows raised as I quickly spin around and go into his bathroom. I am able to find the kit fairly easily since it's in the same spot as in my bathroom.

Setting the supplies on the coffee table, I grab some antiseptic cream and put it on my finger. Putting one hand on the other shoulder, I gently rub the cream into his wound.

He doesn't wince or say anything although I know it must be a little sore. He just stares at me with those intense dark eyes and that "I know you" look. His hair is slightly ruffled and I wonder if it was from our smooch fest or from before. Oddly enough, he looks more vulnerable and attractive to me now than he ever did before.

This is the real Lyncoln.

I grab a cloth bandage and place it on the wound and finish fixing him up. I sigh, handing him some Tylenol and head to get him some water so he can take it.

"Come to think of it, I'm very hurt. I'll be hurt as often as you like if you take care of me like this," he says with a confident grin as he watches me return and hand him the water.

I smile back at him but shake my head as I busy myself picking up the wrappers and putting everything away while he takes the Tylenol. And I know he probably wouldn't take it if I didn't hand it to him, so in a way, he's just humoring me.

I avoid his eyes as I get everything back where it belongs. He could have died this evening and was probably very close to doing so but is acting like it isn't a big deal. Does he have a death wish? If he really cared about the people in his life as much as he thinks he does, would he be so risky?

As I put the first-aid kit back in the bathroom, I turn to find him leaning against the bathroom door, still shirtless, with his muscular arms crossed one over the other, watching me. "What's on your mind, gorgeous?"

I sigh, wishing he couldn't read me like a book. "If you really did care about me like you say you do, you would think twice about putting yourself in a situation where you can get yourself killed. Look at that spot, Lyncoln." I put my hand lightly on his bandage and slowly move my hand lower to his heart. "Six inches lower and you wouldn't be here."

He shrugs. "But I am. I've had closer calls than that if it makes you feel any better."

"No. That certainly does not make me feel better." I pause, shaking my head. "What about your mom and Wyatt? If you don't care about me enough to think twice about it, at least think of them."

"I *do* think of them. That's why I sent them home early when I knew there was a threat. That's why we got the President out. That's why we got everyone downstairs. Ten more minutes and we would have had an assassination or worse on our hands. We originally had it all under control anyway. They were essentially in our trap and we were just waiting for them to come in. But then something happened and they got farther than they should have been able to." He leans in close, taking my hand in his and whispers, "I do care about you that much, and I do think twice. Your safety will always precede mine no matter how many times I think about it."

"Fine. It can precede yours, but you still don't have to risk your life every chance you get. You are a Culling candidate, you should've been with us. What are you trying to prove? You hear of possible danger and just go running towards it? Why do you do this? I just don't get it."

This time he shuts down on me, turning away and walking to the window, ignoring my question.

"Just go," he says softly and it stabs me like a knife.

"No. Talk to me, please. I want to understand. Henry says that loving you involves knowing that you might not come back in one piece but loving you enough to let you go anyway. Why? Why does it have to be like that?" I plead.

"Ask Henry." He keeps his back to me but stiffens as he says his name.

I wrap my hands around his waist in a backward hug in a last-ditch effort to get him to talk to me. "I'm asking you."

He doesn't move my hands or turn but just lets out a deep sigh. "Because I couldn't save my dad." He almost chokes on the words.

I give him a minute. I don't move. I don't say anything. I just keep holding him and waiting for him to tell me. If he was ever going to tell me the whole story, it's now. I'm sure by now he's aware that I know the basics of what happened anyway. I just need to hear from him why he is this way, if his reason is what I suspect. If there is even the smallest chance that we end up together, I need to know if it would be like this all the time. I need to know if I will always be wondering if he is coming home or not.

"When I was thirteen, he was murdered by some drifters. My dad was the head of defense, Taggert's job." He pauses and I can tell this is painful for him to recall. "Two drifters broke into our house and tried to take him, probably to torture him for information. It woke all of us up. I woke up to mom screaming." He pauses again. "When I got to my parents' bedroom, they were telling my dad he had to go with them or they would kill him. He told them he was already dead anyway and made a move to get one of the men's guns. The other man shot him in the head. No one noticed me coming in the room, but I tackled one of the men to the ground and took his gun. We struggled for a while, but I pinned him to the ground and somehow shot him in the chest. He was the one that had shot my dad. Mom went after the other guy, but he took off. They never found him."

I fight back tears as I think of the confident and bold thirteen-year-old boy, barely older than Wyatt, who had to go through that anguish. I still don't really know what a drifter is, other than they are obviously the bad guys. I can't imagine waking up to that and watching your own father get shot in the head.

"Had I been there earlier…" Lyncoln starts and I can hear the emotion in his voice.

"They still probably would have shot him. They were either taking him or killing him and he knew that," I try to reason with him.

He grabs my arms and turns around to wrap his arms around me. He doesn't look at me, just holds me and rests his head on mine as he finishes, "So yeah, sometimes I take unnecessary risks, but I will gladly do it if it spares another family the pain I have had to live with. I will never forget the moment the life left Dad's eyes. Not ever. And now? Now, I enjoy hunting the enemy down. I love the chase. I love taking down an opponent. It's an art. An art I have mastered. An art that may be turning me into a monster."

"You are *not* a monster." I shake my head and move to look at him. My eyes are overflowing with tears by this point, and a few spill onto my cheeks.

"I'm glad you don't think so," he says softly as he wipes some of my tears away with his thumbs.

"But what about *your* family? Your future family? Your wife and kids? Do you want to put them through never knowing if their dad is safe?" I shake my head, imagining a few dark-haired, blue-eyed children.

"If and when that happens, I will stop taking the unnecessary risks. It seems unlikely, though," he says sadly.

"What do you mean?" I ask surprised. By law, it will happen eventually, even if it isn't with me, as tough as that is to swallow right now.

"I never even knew I wanted all that until I met you. And when you choose Henry, it will gut me," he starts. I try to argue but he puts a finger to my lips to shush me, "I don't know how I will ever get over you. I promise I will try to not be as careless. And I won't run into even more danger when you choose him. I'm not that dumb. But know that even when you choose him, I will always protect you. I will always be here protecting you."

He leans down and kisses me softly on the cheek then adds, "Thank you for taking care of me. We have to be up in a few hours. Go get some sleep, sweetheart."

Not knowing what more to say, I know he's probably right though this doesn't feel anything like the end of a conversation. I should go get some sleep, but I don't feel like leaving him. Before I turn to go, I reach up on my tippy toes and give him a quick kiss on the cheek, trying to convey my jumbled up emotions.

Back in my room, it's almost dawn by the time I fall asleep.

But maybe, just maybe, today will be the day I finally find out what the heck is going on here.

Chapter 18

T hings continue as if nothing happened the next morning. No one discusses the attack from the night before because like with everything else we have done so far, none of us really feel like we are supposed to. We head to DIA for defense classes and simulations looking exhausted and confused. Even Attie and I barely talk on the way over, not knowing what to say or how to approach what happened the night before.

A while later, I'm practicing shooting and aiming at different body parts on a target while feeling annoyed and frustrated. Someone could have died last night and they won't even tell us who these "drifters" are? Nothing? Not a single word? Just business as usual? Our targets are flesh colored which also seems to irritate me. Do they really think this will soften us to actually shooting people?

"Why are you skipping the kill shots?" Professor Bennett asks annoyed as he was apparently watching me the last few minutes.

"Because I don't know who I'm shooting and why I'm shooting them," I respond, matching his annoyance and then some.

"Take the kill shot, Ms. Scott," he demands.

I turn to stare him down in defiance. I can see the people around us lower their guns watching our exchange. From across the room, I can see Lyncoln give me a warning look. I need to keep my cool. Professor

Bennett and I have never had any disagreements before. Remembering poor Julia Collins, I'm not sure he is the professor I want to make angry either.

I glare at him a moment before I do what he asks and shoot the target in the heart, not able to shoot a target in the head after hearing Lyncoln's story. I spin around, temper fully out, click the safety on, and hand him my gun, ready to walk away.

He doesn't take it. "Again," Professor Bennett commands while staring me down, stopping me from leaving. If this is some sort of test, I am most certainly about to fail because I'm tired and annoyed and not dealing with this crap another minute.

"I will when you tell me what is really going on here. Is my family in danger?" I point to the targets behind me. "Will those targets someday soon be real enemies?"

Now more people are standing around watching us though I'm trying to speak quietly. Lyncoln's warning stare has turned into one of concern and he starts to make his way over to us. Normally those blue-brown eyes do me in and I cave, but not this time. I think of Ashton and wonder if he is even safe.

"Shoot the gun, Reagan," Professor Bennett warns.

Really letting my temper go for the first time since arriving, I stand my ground and just stare at him in response.

"I'm sorry, did you want to go home?" Professor Bennett sneers.

I turn back around angrily, click off the safety on my gun, and shoot three rounds where the other shot was. I'm actually quite impressed with my shooting though I try not to let him see that. Although they aren't all exactly precise, they are more so than usual. My temper must help my aim. *Note to self.*

I put my gun down, done with whatever this is. "At least I could protect my family there. You could be doing me a favor," I say menacingly, then before I walk away, I turn back to him adding quietly,

"How long will it take? Does someone have to die before you finally tell us what's really going on here?"

I storm out of the range and down the hallway. I don't look back, not even caring about the ramifications of my actions. I don't dare look at Lyncoln because I don't think I could take the disappointment I might find in his eyes. I'm glad Henry was in the simulator for all this too, because I wouldn't be able to stomach the disappointment from both of them.

An hour later, I'm sitting in the simulator waiting room with Henry and Elizabeth watching Bronson go through a simulation when an announcement is made that all candidates are to meet in one of the bigger conference rooms. I should be panicked they are sending me home, but I know if they were, no one else would need to be in the room. Bronson finishes his simulator immediately and all of us head upstairs.

Upon entering the room, I know something important is about to go down. You can just feel it in the air. All the professors are there, along with Elle and Admiral Taggert. Judging by the looks on their faces, this is serious business.

I find my usual spot in-between Henry and Lyncoln and sit in the conference style chair. It takes a while for us all to get there, but in looking around, I see some people look as exhausted and angry as I do. To make more room for the girls to sit as there are only about 15 chairs, some of the boys have to stand. Lyncoln gives up his chair to Attie, who looks at me as if saying, "they better be telling us something".

Once everyone is settled, Professor Bennett starts speaking right away. "It has been brought to my attention that it may not be fair to you candidates to be completely left in the dark about last night's events. Though most of you would have been given some classified information in the near future, the events of last night brought that timetable up." He looks my direction, no longer pissed at me, but looking strangely empathetic instead. "So I have asked none other than our own Head of Defense to shed some light on this situation." He gestures to Taggert.

"Long story short, two men infiltrated Mile High," he says and stops.

Multiple sighs of frustration can be heard in his pause. Other than the "two men" bit, this isn't anything we don't already know. Is that really all they are going to tell us?

He puts up a hand and continues, "I can't tell you all the details. But, here is what I can tell you. You are not allowed to speak a word of this to anyone not in this room without some pretty heavy consequences. In simplest terms, we call them drifters. Our previous history with the drifters begins all the way back to right after Trident. Not all the people overseas died from the virus, just like not all of us did. Some of the North Koreans and their allies, wanting to make sure they got done the job they originally set out to do in taking our country over, came here and started to infiltrate and even fit into our new government in hopes of destroying it once and for all, this time from the inside out.

"Of course we caught on to this eventually and kicked them out, but unfortunately, we let them live. President Walters and his cabinet just couldn't take even more lives after living through Trident. We didn't hear from them again until the third presidency when we found out that President Kane was compromised by them. He wasn't a drifter himself, but he made a deal with them and was doing their bidding. By this time their numbers were increasing, they were multiplying and recruiting anyone that disliked our government, and especially those that we ourselves kicked out on the grounds of expulsion.

"Since then, it has been an ongoing process of finding out who the drifters are, where they are based, and where they will strike next. They don't have a fraction of the technology or military we do, so we normally know when they are coming. Mile High and DIA are the safest places to be in the entire country. They know they can't get in or get very far, but they still see that there is about to be a power switch with a new presidential couple and would love to get their hands on the new President or Madam President. Whether to try to sway like President Kane, or to do harm to, we don't know."

He stops for a moment before continuing as we all try to quickly process what he's telling us. "As for your families and the other townships, we watch them round the clock and have added security details for each of your families from the moment you left. They should be safe. The drifters are sticking to Denver and the Culling. There have never been any attacks on any of the other townships. But even if there were, we are more than prepared. They know better than to try that." He shakes his head with determination and a hint of anger.

"Oh, and one more thing," he pauses dramatically. "The two men who managed to get into Mile High for a short time last night have been caught. Only one is still breathing and is currently feeding us information about how they got as far as they did. We are very, very close to figuring out what happened. We will get to the bottom of it. You can bet on that." He stares around the classroom with his final statement.

Although he's putting on a strong front and seems like he has everything under control, what is he looking for? As he continues watching us, I realize that must mean he is looking for his words to have affected someone...which means he's bluffing. And if he's looking at us, he must think that someone here, a candidate, had something to do with what happened last night.

Holy crap.

Is there a traitor amongst us?

****

Two days later, Elle and Mr. Winters wake me for a verbal in the dead of the night, this time with the lie detector machine on a trolley. I'm not sure why these stupid things always have to happen in the dead of the night, but it's downright annoying. The lie detector present affirms my suspicions that they think someone here is a drifter. I haven't slept much the last two nights dreaming of the traitor and who they are trying to kill. I've had nightmares of being in simulations that I find out are actually real. Every single one ends in Henry dying with there being nothing I can do about it. I'll feel a whole lot better when the traitor is found.

They get me hooked up to all the cords and are kind enough to let me stay sitting in bed. I get the impression this will be a quick verbal. After the typical questions, they start to ask more intense ones. After a few, I cut to the chase.

"Look, I know one of us is a drifter. It isn't me, so you can quit beating around the bush," I say sleepily with a yawn.

"Who were you with most of the night of the ball?" Mr. Winters continues, ignoring my statement.

"Henry and Lyncoln, duh. Lyncoln, who, you know, went after the bad guys. Don't you think he and Henry would know if I were the drifter? Come on, now." I roll my eyes.

Mr. Winters almost smiles but I can tell this is a serious test of sorts. We are all in danger and they have to figure out which one of us is the traitor. I think back to Julia and wonder if this is what she figured out right before she got kicked out. Did she know about the traitor or just the drifters in general? *How* did she know about either of those things? I feel like I was one of the last to know.

"Did you see anything suspicious the night of the ball?" he continues while Elle casually takes a drink of her coffee.

"Yeah, I saw Marisol pretending to be nice."

Elle almost spits out her coffee but manages to keep her composure. Mr. Winters glares at me, looking slightly annoyed and unappreciative at my attempt at humor.

"Mr. Winters, seriously. If I had any pertinent information, I would tell you. People I am starting to really care about are in danger. Not just Lyncoln and Henry, but Attie, Elizabeth, and more. I've been thinking about it since I figured out there was a traitor. I have no idea who it could even be. If it is someone I am good friends with, we are screwed because they are just that darn good at being deceitful." I shake my head and shrug.

"If you could pick anyone, who would it be? Benjamin maybe? Someone overheard you two in an argument." The way he asks acknowledges my being correct on there being a drifter without him having to actually say the words.

"We were arguing because he betrayed me to Marisol, but I don't think he would ever betray the whole State. His mom is sick. He would never do anything to jeopardize her. He's dirty, but not that dirty." I pause as I think on his other question, then begin thinking out loud, "The person in question would have to be good enough, intelligent enough, and trained enough to qualify and excel at the Culling and would also have to go completely under the radar."

I pause for a moment as Mr. Winters cocks his head to the side as he follows my line of thinking. I continue, "I would think it would be a male from a smaller township enabling them to fly in under the radar. But, I doubt it is Benjamin and all the Detroit boys were sent packing. Not Seattle either. Vegas maybe then?"

"Very nice." He nods in approval and looks down at his clipboard for the next question.

All of a sudden, my logic hits me like a slap in the face. "Which is why we are wrong," I say sitting up taller and leaning in excited. I finally found the puzzle piece I have been searching for. For some reason verbalizing it with Mr. Winters and Elle helped me to realize something I have been wondering about for the past few days but not settling on.

"What do you mean?" Mr. Winters asks confused as Elle leans in intrigued.

"Think about it. The drifters have to be smart enough to know that eventually this person would be suspected. If they were suspected, they needed to be what was *not* obvious or logical. First of all, I would bet chocolate cheesecake that it isn't a boy. Second, I bet this person has been in Denver, or at least Vegas, all along learning and gleaning information. There are only four girls from Denver left: Elizabeth, Marisol, Isabella, and Sapphire. One of those girls is your drifter," I say confident and proud of myself for figuring this out on a tired brain.

A part of me feels a stab of fear. Could the drifter be one of my friends?

Mr. Winters looks to Elle and back to me. "That makes sense, actually."

"It does," I nod my head in agreement. I don't want to toot my own horn, but I think I figured it out.

"The funny thing is though, two of those girls you suggested, suggested it was you who had suspicious activity." Mr. Winters stares at me for a moment but looks like he wants to smile.

I do smile. "Because they want me out of the competition. I bet it was Marisol and Sapphire. Do you really think I am the drifter? That I would put my family in danger?" I ask him. "Plus, if I was, I wouldn't be giving Lyncoln the time of day. He's an assassin," I joke.

"No. You aren't the drifter." He doesn't even hesitate in his assessment.

"Well then?" I ask.

"Well then I need to go take this new information to Admiral Taggert while Elle unhooks you." He quickly rises.

He pauses at the door. "Ms. Scott?"

"Yes?"

"This is good reasoning. Very good thinking. We still don't know for sure, of course, but you wouldn't be bad at tactical forces," he says proudly.

I shrug. "Like I could shoot anyone."

"It isn't all about killing. It's about learning to be one step ahead of the enemy, a skill you most certainly possess." He nods to me and leaves.

Elle removes the wires and sticky pads attached to my hands as I am quiet thinking. I know I'm close to figuring out who it is, but I can't put my finger on it. Which one of those girls is a traitor? The obvious answer is Marisol, but because she is the obvious answer, it probably isn't her. I can't believe in my heart that it could be Elizabeth. That leaves Sapphire and Isabella.

I don't know either very well, but Isabella seems like a total sweetheart. I can't imagine it being her. She seems so happy with Oliver and they have been so wrapped up in one another lately that I can't imagine she has the spare time to be a spy. That leaves Sapphire as my best bet. She would have inside information being close to Marisol too.

Is Sapphire the traitor?

****

Before breakfast the next morning, Lyncoln knocks on the door. I barely have time to open it before he comes in, closing the door behind him. He grabs me around the back of my neck and kisses me hard but quick.

"Sweetheart, you're a genius," he says affectionately and almost excited.

Good thing I already brushed my teeth.

"Uhhh, thanks?" I say a little stunned. What a way to open the door and start the morning.

"Winters filled in Taggert on your theory. Seriously, brilliant. You're right. You have to be. I was looking at Vegas girls, but you were right in thinking Denver. Genius." He nods and looks at me with pure pride and a hint of fire in his gaze.

"Thank you," I say and blush. When he looks at me like that, I think I could conquer the world.

"Anyway, I just wanted to tell you while there was no one else to eavesdrop. Well, any more than usual," he says nodding to the watch on my wrist and turns to open the door, "See you downstairs?"

I reach out and put a hand on his arm to stop him. "Wait. Did they figure it out? Which one?" I ask, wanting to be done worrying about the people I am coming to love like family.

"No, but they are going over the last few weeks of footage and we're being monitored now more than ever. If anyone does *anything* remotely suspicious, we'll know." He shrugs. "We've just got to wait it out now."

I respond with a sigh of frustration.

He quickly steps forward and kisses me on the forehead, "You're safe. Promise. Though sometimes I don't want to let you out of my sight, just to be sure. That and you're nice to look at." He grins with that last statement.

I smile. "I worry more about you and Henry than myself," I say honestly.

"Don't. We've got this," he says confidently and kisses me on the forehead again. "We just have to know for sure before we go guns blazing and arrest someone. You know, that whole innocent until proven guilty crap."

Somehow, both his praise and confidence in catching the traitor put me at ease.

After breakfast, we head to DIA for our simulations, target practice, and self-defense class. We are informed that we will begin being tested on shooting and simulations both. We will also start going in with partners to see how we work with others and the simulations will be getting more dangerous. So far, I have only had one simulation and had to kill a coyote that attacked me. Now we will be getting to the hard stuff since we have gotten used to wearing the weird glasses and the simulation room itself. It's about to get a whole lot more real.

****

A whole week later and still nothing. Our days are filled with going to DIA and we even have lunch there now. We have sat in on three different cabinet meetings. They are rather boring and are mostly on the drifter topic. No one seems to be in agreement about anything. Taggert is the only one with an offensive approach, and even his irritates me. I feel like we should be doing something more if they are attacking us.

As for the Culling, no one has been sent home and there has been nothing more said or done about the traitor. I have been careful around all the Denver girls and even tried to eavesdrop on Sapphire and Marisol a few times. Our socials with one another are almost done too. I think back to my social with Sapphire and can't seem to remember anything useful. I am in a constant state of fear that something might happen to any one of my new friends, specifically Henry or Lyncoln.

In the meantime, the simulations have definitely gotten harder. We have to shoot what looks like real life people. It's hard for me, and even harder for Attie. We got to choose a partner that was not of the opposite sex for one simulation to practice as a pair, so Attie and I did ours together. I ended up shooting almost everything just to spare her.

Of course, I've also had to do numerous simulations with Henry and Lyncoln. Oddly enough, I have been "terminated" three times with Henry. Those are the only three times I have been killed, so to speak. As the days progress, the simulations get harder and harder. Some seem so real it's scary. Even the gunshots sound eerily real in the sims. The adrenaline definitely gets pumping in those scenarios.

This whole dating two boys thing is even more confusing as the time goes on. For the past week, Henry comes to my room every night after socials to talk to me about my day and spend more time with me. Lyncoln shows up sometimes too, but has pulled back considerably since the morning he called me genius, kissed me, and left. I'm getting to know them better, and the three of us have oddly formed a working friendship. That might have something to do with the fact that I haven't kissed either of them for a while now, as I promised myself that I needed to cut that out and behave until I know what to do about them. But now that I do know them better, although they have basic similarities, I see how different they really are.

Henry likes spicy food. His favorite color is lime green. He likes studying history and knows more about it than anyone I have ever met. He is also competitive. One night he and Lyncoln played chess. I have never seen a more evenly matched or intense game…but Henry won. Although Henry is extremely outgoing and charismatic, he is also a bookworm and kind of nerdy. Oddly enough, it makes him even more endearing. He is the kindest person I have ever met. The thought of someday maybe having a family with a man like Henry makes me weak in the knees. It's the happily ever after fairy tales are made of. He is definitely prince charming.

Lyncoln, on the other hand, is a meat and potatoes type of guy. He probably doesn't even have a favorite color, although he always seems to wear gray and black ties, so I'm guessing it's gray or black. He is protective to an obsessive extent. He's the hardest worker I know and is just as intelligent as Henry, but in different ways. Henry is book smart and people smart, whereas Lyncoln is common sense smart and strategically smart. If one word could sum up Lyncoln, it would be aggressive. Although he is smooth on the outside and has that "bad boy" relaxed vibe about him, everything he does is aggressive from the way he looks at me, to the way he aims his gun, to the way he walks.

I guess I thought that once I got to know them better, my decision or whatever would be easier to make. One I would fall madly in love with and the other would kind of just fade out. Unfortunately, it is the exact opposite. The more I get to know them, the more impossible a decision seems. Henry is the obvious choice, but for some reason, I just can't fathom saying goodbye to Lyncoln.

If I said goodbye to Lyncoln, I would miss his knowing and fiery stare and the way he knows me better than I even know myself. I would miss the way he smells and his glorious muscles. I would miss the way he stares into my eyes and I know, without a doubt, that he would take a bullet for me.

But if I had to say goodbye to Henry, I would feel like I lost one of my best friends, if not my best friend, and a part of my soul. I would miss the way he always remembers the little stuff and the way he always wants to be near me. I would miss those smooth green eyes and his killer dimples and smile. I would miss just asking him about his day. I would miss laughing and joking around with him, not to mention the way he makes me feel when he kisses me...completely cherished.

With everything going on in the last week, this is the first I have seriously reflected on our situation and only because I'm waiting for my turn for another panel with the Board of Directors. This last week has flown by with simulations and trying to figure out who the traitor is. In addition to our socials finishing up, we have that big test over each other and two big simulator tests coming up, and then another cut will be made.

I'm not ready to leave yet. I kind of wish I would just be sent home before I have to make a choice about Henry and Lyncoln, but the only thing worse than falling for both of them would be being without both of them. Neither is an option. The thought of having to go back to Omaha and marry someone else makes me want to hurl. The thought of marrying anyone at this point makes me want to hurl, but I will do my best to try to kick butt at these tests so that there's a better chance of making it far enough to get to stay in Denver and maybe eventually marry one of them.

I glance in the mirror, finish touching up my makeup, and sigh. I straighten out my skirt suit and put my hair behind my ears. I'm dreading this panel, even more so than last time. I'm not sure what they will tell me this time and I don't even want to know. What I do want to know, is who the traitor is. I can't count the number of times in the past week I have had nightmares about something bad happening to Henry or Lyncoln or both. Why haven't they figured it out yet?

I think of home and feel better knowing that my family is safe and has round the clock security watch. If anything happened to them, I would feel responsible. It's hard to believe I've been gone almost seven weeks now. A lot has changed in seven weeks.

As Sarge drops me off at the panel room, I can't help but feel that something is off. There seems to be a cloud hanging over my head that I just can't escape from. Something isn't right and I can't put my finger on it. Does it have to do with the traitor, or is it something else?

I hear them call my name from just outside the room so I enter and sit down properly as I have been taught to do. The nerves kick in and I hope with everything in me they aren't about to send me home.

Elle smiles, "Ms. Scott. We are pleased to announce that you continue to both surprise and impress us," she starts us off.

"Your basic reasoning and logic are exemplary," Mr. Winters adds, looking down at me from behind his glasses and holding back a slight smile.

"Your etiquette may not always be perfect," Dougall smiles a little too eagerly, "but you have a way with people and putting them at ease. You are a natural charmer due to your wonderful sense of humor. And emotionally, you are very perceptive."

"Your marks on your testing put you among the top in the class. Even your shooting tests and simulators are proving that you are hardworking and deserving to be here for a shot at the Madam Presidency," Professor Zax chips in.

They are all silent a moment and looking at the papers in front of them.

"Why do I get the feeling there is a huge 'but' coming?" I ask honestly, trying hard not to fidget my feet. My hands are sweating as they lie clasped together in my lap.

The evil tester man, Mr. Alexander, speaks this time. "The one area that is still of concern lies in your interactions with people. You are loyal to a fault. In the simulators, you keep taking a bullet for Henry. You literally take a bullet for him and get in his way when he is perfectly capable of making a shot and saving you both. You love people." He stops for a moment. "Which is not a bad thing, but can be when you never think of yourself as having any value. As Madam President, you will have to put yourself above the lives of others. Your country depends on it because your country needs you. There isn't a point in your becoming a leader if you take yourself out of a position to lead."

A few of the others nod. I guess this isn't anything I haven't heard before, and I can kind of see where they are coming from. The way Mr. Alexander describes it, I'm almost being like Lyncoln and running into unnecessary danger. I find myself nodding with them in acknowledgment that it is an area I need to work on.

"Now, unfortunately, we need to address the elephant in the room." Elle smiles empathetically.

I look at the floor, not wanting to look any of them in the eyes out of embarrassment. "The boys?" I feel the heat in my cheeks signaling my blush.

"Yes," Professor Zax nods. "You have yourself in-between some pretty remarkable candidates. I'm sure it wouldn't surprise you much to know that both Henry and Lyncoln are in the top five of the boys."

I know they aren't supposed to tell me that so I don't know why they did. "It doesn't surprise me at all," I shrug.

Professor Bennett takes over. "So, the matter then is what you are going to do. It may be of interest to you that through the simulator tests, you are a better pair with Lyncoln. Through the personality tests, you pair better with Henry. This isn't a decision we can make for you. You will need to think about it long and hard. Who you chose may very well end up being the next president. Part of the reason we are giving you this leeway and not making a decision for you, or rushing it before now, is because they are so closely ranked and at the top. Another part of it is that if we forced your decision, or made it for you, you would forever harbor animosity to the State for not being given an opportunity to choose. But do not be fooled, your lack of decision making is doing them a real disservice and making you look silly. They both should be in the final four theoretically." He pauses. "And despite our urging and nagging, both of them have stubbornly decided that it is with you or not at all."

I feel my hands get even sweatier and the blood drains from my face. *I don't have to decide right now, do I?*

"Taking all things into consideration, we have decided to give you a bit more time," Professor Dougall looks serious and I let out the breath I was holding. "However, a decision will need to be made by the first live interviews. You are normally quite decisive so your lack of decisiveness in this area is causing us concern."

There is a moment of silence as they let that sink in.

Elle pipes in with her kindness after Dougall's blow, "Think of the boys. If the country had to vote today, for the three of you uncoupled, the votes would be split and all three of you would more than likely be sent packing. You want all the votes going to you and whichever one you choose, as a pair, not split three ways. The voters won't vote you in uncoupled, no matter how much they like you. They want to vote for a couple, as it is the only way they know. And it gives you the best shot to win." She pauses a moment then adds, "Normally the panel would help you in making such a big decision, but the truth of the matter is that either of them is completely capable in this case. It just comes down to who you want to be with."

"Makes sense," I nod, glad that she pointed that voting part out. It isn't just about me and my feelings. It's about Henry and Lyncoln. I don't want to jeopardize their shot at the presidency just because I am a confused girl. They each deserve a solid partner who doesn't waver.

"Plus, it doesn't reflect well on the Madam President to be between men and unable to make a decision about it," evil tester man says harshly.

"Excuse me?" I feel the heat in my face again and my temper roars to the surface.

"Like it or not, the Madam President must act in a certain manner. She must be a role model," Professor Dougall comments.

I take a deep breath. "What I don't like is that President Walters, our first president, had the same issue and yet he wasn't forced to decide until he was ready. The Culling was extended a month while he figured it out and dated three different women…and although I don't expect that sort of special treatment, it's different for me because I'm a woman, isn't it?" I squint at them letting my anger be clearly seen. The longer I am in this, the harder it is to rein in my temper. My fuse seems to be getting shorter and shorter.

"Well…" Professor Zax looks uncomfortable and fidgets in his seat.

"Yes," Elle says before he can make an excuse. "Yes, it is."

That infuriates me. If it was Henry with two girls, he would have all the time in the world. For Trident showing us that everyone is equal, for some sick and twisted reason, women are still unequal. We are probably valued more due to being able to bring new life into the world, but because of that, our expectations and standards are even higher. It wouldn't reflect well on the country if a woman had two suitors. Heaven forbid we consider for a moment that I am a person with real feelings instead of just a candidate. And I'm only eighteen freaking years old.

"This may seem harsh, but with the country in its current fragile state, we now more than ever need a strong new and vibrant couple to take over the country. Their bond needs to be unbreakable. The sooner you make a decision, the better and the more comfortable you will become with your choice," Mr. Winters sympathizes.

"In just two weeks from today, on a special Tuesday evening broadcast, we are introducing the couples to the country." Elle smiles politely. "The entire country will be watching. You'll want to have made a decision by then."

"You have two weeks, Ms. Scott," Professor Dougall reiterates sternly.

Chapter 19

fterwards in the hallway by the elevator, I meet up with
October, who has been oddly quiet and missing from action as
of recently. Although I talk to her here and there, she always
seems busy. The life of a double agent, I suppose.

"Hey," she greets me, "You look like you just got the crap kicked
out of you. Rough review?"

I shrug. "I have to make a decision soon." I know she will
understand without prying. "On the way to yours?"

"Yeah. And Ouch. That sucks. I'm sorry, girl." She gives my arm a
squeeze. That means the world to me since I know she's not a huggy
person.

Pulling me aside, farther out of ear shot of our guards, she
whispers, "Listen. Hadenfelt is after the presidency with a vengeance.
The more I snoop, the more power I find out he has. The President hates
him and wants him gone, but he has something over him too. I don't
think he's a drifter or anything, but there is something going on here.
He will stop short of nothing in order to have Marisol win."

"And the good news keeps on a coming," I mumble sarcastically.

"He has one of my guards spying for him so I haven't been able to
talk to you much. I'm probably going home soon since he's making my
job difficult." She sighs.

"I'm sorry, October." She's been sacrificing her time and efforts to help someone else win. That says a lot about her character.

"Don't be. But do whatever is needed to win. Be as ruthless as she is if you have to. Just promise me you will give it your best shot, even if you have to stoop to her level. Take them down, whatever it takes," she whispers.

"I promise," I nod as I turn back toward the elevator.

She stops me. "By the way, the thing with Benjamin was a test too. They put Marisol up to it and she agreed as long as she got the information from it. They played right into her hand and so she obviously went along with it, though what she did with the information was a test for her. But, they made Benjamin betray you to see what you would do and to also see if he would actually do it. You passed and he failed," she says quietly.

"What?" I ask surprised. I was so hard on Benjamin. But they asked him to do it? Why would they do that?

She shrugs. "They were testing his character to see if he would betray someone he cared for. He did. He's too easily swayed so he isn't what they are looking for. Technically, since Marisol tried to manipulate you with the information, she failed too. Not that it matters what she does."

She then starts talking more loudly about her review and asking me about mine even though she already knows all about it. I'm sad to think that October will be going home soon. Happy that she can be with her boyfriend and back to her love of teaching but sad all the same. It also worries me because she and Lyncoln were the only ones not paired.

They told me I have two weeks.

It isn't even about winning anymore. That's on the back burner.

What the heck am I going to do?

****

At dinner that evening, Benjamin and Renae are nowhere to be found and then again at breakfast the next morning. I'm not surprised about that with what October told me, although Renae could be fun hearted when she wanted to be and I will miss her bluntness. I feel a bit of hurt and a little guilty at the fact that Benjamin was so close to being in the final eight couples. If he would have made it just a little farther, could he have made more of a difference in his mom's illness?

I guess some things never change. He wouldn't stand up for a boy when faced with losing his popularity, and he wouldn't stand up for me when asked to betray me. I do wish I could talk with him to make amends. I wonder if his mother hadn't been sick if he would've chosen to betray me. I guess we will never know. Either way, you always have a choice, to take the high road or stab people in the back.

That afternoon, Lyncoln and I have a scheduled sim back at DIA. It's fairly usual now that we can have sims scheduled for all hours of the day. This particular simulation is that we are surrounded and outnumbered by enemies in black while in the woods somewhere. It is clear they will kill us. Most simulations take a while to get going, but this one is a shootout from the start. We stand back-to-back and start shooting our way out as more enemies pop up and surround us.

I use my instincts when I see a fake, somewhat transparent hand of a sim person move and I shoot that person before they can shoot me. We have to terminate them as quickly as we can and try to not get terminated or hit ourselves. It seems impossible since we are greatly outnumbered. We don't have time to talk or strategize who is going for what guy, we just shoot, the quicker the better.

We have four of the ten or so down when one charges at us. Lyncoln moves to shoot him and protect me. Seeing someone move behind him, I reach to protect him at the same time. The result is that we are nose to nose, glasses to glasses, right arms raised, shooting around each other.

We don't even need to look at each other, we just use our instincts and take them all down.

As we finish firing our weapons and the last fake body slumps to the ground, Lyncoln takes a small step back and lowers his gun.

"Nice shooting, babe." He grins a huge grin.

Although his real smile is rare and intoxicating, I see movement behind him. There is another shooter coming from around a tree. Moving without thinking, I reach down and grab a lifeless simulator guy's body, picking it up. It's obviously a simulator body because it weighs nothing, and I don't even know if it will work, but I am banking on it being a shield of sorts. I mean, if we can hide behind stuff in sims, why can't we pick stuff up?

I step in front of Lyncoln with the simulator guy's body in front of me and shoot at the same time the bad guy shoots. Lyncoln turns with his gun drawn but it's too late. The bullet from the shooter hits the simulator body in front of me as my bullet hits him square in the chest and kills him. I successfully saved Lyncoln without having to be terminated myself.

Boom! Take that, panel. I can save us both.

I move my hands to drop the weightless simulator body and look around for movement which would indicate more shooters. Lyncoln does the same.

"I can't believe I fell for that one," Lyncoln groans.

"What, not used to a woman saving your butt?" I tease.

"Well no, but you aren't an ordinary woman either." He says it affectionately though his eyes never move off the surroundings as we look for more intruders.

Just when we are unsure why the simulator is still on if there aren't any more enemies, a random sim turkey walks out from the trees in the distance. I look at Lyncoln incredulously as he looks at me with a smirk.

Without talking to one another, we both raise our guns and shoot it at the same time. It isn't like it's real anyways.

Our bullets hit the turkey at the same time and I immediately find it hilarious. Not that we killed a turkey, but that a turkey was in our sim. Why a turkey? They must have personalized this for us. I start giggling as I feel the simulator shutting off around us and then laugh harder. I'm tired and exhausted, which is why I find it so funny, but I can't stop.

Lyncoln seeing me almost in tears starts laughing too.

"At least you hit that one this time, babe. You know, the one you actually aimed at." He grins as the woods scene fades back to the black rubber-looking walls. "Think that will count as a kill?"

I laugh even harder, removing my glasses to wipe the tears from my eyes.

The doors open and Professor Bennett walks in.

"Ms. Scott, Mr. Reed," he greets us and then rubs his chin thoughtfully, "I just thought you two may want to know that this particular simulation hasn't been passed yet, until now."

"Did they not shoot the turkey?" Lyncoln asks.

I laugh a huge ugly snort before I rein it in.

Professor Bennett smiles and looks amused. "No. The last intruder. So far one or both candidates have been terminated in this particular simulation. It speaks to your relationship that you were able to both make it out unscathed. Great thinking on the fly, Ms. Scott."

I feel myself blush but manage to get out, "Thank you." Then I can't help but start giggling all over again.

****

Later that night after dinner there's a knock on my door. I'm sure it's Henry as usual. I don't hesitate to open the door, and when I do, I find Lyncoln instead. He comes in my room and shuts the door. I notice he never does play by the rules of keeping the door open and no one stops him either. If I didn't trust him, it might bother me. But it doesn't. It feels good to have some semblance of privacy even though we both wear our watches and I'm sure there are other means of monitoring in our rooms as well.

It takes one look at his face to figure out he's upset about something. He's wearing blue jeans and a tight v-neck navy t-shirt. I have noticed that his pec muscles seem to make every shirt he wears look tight. Not that I am complaining or anything, but it's like he can't find a shirt big enough for those bad boys.

"What is it?" I ask, getting straight to the point.

"You need to send me home." His dark blue and brown eyes pierce mine. I see a longing in his gaze that he has been trying to hide. He might not be as open with me about his feelings as Henry is, but I know he deeply cares for me.

"What?" His words and the way he is looking at me are contradictory.

"Send me home," he says more angrily this time.

"I got that part," I snap back. "What did I do? Did they make you do this? Is this a test?"

"No. I'm here on my own. And nothing." He stops and runs a hand through his military short, dark hair. It leaves it looking slightly ruffled, just the way I love it.

"Then why do you want me to do that?" I ask surprised.

"Because it's going to happen anyway. I see you and Henry, what you have. The longer I stay, the more it's going to hurt when you pick him…for you and for me. Just do me a favor and send me home now. That way I can get back to work." Seeing his anguish rips my heart into a million pieces.

I'm not ready to make this choice now and I'm not ready to say goodbye; it has only been one day of my two-week deadline. My eyes start to burn as the tear ducts start working. I know I'm going to have to choose eventually, but I'm just not ready. Not now. My breathing gets heavy and I feel like I can't breathe at all. This time, I might be having a real panic attack. I feel like there is an elephant sitting on my chest about to crush me to death. There isn't enough oxygen in the room for my lungs.

"I can't," I whisper as a tear rolls down my cheek. I take a big gulp of air trying to calm down. I feel like I'm choking and suffocating at the same time.

"Why not?" he asks, this time looking like the one confused for a change.

"Look, I have to make the decision within two weeks. They gave me a deadline," I offer as more ugly tears find their way down my face while I gasp for air in-between words. "I haven't decided anything yet. Just don't make me do it now. Please. Not now."

Seeing my tears, he walks over and wraps his arms around me. "Okay. I didn't mean to upset you. I just thought I'd make this easier for us both now." He brushes the tears off my cheeks.

"I'm sorry," I say as he hugs me. I take a deep smell of him. He always smells so good. My breathing starts to get better as I focus on him and not the lack of air in my lungs.

"For what?" he asks softly.

"For putting you through all of this." I shrug. "For how messed up this is."

"It's okay. Don't get me wrong. I want you. I want you so bad it hurts. If you were to pick me, I would be over the moon. But, I'm not stupid either. I know my chances. I know Henry. I know how he is. You would have to be an idiot to not fall for him." He stops a moment and runs a hand through my hair. "It's going to be okay. I'll stay as long as you need me to, as long as there's a sliver of a chance. Today was so much fun, but it made me realize how much I would miss you if I didn't get to see you every day. I was just trying to make it easier on us. It's okay. If you need more time, take it."

He kisses me once, more softly than I thought he knew how to, and in that moment, I feel like nothing will ever be okay again.

How am I supposed to say goodbye to him?

****

The next day we have a full day of tests. Our socials with one another have finished up and we take a test on how well we know one another. We also have a history test on Trident. They are both very long and mind numbing. More questions are on the test about one another than I thought possible. Each person had to have at least twenty questions about them.

You would think by this point we would all be used to tests. I wish I would've counted how many we've taken. I'm sure it would be at least a hundred. I have answered questions about everything and anything. And the more tests we take, the more I realize I have to learn. It was silly of me to think the tests would be over after that first week in Omaha.

A knock on my door finds both Henry and Lyncoln holding cookies and a deck of cards. I open the door with a smile. It is beyond sad that being with the both of them is starting to be the new normal.

"Hey."

"Hey, beautiful," Henry grins, planting a kiss on my cheek as he walks in.

Both of them are still wearing their dress slacks but their ties are loose and their top couple of buttons on their shirts are open. I can't blame them. I already changed into pajama pants, a t-shirt, and slippers. I should feel bashful being dressed so casually when they are still looking somewhat professional, but I don't.

"Babe." Lyncoln greets me the same as Henry with a kiss, but on the other cheek. Neither seems to mind the other does it, and I am once again mystified by our messed up relationship. This is so not okay.

I reach in the fridge and grab the lemonade that I keep stocked for them and a tea for me.

"So. That question on the test about getting chased around on the playground by a boy that wanted to kiss you, that was totally you wasn't it?" Henry asks as they both plop down on the couch. Lyncoln has his arm around the back of the couch like usual and Henry has his elbows on his knees as he leans in to talk to me.

I sit down in my usual neutral spot, the chair. "Maybe," I smile guilty, wondering how they knew it was me.

"I told you." Lyncoln chuckles and looks at me and shakes his head.

"His name was Gregory Banks and he was actually kind of cute, thank you very much," I say defensively but lightheartedly.

Henry snorts a laugh and Lyncoln punches him saying, "Reminds me of Sammy."

"Sammy?" I ask, eyebrows raised.

"She was my first kiss. She kind of cornered me during our yearly tests and I didn't have any other way out of it, but it was *cute*, I guess," Henry shrugs, borrowing my term and elbows Lyncoln. "Not that Lyncoln here has room to talk."

"And why's that?" I ask smiling.

"Let's just say he did his fair share of kissing on the playground. I wasn't always there, but believe me, I heard all about it." Henry wiggles his eyebrows and Lyncoln stares me down, gauging my reaction.

"I have heard he is quite the ladies' man," I whisper and they both laugh again.

"What about you? Other than ol' Gregory Banks, do we need to head to Omaha to alpha male your past list of admirers?" Henry jokes.

"Uhhh...nope," I say slightly embarrassed. I know they're just teasing, but I don't think either of them fully realizes that until now, I never dated anyone. And now I am semi-dating them both. Just reason number seven hundred and forty-six that this situation is super messed up.

"Nope?" Henry asks playfully but I know they probably both really want to know. Lyncoln kind of already does. I just assumed it was common knowledge by this point.

"I didn't have any boyfriends before coming here. Zero. Not even in junior high," I say honestly and shyly, "Not one."

"We know. We know. But how many unrequited loves were vying for your heart? How many Gregory Bankses tried to smooch ya on the playground?" Henry kisses the air and I laugh. If only he knew how good his lips were at doing just that.

"None." I shrug and smile shyly. "I decked him and all the boys left me alone from then on. They were kind of afraid of me or something. No admirers. No boyfriends. Nothing."

Henry can't seem to believe me. "Seriously?"

"Seriously. The few boys I was attracted to never gave me the time of day. I just wasn't their type." I shrug again, not knowing what else to say.

"Even better." Lyncoln speaks more to Henry than to me and Henry nods in agreement.

"What does that even mean?" I ask confused. He says it a lot.

"It means that you keep getting better the more I know about you," he says while looking at me intensely.

"Amen to that," Henry says, raising a glass in cheers and taking a drink although neither of us cheers him.

[392]

Lyncoln stares at me a bit longer than is needed and then shuffles the cards. We talk awhile about our tests and other random topics. Lyncoln is making fun of Henry and his love for zombie apocalypse literature when there is a knock on my door. I hear two quick knocks followed impatiently by two more.

"Coming, coming!" I sing-song to the door.

I open the door to find a bewildered looking Oliver.

"Come in," I say immediately, taking him by the arm and leading him in.

"I need to talk to you," he says urgently. He sees Henry and Lyncoln as he walks in and adds, "Oh good, you guys are here too."

"Oliver, what is it? I've never seen you so skittish," I ask concerned. I gesture for him to sit down in the chair I was just in. His normal jokester attitude has been replaced by an almost scared one.

He sits and I crouch down to his level and take his hand because I can clearly see that something has him rattled.

"It's Isabella," he blurts out and I put two and two together.

"The drifter?" I ask. Henry and Lyncoln sit up more seriously. Lyncoln immediately going into military mode, jaw clenched, ready to spring into action.

"Yes. I just know it. At first it was little things. Like when we were on lock down the night of the masquerade. Everyone but a few of us were sleeping, remember? Well, anytime she heard a slight noise, I would notice that she would wake up, but was trying to look like she was asleep. That and she seems to be trying to memorize the layout of the buildings or something. She always takes wrong turns at DIA just to see where they go and I know she is smarter than that, but she plays dumb like she got lost or something." He barely breathes between sentences as he explains it to us, "The more simulations we have, the more I can tell she's faking it. She's a far better shot than me and has had far more training in both shooting and self-defense, but is trying to make it look like she doesn't."

[393]

"Has she said anything to you?" Lyncoln is now pacing my room, probably doing everything he can to not go get Isabella right this minute. I'm glad her room isn't on my floor because I might be tempted to let him.

"No. But I know it's her. I just know." He says it defeated and puts his head in his hands. I pat him on the back.

"Oliver she had us all fooled. It isn't your fault," I offer to try to make him feel better.

I can't believe that sweet girl could be plotting against the State. Is she capable of harming us though, or was she just here for information? I think back to conversations I have had with her recently as we have been at target practice. I can't imagine her even saying a curse word, let alone killing anyone. Then again, she did find the hiding spot for our flag during paintball, so maybe she's more strategic than she lets on.

"I should have known sooner. It shouldn't have taken me so long to figure out and I should have said something when I first suspected it the night of the attack," he adds looking at me with remorse, "And I came to you, Reagan, because I knew you would know what to do and you have some pretty powerful boyfriends. If I went to anyone else, she might get suspicious, and I bet she's watching me too. We're friends so this is less suspicious. And I want her caught, but I didn't want to tell someone and have them shoot her or something. She might be bad news, but I'm not sure she deserves to die." He stops and sighs repeating himself, "I just wish I would have known sooner."

"You're telling us now, Oliver. That's all that matters," Henry says kindly. He turns to Lyncoln and swiftly rises. "I'm going to Dad and Taggert with this right away. It'll look like I've just gone home for the night. You three play cards or pretend like you are for the next twenty or so minutes just in case she has an accomplice or eyes somewhere. We don't want her knowing that we have found her out until she's already in custody. I will have them put extra guards on you immediately, Oliver."

Lyncoln nods his agreement to all Henry just said.

"Thanks, guys," Oliver nods.

I walk towards the door as Henry turns to leave. "Please be safe," I whisper.

"I will, beautiful. You too." He kisses me softly on the mouth, fortunately around the corner and out of the view of the others.

There's a lunatic on our hands. Now that we know who she is, we need to get her apprehended before I feel safe. I don't for a second doubt Oliver, but how could sweet Isabella be our traitor?

Chapter 20

The next morning right before breakfast there's a knock on my door. I open it to find Henry standing there in a navy suit with a matching navy tie. He must not be doing sims or training at DIA today. He looks fresh and handsome though. I had never seen anyone look so attractive in a suit until I met Henry.

"Good mor--"

The words aren't even out of my mouth before I am swept up in a kiss and carried back into my room. It literally takes my breath away and I'm hoping that Jamie didn't see it. Not that he can say anything about it anyway, just harass me with his knowing looks.

After a kiss that leaves me feeling dizzy, Henry finally pulls away. I mentally chastise myself for going about a week without kissing either of them to back to kissing both of them.

What is wrong with me? Beginners luck for dating. That has to be it.

"Good morning," he says softly and rests his forehead on my forehead.

"Morning," I manage to get out.

"I just wanted to let you know that we haven't moved on Isabella yet. We want to watch her this morning and will act at DIA." He sighs in frustration. "I know you won't like it and I don't either. I've been fighting against this decision half of the night and again this morning, but I just wanted you to hear it from me. Some think it's safer for everyone if she is arrested there instead of here. Drifters are known for their love of explosives and we want to go through her room before just showing up and arresting her."

"Is Oliver safe at least?" I ask, always the worrier.

"Of course. She shouldn't have any idea we are onto her either. She's scheduled for a sim this morning by herself and that's when we'll move. It's only a few hours from now. Oliver will be at DIA with the rest of us and he won't even be there when it goes down." He shrugs. "His guards have been warned also. We have subtly doubled security this morning. For everyone."

"You're right," I say honestly. "I don't like it."

"Me neither, but Taggert really wants to see what she'll do and if anyone else seems to be involved with her once word of her arrest gets out. The best place to have eyes everywhere is DIA," he explains.

"He has a point I guess." I shrug, still not happy.

"By the way, don't you find it interesting that Oliver came to you? He could have gone to Bennett or Winters, heck even Taggert, but he came to your room not even knowing that we were here." He puts his hands in his pockets in a relaxed way. I love the way he stands in a suit with his hands in his pockets. It's like he doesn't even know the natural power he has with both his body and his personality.

"Yeah?" I ask, wondering what he is getting at.

"It's because he didn't want to be suspicious, but it's also because he knew he could trust you, out of all the people here," he says and looks at me affectionately. I look at him trying to see if he is jealous or why he's bringing it up. Instead of seeing jealousy or anger, I see admiration. "I love that about you, you know." He smiles with those amazing dimples and walks towards me.

I meet him halfway and give him a kiss on the cheek. "Thanks," I smile. I'm trying my hardest to not kiss either Lyncoln or Henry and

Henry is making that dang difficult at the moment. I sensed another kissing session coming on.

"Let's head down for breakfast before we're late. I'm riding with you and Attie to DIA too. I'm not letting you out of my sight this morning. And by the way, you look amazing."

My hair is down but I'm dressed in black gear for DIA. "Right back at you," I say as I give his tie a playful tug.

He gives me a huge grin and takes my hand in his.

****

At DIA, all the guards seem a little tense otherwise things carry on like it's a normal morning. I practice shooting awhile with Oliver while Henry, now in his black gear, is a safe twenty yards down from us at another range. He stays close to me, but not so close it's obvious. Lyncoln is absent and I assume working with Taggert on taking down Isabella. She's at the range too, and much to my dismay, joins us for a bit. I have a bad poker face so I need to rein in my emotions here. I can't just pretend she isn't there like I did at breakfast.

"Hey," I greet her as nice and normal as possible. She can't know that I know she's the traitor. Our safety may depend on it.

"Hey, how are you guys?" she asks nicely. I can't believe this girl is an imposter. She's *so* believable.

"My shooting sucks today. On a scale of shooting like a putz to shooting like Lyncoln…I am pretty much a putz," Oliver says with a laugh as he looks at his target.

She giggles, "Tell me something I don't know."

He pretends to be offended and I laugh. It's hard to carry on like this when I know she's a dirty traitor. Does she want to hurt either of the men in my life? I actually like her. Or liked her. It just doesn't seem like she is capable of doing this.

Why is she doing this?

We shoot around for a bit and I find it odd that Isabella has her last two bullets off of what would otherwise be perfect precision and accuracy. This is what Oliver is talking about. Something isn't right.

As we take a break to watch Oliver shoot again, I try to talk to her and ask her about our big tests yesterday in an effort to treat her like I normally would. We talk back and forth and I just keep reminding myself that any minute now she will be arrested and we will all be safe. Henry is now just two ranges down, staying close and trying to help me feel safe and stay calm.

Isabella moves to put her hand on Oliver's arm. "Hey, I have a solo sim in ten. Walk me down?" she asks sweetly. I feel relieved when she puts her own gun down. These guns aren't real, but they look real, and that was enough to mess with my mind given the circumstances.

"Absolutely," Oliver responds with a smile as he usually would when she asks for something. She turns to leave and Oliver and I exchange a look.

I mouth to him, "Be careful."

He nods.

As soon as they are out of sight, I go straight to Henry to tell him what happened. He talks to his guards while I quickly go in search of Lyncoln. I tell Jamie that I need to find him immediately. He comes down the hallway less than two minutes later like he knew I was looking for him. I'm relieved he isn't wherever Isabella is.

"I was watching you the whole time. What is it?" he asks, looking me over from head to toe worried. His hands naturally land on my hips as he waits for me to tell him what's up.

"Isabella asked Oliver to walk her to her sim. I know it seems completely normal but I have a bad feeling about it," I explain. "We need to get him away from her. He isn't supposed to be with her. She should have already been arrested by now." My voice sounds as frustrated as I feel.

He nods, "I know. I'll talk to Taggert."

He turns but I grab his arm and pull him back towards me. He looks at me confused.

"Not you," I say stubbornly.

"What?" His hands return to my hips.

"Don't go down there. Stay with me," I plead as I hold onto him tight. "Please. I have dreamt this dream a hundred times, a hundred different ways. I need you safe today."

He smiles at me affectionately and reaches to put my hair behind my ear before his hand returns to my hip. "I wasn't going to go anyway, sweetheart. I'm staying here to help protect the candidates. I love you even more for caring though."

Holy crap, did he just say he loved me??

He turns and beckons to his guard standing a few yards back and tells him something briefly before the guard quickly talks into his device and walks down the hallway.

Before I can say anything else, Henry and Knox enter the hallway from the range with Christopher not far behind. My hand is still on Lyncoln's arm and his hands are still at my hips. I feel a bit guilty, but I don't let go. I can't help but wonder if Lyncoln would run into danger if I don't hang on to him for dear life.

I see a flash of jealousy in Henry's eyes, but he smiles at me anyway. It's not his usual smile though because his dimples don't show. I know immediately that something else is wrong because he and Knox both don't look happy.

"Hey, have you seen Attie? She was supposed to be back from her sim ten minutes ago and isn't at the range," Knox asks me with his brows furrowed. "I saw Henry talking to his guards and knew something was up."

"No. I haven't seen her," I respond shaking my head and am immediately more worried. Lyncoln and I exchange a concerned glance. Oliver and Attie are both with the traitor? Why, oh why, didn't they just get her last night in her room when she was sleeping? Who cares if she has explosives? I thought the third floor at DIA was supposed to be cleared for just this. This whole situation is going from bad to worse.

"Want me to head down?" Christopher asks Lyncoln. "Check it out? Make it look like I'm waiting for a sim?" He obviously knows what's going on. Which doesn't surprise me since he is always in those extra meetings with Henry and Lyncoln. Though I don't know his exact rank, I know it isn't as high as Lyncoln's, but it isn't low either.

Lyncoln shakes his head no. "Wait a minute. They should've already moved. Thanks though."

Just then, Taggert and five men in tow round the corner quickly and see us standing there. Not even caring who is in the vicinity, Taggert blurts out, "She has been apprehended."

That was quick.

But before I can take a sigh of relief, I see that he doesn't look happy.

"But?" I ask.

"But Oliver is missing. He was not with her, nor is he anywhere on the third floor," he explains.

I know in my gut something has gone horribly wrong. "So is Attie," I say angrily and glare at him.

It has only taken five minutes or less for this whole situation to go to hell in a handbasket.

****

The next five minutes pass like years. Most of the candidates are rushed back to Mile High with no reason as to why. Lyncoln and Henry try to get me to go, but I strongly decline. Oliver is missing. Attie is missing. I won't leave until I know where they are.

As the guards are going floor by floor, I can't help but wonder how they could've just disappeared. Don't they have surveillance for this? As Henry and I walk the same hallway for the hundredth time, we turn to go down another hallway.

"We aren't even technically allowed here," Henry says frustrated. "This is the second floor."

"I know, but I keep thinking about what Oliver said about her taking wrong turns on purpose to explore," I explain as we get to the end of that hallway and turn around. Probably a dozen guards or so are checking every room on the floor with us. How is it possible that even collectively we still can't find them?

As I turn, taking the same lap we have taken three times now, I hear a soft sound coming from the door at the end, the one for the stairwell.

"Did you hear that?" I ask, stopping and grabbing Henry's hand.

I listen again and hear it. I recognize the voice as a panicked Attie.

"What? The stairs were supposed to be closed off," Henry says, hearing it too. "And cleared already."

I throw open the door to the stairs and go flying down them to ground level. I hear Henry on my heels and Jamie on his. The sight before me is one I will never forget all the days of my life. My gut clenches and I have a hard time not crying out or puking.

Oliver lays in a pool of blood with a knife stabbed into his chest. Attie is trying to stop the bleeding and is using his ripped shirt to put pressure on and soak up the blood. Both Attie and Oliver are covered in blood and Attie is sobbing, which is the sound I heard from the hall.

"Reagan! Henry!" she says absolutely terrified, "Help! My guard went for help, but it isn't fast enough. I need a medical team. Now!"

I turn to Henry and squeeze his hand, "Get those guards. Get anyone you can. And hurry."

He squeezes my hand back and looks me in the eyes as we silently communicate to one another the seriousness of this situation. Henry leaves and I look at Jamie. He gives me the same look. This is bad. Considering the knife to the chest and all the blood on the floor, it is apparent that Oliver needs help or he might not make it. I know if anyone can get help here in time, it's Henry. There is a hospital with medics somewhere here at DIA, so it shouldn't take them long, right?

"We found him here. Someone told us to take the stairs because the elevator wasn't working and we found him like this," Attie says frantically.

Jamie lets out a curse word from behind me.

I kneel down in the blood with Attie. "What can I do, Attie?"

Oliver is rolling his head side to side, barely conscious and looking pale. He has lost so much blood. There is just so much blood. It pours onto the gray cement in an ever expanding pool.

"Me too. What can I do?" Jamie asks, looking bewildered for the first time since I've met him.

"Nothing. He needs surgery. He needs a blood transfusion. I can't remove the knife. It's too deep. And if it stays lodged in there much longer, he'll bleed out anyway." She grabs another piece of his torn shirt as she tries to put pressure on his rib cage, closing the wound around the knife.

"Oliver, stay with me!" I say as I grab ahold of his cheek and his hand while Attie works.

"I don't have anything with me to use. I need a med kit." Attie stops a moment to look me in the eyes and that's when I know Oliver is in even worse shape than I think he is. I haven't seen Attie look like this before.

Seconds feel like hours as we wait, kneeling in his blood that keeps seeping out of him with there being nothing we can do about it. Keep the knife in, and he bleeds to death. Take the knife out, and he bleeds to death faster.

"Oliver. I need you to stay with me. Please," I plead and squeeze his hand trying to keep talking to him. "Help is on the way. Just hang in there."

"Reagan? Attie?" Oliver asks weakly as he comes back to consciousness and spits blood, which runs down his chin. I want to cry out, but I don't want to scare him so I stuff it down. I tear a piece off my own shirt and use it to gently wipe the blood off his chin.

"I'm here. Stay with me," I plead and keep pleading as I repeat it. I hear doors slam and loud voices and Jamie yelling directions, and I know help is on the way. He only needs to hang in there a little bit longer.

Just a little longer.

"Can't," he coughs, "Tell my mom I love her."

He spits blood again. I wipe it away like my wiping can somehow magically heal him.

"You'll tell her. Help is on the way. They'll be here any second," I say and feel the tears now streaming down my face. He is giving up. This is not good. Not good at all.

"Thanks, Attie," he coughs.

"You're welcome, Oliver," she says barely looking at him as she's still working and still panicked.

"Isabella?" He coughs a few weak coughs and looks at me.

"We got her. You did it. You caught the traitor." I smile through my tears and joke, "Now we know why you're ranked so high."

He smiles as much as he can and leans up a little while squeezing my hand with what strength he has left and in-between coughs says, "Well if I can't win, you better."

And with that, his eyes close and he bobs his head. He loses consciousness. I can see the life drain from his face like the way his blood pours out of his wound and onto the cold, hard floor.

"His pulse is fading," Attie says frantically. "I can't do chest compressions because of the blood. He'll bleed out quicker."

Just then the medical team arrives and takes over. At least a half a dozen people immediately begin working around and on Oliver's body. They are checking his vitals, talking about the knife and its location, and using all sorts of medical terms I have never heard of before.

I don't want to let go of Oliver's hand. If I do, I'm not sure I'll ever see him again. So I stay where I am, watching his pale face while they work.

A woman medic turns to me, "We need to move him and fast, you can let go now, Ms. Scott."

I don't move. I don't want to let go. Oliver isn't conscious and it isn't looking good. Their faces tell me it isn't good.

Unexpectedly, I am lifted up by Jamie's arms, losing my grip on Oliver's hand and moved aside. Knox is somehow there and lifts Attie away too as she continues to tell the medical team what has happened and what she has been doing to help him. I reach for her and we hold our bloodied hands together.

They already have an oxygen mask on Oliver and move quickly to get him loaded on a gurney to take him out. It takes less than a minute to get him out of the stairwell once they have him loaded. All that remains is the large red puddle on the floor and the metallic taste of blood in the air.

Henry arrives and Jamie gently passes me off to him. I hold onto him for dear life but keep looking at Attie and holding her hand, wishing more than anything this is all a bad dream or some sort of test.

"Let's go, Attie. You did everything you could, sweetie. Come with me," Knox coaxes her.

I give her a tearful hug and they leave. I stand in the stairwell and stare at Oliver's blood that is everywhere, including all over me. I pull away from Henry and punch the wall with a half scream of frustration. And now there's blood on the wall too.

"I knew something was wrong," I sob. "I've known something wasn't right for days."

"It isn't your fault, Reagan," Henry says softly, standing behind me and wrapping me back in his arms. "It isn't your fault. Let's go. You did everything you could. Let's go get you cleaned up."

I just lean against him and cry. I'll let him take me wherever, but I can't stop the tears.

Understanding that I'm not going to stop crying any time soon, he gently picks me up and carries me out of DIA. I know Jamie is with us the entire time. I don't remember the ride back to Mile High, all I remember is the tears as I cried into Henry's chest and all the questions I have about how it was possible for Isabella to do this.

Chapter 21

Feeling numb, I'm soon sitting in what I assume is Henry's room while he gives orders to his guards, my guards, and Gertie. I still have Oliver's blood all over me and a blanket is wrapped around my shoulders. This is a nightmare. At any moment I will wake up. I don't know as much as Attie about medical things, but I know there was enough blood that Oliver is in bad shape. We were losing him when the medical team arrived. I'm not sure there was much they could even do. The looks on their faces were not encouraging.

"Reagan, honey, I'll be right back." Henry is kneeling in front of me although his face seems blurry. I realize it's because the tears are still just pouring out of my eyes and down my cheeks. My neck and shirt are drenched with them.

He is gone and comes back in less than a minute. I take one look at his face and know what he is about to say. I start sobbing harder if that were possible.

"No. Please, no," I plead with Henry.

He sits down and pulls me across his lap as I sob harder. "I'm so sorry, Reagan. He's gone. We lost him."

"Why?" I choke out. "Why didn't they just arrest her last night?"

"I don't know, beautiful, but I do know that she also injured his guard and killed hers in the process. There shouldn't have been any way that was possible with that much extra personnel and eyes watching. There was a malfunction with the elevators too. They apparently took the elevator to the second floor and then she stuck a shoe in the door to stall it after attacking their guards. Oliver took off for help, and she cornered him in the stairwell. She would have finished him off then, but she heard Attie and her guard from above and took off. She tried to run but we caught her soon after. All of this only took about five minutes or less. We couldn't find them sooner because they were in a blind spot in the stairwell so we couldn't see them on the live feeds. By the time they checked all the cameras and watched the footage back to figure out where they were, you had already found them."

I try to picture Isabella's guard but can't. Two people died and one more was injured. For what purpose? How could someone as sweet as Isabella be capable of something so evil? What has happened to her that she would take someone else's life so easily?

We sit there like that for what seems like hours and I cry more tears than I thought my body had. Sobs rack my body uncontrollably, altering my breathing, and just when I am starting to get myself under control, I hear the door open and close and see Lyncoln. After getting a nod from Henry, he lifts me into his arms and sits down beside Henry, pulling me into his chest. He puts his hands on my face and checks me over from head to toe.

"It's not my blood." I choke on the words, holding back more tears. It's not lost on me that those were the same words he said to me a little more than a week ago.

"I know," he says softly and just holds me, running a hand through my hair.

As Lyncoln holds me against his chest, his beating heart is the only thing that makes sense. I focus on it instead of Oliver, his last words, and all the blood. Henry grabs my hand and I sit there in the lap of one man, hold the hand of the other, and cry out my soul in-between the men I love.

****

Hours later, Lyncoln leaves and Henry convinces me to take a hot bubble bath. As Gertie helps lower me into a tub bigger than I have ever seen, I realize Henry's room is much bigger than mine. Not only does he have a huge tub I could almost swim in, but he has a walk-in shower around the corner that is at least three times the size of mine.

"Where am I?" I ask Gertie even though I know exactly where I am. You would think Henry would have had to stay in a room like the rest of us for the duration of the Culling, not here.

"Henry's wing in the Presidential Quarters," she says with a tight smile, looking at me concerned.

I sit in the hot water until I feel like I'm going numb. Gertie hands me a sponge and although I don't want to move, I know I need to get the blood off.

As I wash Oliver's blood away, I think of the short time I have known him. I think of meeting him on the night of our first ball and our common bond over Marcia. I think of our group project and his humor and crazy, constant hand gestures. I think of his kindness when we overheard Sapphire and Jade talking about me in the hall. I think of how excited he was to see his parents when our team won the paintball competition. I think about the little conversations in the hallways or comments during class. How can someone so full of life be gone so quickly?

Later, after a second and third bath full of hot water since the first one turned reddish brown in color from all the blood, Gertie helps me out of the tub and gives me some pajamas. They are silky soft and the smoothest thing I have ever felt. I brush my teeth next because it seems like a normal thing to do and I need to do something or I'm going to go crazy. I'm not sure I can cry anymore. I'm beyond that point now. Now

I just feel numb. Not shock, but maybe just disbelief. This cannot be happening. This cannot be real.

I sit down on Henry's huge, soft couch and he puts some water, crackers, and cheese in front of me.

"Can you try to eat or at least drink something for me, beautiful?" he asks softly. He has slightly wet hair and a new shirt and jeans. He must have showered somewhere else while I was in the bath.

"Sure," I respond even though I'm not sure I can try. I take a sip of water anyway. It oddly feels good as the cool water goes down my throat.

Seeing my wet hair sticking to my skin, Henry asks Gertie, "Can you get me a hair dryer? My mom should have had one in the master bath somewhere."

"Sure. I'll get it," Gertie responds and leaves, returning in just a few minutes with the dryer and my hair brush both. She plugs it in and is about to start drying my hair, but he stops her.

"I can do it," he says smiling at her nicely. "Thanks for all your help today."

"Please have the guards get me if she needs anything at all." Gertie leaves again despite looking like she wants to stay as Henry turns the hair dryer on low.

"It can just air dry," I say dismissively over the hum of the dryer.

"I want to."

He turns it on and gently pulls my hair with the brush. Something about his kind gesture breaks my heart. It feels amazing. What man would think of drying a woman's hair? Henry would. He would think that wet hair would be uncomfortable and he would want to take care of me. He's always doing things like that.

Minutes later, with now dry hair, he turns off the dryer and leans in to give me a kiss on the cheek.

"How are you doing?" I ask him, realizing that he was there with me and is probably affected by what we saw also.

"I'm okay. Glad she was caught. It could've been even worse." He shakes his head, his disbelief mirroring my own. "And like you, I want answers. How did she have the code for the second floor? How did she know we were on to her?"

I sigh in silent agreement.

"Obviously our schedules for the day have been cancelled," he informs me. "It's really only just after lunch, but why don't you try to get some rest?"

I nod, realizing I'm absolutely fried but am not sure I will be able to sleep either.

He pulls back the covers on his bed and I crawl in. I didn't think it was possible to have a bed comfier than mine, but he does. I lay down and he pulls the curtains making the room darker.

"Anything else I can get you?" he asks softly.

"Can you just lay here with me so I can fall asleep?" I ask. Every time I want to close my eyes, all I can think about or see is the blood.

"Absolutely," he says. "There's no way I wasn't going to do that anyway."

Instead of getting under the covers with me, he lays on top of them and puts his arms around me. He smells fresh and manly and it helps distract my senses from the horror they have just been through.

I lay there as he runs his fingers up and down my arm and gently massages my neck and back. It takes a while, but I finally relax enough to drift off.

****

I wake to Lyncoln waking Henry and them walking around the corner where the big couch is to have a discussion. I feel guilty about Lyncoln finding us like that, but all things considered, I'm sure he understands.

I sit up and run a hand through my hair. I look at the clock. It's almost dinner time. I slept three hours.

Henry and Lyncoln walk back in the room as I take a drink of water.

"Beautiful, I need to go see my dad for a bit," he leans down and kisses me on the cheek.

"Okay," I respond softly, my voice sounding hoarse, probably from all the crying.

"Not to worry. Lyncoln is staying. We aren't going to leave you alone," he says affectionately and looks me over head to toe as if to make sure I am okay before he leaves. I would be annoyed with their thinking that I need a babysitter, but his concern for me is so genuine that I can't at all be mad. And I don't want to be alone either.

Lyncoln plops down his backpack and then sits at the end of the bed with his hand on my feet. Although the days' events are blurry, I vaguely remember him telling me he loved me. Well, kind-of, sort-of.

"Say something, sweetheart," he says with those deep blue-brown eyes boring into my soul. "I know asking you if you are okay is stupid, because you aren't."

"I just don't understand how it could've happened," I shake my head while looking at him.

"Me either. That's why I went back to DIA to hound Taggert, well until he kicked me out. There has to be a mole in the security detail. How else would someone know that she was going to be arrested and how else would she know the codes for the second floor even though she had never been down there before?" He shrugs.

"Great. So I finally think that we are safe since Isabella is locked up, but really we aren't." I sigh frustrated and play with my hands. How much more worrying can I take? I don't want to go through the hurt of having this happen to another one of my friends.

He pulls my chin up to meet his gaze. "I'll make sure you're safe, Regs." His velvety voice is full of emotion.

"And who'll make sure you're safe?"

He doesn't even hesitate. "I will." He smiles that confident arrogant smile that I both love and hate.

"Have you seen her?" I ask, knowing he knows who I'm talking about.

"Briefly. Through interrogation glass though, not face to face. I didn't dare enter the room with her. My parents taught me to not ever hit a woman, and she was making that difficult after what she did to Oliver, Austin, and Zeg. After we got her to drop false pretenses and her fake sweetness, she got really spiteful," he stops to shake his head and clench his jaw in anger. "I just don't understand how she can be full of so much hate. Seeing her today, it's kind of remarkable she didn't lash out before now. She was a ticking time bomb."

"Do we know anything about her background? Does she think the State was somehow unjust to her?" I ask feeling confused about it myself.

"Nothing. And the accusations she is throwing out are definitely not things we have done either. It's getting really confusing."

I think of the little I know about her background and randomly think of when we won the paintball competition. I thought I remembered her saying something about seeing her dad. "What about her family? When we won the paintball competition, didn't she get to see her family? Are they all drifters too?"

He nods. "Just her dad, she has no siblings that we know of, and she said her mom died when she was little. It looks like her dad here is actually her real dad though. He apparently went missing a few days after she saw him. We've watched their whole exchange looking for any hints of her tipping him off but found nothing. And I can't get over that they were here in Denver, both playing their parts for years. We are looking into how and when they even got here."

"Weird."

He's quiet a moment in agreement with me and then his demeanor gets softer as he says, "So after Dad died, I did anything I could to just keep doing something. Do you want to play cards? I can probably get you a movie? Do you want to help me work? Do you want to go for a walk? Do nothing? More sleep? What do you need?"

"Eventually, I want to go check on Attie, but I'm not sure I'm ready for that yet. How about work?" I shrug.

He nods. "Okay. Knox is with Attie and won't leave her side, by the way. They gave her some meds to help her sleep and she is out, for now. Do you want to help me go through files of Taggert's personnel or is that too close to home?" He looks at me concerned.

"I want to help. Especially if it helps to keep us all safe. And if I have clearance," I offer.

He just rolls his eyes and hands me a file out of his backpack.

"Rules are rules," I say, repeating what he first told Langly the morning after the Grady incident.

"As far as I'm concerned, you have clearance now. No rules broken. And you are probably better intuitively about this stuff than most of my men."

I give him a nod and that's that. We get to work.

An hour later, we are sitting side by side with files spread out over Henry's bed. We have a for sure "no" pile of people we trust or who were busy or with someone when Isabella stabbed Oliver. We have a "maybe" and we have a "most suspicious" pile. I don't know a lot of the people we are looking at, but Lyncoln explains each one and what they do. I understand that he cares more about his job than he lets on. These men are brothers to him, the only brothers he has.

Lyncoln picks up the file with the picture of Marisol's father and moves it to the "no" pile.

Seeing the look on my face, he feels the need to explain, "I don't like him either. He's a total ass. However, he was in the infirmary getting things ready for Isabella's arrest as the Head of Interrogations. He was with four other military men the whole time. Not to mention his extreme hate for all things drifter would be pretty hard to fake."

"I feel like the President has two enemies, the drifters and the Hadenfelts," I shake my head in disgust.

"You may be right about that." He stops to reach over and rub my shoulder. "She won't win, Regs. Don't worry."

A few files later we feel like we have narrowed down the possibilities to about a dozen or so people. I actually start to feel hopeful we are onto something when I reach down to pick up the next file and I see a red-brown color stuck under my thumbnail. The scene we found Oliver in comes rushing back to life. There was just *so much blood.*

"Regs?" Lyncoln asks, seeing the blood drain from my face.

I feel the tears, back with a vengeance. "It's my nails."

He picks up my hand and places it in his larger one, trying to figure out how I'm hurt.

"I scrubbed and scrubbed and scrubbed and I can't get the blood out." I choke on a sob.

"Babe." He picks me up and gently places me across his lap. He then pulls out a pocket knife and flicks it open. "Trust me?"

I nod.

He takes the pocket knife and uses it to go underneath my fingernails and get out all of the dried blood. One arm stays around me as he uses both hands to help get it out. It isn't perfect, but they look much better than before. The blood is finally almost all gone, except from my memory. And I'm sure it will remain there for a very long time.

"Thank you," I say sniffling when he is done.

"Anything, anytime," he whispers, giving me a kiss on the forehead.

****

Later that evening after he meets with a couple of military officials for what I assume is updates, Lyncoln takes me down to see Attie. We hug and cry only a small amount given the horror we have just experienced. She seems sad and angry, but is dealing with Oliver's death about as good as can be expected. I'm impressed with her grace all over again. I'm also impressed that Knox is taking care of her like a true gentleman. They will make a great presidential couple.

After a meal of hot roast beef with both Henry and Lyncoln, they inform me that I am staying the night in Henry's room. I try to argue my way out of it but am outnumbered. Much to my dismay, they both stay also. I sleep in Henry's massive bed while the two of them cozy up on Henry's couch just around the corner. Well, they would be cozy, but it's so huge that they both have plenty of room to sprawl out.

In the dark of the night, I have a hard time falling asleep. Even when I close my eyes, all I see is Oliver's blood. I can't believe he is really gone. I try to cling to all my good memories of him instead of the way we found him. Maybe they were right about leaving me alone in my own room for tonight.

I must have fallen asleep at some point because I wake up with a jolt and my heart pounding. I hope that I screamed only in my dreams and not out loud.

A lamp turns on, and Lyncoln is there at the end of the bed looking sleepy but concerned.

"I thought I heard you," he says, looking me over affectionately, making sure I'm okay.

Although I don't remember what I was dreaming about, it was obviously horrible and had to do with Oliver. I feel sweaty. And helpless. Seems about right.

"I'm sorry I woke you," I say embarrassed. "It was just a dream."

"Please don't be. Mom woke up screaming for weeks after Dad died. It's natural you would have nightmares after seeing what you saw," he says as he sits down, crossing one leg over the other over the edge of the bed and holding my hand while his thumb rubs circles over my palm.

"Did you?" I ask curiously, "Have nightmares?"

He shrugs and looks at our hands instead of at me. "I tried not to sleep at all. I was too afraid of falling asleep. Even today, if I hear the slightest noise, I'm immediately awake."

It breaks my heart to think that Lyncoln saw something so horrifying at such a young age. I understand more now than ever how hard that must have been for him. It's a miracle he's such a good man today. I'm sure his relationship with his mom is a big reason for that.

Tears burn my eyes and I squeeze his hand, "I'm sorry you had to go through that. Knowing how much pain I am in, I would do anything to have taken yours away. You were so young. And it was your dad."

He puts a hand around my neck with his thumb resting on my jaw and looks me in the eyes with that intense gaze of his. "I let it consume and absorb me for a while. It controlled every part of my life. Then I started to slowly get control back. Just so you know, Regs, the pain never really goes away. It lessens and fades and you think you are finally standing in the sunlight on the other side of it, and then one day it will just kick your knees out from under you and hit you all over again." He shakes his head. "When Dad was ripped out of my life I had a long battle with grief. Grief is anything but kind. You, too, have a long road ahead and I'm here. Even when you pick Henry, I'm still here."

I reach in and give him a quick kiss on the cheek before wrapping my arms around him, not knowing how to form words to express what I feel.

Chapter 22

"It may seem insensitive for you to be sworn in because of the event of Oliver's death, but if you will pause and think about the State for a moment..." Professor Bennett has told the rest of the Culling candidates about the details of yesterday and has just begun explaining to us that we are to keep it a secret and will be sworn in to do so. "If the general population knew that we were being attacked, panic would ensue. Until we know more, and until we know how to act, this needs to be kept quiet, on a need to know basis."

I hear some murmurs of disagreement to his statement. Marisol is sobbing uncontrollably, putting on another show. She isn't the only one crying. Attie is trying her best not to, but I can tell she is struggling. Elizabeth looks even more beautiful as she silently cries and Maverick consoles her. Morgan is wiping at her tears. I don't have any more tears to cry, so I just sit there numb to the conversations going on around me. Henry has his arm on the back of my chair in support and Lyncoln is somewhere in the back.

"It also further protects your families," Taggert chimes in. "The less they know, the safer they are. The other townships are safe right now. We don't want to jeopardize that in any way, shape, or form."

"We aren't at all saying you can't talk about it. But if you need to talk about it with someone, it must be the people within this room, even one of us," Dougall says in a moment of kindness before switching to her typical cold self. "Letting this information out to the public will not only be grounds for dismissal, but even harsher punishments. Our country's safety is at risk here."

What they are telling us makes sense even though they are also threatening us into doing their bidding. I think of Oliver's last words and his want for me to tell his mom he loved her. What about his family? Don't they deserve to know that he died a hero? When his actions may have prevented something even more tragic? It feels like yesterday he was giddily talking about lunch with his parents when they were flown in as our prize for winning the paintball competition.

In a moment of silence, I gather my courage and decide to find my voice. "His mom. What about her?"

I'm surprised to hear that my voice doesn't falter. I think of the way Oliver mentioned his mom and the softness in his eyes as he was coughing up blood and about to die. Henry squeezes my shoulder and I think it's the only thing keeping me together.

Professor Bennett drops his head in shame. "We will have to tell her it was an accident. A training accident."

"Excuse me?" My temper flares to life as my eyebrows raise in astonishment.

"It's the only way, Ms. Scott," Taggert says sympathetically.

I stand, finding a strength I didn't know I had. "No. It isn't. His actions saved all of us. If he wouldn't have stepped forward and told us it was Isabella, it could have been any one of us in that coffin, including you," I spit the words towards Taggert. "His mother deserves to know he died bringing down an enemy or at least helping others. He died a hero. Maybe if she knew that, she could make some sense out of his death. Don't tell me that's the only way. Find another way."

With that, before I really freak out and lose my temper even more, I storm out of the room and down the hallway. Sarge is on my heels and looks concerned. I manage to get into the elevator before Henry or Lyncoln catch up. I just need a moment alone.

In the elevator, I lose it when Sarge puts an arm around me and says, "I heard what you said back there and I couldn't be prouder of you if you were my own daughter."

****

I ask for Sarge to bring me lunch while I get ready. I already put my hand on the bible yesterday and got sworn in, thus sealing Oliver's secret and chivalry among other things. Since the rest of the world will never know Oliver died a hero, they decided to hold a funeral for him here in Denver with just the Culling candidates and professors before taking his body home to his family. It will be our way to say goodbye. Elle asked me if I would say a few words and I told her I would. I have no idea what to say. Nothing I can say will make this situation better.

Frank and Gertie are trying to be cheerful and not mention the seriousness of a funeral, but they both seem worried about me. I wear a long sleeved black dress. It is tighter fitting and all solid black except for the spot on the back from my bra line up, which is lace. I wear my hair up in a bun and Frank applies light makeup. I have seen movies from before Trident. I look exactly how they looked at funerals, like someone in mourning.

I dread the time to leave as the clock ticks on, and yet all too soon it is time to go. Henry meets me at my door and we go down hand in hand. We enter the ballroom, which has been transformed with white flowers and chairs for the funeral. The lighting of the room is dim and sad and matches the emotions of the event. Although the drapes of the windows are pulled open so we can see out, it is still cloudy outside and dreary. At the end of the room there lays a casket beside a picture of a smiling Oliver.

Is Oliver's body really in there? I don't know. I don't even care. He's gone. All life has drained from his body. I saw it happen with my own eyes. Everything that makes Oliver, Oliver, is now gone.

We find a spot by Maverick and Elizabeth. I'm about to ask if we need to save a spot for Lyncoln when Henry shakes his head as he places his arm around me.

"He doesn't do funerals," he says as if reading my mind and I nod in understanding. It must bring back a flood of emotions for Lyncoln, forcing him to relive the hours after the horrifying way his father died.

"I'm sure you don't '*do*' them either. Are you doing okay?" I ask, reaching across Henry's lap to squeeze his hand not already around me. This is probably bringing back all sorts of memories of his mom's grandiose funeral. Which was probably also in this room.

He nods grimly. "I'm good. I had to decline doing a speech though. I did one for Mom's and can't bring myself to do it again."

I smile understanding, knowing that today is going to be hard on the both of us. "Well afterwards if you need to go for a walk, or talk, or just need someone to sit there in silence with you, let me know, okay?"

He looks at me, emerald eyes full of emotion, a stark contrast to his black suit and tie. "I will. Thank you, Reagan. And right back at you."

He gives my hand a squeeze and I nod.

The funeral begins with the typical funeral readings and a violin player playing a beautiful song. Before I have time to figure out what I'm going to say, the candidates' speeches are starting. Maverick gives a short but meaningful speech. Marisol cries and blubbers about what a great person Oliver was and how much she liked him. Her words are beautiful and would be quite moving, except I know she never even gave him the time of day. As Trent starts speaking, I realize it's my turn next and I still have no idea what I'm going to say.

"Do you want me to go up there with you?" Henry asks, squeezing my hand as if trying to channel me more confidence. I know he doesn't want to be up there at all, so the fact that he's offered to do it anyway means a lot to me. He would sacrifice his own discomfort and battle with his own demons in order to be there for me.

"No. Thank you, but I think I have to do this alone." I smile at him affectionately. He has given me space when I needed it and held me when I needed it. Henry is a great partner even through this nightmare.

As Trent finishes, I walk to the stage and stand at the front of the room, taking out my notecard and placing it on the podium before me. The notecard is blank but will give me something to look at if I stumble or need a break. I take a deep breath. Here goes nothing.

"When I first met Oliver, I was genuinely surprised at how kind and funny he was," I begin. "If there is one word to describe Oliver, it is joyful. He was always making a joke or making someone laugh without even meaning to. He also had a kind heart and would be there if you ever needed him." I stop a moment, take a shaky breath, and look around the room. I spot Lyncoln leaning against the wall beside the door, also in a black suit and tie. He looks me straight in the eyes and I look back at him, trying to use his affectionate gaze as fuel to get me through this in one piece.

I take a deep breath, look at my notecard, and keep going. "That being said, now when I think of Oliver, I struggle not to remember the tragic manner in which he died and that he died saving us all. How can someone so vibrant and full of joy be gone? Could anything have been done to prevent his death? Would I still be here today if it weren't for him?" I breathe out a deep breath again, trying not to cry. "But this is what I am learning of grief...grief demands answers to unwarranted questions. It is completely relentless and consuming...and cruel."

I stop and look Lyncoln dead in the eyes. His eyes are full of emotion and although he isn't crying, he looks like he could, which is shocking because he always, always keeps his emotions in check. I almost lose it, but take a steadying breath instead. I feel the tears pooling in my eyes but force them to not spill over, blinking forcefully a few times to make sure they don't.

"The thing is though, if Oliver were here, he wouldn't want any of that. He would tell a joke to try to make it better, or use one of his thousands of hilarious hand gestures." I pause as people softly chuckle and smile as they remember. "So in order to honor Oliver as we battle being completely absorbed by our grief, instead of remembering him by the manner in which he died, we must remember him by the manner in which he lived." I pause again as tears threaten to spill over. I look at Henry who is also teary eyed. He waves to me with two fingers like when we met. His gesture wills me to have the strength to continue and finish.

"Because he lived. He *really* lived." I almost lose it again, but keep it together somehow when I look at the blank notecard. "We need to honor him for the courageous, vibrant, and animated way he lived. Anything less than that would be an insult to his legacy. So please join me in a round of applause. To Oliver. May we follow his example and live our lives joyfully and selflessly. Well done, Oliver. We will miss you." As I finish, a lone tear escapes and falls down my cheek. I turn towards his casket and start clapping.

Henry is the first to stand as he claps and the rest of the room joins. We clap for a while in appreciation for Oliver and the life he lived. With the claps still going, I turn to leave the podium and none other than the President himself is there clapping.

I shake his hand, smile, and turn to go back to my seat. Everyone else sits back down for the next speech, his.

The President grabs my arm gently. "Here, Ms. Scott. You forgot your notecard." He says it softly and then his eyebrows furrow in confusion as he flips it over and then back over.

I take it from him anyway. "Thank you."

He raises his eyebrows. "That was straight from the hip?" He shakes his head, smiling at me kindly, and then turns to the podium and begins speaking. He talks about loss and the honor Oliver died with.

I listen but just feel relieved and glad to be back in my seat. Henry's arm around my shoulder warms me. He rests his head against mine for a minute and I know what he's thinking, that we've almost made it through this thing.

"A famous quote reads, 'It's not the years in your life that count, but the life in your years,' " President Maxwell finishes. "If that were the case with Oliver, he lived a short but full life."

Chapter 23

The next day we are to be busy back at it with simulations, practice at the range, and Dougall starting our training for the live interviews for the nation. I am so numb from losing Oliver that I don't even realize that I have made the final eight couples until October brings it up that morning at breakfast. I came down early making a point to chat with her since I wasn't doing much sleeping anyway. I feel like I keep getting close to people and then they leave…or worse. October suspects she is going home soon, so I'm trying to enjoy the time I do have left with this quirky and genius girl.

"Wow. I had no idea," I say surprised when October reminds me about the promotions.

I got this far. I got my parents more influence and two promotions. I know this will mean the world to them. Now they will be reevaluated for leadership positions. I want to make it to the final four, not just so I can have the opportunity to stay in Denver with the men in my life, but I also want to make it farther for me. Can I do this? Do I have what it takes? After the past few days, I'm not so sure. But then I remember Oliver telling me to win.

I have to give it all I've got.

"I bet they'll wait a week and then make the next cut." October shrugs. "I don't think they would send anyone home right after all this.

And plus, whoever they send home now will have to go through the debriefing process."

"I hope no more cuts are made for a while." The lunch room now has only one long table instead of three. Marisol, Sapphire, Christopher, and Hugh sit at the opposite end of the table as I do. Haley, Bronson, Morgan, and Trent usually pose as the barrier between them and us, mostly because both couples are good at breaking the tension with a quick joke or inappropriate comment. No one can be angry or mad especially in the presence of Trent.

"Well whenever I go, know that I won't be mad," October smiles.

"I bet you are ready to see Lucas." I never could fathom the need to be around someone so often before coming here. I thought it was needy or clingy that girls would talk about missing their boyfriends. Now that I have a "boyfriend", or two, I see why all these girls were so enamored. I would definitely miss Henry or Lyncoln if they were gone.

"I am," she smiles shyly. "And it has been hard, but I appreciate him more because of it. I just want to get back to normal although I'm not sure what normal is now. I will constantly be thinking about Denver and the drifters and what is going on. It's hard to play dumb when you've been dealt the perfect hand. I don't know how to go back to just teaching now."

Knowing that October's mind never stops, I understand what she means. If I were to go home today, I would constantly be in fear for my family. I'm not sure it's even fair to keep the rest of the country in the dark. I know the powers to be think they are keeping everyone safe, but wouldn't everyone feel more united if they knew? And is October supposed to keep this secret from Lucas? Even when they are married? Is that fair to her?

October looks around suspiciously before lowering her voice, "So, have you decided what you are going to do yet? I'm supposed to find out for Marisol. Not to worry, I won't tell her anything. Didn't tell her you had a deadline either." She smirks and grins a sly smile that looks almost evil.

"Remind me to stay on your good side." I stop to laugh. "And no. I haven't." I pause again, this time to think. "Either way I will be judged. Either people will think I chose Henry because of who he is or they'll think I chose Lyncoln because he is essentially a military star."

"Want some advice?" she asks kindly.

"Absolutely," I sigh.

"Don't pick who is best for the country, because either of them are fine choices. Don't pick who is best for winning, because it isn't all about winning. Pick who you want to pick. Think about meeting them back home in Omaha, not in this crazy situation. Who would you pick if you just randomly met them? No sims, no tests, no important parents or careers, no nothing. Blur it all out. It's just you and this person and no one else on Earth. Who do you want there? Who do you want to walk down that aisle towards?"

"My problem is that my head and my gut aren't agreeing." I shake my head while thinking about what she said, which may be the most romantic and unpractical thing October has ever said in her life.

"Take it from me, who values intelligence over everything else, the brain is your fear mechanism whereas your heart is the gateway to your soul. Ignore all the details and just go with your heart."

****

After breakfast, we are informed we will be starting our longer sims. Starting today they will be two-hours long, tomorrow doubling to four hours, and then double again to our big eight-hour sim test. An eight-hour sim? Come on. That's gunna suck.

On a whim, Elizabeth, Attie, October, and I decide to go together for a two-hour sim.

"All girls?" Bennett looks at us almost scolding, settling his eyes on me as if I'm to blame.

"Yeah." I shrug. I don't think I've been his favorite person as of late.

"You realize without your significant other, your partner, your chances of termination are greatly increased? And this does go towards your total rank?" he asks, staring at us all seriously.

"Actually, Professor Bennett, as long as it's someone you trust, we should be fine. Why not let us and just see what happens?" October corrects him and then tries to persuade him.

He finally gives in. Two hours later, we all walk away victorious. Not even meaning to, we kind of made a statement. We are all women and we could defend ourselves just fine. I feel oddly invigorated and know that Oliver would salute us if he were here. Having had such a great time together, we decide to get together tonight for a girls night. Who knows how long we have with each other anyway.

At dinner that evening, Henry gives me a kiss on the cheek as he sits down beside me. He seems tired and worried. I almost think about canceling girls' night right then and there, but can't bring myself to do it. I grab his hand and give it a squeeze under the table. I have no idea how I would've gotten through the last 72 hours without him.

"Hey, I heard you had an all-girls sim." He smiles, dimples out.

"Ummm, yeah, we did! And we kicked--what's the word again, Knox?" Attie asks.

"Tukis." Knox rolls his eyes but smiles.

"Tukis," Attie says in confidence. "Knox tells me it is a more sophisticated word for butt."

October just shakes her head. "Good luck with that one," she smiles to Knox while pointing to Attie then she turns to point to Henry. "You. We are all getting together tonight for a girls' night, so don't think you get to steal her," she points at me, "from us."

"Did I just hear the words, 'girls' night'?" Lyncoln asks, setting his tray down and sitting on the other side of me.

"You did. But it isn't all the girls so do try to contain yourself. We all know you have an issue with being gossipy," October jokes. Having never seen her call someone out or be so jovial, I almost spit out the tea I was taking a drink of. Lyncoln shakes his head amused and pats me on the back as I cough.

"Not again," Maverick shakes his head. "This girl can't hang."

Elizabeth is giggling away and I'm not sure if it is at what October said, or at my choking on my tea, or both.

"Are you talking about me or Reagan?" she asks as she giggles harder.

"Yes," Maverick responds and we all laugh. Laughter feels oddly welcomed after Oliver's death. I know it is what he would have wanted.

It's times like these that this doesn't even seem like a competition and I don't want it to come to an end. Not just because I have to make a decision between Henry and Lyncoln soon, but because I will miss all of them. I think of Marcia, Vanessa, and even Renae. I spend all this time with these people and then just never get to see them again? They aren't just friends. If there is anything that Oliver's death has taught me, it's that I care for these people like family.

****

After making fun of people and laughing for hours, the girl talk takes a serious turn. October tells the others she was spying and that Marisol has a lot of power and to look out. We ask about each other's love lives. Naturally, I don't feel like chipping in and they call me on it.

"So Reagan?" Attie asks kindly. "Do you want to talk about it?"

"Yes and no. I have to make a decision soon. I just have never been *that* girl before, that girl that gets the boys, or even a half a second of their attention, and yet here I am trying to decide between two men who are..." I shrug not even knowing how to describe the both of them.

"I'm sorry," Elizabeth offers sympathetically. Since she had seven or eight suitors that first night, she might understand what I'm feeling.

"Me too," Attie sympathizes and pauses before shouting, "Group hug!" She launches herself at me while Elizabeth hugs me from the other side and October, in true October fashion, just stands there with her eyebrows up.

"Do you know what you are going to do yet?" Elizabeth asks after they finally release me.

I sigh. "I think so. And that's the problem. It's going to suck and it's going to hurt."

****

The next day for our four-hour sim, Bennett tells me I need to do two, one with Henry in the morning and one with Lyncoln after dinner, lasting probably until about midnight. Our schedules are different now having finished up our self-defense class. We go to sims when we are scheduled. We go to Dougall when we can and when we aren't in sims. Sometimes we go alone, sometimes there is a group. Sometimes Dougall is at DIA and sometimes at Mile High. And when we aren't doing either of those things, we are to be at the range doing drills that they set up for us, although by this point most of us have mastered shooting a gun.

The sim with Henry goes well and I try not to step into any line of fire that I don't need to. The thing with these long sims is that it adds an element of survival. You get away and must find a fake hole or cave or something, use whatever the sim gives you, to lay low as you go into hiding. Then you wait. And they will find you. They always do in a sim. The bad news is, since you are hiding, you can't even talk to one another. Or shouldn't. Normally four hours of being with Henry would sound amazing, but since we can't talk, it's rather boring. We sit on the mouth of a fake cave, one at each corner with guns drawn and pluck off the enemy as they come from below us. In the end, I'm not terminated but do sustain an injury to the arm. I will be docked for that.

After lunch, we both have a short break and Henry comes to hang out with me in my room. It feels good to finally be able to talk to him. Four hours of keeping my mouth shut and wearing those super unattractive glasses weren't fun. I don't know how I didn't fall asleep. Probably the faces Henry kept making at me to entertain me.

"I was just sure it was going to be a zombie sim this time," Henry jokes, one arm around the back of the couch behind us as he sits facing me.

I shake my head. "You and zombies."

"Just saying. It's a good way to go, way better than Trident. I could survive forever on my own, or like to pretend I could. Probably because I was never allowed to be on my own growing up." He smiles charmingly and adds, "Plus, I'm a really good shot."

"That you are." I've seen him in the practice range and sims. I know he's right. He and Lyncoln always have competitions that often end in a tie because neither one of them miss the bullseye. *Showoffs.*

I think about what he said and realize that although he wasn't ever left alone, he would have no problem surviving on his own. I don't doubt it for a second. It makes me wonder what Henry would be like if he wasn't raised so privileged. I have no doubt he would still be ranked at the top in the Culling, but what would he do if his life wasn't submerged in politics? Would he seem less perfect? Somehow I doubt it. From day one, I have never liked Henry for his status. I have always been attracted to his personality instead.

"What would you do, if there were no politics and no Culling? I mean, what if we had met somewhere else? What would you want to do if you could do anything you wanted?" I ask.

"Besides for writing insanely awesome zombie literature?" he asks with a bounce of his eyebrows and I know he is only half joking.

"Yes. Besides zombie literature." I roll my eyes with a smile.

He pauses for a moment. "If we are talking pre-Trident, I probably would have wanted to be a teacher or a coach of some sort. Post-trident, I think I would prefer to be a military training instructor. Why? What would you do?"

I shrug with both shoulders and a gesture for extra emphasis. "I don't really know. I listen to Marcia talk about the advances Seattle is making and I'm fascinated and think I would work in water. I listen to Attie talk about how lacking other townships are in their medical advances and I think that I would want to help with the poor helpless babies. I guess, when it comes down to it, I just want to somehow help people and fix things. I don't know what job that is."

"Well, I think you are headed in the right direction." He smiles a huge grin, dimples bouncing, and squeezes my hand with the hand not around the couch.

"So are you. You could essentially run the military."

"Yeah…but I would want to do more than that. I'm talking about the day to day training, teaching them how to shoot, how to kill, the physical demands, the mental toughness, and the camaraderie of it all. Lyncoln and I went into training as strangers and came out brothers. *That* is what I want to be a part of." His face gets so animated when he's talking about it that I can tell it's something he really cares about.

I wonder if that's what he would do if he doesn't get the presidency. I try not to think about Henry as the president or Henry not as the president. For the most part, I just like to think of Henry as my boyfriend. I'm beginning to see that it's very selfish of me to take only that part of him into consideration. He is so much more.

****

After another completely boring interview session with Dougall and dinner with the rest of the gang, Lyncoln and I head back over to DIA for my second four-hour sim. The good news is I won't have another sim for at least another two days while everyone finishes up theirs.

"You are going to have to kick me to make sure I don't fall asleep," I joke on the ride back to DIA.

He half-smiles, "Past your bedtime, sweetheart?"

I nod two slow nods and yawn. He almost laughs.

"You are a superhuman. Not all of us can roll on three or four hours of sleep," I offer.

"Not all of us can shoot a turkey either," he winks.

"If I recall correctly, we both shot the sim turkey." I laugh and try to lightly punch him, which he of course easily deflects.

"Nope. I only remember my bullet. Which, of course, hit it."

"Of course," I shake my head mocking him. Typical Lyncoln, oozing confidence with every word.

We ride in silence for a while, but it doesn't feel awkward. Lyncoln may be dark and intense and intimidating to most people, but if you really get to know him, he isn't scary at all. Except scary attractive maybe. Scary muscular. Scarily good at the art of the smooch.

I feel my chin turned toward him as he asks, "What were you thinking of just then?"

I blush and he smiles a huge grin as he looks me in the eyes affectionately. "Okay, then."

"I was thinking about how many push-ups you must have done in order to get your neck like that?" I point to it. "Seriously, what is it with you Denver boys? You are all huge! But your neck specifically…" I shake my head unable to come up with an accurate descriptor.

"We have to start weight lifting and physical training sooner than the rest of the bunch. That's all. It isn't really a big deal." He shrugs.

"Tell that to your biceps," I say, poking them and making him grin. I think if he could blush, he might have. "How are your mom and Wyatt?" I ask after a few seconds, liking the playful Lyncoln beside me.

"They're good. I saw mom the other day on her way to a meeting. She says Wyatt asks about you often. You left quite the impression." He shakes his head. "He keeps blabbering on about some game you are going to teach him."

"Really? I did?" I ask kind of surprised. Since he's just a child, I was sure he had moved on to something more interesting. He seems like the type of kid that barely focuses on anything for longer than a few minutes.

"You always do. He told the kids at school the next madam president was going to teach them all a new way to play kickball." He smirks.

"I would do that even if I wasn't Madam President," I say quietly, looking down at my hands.

Am I really going to be the next Madam President? Am I really going to start going after it? What is holding me back? This decision looming over my head?

"I know you would," he says softly and takes my hand in reassurance.

I sigh in contentment and look back out the window.

"Regs," he interrupts the silence shortly after.

"Lync," I smile softly, wondering what he is about to say because he seems uncomfortable. Not his usual confident self.

"Your speech at Oliver's funeral was beautiful. I wish someone would have said something like that for my dad. You'll make a great madam president," he says in a rare moment of shyness and squeezes my hand he's still holding.

I swallow a lump that is apparently lodged in my throat and manage to get out, "Thanks."

"And yes, I think it'll be you. I can see you are doubting yourself after this last week." He rubs his thumb along my hand.

"Thank you." I sigh. I look back out the window, lost in my thoughts, reminding myself that the deadline is inching closer day by day. One of these mornings I will wake up and it will be here.

What on earth am I going to do?

****

During our sim, much like the one with Henry, we are in a wooded area and rather than head for a cave of sorts, Lyncoln finds some brush and a hidden area low to the ground in a spot in the corner of the sim that allows us to see who will be coming at us. The good news is, I can relax and just sit there while we wait and not have to worry about being on the lookout so much. The bad news is that there isn't much room and our bodies are shoulder to shoulder. Maybe that's the good news actually, I'm not sure.

It's a good thing the shrubbery we hide in isn't real, or the twigs would be stabbing into us as we take our positions sitting down. I sit cross legged with my gun in my lap. He sits with a knee pulled in and his left arm lazily draped across the knee to help stabilize his gun which he holds in the other hand. If someone could see us without the sim on, we would look hilarious just sitting on the ground in the corner.

"Isn't being lower to the ground not as safe?" I whisper, wondering what his strategy is here. Lyncoln always has a strategy.

"Yes," Lyncoln responds, looking at me intensely. Although it is almost 2000 hours and all but dark outside, the sun is just beginning to set in our sim.

"So why are we doing it then?" I ask.

"Because everyone else will choose high ground and the cave. I want to know what the sim will do if we don't do what is expected of us," he whispers as if the bad guys were real and could hear us. He always takes the sims super seriously, trained assassin that he is.

I shrug. "Okay." I trust his judgment. If this is what he wants to do, I'll do it.

"Let's just hope we don't get attacked by an army of turkeys down here," he jokes and I stifle a laugh.

After a while, I feel myself start to fall asleep. After jerking once or twice as my body tries to nod off, I try holding my gun but it feels way too heavy. I hold onto my gun in my left hand and wrap my arm around Lyncoln's huge bicep instead.

"One hour down, babe," he whispers affectionately.

The darker our sim gets, the harder it is for me to stay awake. Lyncoln puts his hand on mine and helps keep me awake by squeezing or rubbing circles on my hand. The time drags on and I am getting sleepier by the second. I grab Lyncoln's arm and turn it palm up. I trace along the veins in his palm first, then up his forearm where he has a scar, and then up his bicep. I'm not even paying attention to the fact that what I am doing is affecting him; I'm just exploring the veins on his glorious body with curiosity, wondering if his body has been through as many bang-ups as his soul. What happened to him? His scar on his forearm reminds me of the scar on his abdomen I saw when he was shirtless.

He catches his breath once and I can almost feel his heart pounding beside me. I turn to look at him and he has his fiery gaze on me. I hear my own breath hitch and I'm just sure he will lean in to kiss me. The air seems to sizzle around us.

"Not here, Regs. Not here. You're killin' me," he whispers. He rests his head on mine for a second and then continues listening and looking out the small holes in the fake shrubbery.

I quickly do the same, realizing where we are and what we are supposed to be doing though I do feel a bit rejected. Eventually, I hear some movement but don't see anyone. After what feels like an eternity, the sim fades and we are back at DIA. They didn't find us. Wasn't that the point?

"Well, done," Professor Bennett says cheerfully with a clap as we come out of the sim. "Interesting choice of the shrubs."

"Pretty boring if you ask me." Lyncoln shrugs.

"Mr. Reed, will you go check in with Taggert for the evening report while I speak with Ms. Scott for a moment before you leave?" he asks.

Lyncoln nods saying, "Yes, sir," and swiftly walks away. I'm left wondering who really has the higher rank between the two of them. Although Lyncoln said "sir", I feel like it was more out of respect than necessity.

"Ms. Scott, have a seat will you?" He gestures to the couch in the viewing room of the sims.

"Sure," I say with a shrug as he hands me a cold bottle of water.

"These particular sims weren't about terminating the enemy this time, my dear," he starts.

I twist the bottle around in my hands feeling the sweaty plastic. "They weren't?" I feel confused and tired. I have never wanted to sleep in my bed more than I do right now. Sims are exhausting. And this one was a total waste of time.

"No. They were about putting aside your attraction and sexual tension to see if you would listen and be prepared or if you would be so enthralled with one another that you would let the enemy sneak up on you in the heat of the moment," he says, looking at me carefully.

"Okay?" I'm wondering what he's getting at. I passed both times then, right?

"I just thought you should find it interesting you came closer to losing focus with Lyncoln today than with Henry. You can blame tonight on that you're tired and it's dark, but time and time again, you are physically drawn to Lyncoln. And in times of crises, you are drawn to one another like some sort of magnetic pull." He smiles warmly then sits down.

I start to panic, concerned this conversation is heading in the direction of my impending deadline, when he adds, "Look. All I'm saying is that you can't ignore that connection, which is what I tried to point out after your simulation with the turkey. You are such a smart and logical girl that I know you would push the physical part of it away thinking it doesn't matter. Take it from a happily married man, the physical part matters too. I'm not saying you aren't attracted to Henry. I'm not saying you shouldn't pick him. What I am saying is you and Lyncoln have a rare but powerful attraction to one another. Even when both of your brains are telling you to stay away from one another this entire time, your bodies have a hard time listening. As a spectator just along for the ride, I just wanted to make sure you realized all that. As I see you struggling with this decision, you remind me of my own daughter and I just wanted to try to help."

I look down at my hands in embarrassment and blush. For some reason what he is telling me is making me feel like I have cheated on Henry, and in a way, I guess I have. I'm also weirded out that he has alluded to the fact they have been watching me with each of them. *Awkward.*

"Thank you. I just don't know exactly how to handle what you've said," I respond honestly.

"Just take it into consideration," he says as he pats my shoulder twice in comfort.

Bennett then walks me down to the vehicle waiting to take us back to Mile High. It is a quiet and awkward few minutes so I keep fiddling with the water bottle in my hands. When we get downstairs, I see Lyncoln is already ready to go.

Before Sarge opens the door to the SUV and while Lyncoln walks around the vehicle to the other side, Bennett says quietly, "You don't really have a wrong choice here, Reagan, I hope you see that. I'm just hoping to point out that you can be happy, too. Don't over think it and make it harder than it has to be."

As we get in and settled, Lyncoln picks up on my dampened mood. "Everything alright?" he asks and reaches for my hand, validating what Bennett just pointed out. I'm not sure if it makes me feel better or worse.

"Yeah," I respond quietly.

"Did he tell you the real reason for our sim?"

"You knew?" I ask astonished. Why didn't he tell me? I made a pass at him in there and he didn't warn me. It makes me want to grab my hand back.

"No. I mean, yeah, I figured it out." He squeezes my hand. "Why would they have a sim where we do nothing? They wouldn't. They wanted to see if we would behave." He shrugs.

"Why couldn't I figure that out?" I'm disappointed in myself. And I'm glad these were closed sims. Normally we can watch each other, but not for this set of sims. I am relieved neither Henry nor Lyncoln know how I handled the others' sim, especially since Lyncoln knows the reason. And now he probably knows I feel guilty, but he doesn't know why or how I handled each one.

"You probably could've figured it out if you would've had the chance. Taggert had two things to say to me and then I was waiting for you." He shrugs.

"You are very perceptive, have I ever told you that?" I say honestly.

He just smirks and then looks at me playfully. "Had I known that was the real purpose of the sim, I would have kissed you senseless at the beginning and saved us both four hours. At least then we maybe could've shot something."

I can't help but smile knowing that he would have done just that. Although I keep holding his hand, I'm quiet the rest of the way back to Mile High. When we get there, Lyncoln walks me up to my room like he usually does, knowing that I'm still mulling over whatever Professor Bennett said to me. As I take off my boots in my room, he asks me for the third time if I am okay as he stands at his usual spot, leaning against the wall by my bathroom and kitchen.

"Yes." I look him in the eyes, which I have been avoiding until now.

"Do you want to talk about it?" he asks. I can see his genuine concern there.

"No."

All of a sudden, I am hit with the urge to kiss him. Really kiss him, like the night of the attack when I thought he might be dead. Is what Bennett said true? If I shut off my mind and just give in, what would it be like? Would it be like that every time?

"Do you just want me to go?"

"No."

Before I can over think it, I quickly go towards him. I slow down once I get to him, becoming shyer. I place my hand on his chest while he puts a hand on my waist like he usually does. I feel his heart beat under my sweaty hand. I grab onto his shirt and lean in for the kiss. It starts soft and caring then gets more urgent. I shut my mind off and just listen to my body.

Don't think. Just feel.

Minutes later, I feel a coldness as he pulls away abruptly. I open my eyes to see that I'm once again against the wall and vaguely remember him moving me there. We are both breathing heavily and his eyes are...*sensuous*. Downright sensuous. Somehow my hands have traveled up to his hair, which is looking a little messy.

We just breathe heavily for a moment while we look at one another and he takes a step back.

I grin. "Why always the wall?"

"It's either that or the bed and that seems a bit inappropriate," he says out of breath and then clenches his jaw adding, "Tell me that wasn't goodbye?"

I can clearly see the pain he is trying and failing to mask. I take a deep breath and slowly smile, shaking my head. "I have no idea what that was, but no, I don't think that was goodbye."

He crashes into me again and there is more kissing. Though he is a man of few words, I know that he is telling me how much he cares, that he doesn't want to lose me. His hands roam up my arms and down over my back, resting on my lower back as he pulls me even closer.

He pulls away suddenly and we are both breathing heavy again.

"I'm leaving." He shakes his head.

"Okay..." I say with a deep breath and wonder if I did something wrong. Other than the obvious.

"Before we get out of control," he adds, trying not to smile as he stares me down.

I blush and start to feel bad for what just happened. For the first time in my life I wonder what it would be like to go that far, cross that line. I have always kind of thought of sex and the whole reproducing thing as a chore since having children is required by law and all, but now I'm thinking it might not be so bad after all. Not that I am ready to find out or anything.

Yikes. Double yikes. Yikes on yikes.

He reaches for my hand in reassurance. "I don't mean that, Reagan. You aren't the kind of girl that sleeps around. I know that and respect that. More than you know. We wouldn't do that unless we were married. You don't even have to worry about it with me. We won't be crossing *that* line any time soon. I just meant I didn't want to get carried away. You aren't mine to get carried away with."

Other than feeling a huge, drowning dose of guilt, his words both excite me and pain me, and I wonder what it would be like to be Lyncoln's wife. He takes my face in both of his hands and gives me one last kiss on the forehead and then quickly leaves.

I change into my pajamas although the thought of staying in my gear is intriguing now that I smell like Lyncoln. By the time my head hits the pillow, I know what a horrible mistake I've made. I know now, without a doubt, that I love two different men. When exactly did that happen?

And even worse, if I turn off my brain like Bennett said and let them have an equal chance, who will I choose? No one else is going to make this decision for me. It's one I have to make for myself.

Chapter 24

The next morning while others begin their sims, Lyncoln, Henry, and I are pulled into a room with Attie, Knox, Taggert, and Bennett. I feel awkward around Bennett because of our conversation the night before, but try to put on a good face. Too bad I can never conceal my emotions very well. I know I am doing a poor job of it because Lyncoln's hand finds its way to my knee under the table, which is what he always does when he knows I'm struggling with some sort of inner demon.

"So two things today," Taggert begins with an air of seriousness. "The first of which is that you will be given confidential information we have on the leaders of the drifters. You will know their faces, their names, and some of the evil things they have been up to. We want you to know as much as you can about these people."

He pauses and then continues, "The second of which is that you will begin to sit in on the interrogations of the drifters we have in custody starting tomorrow."

I feel the blood drain from my face as Lyncoln gives my knee a squeeze. By interrogations, he really means torture. I am going to "sit in" on torture? If they are so worried about me being ladylike, is that really ladylike at all? Then I think of Isabella and have to refrain from running to vomit in the trash can. I don't want to see her face. Ever.

"And what exactly will that entail?" Attie asks nervously. I smile at her, appreciative for her asking so I didn't have to. We are both dealing with Oliver's death and Isabella's betrayal the best way we know how, but that doesn't mean it's always pretty. And seeing his murderer doesn't seem like the best way to help us with that grief either.

"You might as well see it all. In order to lead our country, you need to know all that goes on to keep it safe. The good, the bad, and the downright ugly," Taggert says ominously. "But we will, of course, debrief afterwards."

Great. Sounds lovely.

Henry and Lyncoln look equally as excited as I do and I wonder what of all this they already know or have seen and what will be new to them.

Bennett then starts a slideshow on some of the drifters. I look at picture after picture. You would think since we blame the spread of Trident on North Korea, more of them would look like they came from there. But less than half of them look like they have any sort of Asian heritage. They have a variety of skin color combinations just as we do. I begin to wonder what made these normal, every-day-looking people so angry they would feel it necessary to take lives in the post-Trident era. Has there not been enough death for them? Will they take down what is left of the United States' government at the cost of the entire human race?

We take a quiz on the major drifter leaders at the end of the afternoon and Attie, Knox and I are all exhausted from trying to memorize this new information. Lyncoln and Henry not as much because they probably already knew it. I put a lot of pressure on myself to retain the information because I feel the more we know, the better prepared we are to prevent future attacks.

The cloud of what we will witness tomorrow is also hanging over my head. I wonder if all the couples got that information today or if it was just the group I was in. I sure hope I don't have to watch Isabella being tortured tomorrow. I don't want to see her ever again. End of discussion. Period.

Dinner time with my new group of friends is the only thing that gets me through most days, and especially this day; Oliver's death has brought us all even closer. Trent and Knox, both from Galveston, banter back and forth and have us all laughing. We rarely leave the cafeteria before 2000 hours these days, liking the extra time spent with one another. I can't imagine what it will be like when there are fewer of us, even worse if Marisol is still in the bunch, although even she has been making more of an effort to be not as hateful since Oliver's death.

That night before I go to bed, I dream of Isabella being tortured. Even after what she did to Oliver, I'm not sure I can stomach the sight of what I will see tomorrow.

****

The next morning, much to my dismay, October, Sapphire, and Hugh are all gone. I knew it was bound to happen eventually, but it doesn't lessen the blow any. I'm also pretty quick with math to notice that there are seven couples, plus one. That "plus one" is my doing and a big decision I will have to make soon, within five days to be exact. Although I have made it to the final 15 of the Culling candidates, I feel as if this is the hardest thing I have ever done and it is only going to get harder. Today is the day I have to see the torture.

Yay.

At DIA, Henry sits beside me with Knox and Attie behind us. Lyncoln is nowhere to be found, probably doing whatever it is he does. We are behind some sort of glass. We can see the interrogation room, but the interrogation room can't see us, thus we are in what they call "the observation room". Somewhere on the opposite wall, hides a

[446]

similar room, "the control room", which has the only door that leads directly into the interrogation room. That's where the dudes that decide what method of torture to try next sit and watch. So Hadenfelt is somewhere on the opposite side of the room I am looking in.

Fortunately, when they bring in the subject of today's interrogation, I find it's a man instead of Isabella. I let out a breath of air in relief but stop as I take a good look at him. I assume he is the lone surviving drifter from the night of the masquerade. They roughly tie him, hands behind his back, to a chair in the middle of the room and we are ready to begin.

The man before us in "interrogation" looks like he hasn't had a bite to eat since the night of the attack, which was almost three weeks ago. The fact that it's hard to determine what ethnicity he is means he probably has multiple. His skin is only slightly darker than Lyncoln's naturally dark complexion. This man isn't a huge man, but he isn't small either. Though he's sitting so it's hard to tell, I would guess he was five foot nine or so. And way too thin currently. In the way he sits calm and aware as he looks at his interrogators, I get the sense that he is a very intelligent fella. Apparently just not intelligent enough to not attack us.

We are only about ten minutes in when I can feel the bile climbing up my throat. What type of person does it take to conduct these things? After Oliver's death, I thought I had experienced enough violence for a lifetime.

"You have told us that you answer to Marcel." An evil-looking soldier paces in front of the drifter, formalities now taken care of. He has a huge jug of water and a towel in his hands. Surely nothing too harmful can come from those weapons, right?

"Now. I would like to know who specifically you were sent for."

"I told you..." the drifter starts. He has blood stains and dirt everywhere. I'm sure he smells like urine. He has no shirt and his pants are torn. The fact that he is bruised and missing a fingernail tells me this isn't the beginning of the torture for him.

It makes me feel absolutely hateful. And not towards the man being tortured.

Before he has a chance to finish and answer the question, another solider helps hold him down and tilt the chair back. They place the towel over his face and start slowly dumping the water onto the towel and his face. They don't stop until the entire jug is gone. The man is coughing, spitting, and struggling to breathe.

They are going to drown him. That is my only thought in watching this all go down. Why? How is this effective? Does he fear for his life? Yes. But more than anything he just hates his captors. I bet he even hates us more than he did before he took part in the attack.

The drifter refuses to give them any new information and they move next time to two jugs, continuing all the way up to four. I have no idea how the drifter survives, and for a moment I think he is gone, but they stop, allowing him to puke up a bunch of water. As the interrogation finishes, the drifter too weak to continue on, I realize I have been squeezing Henry's hand so hard he is starting to lose circulation to some of his fingers.

"I'm sorry," I say to him while fighting back tears. I have just seen the ugliness of humans at its finest.

"It's okay, beautiful," he says softly and rubs my back with his freshly released hand. I know from the look on his face that this is something he has seen before. He knew it was going to be like this. I also know he isn't a fan of it as his green eyes seem icy with dislike for the process. "Are you okay?" he asks concerned as he looks me over.

"I don't know. I don't think I'm okay with this," I say knowing that I one-hundred-percent am not.

"Yeah, me neither. I kind of like Lyncoln's outlook on it," he says with a shrug.

"Which is?"

"Which is if they are dumb enough to provoke us and shoot at us, then they are dumb enough to deserve to die." He pauses. "Seems pretty brutal, but it's actually a way more humane way of dealing with the drifters."

I'm not sure I like either option but before I can think it through Henry adds, "What are we supposed to do, Reagan? If we let them go, there will be more incidents like the night of the masquerade. If we torture them, we are stooping to their level. There isn't an easy right answer here."

Knowing he is right and just wanting to get out of there, we stand to leave to go to our debriefing room. I give a sobbing Attie a hug around her shoulders where she sits. I know the entire time she was thinking of ways she could save the drifter instead of ways she could harm him. As hard as this is on me, I'm sure it's even harder on her. Knox seems oddly fine. Of all of us, he seems to be dealing with it the best, on the outside anyway. For as intelligent as he is, I wonder what his opinions on this would be.

Unfortunately, the Head of Interrogations, Marisol's father, runs our debriefing with Taggert. Listening to him spout out the research and meaning behind what I just saw makes my hatred for it intensify. None of us seem okay with what he is talking about. And he's talking about torture methods so nonchalantly.

This is messed up.

As he is explaining yet another method of torture, an archaic form of whipping, and why it is effective, I quickly rub my temple to prevent myself from saying something I shouldn't. I just need to get out of this room before I get myself in trouble. Henry has his arm around the chair I'm sitting in and reaches across to hold my hand as well.

Hadenfelt notices it and hones in on us.

"What?" he snaps. Seeing his haughty stare, so eerily similar to his daughter's, is enough to make my temper flare. "We've done the research and trained for this for years. My interrogations are a well-oiled machine. We get results," he says loudly.

"No," I pipe up. "You get more hatred and a whole slug of false information. If you got results we wouldn't be in a war right now."

Hadenfelt glares, his own temper now showing through. Henry tenses beside me, like he's ready to defend me at any given moment.

"You think there's a better way?" he laughs in my face.

I don't hesitate. "I know there has to be."

He smiles. And it's terrifying. "Be my guest then. You wanna lead the interrogations tomorrow?" he challenges.

Henry stands abruptly, surprising me.

"Maxwell," Taggert warns him.

Henry turns to Taggert, looking livid. "I'm not going to let him bait her."

Taggert nods and sends Hadenfelt a glare that has him sitting down. "We're done here today, kids. Emotions are obviously running high and I can understand that given what you just saw. Interrogations resume tomorrow."

Henry doesn't hesitate to grab my hand and get us out of there, with Attie and Knox not far behind.

In the hallway I whisper to Henry, "Thanks for having my back."

He smirks. "Anytime, beautiful. Did you see his face though? 'If you got results we wouldn't be in a war right now.' I swear you could put the devil himself right in his place." He laughs and shakes his head.

That makes me laugh, and by the time we head to supper, I'm feeling better despite what I was forced to see today.

****

The next day we are on bottle four of waterboarding with the same drifter. Lyncoln and Henry are both in the observation room with Knox,

Attie, and I when I can't take it any longer. I stand up and move to leave, not caring if I fail whatever test this is.

They are going to kill that man. Eventually, they will kill him. I'm sure of it. I refuse to sit there and watch it happen. His lungs cannot take much more. Lyncoln is sitting closest to the door and tries to stop me, but I throw his arm away and slam the door shut on my way out. I refuse to sit by and watch someone die. *Someone else.*

In the hallway, I try to decide if I want to go back to the practice range to shoot off some steam or go back to Mile High to my room, anywhere but here really. But instead of either of those reasonable options, I keep thinking of Hadenfelt's challenge from the day before and decide to act rashly. I am probably going to regret what I am about to do, and it may or may not get me sent home. I know either Henry or Lyncoln is about to come check on me, so I don't have the chance to think anything through.

The only thought I have is, *"I'm going to get in deep crap for this."*

I ignore a warning glance from Jamie and open the next door, to what I assume is the control room for the interrogation. I find I am correct as I stand in a room similar to the one I was just sitting in. Four people sit at a desk with papers everywhere and all turn their heads my direction in surprise. I'm fortunate that Henry and Lyncoln can't see in this room or they would be here in a heartbeat to stop me from what I am about to do.

"You can't be in here," Hadenfelt snaps and I can feel through his stare that he doesn't like me one bit. Like Henry's comparison, I think I might be staring into the eyes of the devil himself. And he has crumbs on his shirt. Was he actually eating while watching a man being tortured?

"What do you think you're doing?" another man I've never seen before asks, almost matching Hadenfelt in the degree of hate radiating off of him.

"I think I want a shot at it," I say boldly even though I'm so nervous I think I might pass out.

My heart is pounding a mile a minute and my hands are sweaty. Jamie is right beside me shifting back and forth on his feet and looks like he is thinking about picking me up and carrying me out of here.

"Excuse me?" Hadenfelt looks at me incredulously and then rudely laughs. He actually leans in to laugh in my face, for the second day in a row, while the other two just look on curiously.

"I would like to try to get more information out of him. You asked me if I wanted to lead interrogations today and I do." I try to say it nicely even though I know I'm quickly starting to violently hate the man before me. More than I have ever hated anyone.

Hadenfelt puts his head back and laughs again, this time harder. The others join in, but I don't budge.

"You can't be serious?" the other man asks with sarcasm dripping off his tongue.

"Well, what you're doing obviously isn't working," I say pointedly and turn to Hadenfelt. "So what is the harm in letting me have a go at it? You asked me. More than likely to make me look like a fool. I'm calling your bluff. Give me a shot."

"Our men have been trained for this for years. You can't just up and walk in there," Hadenfelt says defensively.

"So by letting me in there, you would only further your point. You challenged me to do this and I accept your offer. Unless you don't want me to go in there because you're afraid I'll make *you* look bad." I try to lure him with my logic. I need to speed this along if I am going to save that man before Henry or Lyncoln come storming in, or before Jamie caves and carries me out of here.

Hadenfelt snorts, clearly insulted.

"Sir. Just let her. This will be great," the other man offers.

Hadenfelt thinks a moment, actually considering it.

"Fine. Go ahead, Ms. Scott. Be my guest. Do know that you will be graded on this," he reminds me rudely.

"Aren't I always?" I reply in matching rudeness.

I look at the other man commanding, "I need a bottle of water."

"You what?" he says taken aback and super annoyed with my bossiness.

"I don't recall stuttering." I'm really beginning to hate all of the people in this room. These men are just bullies with power and I refuse to cower to them.

"For God's sake, Williams, just get her a damn bottle of water so we can get this over with," Hadenfelt spits at him before turning back to me. "You have five minutes."

The man named Williams does so quickly and then I'm facing the door into the actual interrogation room. It takes every fiber of my being to not vomit all over myself. I take a deep breath and wipe my hands on my pants. I'm glad I'm in my black DIA gear since it makes me look important. I need to be commanding or this will never work. I have to channel some sort of inner power I have never had. If I don't, they are going to kill that man. I'm his last chance.

And I don't want to watch another person die.

Jamie is fidgeting beside me and I know he's pissed at me, but I don't dare look at him. He isn't supposed to intervene, but he doesn't like this one bit. He isn't about to leave my side either though.

I gather all my courage and open the door as they are pouring another jug of water over the drifter. There is water everywhere, flowing to the drain in the center of the room. The two men stop when they see me, eyes wide and full of surprise. For a moment they forget to remove the towel over the drifter's face until I gesture for them to lift it off.

"Who authorized this?" the one man says venomously.

"Hadenfelt. And you are dismissed," I respond then point to the other interrogator, "You. Sit him up and then stay posted at the door."

Well, I sounded bossy. Now I just need to not puke.

The first man storms off angrily and I can already hear him yelling in the room I was just in as the door shuts. Although the other man took part in the torturing too, he somehow seems softer, which is why I decided to let him stay. That and I might need backup because if the drifter comes at me, tied to a chair or not, I will pass out on the spot.

I take a step towards the drifter and pace back and forth. I have no idea what I am about to do or what I am about to say. I just know that for some weird reason, he needs to talk first and he needs to know that I hold his life in my hands. Because I really do. If I don't do this right, he's a goner. If not today, then tomorrow. And I will probably be forced to sit in the observation room and watch it happen.

So I pace, with authority, putting on an act. And also because my nerves are going psychotic at the moment and it seems to help. I'm still not sure I'm not going to vomit. This room not only smells like urine but also blood and puke. From the blood stains on the floor, I wonder what other than the fingernails and water-boarding has been done to this man.

Finally, after what feels like forever, the drifter speaks up.

"Are you here to try to seduce me? That's a technique they haven't tried yet," he speaks so hoarsely it makes me cringe. With the amount of water they are dumping on him and into his lungs, he probably has a bad case of pneumonia. I'm sure he wouldn't have lasted many more days of this.

I look at him with a death glare, "No."

His logic even at his current state is impressive though. I would think the same thing in his situation. Tortured for days and then all of a sudden a young girl comes in confusing his interrogators? He must think we are trying to soften him up to get him to talk.

"Then why are you here?" he coughs the last part. Right to the point. Smart man.

"I'm pretty sure I'm your last hope, before they properly dispose of you," I say strongly. I don't falter or sugar coat it. I'm not lying either.

The man before me just lets out a defeated sigh, knowing that I'm speaking the truth.

"Do you have any siblings?" I ask, finding somewhere to begin. I have to find some way to relate to this person or this will never work. In his eyes, I see pure hatred. I have to find a way not to necessarily absolve it, but to work with it, bring him down from all that hate. I need to remind him of something good in the world.

"You are my last hope and that's what you start out with? I'm already dead," he says sarcastically and closes his eyes.

I walk up to him and put my face in his face. The up front and personal stench radiating off of him makes me taste bile, but I swallow it down.

"You more than likely are, yes." I stare him down.

A few seconds pass as I just stand there staring him down and don't move, mainly because if I move too quickly, I'm afraid I'll pass out. After he realizes I'm not backing down, he calmly states, "I have a sister."

Bingo. Common ground. Now I need to get him to trust me just a small, minuscule amount.

I start pacing again. "I have a brother."

"Congratulations," he says sarcastically again.

Although I would never, ever use it, to get him to shut up, I walk over and grab a pistol off the counter. I cock it and turn the safety off and back on again to let him know that I do indeed know how to use it. I can see him gulp down his fear before me.

"So as I was saying." I smile like a lunatic. "I have a brother. We are pretty close. Close enough that I would never do anything as stupid as risking my life on a suicide mission. You knew you were either going to get caught or die. You knew what you signed up for. So why do it?" I ask pacing and gesturing with the gun as I swing it around. I'm careful to never have it pointing at anyone though the safety is back on. The guard in the room is looking at me like I'm crazy and winces on more than one occasion but doesn't say a word. I don't dare look at Jamie because I know he is absolutely livid with me.

"You're smart. You figure it out," he says. He isn't insulting, but borderline. I would still be fuming too if I was tortured like he was.

"Well, the obvious theory would be to kill the President. But why him, and especially now if there is going to be a new one? Nope. That's not it." I shrug and swing the gun around. He listens to me but never takes his eyes off the gun. I realize I am acting crazy, but that is just where I want him. I want him to believe I am crazy. Heck, I believe I am crazy right now. Why did I waltz in here like I owned the place again?

What am I doing?!

"So the next theory would be that you were after a Culling candidate?" I spin and look at him. "Who were you after?"

He just stares at me.

Knowing my five minutes are about up, I stop for a moment and let my arms dangle at my sides, and then I angrily start to approach him. "Do you know what it's like? Do you know that your drifter candidate killed a friend of mine? Do you know what it feels like to hold him in a pool of his own blood that you can't stop from oozing out of the hole in his chest? Do you know what it feels like to see the life drain out of his eyes? Do you know how much that infuriates a person? So let me be clear. Your actions killed my friend. No. You didn't personally put the knife in his chest, but you damned well helped it along."

"Oliver wasn't supposed to die," he sighs and says quietly when I am only a foot away from him.

Oliver's name on the drifter's lips makes me see red. "Don't you dare say his name," I say violently as I am now right in front of him.

"Sorry," he winces. "He wasn't supposed to die, Reagan."

I notice his use of both of our names and wonder how in the heck a person who has been in custody the entire time knows so much. Maybe from earlier torturing questions? I don't know, but something is fishy here.

"Who was supposed to die?"

He doesn't look uncomfortable. No fidgeting. Nothing. I'm not close enough to the truth yet. So if no one was supposed to die, what was the point?

"No? Who were you supposed to get then?" I ask next.

This time his left foot moves a touch. Bingo. Getting close. I take my gun and make tick-tock noises trying both to annoy him and let him know we are running out of time.

"Anyone really. Anyone we could find, as long as they were a Culling candidate and male," he sighs in frustration.

"Why? When you already had an insider?" I ask confused. That doesn't make much sense. Is he just trying to cover his own rear, or was there another plan? Were Henry and Lyncoln at the top of that list? "Why not just take Oliver? She was spending enough time with him it can't have been that hard?"

"You might as well know since it will never happen now anyway," he says annoyed and with hatred in his voice as he starts yelling in frustration. It isn't a very loud yell because he sounds so hoarse. "We were supposed to get Isabella and one more, it didn't really matter who, but preferably her partner. That's why I said Oliver wasn't supposed to die. We were to pose a kidnapping. The goal was to lure out the military. Release to the public their kidnapping and finally shed light about our existence to the rest of the townships. Then Isabella, having survived a kidnapping and returned relatively unharmed, would have all the sympathy votes necessary to win."

"So the goal was to have Isabella as Madam President?" I reiterate.

He nods once. "Had we been successful, Oliver would have been President."

I walk over to the metal table and put the gun down and grab a knife walking towards him purposefully. He looks at me confused and then closes his eyes and braces for what he thinks might be death.

Does he really think I'm going to kill him now that he's talked?

Instead, I untie one of his hands. Then I hand him the bottle of water.

He looks at me confused and I shrug.

"You are crazy on a whole other level of crazy," he says honestly.

"I'm going to take that as a compliment," I reply with a smirk.

He takes a drink of water and coughs it down. "Who would think I would be thirsty," he says hoarsely as he takes another drink.

"I figured your throat was raw."

"What now?" he asks tired.

"I'm going to get you a cot and some sleep," I say half to him and half to the people on the other side of the glass.

"Why would you help me?" he asks incredulously. "You said it, I was partially responsible for Ol--I mean in the death of your friend."

"Because for the life of me, I don't understand this war and have a million questions. How can there be this much hatred? Didn't Trident show us our greed is capable of killing off the human race? So why are we still fighting after all these years? To what point will the drifters finally be happy? When everyone is dead? And why did my friend have to be collateral damage in a war with no point?" I blurt out honestly and fight back the tears that threaten to spill over.

"I don't know the answers to your questions, but I do know that just as you have been raised loyal to the State, I have been raised loyal to my side. Do you understand that there was an entire group of us that needed your help? When things got really bad, we reached out. It was either you help us or we starve. We starved," he says viciously. "So don't act all high and mighty until you know all the facts."

"When?" I demand, wanting to know more about this new information.

"About ten years ago. I was fourteen. And I watched my mom starve to death." He stops to cough. "She starved herself so that my sister and I could live."

My mind is spinning with questions, but I know he's exhausted. He looks like he's about to fall asleep. I myself feel emotionally exhausted. And I need to get away from the smell in this room.

"We are done for today." I nod with authority and turn to leave the room.

I finally look at Jamie, who still looks livid, but is relieved we are leaving and possibly even slightly impressed. I pat him on the arm, as if apologizing for what I just put him through.

I open the door to the control room and realize my hands have never really stopped sweating or shaking. I assume the drifter didn't know, or he probably would have called me out on it. As I step back into the small room where Hadenfelt resides over the interrogations, I am met with a room full of people staring at me, most of which are as livid as Jamie looks. I lean my back against the cold door I just came through and grip it as I try to calm down, feeling rattled by what I just did.

Hadenfelt is fuming and is glaring daggers at me. Lyncoln is there and has a slightly bloody lip. The other guy who Hadenfelt called Williams looks worse and his eye is already starting to swell shut. Henry is there and seems to be holding Lyncoln back, although he is fuming too. But, the most powerful presence in the room is Admiral Taggert himself. I have so many questions about the scene before me, but now is not the time to ask. I seem to have interrupted a brawl of sorts, one that I also seem to have started.

"Nicely done," Taggert simply nods to me.

"He needs a cot, a change of clothes, and for God sakes get him a room that doesn't smell like his own pee. Maybe some hot tea for his throat and some warm food," I demand, feeling all of a sudden exhausted by the afternoon's events.

"You heard the woman," Taggert says pointedly at Hadenfelt.

"I don't think that--" Hadenfelt starts.

Taggert interrupts him right away. I have never seen him look so violent before, and now I definitely know why Taggert holds the position he does. "I don't recall asking for your opinion. You will do as she said. She is doing your job better than you are and it's her first day. She is now in charge of interrogations with this drifter because she has established a connection with him and got him to talk. No one talks to that man but her from here on out. Do I make myself clear?" As he speaks he reminds me of a snake and the way they coil their powerful bodies around their prey and squeeze them to death. And to think I once thought the man looked like Santa Claus.

"Yes, sir," Hadenfelt spits out.

Taggert looks to me. "You have the rest of the day off. I'll see to it." He gestures his head toward the door out. "Your interrogation resumes tomorrow."

"Yes, sir," I say softly, having just seen him verbally destroy Hadenfelt. I kind of want to high-five him on the way out, but I'm not sure that will help Hadenfelt hate me any less.

Henry and Lincoln follow me into the hallway. I don't say anything and neither do they. We load the elevator with our guards when Henry finally can't take the silence anymore.

"Have you lost your mind?" he asks frustrated and angry.

I shrug and bring my arms up to cross them over my body. I'm pretty sure I have lost my mind, but I don't really think I need to admit that to them at this point. My hands won't seem to stop shaking either.

"What were you thinking? You can't just pull crap like that." His voice gets even louder as he turns, his back to the elevator doors as he glares at me, ripping me out despite an elevator full of people.

"Lay off," Lincoln warns and moves forward like he wants to step between us.

I have a feeling part of the reason Henry is mad at me instead of Lincoln has to do with the way Lincoln made Williams's face look. Lincoln had a punching bag while Henry had to bottle it. Still, I have never seen Henry so mad. He was mad at Hadenfelt yesterday, but that still wasn't like this. This is disappointment wrapped up in anger. And it sucks.

"No." He glares at Lyncoln briefly and then turns his anger back on me. "Do you not understand that you have people that care about you? You two are just the same," he looks at Lyncoln accusingly and then back at me as he implies that I am like Lyncoln, voluntarily putting myself in harm's way. Though he might not approve of it, Lyncoln can wrap his head around why I did what I did because he does it all the time.

His statement hits me right in the gut. The tears start to fill my eyes and I try to be strong and fight it with everything I have. I'm almost gasping for air trying to contain them as the events from today and yesterday hit me like a ton of bricks. Henry looks at me remorseful and reaches for me, but I step away.

In-between sobs, I manage to yell at him, "No. I put myself in danger because no one else would save that man. They were going to kill him. And you would've sat there and let it happen! I didn't want to watch anyone else die. One was enough for me."

And with that, the elevator doors open and I brush past Henry and run down the hallway towards my room with Jamie on my heels.

Chapter 25

I choose to eat supper in my room in my pajamas, not feeling up to seeing everyone else although I'm dying to know what happened in the control room after I took over the interrogation. Jamie and Sarge have checked on me at least five times and I'm thinking about calling it a day and just going to bed early when I hear a knock on my door. I don't even check to see who it is. Since Lyncoln briefly stopped by to check on me about a half an hour ago, I'm assuming it's Henry.

Upon opening the door, I see that I was mistaken. None other than the President himself is before me. I suppose I should be nervous he's going to give me the boot after what I pulled today, but I don't think the President himself would do it. That honor would be reserved for Dougall or one of the other professors.

"May I come in?" he asks kindly.

"Yes, please do." I smile tightly, feeling embarrassed to be wearing my pajamas and probably looking worse for wear.

I grab a bottle of water for him as he sets a box down on my coffee table. Two of his guards are outside of my room, and two are inside with us. I'm sure there are two more down the hall and two more at the elevators. This man is never without an entourage.

"It is my understanding you had a rough day, so I brought a little something to brighten it." He smiles apologetically as he sits down.

"Let me guess. Chocolate cheesecake?" I ask with a smile.

"You got it. With peanut butter this time." He smiles back then sighs before he begins, "Sometimes you remind me so much of my Essie. I am truly sorry for the events that transpired today. You never should have been let in that room," he says firmly.

"But they were going to kill him," I interject. "I couldn't just sit there and watch them kill him. I know he wasn't completely innocent, but did he really deserve to die?"

"No. It never should have gotten that far either. Hadenfelt has been stretching the rules a bit as of late." The way in which he says it makes the underlying tension bubble to the surface. "Regardless, there is something you should know that will help you with your interrogation tomorrow, should you chose to go back."

"Okay?" He definitely has my attention.

"When Mr. Nolan Samson, the drifter you intervened with today, referred to the State turning down the drifters and a bunch of them starving, he is absolutely correct," the President admits with sadness. He runs a hand through his thin, gray hair, thinking about what to say next. "We didn't handle it the best. There was a famine where they were located. They sent some men to ask for help. We thought they were decoys trying to lure us out. How were we to give them food but keep ourselves safe at the same time? How did I know it wasn't some big ploy? How did they not have food with a booming wildlife population?"

He shakes his head and looks at me sadly. "We went back and forth for hours. Finally, my cabinet voted to deny their request. We gave the three that came more than enough food and lots of dried goods like rice that would last them a while, but we sent them on their way."

I nod thinking about his reasoning. In Omaha we can barely keep up with feeding our current population as is anyway. *So what would I have done?*

"This decision ate at Essie and me. We had the moves in place to finally form a truce and use their situation to our benefit, but we didn't know it and were running scared. They had just attempted an attack on Denver and we were reeling from that. I just couldn't take the risk of more of my people dying.

"As a result, some of their people died. By the time we knew how bad it really got, it was too little too late. I'm not proud of this decision, but I did what I thought was right at the time. Later we would find out there was a disease in the deer population that made all the wildlife numbers greatly fluctuate. That in combination with some bad weather and being in the wrong spot at the wrong time, made them starve. If they hadn't planted it themselves, they had zero food. And since the drifters are known for hopping camps and being nomads, they hadn't planted a thing. We just didn't know. We had no idea how bad it really got." He shakes his head and I see him struggle with the guilt he has been dealing with for the past ten years.

I put my hand on his hand and give it a quick squeeze saying, "I understand." The longer I am in the Culling, the more I see the gray areas in which the right thing to do doesn't seem so straightforward. This was one of those instances.

He nods then adds, "You absolutely do not have to go back tomorrow. I need you to know that. This isn't your responsibility. It's mine."

"But will Hadenfelt be in charge if I don't?" I ask, not even attempting to hide my dislike for the man.

"Unfortunately, yes. Taggert will watch him closely though." He shakes his head like there is nothing he can do about it.

"Then I don't have a choice. I'm going," I say determined.

****

Out of pure exhaustion, I fall asleep almost as soon as my head hits the pillow after President Maxwell leaves. I am awakened from a deep sleep to a knock on my door. I lazily get out of bed and yawn. I feel annoyed towards whoever is coming to disturb me. I barely get enough sleep these days.

I open the door to a distraught looking Henry. "Hey," he says softly.

"Hey," I respond with a yawn.

"Can I come in?" he asks unsure.

"Of course." I shrug and move to prop open the door.

Before we get as far as the couch, he wraps me in his arms. "I am so sorry. So, so sorry. I lost my cool." He pauses. "There is no excuse."

"It's okay," I respond softly, my annoyance with him waking me now gone given his heartfelt apology. "It was just a messed up situation. I shouldn't have done it, but I had no other option. I think Hadenfelt wanted to kill him in front of us just to mess with us."

He then kisses me fervently, pulling back after a minute then kissing me once more on the cheek.

"You drive me crazy," he whispers in my ear.

"Welcome to my fan club," I joke.

He pulls away and holds my small hands in each of his larger ones and looks at me affectionately. "I can't even think right when I think you are in danger. You did amazing today. Amazing. You did better in interrogation than people that have had training for years, but I was so worried about you that I couldn't even focus on that. I lost my mind when I couldn't find you and then saw you in that room. I have no idea how I could run the country when I am in a constant state of worry over the woman I love."

My mouth drops open. Did he really just say what I think he said or am I still dreaming?

"You..." I don't even know if I want to ask if he is sure he loves me because I want it to be true.

"I do." He grins with those killer dimples and searches my eyes as if wanting to remove all my doubts. "I love you, Reagan Scott, and it scares the crap out of me."

We are kissing again before I have a chance to say anything or process it. Before I know it, he pulls away and I am left breathless and confused. My lips feel swollen and tingly and my senses have definitely woken up.

"You need some sleep. I was going to do this in the morning, but I just couldn't end this day with things how we left them. I'm going to go now, beautiful." He smiles and kisses me on the cheek again.

"Hey," I grab his arm to stop him.

"Yeah?" he asks, turning.

"I'm sorry, too, for what I said to you earlier. It was a bit harsh."

"Don't be. I deserved it and I like that you aren't afraid to put me in my spot." He smiles sheepishly and then adds, "Especially if my spot is right beside you." He chuckles. "So cheesy, but so true."

And with that, he leaves. I have a hard time falling back asleep. Both Henry and Lyncoln have now told me they loved me, although Henry's was downright and Lyncoln's was implied. Despite knowing how they both feel, I feel like my heart is fracturing. And it's not a clean break either, it's a slow and painful one.

What am I going to do? Just when I think I know what I should do, I am with one or the other and they say or do something that makes me question everything.

How will I ever choose?

****

The next day I'm excused from sims and the range for interrogating so I throw myself into my work with Samson to avoid the big decision that is rapidly approaching. I limit our sessions to two hours in the morning and two hours in the afternoon. I allow him a shower, a meal, some clothes, and a new room. I also have a medic check his pneumonia, which he does have like I originally suspected.

Instead of meeting in a room with torture equipment, we meet in a different type of interrogation room without all of that. There is a table in which we sit across from one another and talk like civil human beings, though he is tied down. And of course, Hadenfelt and his cronies are on the other side of the window in the control room, always present and always watching. Jamie is in the room with me, right by my side. Henry, Lyncoln, Knox and Attie are in the observation room too. I am never alone in this.

It's a long day, but the interrogating is coming along. There is still animosity on both sides, but in the morning session we were talking more about why each side hates the other. He hasn't given us any solid information on their future plans, but he elaborated on the attack plan for the masquerade and has hinted at more information that is helping us find the mole here. It is slow going, but it is progress nonetheless. 24 hours ago he was almost a dead man.

Ending our session for the day, I look at him with tears in my eyes. "Please help me make sure what happened to Oliver doesn't happen again," I say softly. I'm tired of having nightmares that find me at Henry or Lyncoln's funerals.

He sighs and I can tell he is having some sort of inner struggle.

"Even though the guy is on my side, I still don't like him." He shakes his head in reference to the mole. He is still bruised, has a horrible cough, and looks too thin, but he looks marginally better than he did a day ago.

"Then what's the issue?" I ask, eyebrows raised.

"Other than if I tell you, he will come find me and kill me?" He shakes his head. "I'll be a traitor."

"Well here, you already are one," I state the obvious.

"Yes. And I'm not naive enough to think I will ever leave here, but I don't want to become one of you either. Once you get as much information out of me as you can, you will be done with me and kill me. That's how this works," he ends his explanation angrily.

"Why do you have to think about it in terms of us and them? I can't promise you immunity, or even freedom, but this is about doing the right thing. Do you want more blood on your hands?" Although I get to play boss lady, I'm not in charge here and can't make him any promises. With Hadenfelt in charge, he is probably right that he will be killed when we are done with him. But as long as he keeps helping us, he secures his future for one more day.

"That piece of information is the last bargaining chip for my life, so I will keep it awhile if you don't mind," he says sadly.

Knowing our session for the day is over, I leave and plan on talking with Taggert the next day to figure out some sort of way to save the drifter's life. I understand he can't go free, but he shouldn't die either. I'll be going over Hadenfelt's head for this but Hadenfelt won't cooperate with me at all, so I'll just deal with Taggert personally.

****

Back at Mile High, Dougall is trying to train me for the interviews. In a rare occurrence it is just the two of us, but it is after dinner since that was the only time she could corner me. After prepping for a few questions on my political views, the conversation turns more serious.

"It has been 11 days," Dougall points out.

"Yes, ma'am." I release a huge sigh, feeling the weight of the world on my shoulders.

"Do you know what you are going to do? It may be wise to do it just a day or two before the deadline, show the panel your decisiveness. And you can be that much more ready for the interviews too," she offers.

"So you want me to do it tomorrow?" I ask shocked. My heart rate picks up and my hands begin to feel clammy.

"Or the next day." Then she pats my hand in a rare moment of softness. "You knew this was going to have to happen eventually."

I just shrug sadly. Either way, a piece of me is going to leave when one of them leaves. I only have three days left.

Three days.

****

Though it's a Sunday and supposed to be our slow day, I plan to hit interrogations hard. After my discussion right away in the morning with Taggert, Henry, and Lyncoln, I head to the interrogation room to begin my first session with Samson. Henry is heading to his big eight-hour solo sim. And Lyncoln, who has surprisingly been the biggest supporter of my interrogations, is finishing brainstorming with Taggert a deal we can offer Samson before sitting in on my interrogating. I left without him to come to the interrogation rooms because I don't like Samson waiting for me, especially with Hadenfelt and his evil minions sitting there on the other side of the glass of the control room.

I greet Attie and Knox already in the observation room and then enter the next door to the control room. I can feel the hatred boiling off of Hadenfelt and Williams as soon as I hit the door. The better I do, the worse they look. And since I am doing pretty well, they are looking pretty bad. Hadenfelt baited me into that interrogation room, hoping to prove a point and make me look like a fool. Who's the fool now?

"May I ask a favor?" Hadenfelt asks right away in a fake sweet voice, the same one I have heard his daughter use often. Now I know where she gets all her shady characteristics from.

"What?" I sound as annoyed as I feel.

"Since you have been so successful with this drifter, we were wondering if you could work with Isabella. She is being difficult and today may be her last day here." He gives me a look that has me catching what he is implying.

Although I feel like he is trapping me, baiting me again, I also know what he is saying. She isn't helping them and they are going to kill her today if she doesn't give anything up. Although I don't feel like facing the person who killed my friend, I don't feel like making a conscious decision to let her die either. I hate that he just put that choice upon my shoulders, too. I don't want to decide if she lives or dies.

I sigh. "When?"

"Well, while Taggert figures out what to do with your drifter, why don't you try now? Doesn't have to be long, maybe ten or so minutes? Just you and her, no extras, no other distractions. That seems to be working," Hadenfelt offers and is doing his best to say it without animosity. "I have her all ready to go a few rooms over. You can go for a few minutes now, and by the time you finish up with her, you might have something more solid to offer Samson."

I know I'm giving him what he wants which is why his hatred for me has been replaced with indifference. Am I even going to be able to handle being in the same room with Isabella after what she did to Oliver? But does she deserve to die, and in the most inhumane way at that? Why is he putting her life in my hands? I don't want this responsibility! Is he just trying to mess with me, knowing that being in the same room as her will affect me?

"Fine," I finally decide, determined to prove him wrong yet again. I know I have to at least give it a shot. Here's hoping I can make him look like a fool both times he's baited me like this.

"Good. Williams will take you and stay posted in the control room," Hadenfelt nods to the other man, who is still quite bruised from his run in with Lyncoln.

"Yes, sir," Williams says, looking as hateful as ever.

We walk in silence down the hallway and around a corner and my gut starts to churn. Can I do this? Can I face Isabella? I would feel better if Henry or Lyncoln were here. I know Lyncoln will be down shortly and Attie and Knox are just a few doors down. Jamie looks uncomfortable with this too, but he is still here. So I am not alone. *I am not alone.*

Williams enters the door into to the control room for this interrogation room and hands me a water bottle from the counter knowing that I was going to ask for it. He seems to be in just as big of a hurry to get this over with as I am. Through the glass of the control room, I can see Isabella, who looks to be in about the same state as Samson was. She is tied down and sitting in a chair in the middle of the room. Evidently waiting for me.

"You are not going in there alone," Jamie demands. "I know Hadenfelt said no extras, but I don't care. Let me call this in. At least get Lyncoln down here to observe. Then we'll go in."

I know by "calling it in", he means to fill in Taggert and my boy toys on what is going on. Hadenfelt is throwing me for a loop and he wants the others informed. Immediately.

"She's tied up," I say feeling anything but brave. "Call it in and then come on in. I want to get this over with before I bail. Just five minutes. We will only be in there five minutes max. Go ahead and call it in. I'm going to go get started."

I want to get this over with, but I also want Taggert involved as soon as possible. The sooner Jamie calls it in, the better. I can survive the first thirty seconds without him.

He nods. "I'll be right here."

Before I lose my nerve, I open the door that brings me face-to-face with Oliver's murderer.

She isn't awake but comes around upon my entering the room.

"Reagan?" she asks confused.

"Yeah," I answer coolly. Every fiber of my being wants to turn around and leave this room immediately.

"Did you take a wrong turn?" she asks mockingly.

I see what Lyncoln means about her being so full of hate. Where is the sweet girl that always joked around with Oliver? Was this monster hiding beneath the surface the entire time? I already regret my decision to come in here.

"No. They have me helping with interrogations," I respond hatefully and begin pacing. Is Jamie back from calling it in yet? I would feel better with him in here. This is too weird. Too painful.

"I wouldn't think you would have that in you," she laughs a good hard laugh at my expense.

"You'd be surprised what people are really capable of," I respond without faltering.

"Well, I'm glad you're here. I've been meaning to talk to you about Lyncoln. Isn't he just the best kisser?" she says dreamily.

I know she's trying to get a rise out of me. She might be lying, she might not be. It isn't a secret that Denver girls have been chasing Lyncoln for a while now, and I can't say I can blame them. Either way, I can't let her get to me.

"He is," I simply nod in agreement. "But while we are here, let's talk about Oliver."

I feel the hatred boiling to the surface of my skin. *She killed my friend.* That needs to be on the forefront of my mind. Unlike Samson, she killed someone in cold blooded murder. I'm not sure she deserves a second chance. Or to be reasoned with. Part of me just wants Hadenfelt's men to do whatever they do. If she dies, whatever. But, the other part of me wouldn't be able to sleep at night if I were to do that.

"You may hate this country. You may hate me. But I can't for the life of me figure out why you would stab and kill the *one* person who would have given you the world," I say more coldly than I have ever spoken to another human being before.

[472]

"He didn't love me. Not the real me," she argues.

"True, but even when he figured out you were the traitor, he wanted to make sure they weren't going to kill you. That's the type of person he was, much unlike yourself." By the time I'm done, I'm spitting the words towards her, hatred rolling off of me in waves.

"He ruined my plan, my whole life's work." She shakes her head like it's ridiculous of me to question her actions. "Do you know how annoying that is?"

"So injure him. Punch him in the face." I pause, trying to rein in my temper. "You didn't have to kill him."

"He got in my way," she shrugs annoyed.

Knowing this whole thing is useless, I plan on getting out of here. But before I do, I walk towards her, lean down to her level, and look her in the eyes. "You were never going to be Madam President, Isabella. Get over it. Your life's work was a complete and total waste."

I'm not sure if it's my knowledge of her plan or just her natural hatred for anything and everything, but at that moment, as I turn to walk away, she launches herself at me. Knowing she is tied up, I slowly turn back towards her and take a huge step back, but not quick enough or big enough. Unbeknownst to me, one of her hands is loose and quickly fastens around my neck, with her thumb digging into my airway.

I try to fight her hand around my neck and get free, but I can't get it off. Her ankles are still tied to the bottom of the chair and one arm is looped around the back, but loose enough she can stand. How can someone with only one hand have so much strength and know exactly where to put the pressure to cut off my airway? She was trained to do so, that's how. Knowing I can't make her budge and that Jamie and Williams will be coming to my rescue soon, I try to reason with her.

"They'll kill you," I gasp for air and try to warn her.

"Not before I kill you," she grins confidently as she presses in harder. Her eyes look absolutely violent and evil. I wonder if this is what she looked like when she stabbed Oliver. Killing people is obviously a hobby of hers.

The more I struggle trying to get her off, the harder she presses. I try to use the moves they taught us in self-defense and aim for her face or try to knock her arm away or move back to get out of her reach, but it's no use. She anticipates all my moves and is strong enough to keep her hold, even with only one hand. And when I try to move away, I'm dragging her body weight with my own so I don't get far.

As I begin to run out of air, I realize that Williams isn't coming to my rescue and something is terribly wrong because the minute she jumped me, Jamie would've been in here. Realizing she had a hand free to begin with, I quickly sense that I've been set up.

How? I wasn't supposed to be alone. Where is Jamie? Or Lyncoln?

I try one last time to release her hand from around my neck, but it doesn't work. I try to poke her in the eye and hit her arm again, but nothing is releasing her death grip from my neck. I even try kicking her legs still attached to the chair, but she just won't budge. If anything, she tightens her grip.

I am completely alone.

No one is coming to help me.

This is bad.

Starting to feel dizzy and lightheaded from over exertion and realizing this could be the end of the road for me, I reach behind my back and pull out the gun that Lyncoln handpicked and insisted I wear at all times during interrogations. Black spots dance across my vision which is becoming blurry. I know, without a doubt, I have only seconds of air left before I pass out and then she finishes me off. I move quickly without thinking about it. I use one finger to switch the safety while it's still behind my back, then I bring it around and barely take time to aim before I pull the trigger. Isabella never sees it coming.

Isabella and the chair fall to the floor immediately, the metal chair banging loudly. A pool of blood begins flowing from her upper stomach. I drop my gun, gasping for air, and fall to my knees as my hands go to my neck. My throat is on fire as I gulp sweet oxygen back into my lungs.

As she loses blood and I sit there gasping for air, I realize she probably isn't going to live through this injury. She's losing blood too fast, just like Oliver did. And unlike with Oliver, no one will be in a hurry to save her.

She looks up at me in obvious pain. She doesn't say anything, but looks oddly peaceful. As she closes her eyes, I see her face turn even more peaceful. Funny that in the moment where she is in the most pain, she finally seems to forget about everything else. Not able to stomach standing there and watching her die, I scramble to my feet and run out the door.

In the control room, Williams is nowhere to be found. Jamie is unconscious and sitting slumped to the floor by the door I just came through. The way he's facing looks like he was watching me and about to come in and was hit from behind. I check his pulse and am relieved to find that he is still breathing. He's just knocked out.

I open the door to the hallway, a hand still around my neck as my breathing is still on fire, and run down the hall back around the corner to the observation room of the other interrogation room where I know Attie and Knox will be.

I've been set up. I need help. Jamie needs help. I need someone I trust. My friends.

Seeing my bewilderment, Attie and Knox immediately stand when I enter.

"Reagan…?" Attie asks worried.

"I was set up. Jamie needs help. Help." I'm frantic. I grip the door frame and look to their guards, "Get help. Quickly. Please. Please help."

"What do you need?" Knox asks. "How can we help?"

"Lyncoln. I need Lyncoln."

Knox turns to look at Attie like he doesn't want to leave her alone and she says, "My guard is here and so is yours. Go."

He looks at her and they communicate through a look and then he leaves the room. Their guards are rapidly talking on their radios getting help too. I move out of the way to the wall by the door.

"What happened? What can I do?" Attie asks as she approaches me and moves my hands to look at my neck.

"Isabella. Hadenfelt wanted me to interrogate her. He set me up." That's all I manage as I lean against the wall in disbelief, then repeat, "I need Lyncoln."

"Knox is getting him, sweetie." She runs a hand through my hair and looks the rest of me over, taking my pulse and going back to nurse mode. "They'll be right back. I can't believe this; I just saw you not even ten minutes ago."

Then the tears start coming and I am sobbing. I slide down the wall at my back until I'm sitting with my head in my hands and my knees pulled up. I think of Henry and that I should be asking for him too, but in this moment I realize that I don't want to see Henry anyway though I know he is busy with the long sim. He would have been smart enough to shoot her in the foot, or figured out a way to save her. Henry is too good of a man to ever kill another human being.

I just killed someone.

Within minutes I hear stomping as Lyncoln, his guard, and two other men come barreling down the hallway at a sprint and into the observation room. I keep my head in my hands and don't dare look up at him.

"What the hell happened here?" Lyncoln demands and I can hear the panic in his voice right before I feel his hands on me, checking me over.

"Help Jamie. He's unconscious. Please," I start. I avoid his eyes.

"What happened?" he repeats as he takes my face in his hands. That's when he notices my neck, which must be really red. He moves my head to the side and runs a finger softly along the spot that feels sore.

"Please. Help Jamie. He's unconscious. I was set up. Williams and Hadenfelt must have set me up." That's as much as I can get out between sobs.

He looks to one of the men with him and nods as two of them go to help Jamie like I asked.

"Okay. Jamie is getting help. Now, what happened? Please. Tell me what happened." He looks confused at Attie and Knox, who just shrug, and then he turns back to me. "Reagan. What happened, sweetheart?" He says it softly, like it's just the two of us. He lifts my chin up so I look him in the eyes. I see the concern etched all over his face. His eyes flicker down to my neck again, and he clenches his jaw angrily.

"Hadenfelt had me interrogate Isabella," I begin.

"Isabella did this? She wasn't tied up?" he interrupts, fuming. He stands back up and I see his expression click into kill mode. Jaw clenched, hands clenched, he is about to kick some serious butt.

"Don't bother going in there," I say quietly in-between sobs and reach for his hand to pull him back down. Every word I say hurts more and more. The sobbing makes my throat feel worse from all the gasping for air I did in my struggle with Isabella, but I can't seem to stop crying.

"Why not, sweetheart? I promise I won't kill her, but I will personally make sure her life is a living hell." He comes back down to my level, rubbing my shoulders and wiping away my tears.

I search his eyes helplessly, wishing I didn't ever have to say the words I am about to say to him.

"You can't kill her. Because I already did."

Chapter 26

I only remember Lyncoln lifting me up and carrying me out of there. I do know there was a lot else happening around us though. Lots and lots of men in uniform. Radios were going constantly. Taggert's name was being used frequently. I think I remember Lyncoln telling me that Henry was being notified and going to leave his sim early too. Everything felt fuzzy, like a disconnect from reality, and I couldn't seem to focus on my surroundings.

Still in Lyncoln's arms and assuming we arrived at my room back at Mile High, I'm surprised when Lyncoln knocks on a door. The President opens immediately, looking alarmed and outraged.

To me he says, "Reagan, I am truly sorry, and am both relieved and glad you are okay." Then to Lyncoln, he adds, "I'm having a meeting down with Taggert and Henry as soon as they arrive. Are you coming?"

Not even pausing to chitchat, as he walks away, Lyncoln says over his shoulder, "No."

Before I know it, I'm sitting on a cold floor. Then water is all around me. A shower. I'm not on a floor, I'm in a gigantic shower. Henry's shower? All of my clothes are still on though. I don't even remember Lyncoln putting me down.

"Why did you bring me here?" I ask hoarsely, snapping back to reality.

He sits down on the shower floor with me, also fully clothed, and holds onto my cheek. "Well, either Williams is a drifter and just tried to get you killed, or Hadenfelt is even more of a despicable creature than we all imagined. Either way, I need to make sure you are safe. And this is the safest place in the entire country."

I just nod as the water falls all around me and Lyncoln rubs the back of my neck.

After a few minutes of silence, Lyncoln scoots me forward and moves behind me. He undoes my hair tie and begins to wash my hair. What is it with these boys and my hair, anyway? One blow dries my hair, the other wants to wash it? This would be funny, except that it isn't.

I try to brush him off, but he continues.

"Stop," I demand. I don't feel worthy of his kindness after what I've just done.

"Reagan." He says my name softly. More softly than he ever has before.

"I murdered her," I choke the words out. "I am a murderer."

He's in front of me again, eye level. "So am I. Remember? The first time when I killed one of the men that killed my father."

I nod. He was thirteen. Thirteen years old! I can't imagine the pain he went through as a just-turned-teenager. He killed a man and watched his father die at the same time. Terrible doesn't even begin to describe it.

"It's going to be okay, Regs. You did what you had to do, to live." He brushes his thumb over my lips.

"Why didn't I shoot her in the stupid foot?" I argue. It hurts to talk, but it hurts to realize that I'm capable of killing someone in cold blood. Am I just as bad as she was?

"She had you by the throat. You couldn't breathe. You didn't have time. I'm sure you waited until the last possible moment too, thinking that Williams, or Jamie, or me, or someone would come. And we both know she was going to die anyway." He wipes the tears from my cheeks I didn't even realize were falling because of the water from the shower also on my face.

I know he's right but I still feel the guilt eating away at my soul. *I took a life.*

"You shouldn't have been in that room. Hadenfelt *will* pay for this," Lyncoln says with raw protectiveness in his eyes. "Even if I have to do it myself."

He wraps me in his arms and we just sit there, fully clothed, while the shower water falls down around us.

I eventually let him wash my hair because I don't have any fight left in me, and I don't think I can talk anymore to argue. After sitting there for forever, he sees that my skin is starting to get "pruney", as my mom calls it, so he gets out of the shower. He leaves me to quick change into jeans and a t-shirt and then comes back in with a huge towel.

He reaches in and shuts off the water while I continue to sit there. The shampoo smell from my hair that smells like Henry is weirdly comforting.

"Reagan, I need you to take off your wet gear and get in this towel okay? I mean I would love to do it for you and get to see you naked and all, but I'm pretty sure we both don't want it to go down like this. I'm going to be right around the corner."

His use of the word "naked" gets me moving. Knowing he is just around the tiled corner, and that he will come back if I don't do as he commands, I quickly take off my boots. My pants are hard to get off soaked through. As quickly as I can, I do as he says and wrap the oversized towel around myself.

"All clear?" Lyncoln asks shortly after. I'm amused by his military terms and would find it hilarious in a different situation.

"Yeah," I respond, stepping out of the shower. "All clear."

He comes back around the corner with another towel and dries my hair and shoulders. Knowing I am naked under the towel, I feel awkward and just stare at his feet. I have never seen him barefoot before. I decide I like it. He seems more human and less military legendy in his bare feet.

He quickly runs a hair brush through my hair and says, "There is a toothbrush right here if you want it. And here are some clothes." He points to a pile of clothes. "They are mine for now. I had my guard grab me some and he brought me an extra pair for you. Sarge is in the meeting and Jamie is still getting checked out so I couldn't get you any of yours until Gertie arrives, is that okay?" he asks.

I nod. "Jamie is okay?"

He nods and smirks, "Pissed off. They almost had to tranq him. He might kill Hadenfelt before the night is up."

I breathe out in relief. *Jamie is okay.*

Lyncoln pauses at the door of the bathroom a moment. His blue-brown eyes are worried and angry and something else I can't put my finger on. He kisses me on the forehead and leaves me to change. I do so, brush my teeth, and throw my hair up into a bun on top of my head. When I come out of the bathroom, he has a cup of tea ready for me in the living room of Henry's quarters.

"Your throat must be burning." His tone of voice throughout all of this tears at me. I once thought he might not be capable of being this tender. I was wrong.

"Are you sure you don't want to go to that meeting?" I ask as I sit on the couch beside him, knowing that he would want to go. He enjoys the hunt and has just been handed a new prey, Hadenfelt.

"I'm not leaving you, at least not until Henry gets here." He looks me straight in the eyes intensely while he says it and moves in closer to wrap his arms around me. He then whispers into my hair, "Thank you for fighting back. Thank you for still being here. I don't know what I would've done if I would've lost you." I can hear the emotion in his voice as he takes a shaky breath.

His words make me feel better as I realize that I did do the right thing in fighting back. I feel bad because I shot her in the wrong spot, but I did fight back. I honored Oliver in not allowing her to take down the both of us. Lyncoln's words also make me come unglued as I realize I was supposed to be making a decision about him and Henry any moment now. I'm going to have to lose one of them, one way or another.

Lyncoln then picks me up and carries me to Henry's huge bed where he holds me as I cry it out for the second time in less than two weeks.

****

I wake up to a familiar smell and realize that I'm still wearing Lyncoln's shirt. I hear voices and then Lyncoln walks in the room. Seeing I'm awake, he sits on the bed beside me and takes my hand.

"That was Henry radioing in. He went straight to the meeting since I'm here and you were out. Then he will be here as soon as he can. Or I can go get him now if you want, since you're awake." He pauses then when I don't say anything adds, "Also. Due to the obvious dangerous nature of this Culling, the President and Culling Board have decided to send all but the final four couples home."

"What?" I snap my head up and sit straighter.

Holy crap.

"You and Henry, Knox and Attie, Mav and Elizabeth, and sadly Chris and Marisol," he explains.

The blood drains from my face. Did they send him home?

"What about you?" I ask, trying to calm the horrified look I am sure is on my face.

[482]

"I'm still here for now." He gives me that signature half-smile.

I let out a breath I was holding and close my eyes in relief. "I don't want you to go."

"I don't want to go either. Other than all this drifter crap, I'm kind of starting to like the Culling, which surprises you and me both." He kisses me on the forehead and then changes the subject, "So the Hadenfelts must think they have this thing in the bag now. You realize you have to take them down, right?"

I sigh. "I don't even know if I want it anymore. Omaha sounds pretty nice and boring right about now."

Once it's out of my mouth, I know it's how I've been feeling since Oliver's death and all the knowledge about the drifters and this ongoing war. And although I miss my family immensely and want to protect them, I know I can do more for them here than I can do in Omaha. I want to go home, but I know I would be miserable there knowing what I now know. I'm just like October described before leaving.

"Reagan. We both know that's out of the question. Attie is too tenderhearted. Elizabeth and Maverick are too idealized. It's going to come down to you and Marisol. Are you really going to leave knowing that she'll become Madam President?" he reasons. "You're just going to hand it over to her like that?"

"No." I know he's right, I just wish I had more of a choice in the matter.

"Plus, now you can officially stay in Denver, even if you don't win." He winks.

I just gulp. I don't know how I feel about that right now. For the longest time I was so nervous I would be sent home, and one or both of them would still be here in the Culling moving on with someone else. Now, I finally don't have to worry about that anymore. But with everything else going on, I have a hard time feeling relieved.

"What's the deal with Christopher anyway?" I ask Lyncoln, knowing that he knows him better. "He doesn't even seem to like

Marisol that much. He's always been nice to me, but I don't really know him that well."

"I don't think he does like her that much though they do have a history. They used to date before she went all manipulative and mean. But, Chris is a very smart man, very calculated, and to be honest, he wouldn't be a half-bad President. He just saw a way to get to the end and he took it. He doesn't have to be in love with her to be the president. It's as simple as that."

"But what about the whole family image thing the Presidential Couple is supposed to portray?"

"Ha. I would wager that if they won, they would both have someone on the side shortly after. The kids might not even end up his." He shrugs. "Not that they would check or anything."

"She can't win," I say disgusted. Her father pretty much sent me to my death earlier today and if she wins, he will have even more power. She could appoint him *"how she deems necessary"* and that right there is a disaster waiting to happen. I venture to say he would run the country more than she even would.

"Then you will." He stares me down affectionately.

I blush at his confidence in me. "So now what?" I ask, needing something to do.

"Now we wait to hear what they decided in the meeting to do about Hadenfelt and Williams. Williams is gone. There was a lockdown while we searched the entire building, but the surveillance footage showed him leaving DIA shortly after leaving you with Isabella. He knocked Jamie out cold with the butt of his gun as soon as you opened the door and ran for it. And though it sucks that he is a drifter, or compromised in the very least, it could've been far worse. He was fully armed and didn't kill you himself." He pauses a moment to clench his jaw angrily before continuing, "Meanwhile Hadenfelt, of course, is blaming this all on Williams, saying it was his idea to let you in there with Isabella. He acts as if Williams did all of this on his own. He says he had no idea."

"Well isn't this just great. Hadenfelt has the perfect alibi in Williams being gone and seemingly our drifter mole. I know Hadenfelt was in on it somehow. He might not have known that she would try to kill me, but he wanted me in that room. He wanted me at the very least scared. He wanted me knocked down a peg or two. I just wish I knew how far he was in on it. He could be working with the drifters too since the mole was one of his trusted men." I'm so angry as I finish speaking, I just want to punch something or scream out in frustration. The only reason I don't is that Lyncoln is rubbing my palm trying to calm me down.

"And we might not ever know. Hadenfelt may have just committed treason, but we'll never have evidence enough to call him on it," Lyncoln adds intelligently.

"Except we have Samson." I smile then stop smiling right away as I worry. "Wait, is he safe? Hadenfelt would take care of him just to save himself. And Samson was worried about the mole coming after him. If it was Williams, he was right about being in danger. The mole could hear his every word."

"Yeah. He's fine. Taggert and I were on our way down the minute Attie and Knox's guards called for backup. I met Knox at the elevators. I came to you and Taggert went to Samson and Hadenfelt. It's a good thing your interrogation with Isabella didn't last long, or we could've lost Samson too. Hadenfelt obviously underestimated you. He took Samson in a different room where Attie and Knox wouldn't be able to see and had one of his men working his evil magic on him." He shakes his head and I wonder what exactly went down. "Samson is a bit banged up and says he will deal with no one but you from here on out."

"What a mess." I shake my head.

"I know." He rubs my shoulder trying to take away all the stress I feel.

What a day. What. A. Day. I just sit there a moment taking it all in.

"Wanna go cook something in the Presidential Kitchen while we wait for Henry?" he asks, standing and reaching for my hand.

I nod my head in surprise. "You? Can cook?"

"Oh please, gorgeous. You have yet to see all my talents," he says playfully as I take his hand. "I called in the doctor that serves in my unit too. Please don't fight me on this. Just let him take a quick look at your throat and then let me wine and dine you."

I still feel like a horrible person for what happened with Isabella, but the more I sit around doing nothing but thinking about it, the more I feel like a weight is pressing down on my body and going to either suffocate me or flatten me into a million tiny pieces. So I guess I will see this doctor and then see what Lyncoln is going to cook me.

****

I sip on a glass of iced tea and stir some sort of white wine pasta sauce while Lyncoln slices, dices, and spices into the concoction I'm stirring. We talk back and forth and as the day drags on, I feel less and less guilty for what happened with Isabella. She attacked me, not the other way around. I just wish I would've been with it enough to shoot her in her stupid traitorous foot. Yes, it's probably true that she may have died today whether it was by my hand or not, but I just wish I didn't have to deal with the ramifications of taking a life. Then again, her grip on my throat was so good, would anything but a kill shot have stopped her from killing me?

I guess now we'll never know.

Cooking dinner with Lyncoln is oddly soothing. That and the fact that though I have now killed a person, he has never once looked at or treated me differently. I love him for that.

"So, if you could do anything and there was no Culling, what would you do?" I ask Lyncoln, thinking of when I asked Henry that same question. I want to get my mind off of Isabella, who my train of thought always seems to be returning to.

"Career-wise, I would still be in the military. It's all I've ever known. It saved me from a dark time in my life." He shrugs. "I have no idea what I wanted to do before my dad died, but I'm not even the same person as then. Otherwise, more than anything, I want to have my own family. In meeting you, I've realized how much I want that. I think it will be therapeutic for me in a way. A way to honor the memory of my dad, in being the best damn dad I can be."

This somewhat surprises me and breaks my heart. The aggressive and all-empowering Lyncoln Reed just wants to be a dad? Lord have mercy.

"Don't look at me like that. Yeah, I'm dark and mysterious or whatever you call it, but losing what siblings I would have had in addition to my dad has always made me want a big family. I want…I don't know? At least four kids? I want the craziness of a bunch of runny noses and dirty diapers and all that. I want…" he drifts off as if thinking.

"Go on," I urge and take a sip of my iced tea, trying to cool my hormones.

"I want you. I want this." As he says it he uses his knife to point to him and point back to me and sighs. "I want a wife I can respect and love like I do you. It scares the heck out of me to think that you are the only person on the planet that could ever be that to me. I respect you just as much as I love you."

I stir the sauce in front of me not knowing what to say to that. The image he paints of his future family makes me want to be the one there with him. He deserves a happy ending, that's for dang sure. I try my hardest not to start tearing up as I continue to stir.

Seeing my lack of response he adds, "I'm not meaning to be persuasive or add more pressure on you or anything. I was just being honest. Please don't pity me. I hate it when people do that." He reaches to add more stuff to the sauce then runs his hand down my arm as if reassuring me he's fine. "How about you, what would you do?"

[487]

As he goes to the fridge to get another ingredient, I repeat the same basic thing I said to Henry, "I don't know, but I know I like helping people."

He stops at the open refrigerator door and turns to me with his signature half-smile, "That you do. You will go all psycho and enter an interrogation room to save even an enemy, even when we were given specific instructions to only sit there and watch."

"Hey, now." I pretend to be offended and turn back to my sauce, like he isn't there.

Except he is. The air seems to spark as I feel him near me before I see or know for sure that he is. I feel his breath on my shoulder and neck. I know once we start, with the day I've had, my body will not want him to stop kissing me. But then again, after the day I've had, I need one of those mind-numbing make-out sessions pretty bad.

"Did you kiss Isabella?" I blurt out so I don't throw myself at him. "I don't mean to ruin the mood, she just...uh...said something."

He sighs. "Yeah I did. I was young and dumb and girls were giving me attention. She isn't the only one."

"Okay," I respond with a shrug and continue stirring.

"Reagan." His velvety voice says my name softly as he puts down my spoon, turns the burner down, and turns me around so I'm facing him. He looks...shy? Sheepish? Something.

"What?" I ask, wondering what he seems so weird about. I mean, his track record with girls isn't really a secret here in Denver.

"I slept with two of them and kissed more than I can even count or care to remember. I'm sorry if that affects your image of me, but you deserve to know. It was right around when I started the military. It was a *long* time ago. I realize I have less than a ten-percent chance with you. But on the very remote chance that you do choose me, I want you to know exactly what you're getting yourself into. No surprises, no regrets." He then switches his weight from one foot to the other as he awaits my response while searching my eyes for a glimmer of hope.

[488]

I look at him and slowly blink a few times. "Okay," I say with the same tone as before. Do I like what I am hearing? No. Does it surprise me? No. I know how much of a mess he was, so how can I judge him for a hard time in his life?

"Okay?" he repeats, wanting me to elaborate.

"Am I jealous that you have a past and I do not? Heck yeah, I am. But, I'm not going to change my opinion of you for something you did in the past. All of that," I gesture, "made you the man you are today, and *that* man is pretty darn impressive. Besides, given my current situation, I'm trying my best not to judge."

He wraps his arms around me as he lets out a big breath and kisses my hair. "Thank you, Regs."

I don't know what to say so we just stand there a while. We hear voices coming down the hallway and break apart back to our duties although he stands closer to me than necessary with our arms touching.

"There you guys are." I hear Henry's worried voice and moments later am in his arms. He kisses me on the mouth quickly and soundly, and then holds me while looking at me with his worried emerald eyes. "I have never been more scared in my entire life as when they called me out of my sim."

"Taggert, Mr. President." Lyncoln steps away to greet the other two men as he gives Henry a moment with me. It breaks my heart to know that they are both the jealous type, but both give each other time with me. Reason number five million and forty-three that this situation is messed up and has gone on for far too long. This needs to end. They deserve better than this.

"Ms. Scott, again, I am truly sorry for what you had to go through," the President says as he plops himself on a stool on the other side of the counter. It's weird to see the most powerful man in the world sitting somewhere as casual as a kitchen bar stool.

"Thank you." I shrug and turn back to the sauce to keep stirring. Does he realize this is the second time in the last week he has had to apologize to me? I'm not going to tell him it's okay because it isn't. I shouldn't have had to kill Isabella today. I shouldn't have had to save Samson. Both of those things should have never gotten to that point.

Henry refills my tea, gets some bottles of water for everyone else, and then joins his dad and Taggert on the bar stools while Lyncoln and I continue cooking.

"So?" Lyncoln asks and switches to work mode although he stays close to me, even giving my hand a random squeeze at moments when the others aren't looking.

"So Hadenfelt is getting demoted and suspended for 30 days. Without a confession from Williams, we don't know how guilty or how deep Hadenfelt was in this," Taggert begins and Lyncoln clenches his jaw. Taggert holds up a finger to stop whatever argument he's about to make and continues, "But since he was dumb enough to be waterboarding Samson when we found them and stormed in there, he still disobeyed direct orders. So we are demoting him and watching him. Unfortunately, that is all we can do for now. One more false move though, and he's gone."

"Gone?" I ask. Gone as in killed, or gone from DIA?

"As the Head of Interrogations, and completely gone from DIA," the President chips in. "Trust me, stripping him of all power and watching him live like an ordinary civilian will be the cruelest form of punishment for him."

There seems to be no lost love between those two. So why does Hadenfelt still have his job again?

"When?" Lyncoln asks.

"Already happened. He threw quite the fit, made all sorts of threats, and was escorted home. He's being watched round the clock." Taggert rolls his eyes in disgust.

"And what about the obvious?" Lyncoln asks. "If Williams is the other drifter, he was in contact with Hadenfelt every day. We all know Hadenfelt is a sick bastard. He was torturing the drifters worse than we thought, so it's highly unlikely he is one, but who's to say he wouldn't make a deal with the drifters? Especially in regards to this Culling? This isn't good enough. His plan could already be in place." He reaches down to squeeze my hand again. "How do we know he isn't compromised?"

"We won't know, all we can do is watch him, and that we will. When he makes a move, we'll know," the President promises and adds, "And your point is exactly why we sent the other candidates home. We already knew our final four and we didn't want the others in danger any longer than necessary."

"Marisol should have been sent home too," Henry says angrily. "A while ago. Remove all chances for Hadenfelt to gain more power. Before the vote."

"You know it and I know it, son. Hadenfelt has influence on the board. None of them want her to win, but they are too scared to send her home," the President explains. "They just hope she doesn't have the votes to actually make a run at it."

"Can't you just make it a vote of the cabinet instead of waiting for the voting?" I offer, agreeing with Henry. I send him an affectionate smile trying to communicate so.

"Same story, different version." Taggert gestures with his hands and shakes his head.

"So how exactly do we make sure the Hadenfelts get stripped of their power then?" I ask confused.

"You or your friends win the Culling, dear," Taggert says looking at me dead on. "You have thirty days."

"Fantastic. More deadlines," I mumble. And even more pressure now too. This Culling could have a very disastrous ending, in more than one way.

"One more thing," Taggert says, looking at Henry and then to me.

"What?" I ask as everyone ends up looking in my direction.

"Henry wants you relieved of your interrogating duties. And I agree." He nods and pauses. "This is on me and not at all your responsibility. However, I tried speaking with Samson this afternoon to confirm that Williams is the drifter, and he will not budge. He is asking for you and only you."

"I'll do it," I say without hesitating.

"No. You don't have to," Henry insists. "Especially after today. I want you to feel like you at least have a choice. You don't have to do anything you don't want to. You're a Culling candidate, not an interrogator. The Culling is hard enough without adding that to your plate. We are all required to observe interrogations, but you are definitely not required to lead them. "

"I don't have to, but I will," I argue, thinking aloud. "I started it and I want to finish it. I'm not afraid of Samson either. And now more than ever we need to know as much information as we can. We needed to know yesterday if Williams is for sure the drifter. I don't know which outcome I prefer, that he is and that makes Hadenfelt dirty, or he isn't and Hadenfelt is just even more evil. Either way, he needs dealt with. We can't deal with an outside threat if we have an internal one."

Taggert smiles. "I really should think about recruiting women from Omaha for interrogations. You are one smart cookie."

I feel myself blush. "Thanks."

The President claps his hands together and smiles excitedly. "So now that's all settled. This smell! What are you making me for dinner this time, Lyncoln, my boy?"

****

Later that evening, after the most amazing pasta I have ever eaten, I play cards with the President as Henry and Lyncoln take a turn in a meeting of sorts with Taggert. Apparently, there is a full conference room just one floor below us within the Presidential Suite so they don't have to go far. They'll conference in with the others back at DIA. I find I don't mind the meeting because I know that other than myself, Henry and Lyncoln are the two people I know of that most want Hadenfelt gone. The more of us that are pushing for him to be removed, the better.

Afterward, Henry and I talk in his room on the ginormous couch.

"Pancakes or waffles?" Henry asks. Playing *This or That* has become our ritual.

"Waffles," I respond without hesitation.

"Books or movies?" he asks.

"Books."

"Rain or snow?"

I groan. "Neither with where I'm from since we have to work in it. But probably rain."

He shakes his head. "I disagree. I like the snow. Alien take-over or zombies?"

I laugh out loud, which is the last thing I expected to be doing today. "How about aliens deliver zombies as a means to take over our world?"

"God, I love you," he grins, not at all seeming to notice how easily he says those words to me. "I think I know this one, sweet or salty?"

"Is that even a real question?" I laugh. "But you like salty things better right?"

He nods and grins again, then stops after a moment. "Would it help if I offered to just run away with you?" he asks with a worried expression.

"What?"

"We can go wherever you want. Omaha. Here. Live like the banished. I don't care." He shrugs and rubs my arm with one hand, while the other lazily holds his chin over the back of the couch.

"What are you talking about?" I shake my head confused.

"I used to want to do this for Dad's legacy. He worked so hard and because of this huge mess with the drifters, the country is still in a fragile state. I'm starting to believe that there isn't much I can do about that; there isn't a quick fix. Now that you're in the picture, all I can think about is how to keep you safe. Do you realize that for the last two years, my dad hasn't left here much? Sure, to make his appearances, but the cabinet even meets here or he videos in. Remember the room we were in on the night of the attack?" he asks.

I nod.

"There is a room like that within these walls. His office, the bedrooms, and bathrooms are all bullet-proof and blast-proof. So when things got more intense with the drifters, he was confined here," he explains then adds, "And I don't want that life for you. I don't want you to feel like the only place you are safe is up here. I want you to be able to get some fresh air without fearing for your life. And I'd drop out of the Culling in a heartbeat if you wanted to. I'd do anything for you."

I sigh and bring a hand to his cheek, "I love you for that, but I would fear for my life even in Omaha. Now that I know what is going on, I won't be able to let go of it until I know it's handled. I'm a problem solver and have just been handed this huge problem to fix. I fear for my family every day, but I know that the best way to protect them is to stay here and figure out a way to end this war that never seems to stop."

"You do know that could take years, right?" Henry asks sadly. "Decades?"

"Yes," I answer confidently.

"And you know it isn't your responsibility, right?" he adds.

"Yes," I answer again.

He sighs but still smiles, leaning in to give me a kiss on the cheek. "That's what I was afraid you would say."

****

The next day, I convince Taggert to let me take Samson outside for some fresh air. At first he called me crazy since Williams is still on the loose. I assured him we could take as many guards as he wanted and Samson could stay tied up. I'm not sure if I pushed it so hard for Samson's sake or my own, but with the help of the men in my life, I got my way. We walk around in the same open field from when we had our paintball competition. At least ten guards are with us even though DIA sets right there in the background.

I wear my heavy jacket and gloves as the weather in Denver is turning quite cold. A November day like this makes me wonder what my parents are up to. Is harvest over or just beginning? Are they beginning working in the greenhouses? This morning there is enough moisture in the air and it is cold enough that I can see my breath when I talk. I know there would be leaves all over the ground at home that would crunch beneath your feet when you walk, much like here.

"So," Samson says quietly. He is also wearing a jacket. His feet are removed from their ties, but not his hands which are down at his sides both cuffed and roped. We walked an entire lap of the field in silence before he spoke first.

Jamie is right beside me and seems to be on pins and needles. He feels somewhat responsible for what happened with Isabella even though I have assured him he isn't. Needless to say, he will be present for every second of all interrogations now. He doesn't trust Samson at all. Oddly enough, I do. He isn't a monster like she was. I can't explain it. If anything, I trust Samson even more now.

"So." I nod once. I'm not even in the mood to talk much because I'm in my own head right now. My deadline is tomorrow and then there is the immediate matter at hand. Was Williams for sure the other drifter? He had to be if he felt comfortable just leaving Denver like that. Right?

"So are you ever going to tell me why your neck is red and why I was tortured by that sadistic jerk yesterday before a bunch of guys came in and removed him?" he asks, straight to the point.

He tried asking me the same thing earlier this morning, but I wasn't ready to talk about it and kind of just ignored him. Our interrogation session didn't get very far or last very long. Maybe all of ten minutes before I needed to bail before having a panic attack about having killed Isabella. Then I had the idea of coming outside just like I did with Sarge the night Marcia left the Culling. I just simply needed the fresh air. It's almost lunch time now, but I still thought a shorter session out here might help.

"I was with Isabella." I stop to rephrase. "Correction. I was manipulated into going to interrogate Isabella," I explain.

"And the other guy?"

"Is an idiot," I say like it's the most obvious explanation in the world.

"Wasn't she tied down?" he asks confused as his eyes rest on my jacket where my neck is hidden.

"Mysteriously one hand was free," I say pointedly and feel Jamie tense beside me as I bring it up. I look at him and shake my head as if to tell him to stop blaming himself. He was knocked unconscious. There was nothing he could do.

"I bet she will pay for that," Samson says with a shake of his head.

"She did. With her life. Williams left me alone in the room with her and knocked my guard unconscious, evidently hoping that I would be killed. When she wouldn't let go and I was running out of air, I had no other choice but to pull out my pistol and shoot her," I say the words bitterly. I'm not sure if I'm bitter at Isabella for putting me in such a situation, or bitter at myself for shooting to kill. I take a deep breath and remind myself that she did kill Oliver. These "what ifs" will drive me bonkers.

"Wow." Samson lets out a deep breath.

"So, like I said, I need to know right now if Williams is for sure the other drifter here. If he is, why didn't he just free Isabella instead of having her try to kill me? He could have taken her with him. It must mean he has a plan with Hadenfelt or that the drifters wanted me dead. And if he isn't the drifter, Hadenfelt is to blame. At this point, we are pretty sure he isn't a drifter, just a naturally evil man. So which is it?" I demand.

"Look. I never thought not telling you would put your life at risk," he says apologetically.

"And yours too." I stare him down waiting for an answer.

He finally sighs in surrender. "Yeah, Williams was a drifter, although that isn't his real name of course."

It's my turn to sigh, with frustration. In his position, Williams could have freed Isabella, and Samson too even, and made a break for it. But, he specifically wanted me out of the picture, or in the very least wanted to scare me. Why? Was it under the orders from the drifters or Hadenfelt himself? Or did he just think that it would be harder for more than one person to disappear and took the chance he had while he had it?

"Is Hadenfelt?" I wonder aloud even though I'm pretty sure I already know the answer.

"Heck no," he says confidently.

Okay, well, that doesn't exactly mean he's loyal to the State either. It seems the only thing Hadenfelt is loyal to, is his position of power. So did he make the call to have me killed? Or was he really just as innocent in this as I was and just wanted to rattle me by having me interrogate Isabella? I have a hard time believing that. When pigs fly, as we say in Omaha.

He interrupts my thinking and adds, "You, specifically, were never on our agenda. And to my knowledge, Williams was supposed to stay here as long as possible."

"Are there any others?" I ask, wondering when I will get to stop living my life in constant fear that someone I love, or myself, is in danger.

He shakes his head. "Not that I know of, but…"

"But?"

"I know that Williams was part of our plan, and a backup to our plan with Isabella. Williams would be killed if he returned on his own will after not following through with his mission. That must mean there is a backup to the backup, or…"

"Or something has changed," I finish for him.

He nods and gestures with his tied together hands. "There is always a backup, usually three. I wouldn't be surprised in this case if there were more."

"Great," I say sarcastically.

"So what was Williams' mission?" I ask.

"I'm not completely sure. I only knew of his part in our attack plan and in ensuring Isabella's safety and cover for the Culling. I'm sure he had multiple scenarios based on how our attack went. He's been here for years." He shrugs and then adds, "I never liked him. From what I know the guy is a sadist too, much like your Hadenfelt."

"I never did like either of them," I say honestly and think of Williams and Lyncoln's fight. At the moment, I wish I could take a swing at Williams. At least Lyncoln gave him a black eye though. There is that.

"Now what?" he asks and I know he is referring to his well-being. What are we going to do with him?

"Now you help me figure it out. You won't lead us to their location, correct?" I ask since this is one of the main topics Taggert has asked me to push.

[498]

"No. And since it changes often, they would know you were with me before we got there anyway. It would be suicide." He shrugs.

"And you don't want anything to do with the State?"

"No. I understand now that not all of you are evil and had no idea what was going on all those years ago. I just can't help you destroy everyone I've ever known. We have good people too."

I nod in understanding. "So that leaves it as you helping us figure out what their game plan is. For now," I offer.

"Okay," he nods in agreement although he doesn't have a choice in the matter.

"Are there others like you?" I ask randomly as an afterthought as we head back toward DIA.

"What do you mean?"

"Are there more of you that don't like the leadership of some of the drifters and are just choosing what they believe is the lesser of two evils?"

"Yeah, I mean, just like this Hadenfelt dude is pure evil, we have our own like that."

"Interesting," I say as a plan starts to wiggle its way into my brain.

****

After dinner that evening, I am with Dougall about to get started on interview prep, when a guard I have never seen walks in interrupting.

"Ms. Scott?" he asks.

"Yes? Is everything okay?" My heart begins rapidly thumping in my chest as I wonder who got hurt or what a drifter did this time.

"Yes. Quite okay. I have orders to show you something," he says with a tight smile and stands at attention, waiting for my move.

"Can this wait? I rarely get enough time with her as it is. The first interview is tomorrow evening for God's sake," Dougall says with an annoyed gesture.

"I'm afraid not. Direct orders, Professor Dougall." The guard stands firm.

"And who am I going to have to argue with about this later?" she asks, clearly annoyed.

"Uh. The former Madam President, ma'am." He nods and stands his ground again.

"What?" Dougall and I say at the same time. Then Dougall nods to me, "You better go."

I try to ask the guard what he is talking about on the way to the elevator, but all he says is, "You'll see."

Whatever that means. I'm pleasantly surprised I get to get away from Dougall though. I was fully prepared to get reamed for not having made my decision yet. I'm hours away from the hardest thing I am ever going to have to do. My deadline is tomorrow. And I didn't do it early like she asked either. I was busy with Isabella and the ramifications of our showdown. So this interruption, whatever it is, is welcomed. I don't need Dougall to remind me tomorrow is my deadline. I've been counting down days and hours since she gave it to me.

I'm even more surprised by this whole thing when the guard takes me up to the Presidential Suite. I'm not taken to Henry's wing but to a different room with a huge couch and television and none other than President Maxwell sitting on the couch. No Henry in sight.

"Honestly, Fredericks, this couldn't wait?" President Maxwell asks more annoyed than I think I've ever seen him.

The guard evidently named Fredericks moves to the TV and is pushing buttons and connecting a computer to the TV with a cord.

"This has got to be the oddest thing I have seen this week and that is saying something," the President says to me warmly with a smile.

"You don't know what this is about?" I ask.

"No. Apparently you don't either."

I shake my head. "No, sir."

Before Fredericks has a chance to explain, I hear a lovely voice say, "Are we rolling? Okay, good."

The President catches his breath, snaps his head to the screen, and cannot peel his eyes away. If I hadn't been given the clue earlier, I would have most definitely figured out that the woman before me is his late wife. She looks old, very thin, and sick. Her skin is pale and she wears a scarf around her head because I assume she has little to no hair. Although she looks frail, she still has some life in her eyes. Her facial features are soft and she has a caring look about her, like she was the best mom in the world.

"Hello," she says smiling to the camera. "I want to say how happy I am to meet you, well kind of. If you are watching this, it is because you have made it to the final four couples in the Culling with my son." She smiles bigger then looks almost sad as she adds, "And I am no longer there to meet you personally.

I catch my breath and sit down on the couch. Holy crap! She left this for me?

"I know you are an amazing and strong woman, and I know that my son would do anything in the world for you." I can see tears fill her eyes with love for her son. "I want nothing but the best for both of you, and I love you, my future daughter-in-law, already.

"I am leaving you this message though, to be given to you upon making the final four, so that you really consider what I am about to say. First off, I love my husband more than I can express. Max, you are my one and only. You are stubborn and strong and a big pain in my butt," she laughs as she wipes at a few tears that threaten to spill over. She pauses and smiles again, getting control of her emotions.

"This job, the presidency, is messy. I'm sure it hasn't been long since my passing for the Culling to be called because I know Max was ready to be done long before I got sick. This job is just..." she takes a deep breath and sighs, "messy."

"I want you to understand that it almost ate my husband alive. The decisions you have to make gnaw at you as you wonder if you made the right choices, especially now as we continue to try to take down our enemy. You absolutely can do this if you want to. You can make it work. You can be there for one another just as we were. But, I also want you to know, that you don't have to. It isn't your personal responsibility to fix things because quite honestly, like us, you could live your whole life and still not see them fixed. It is beyond exhausting.

"I raised three children and feared for their lives every day. They were mostly kept locked up here because of that. That is no way to have a childhood and as scary as it is knowing your husband is constantly risking his life by running the country, it is a hundred times worse when it is your own children at risk." She stops a moment and brings a tissue to the tip of her nose.

"I just want you to understand that and really consider it. I know you love my Henry. I know you love your country and are doing your best. But, I also want you to know that Max and I would be just as proud of you watching you start your family with the general public as we would be of you as the Presidential Couple.

"The choice is up to the both of you. Think of Henry. Think of yourself. And think of your future children. Do you really want this? If so, I couldn't be more proud. If not, I couldn't be more proud. I just want you both to be happy and wanted you to understand that our legacy is no responsibility of your own. Henry has grown up his entire life knowing there would be a Culling when he came of age. Knowing he would have an upper hand and could possibly run the country someday. I just want you to know it's not the only way. We don't expect you to make the same choices we did. And you don't have to win the presidency to be able to make a difference in this world.

"And please, please, show this to Henry when you are done. I want him to see this too, but not with his future wife because I want her to be able to see it uninhibited. Henry, I love you son. I would give you the world if I could. I know you want to further your father's legacy. It's all you have talked about lately. Just know that he and I love you no matter what. I hope you've found a love like ours. Hold onto it and cherish it, son.

"Max. I love you. I will always love you and be looking down on you. Please don't go lonely the rest of your life. Please find someone and not feel a bit guilty when you begin to feel happy again. I fought this cancer hard trying to stay with you and I just couldn't quite beat it. The only thing I ask of you is to please, please, don't be lonely. You owe it to me to find a way to be happy again."

She stops to cough into her tissue and it makes me wonder how much longer she lived after this.

"I have to go now. I love you all, always. Just think about what I have said." She smiles one last time, trying to keep all sorts of tears and emotions at bay, and the recording flickers off, the screen going blue.

The President, who is wiping his tears away says, "But how?"

Fredericks answers, "She left that and all the very specific instructions with it to a group of us three months before she passed, sir. We were not supposed to show it to any of you or speak a word of it until now. There are a few more for later dates as well."

I feel like my chest is about to explode. This woman is a woman that I could never fill the shoes of, could never emulate. She is one in a million. She confidently said those things about the woman she knows Henry loves. What if she were here to see that woman also has another man she loves? She would be ashamed. I have broken her heart and she isn't even here to feel it.

I have twelve hours or less to make a decision and this definitely didn't help me any; I just feel worse. Helpless. Torn apart.

What in the world am I going to do now?

****

I tell Sarge to send word to Henry that I will come up to see him first thing early in the morning and that I'm just worn out and going to bed. The truth is, I need time. I need more time with the both of them. I have to make an impossible decision, and like on many of the tests I have taken for the Culling, there isn't a right answer and there isn't an easy answer. The answer I want to make and the answer I feel like I should be making are not the same.

This is gunna suck.

I pace my room and think it over. I try to sleep and soon give up. I get some hot tea and make a list of things I love about each of them. That just starts the tears, so I chuck it in the trash. Although anyone seldom prays anymore, I do that too. I try everything I can think of to figure out what I am going to do.

This isn't just a simple decision. It's a decision that will more than likely last the rest of my life as it is implied that I will marry this person, winning the Culling or not. This is a forever type of decision; I can't take it back. So is what I think I am going to do the best thing? The best thing for me? Or the best thing for the country?

I wish more than anything that my mom was here to talk about this with. It is around two in the morning when I remember her words from when they came to Denver…"*Listen to your heart, double check with your brain, and then go with your gut.*"

Okay, mom. *Okay.*

Chapter 27

I knock on Henry's door the next morning after both coffee and tea. I didn't sleep much and don't normally drink coffee, but desperate times call for desperate measures. I tried to put on a bit of makeup since it's before Frank and Gertie were set to arrive, but I know I probably still look exhausted.

"Hey, beautiful," Henry says with a smile, looking striking in his dress shirt and tie. He doesn't have his jacket on yet and I love this look on him.

"Hey," I smile.

He kisses me gently and then pulls me into a huge hug. "I wish you would've let me see you last night," he says and then kisses me on the cheek. He smiles his affectionate smile and his dimples are distracting. "So you met mom."

"She is an amazing woman," I say sincerely. "I don't think amazing is even an accurate enough word."

"I think she's pretty great too," he nods and kisses me quickly again, then rubs his hands up and down my arms like he's trying to warm me. "Ready to go down for an early breakfast before your interrogations?" he asks. "I got up early to come to you, but you already beat me to it."

"Not quite," I respond nervously.

"Okay, what's up? You forget something in your room? We can go get it," he offers as he grabs his suit jacket off a nearby chair and then returns rubbing my arm up and down with the hand that doesn't now hold his jacket.

Before I chicken out, I wrap my arms around him hard and don't let go. I focus on breathing in and out as I think I might pass out.

"What's wrong, beautiful?" he asks concerned as he wraps his arms around me. He tries to move me back a little to look at me, but I won't let go.

"I can't." I haven't even started and the tears have already arrived. "I can't do this to you. Or with you. I'm so sorry. I do love you, Henry Maxwell. More than you know. You are the absolute best person I know. You deserve better than this. You deserve more than the presidency. I love you, not enough to drop out of this, but enough to save you from it. Enough to let you find someone you deserve. Enough to let you find someone worthy of those things your mom said in the video."

He drops his jacket on the floor and jerks me back to look in my eyes as tears keep falling down my face. He brushes them away. "But I just want *you*, Reagan. I don't care if it's with the presidency or not. Do you get that?"

I nod my head. He closes his eyes and I see the emotion of pain cross his facial features.

"Answer me one thing then. One thing and I will try to accept this." I see the tears spring into his green eyes as he fights down his own emotions. "Do you love Lyncoln? Are you picking him? Or are you just doing this to save me because you're always trying to save people?"

"I do love him," I say wholeheartedly. "I never thought it was possible, but I love you both, just in different ways. I don't want to make this choice. Especially not today. But your mom is right, this job is messy. I want you to live your dreams. I want you to have a family and not have to worry about your children. I want you to have it all. And I love you...I just..."

"You don't love me as much. Or enough," he finishes for me.

My heart shatters as I realize he's right. And it's cruel to put it that way, but it's the truth.

"I just wanted *you!*" he says frustrated. He embraces me again then shakes his head and says more quietly, "I just wanted you. I don't know how to have it all without you. Please don't do this, Reagan."

"I am so sorry." I sob huge, heavy sobs with my words. "So, so sorry."

We stand there for a while, each of us battling our emotions. He wipes a hand at his nose and runs the other one through his hair. "Did you make this decision before you saw the video?"

"Actually, yes. I was just second guessing myself and going through all sorts of 'what ifs' before I saw it. Seeing the video made me feel almost relieved as it confirmed what I was feeling about the presidency. I felt guilty too, like I was betraying your mother. If she knew that the woman you loved, loved two different men and couldn't decide between them, she would have been *so* disappointed. It made me feel ashamed. I knew that was confirmation enough for me," I respond, fighting back more tears. "Not that it made this any easier."

"Actually, if she knew you, really knew you, she would have said more good things about you than what she said on that video. You are one in a million, Reagan Scott. If this is really what you want, it will hurt like hell, but I will figure it out. Please tell me this is really what *you* want," he says softly and raises a hand to my cheek, looking for any last traces of hope.

"It is. I have to choose Lyncoln. I want to choose Lyncoln. I hope this isn't goodbye though. I love you, Henry. I really do. I feel like I'm saying goodbye to a part of my soul." I choke as more tears spill over.

I reach in to kiss him on the cheek. He turns to kiss me on the lips, kissing me like he is trying to convince me to stay. When I finally pull back, knowing that this is not making things any easier, I say, "I don't want to say goodbye to you. I don't want to leave you, but I have to go.

I can't keep doing this to the both of you. It's gone on for far too long and I hate it. I am so sorry. So, so sorry. My head wanted it to be you. My heart just can't."

Before he can try to console me and make me feel even worse, I spin around and leave as quickly as my legs will carry me.

****

I cry in the hallway as Sarge and I race to the elevator. I cry in the elevator. I cry in the next hallway. Sarge grabs my hand and asks me if I am okay. I nod and then continue to cry as he breaks protocol and hugs me. My heart is completely and utterly broken, and yet I also feel so relieved that this back and forth between two guys thing is over. I then cry as I feel guilty about feeling relieved. So very many ugly tears.

Finally, we get to where we are going and I knock on the door. Sarge has to know by now what is going on but he lets me be.

A shirtless Lyncoln answers the door. "Babe," he greets softly before he takes in my tears and then repeats worriedly, "Babe?"

"Can I please come in?" I ask through the sobs. I have to look a mess by now. Mascara everywhere, snot streaming out of my nose. One huge ball of emotion.

"Of course," he says concerned. He looks to Sarge, who just shrugs.

He closes the door and wraps me in his arms, right there in the doorway. "Is everything okay?" he asks after a moment or two. His warm, bare skin on mine helps, but I still can't stop the tears.

"No," I say and mean it.

He seems to know why I'm here.

"Oh hell, Reagan. It's okay," he says and leans back to look me in the eyes. Those deep blue-brown eyes make me feel even worse. "I know what this is about. I'll be okay. It's okay, sweetheart."

He brings me in closer and I can't even find the words I need to say. He has it all wrong, but his bare chest is intoxicating and he just smells...*like home.*

"I will always love you though." Hearing his words both breaks my heart and makes my heart flutter at the same time. "Always."

"No." I push him off as I walk farther into his room.

"It's okay, Regs," he says as he moves towards me and tries to grab me again. "It had to happen eventually."

"No," I say more firmly this time and step back.

"Hey." He takes my hand and kisses my knuckles. "It's okay."

"Would you just shut up already?" I snap annoyed as I whip my hand away and try to breathe normally again. I hold up a hand to stop him from touching me. "If you say 'it's okay' one more time, I swear to God I will kick you."

This stops him and finally shuts him up as he looks to me confused and a bit amused at my empty threat.

I take a deep breath, gulp down my emotions, and get serious. "I never wanted this. I had never kissed a boy, much less dated one, before coming here. Now I love both of you," I say emphatically as he nods his head in understanding. He tries to move closer to me, but I hold up a hand again to stop him and take another step backward. "My heart is in a million pieces right now and I don't know how to fix it, but you have to help me try to put myself back together...*please.*"

"What?" he asks surprised. I see a glimmer of an emotion cross his face that I haven't seen before. Hope maybe? Shock?

"I love you. And sometimes I hate you. But if I drown out everything...the Culling, the drifters, Hadenfelt..." I stop to gesture, "Everything. If I just listen to my heart...it's you. It always has been."

I don't have time to take a breath and finish my speech before I feel his lips crashing into mine. He kisses me breathless like that first kiss in the trees and pulls away a long, long time later.

"Tell me this is real. Tell me this isn't a dream right now," he says, pressing his forehead into mine and taking a deep breath like he is trying to breathe me in.

"It's real," I whisper.

"I love you, Reagan. I know you love Henry, too," he pauses as I see him get emotional, not teary-eyed--but emotion nonetheless. He closes his eyes for a brief moment to keep his composure and then he puts a hand on my face and brushes his thumb across my lips, "Other than having my dad back, you are the only thing I have ever wanted in this life. I don't know how or why this happened. I don't think I have ever been more surprised...or happy."

More tears stream down my face, and this time they are the happy kind.

"Are you really mine?" he asks incredulously.

"I'm yours." I nod.

He grins. "Even better."

****

We decide to have breakfast in his room since I look like a mess and don't feel like being around everyone else. While we are eating, there is a knock on the door.

Lyncoln goes to answer it and then comes back in and says, "It's for you."

"Ms. Scott." Professor Dougall steps in the room and greets me. "A word? Today is your deadline." She looks at me, taking in my disheveled appearance disapprovingly, looks to Lyncoln, and then back to me again as if she wants to talk to me in private.

"I've made my decision, Professor Dougall," I say sadly and fight back more tears. How can my emotions switch from so happy to so sad within seconds? Will this always hurt this bad? Knowing I caused someone I care so much about such heartache? I had to crush Henry's heart in order to follow my own. And I crushed not only his heart, but his presidency shot too.

"Okay?" Dougall asks uncomfortably and looks from me to Lyncoln and back again.

"Well don't act so surprised," Lyncoln says, squinting at her like he's mad. "She chose me." He gives her a rare real grin and winks at her.

She looks to me and I nod.

"I take it Henry knows?" she asks gently.

I nod and feel that pain in my gut again, "He does." Lyncoln places his hand on my knee and gives it a squeeze of support.

"Oh. Okay then," she says immediately more chipper than before, "Well, I need a minimum of three hours with you before the interviews tonight, and Lyncoln will need to be there for at least half of it, if not all of it. Also, when I stopped by your room, Frank and Gertie were a bit flustered and trying to find you." She shrugs. "You may want to speak with them."

"So what you are telling me is that there won't be interrogations today?" I ask annoyed.

"Definitely not." She purses her lips in a thin line to show her displeasure.

"Okay then," I say feeling bummed. I was happy with the progress I was making yesterday with Samson. And I was looking for a break from all of this guilt that is gnawing at me.

"I will go inform the other board members of your decision. You have two hours," she tells me. She gives Lyncoln a smile and leaves.

I stand up and brush my hands off. "I suppose I better go check in with Frank. This morning we were supposed to do the last fitting for my gown for tonight, but I left before they got there."

I start for the door.

"Wait a minute. I have to go the whole morning without seeing you?" he asks like he is wounded.

"Don't you usually?" I turn back around to roll my eyes at him.

He stands and moves so quickly I don't know how it's humanly possible. He grabs me by the hand and pulls me into his chest, which unfortunately now has a shirt on it. "Well yeah, but that was before."

He kisses me in such a way that I know I made the right decision.

Henry is the perfect guy. I always felt like I was trying to be the best version of myself to keep up with him. Lyncoln is far from perfect, but he sees me as is, in all my flaws and strengths, and meets me there in the muck of it all. I can just be me with Lyncoln. I realized a while ago that I am more myself around Lyncoln than I ever was around Henry. Henry somehow mostly saw the good me because that is who I was trying to be around him. Whereas Lyncoln just sees me, good or bad or messy or mad. *Just me.*

The reason I was so afraid of giving in to my feelings for Lyncoln was that I knew the power he had over me and it terrified me. I love his passion. I love his darkness. I love his mystery. I love everything about him from the way he walks to the way he talks. I tried to distance myself from him because I was afraid of my feelings, afraid of how much I cared for him and how out of control it made me feel. But, I pull him out of his darkness and he pulls my strengths out of me. We are a perfect team. We might not be perfect people, but we are perfect together.

Chapter 28

Frank takes one look at my face and says, "What happened? Did you sleep at all last night, darling?"

"A couple hours maybe," I lie.

"I swear as soon as they had you work in interrogations you have been getting less and less sleep," he says angrily.

"That wasn't it, Frank," I say with a sly smile. I do enjoy spending every morning with my attendants.

"Is it Hadenfelt? That evil man. I swear. I haven't been in active military for many a moons, as they say, but if I see him in the hallways..."

"Dear, shut up. She's trying to tell you." Gertie playfully smacks him in the chest to shut him up.

"Two weeks ago they gave me a deadline about Henry and Lyncoln. I had to choose. Today was the deadline." I shake my head, still feeling absolutely gutted by having to hurt Henry like I did.

Gertie gives me a side hug. "I am so sorry, especially after all that you have gone through the last few weeks. I can't believe they made you do that. It hardly seems fair given the stress you are already under. Are you doing okay?"

"I think so. I picked Lyncoln by the way," I admit shyly.

When I figured out I wanted to pick Lyncoln, I knew that people weren't going to understand. Henry was my shoe-in for the presidency. Not that Lyncoln is a bad choice, but I pretty much had it in the bag if I picked Henry. So I'm sure that's what everyone expected me to do. October helped to point out to me that none of that matters. Plus, if I can't win with a man like Lyncoln and win only because of who Henry's dad is, then I don't want it anyway.

"I'm so glad," Gertie says, surprising me. I look at her with raised eyebrows and she continues, "Henry is your best friend and you have an incredible bond, but you and Lyncoln. Ahhh, fireworks happen when you are near one another."

I like the way she describes that even though she reminds me I will be missing my best friend.

"I'm happy you've made a decision and have that behind you. I would have supported you either way, darling," Frank adds.

"Thank you, Frank." I smile affectionately at them both and know Frank is about to go crazy if we don't address my attire for the evening. "So burgundy in the style we discussed?"

"Yes, and it is just marvelous." He nods, eyes twinkling in excitement.

****

"You need to look cozier than that," Dougall commands. This is about the third rude remark she has said in the last five minutes.

We are sitting answering her millions of questions in interview prep. Dougall will be asking the questions tonight also. She has been threatening to throw in questions we aren't prepared for, but I highly doubt it is in Dougall to do something she doesn't already know the outcome of. She just wants us prepared for anything.

"Can you give her a break? She's had a rough day and a rough couple of weeks. Even without a deadline, I might add," Lyncoln snaps at her while rubbing my back with the hand he has draped over the back of my chair. He already knew about the deadline but was shocked that with Oliver and Isabella and everything going on that the board was so cruel in making me keep to it. He's happy with the outcome though.

We are answering all of her questions right too, she just wants us to feel more like a lovey dovey couple. And we are, we definitely are behind closed doors, it's just that as I sit there at Mile High cozied up to Lyncoln, I also have in the back of my mind that Henry is upstairs and broken hearted somewhere. I have a hard time letting myself be happy today when I broke someone else's heart this morning. Maybe she was right. Maybe I should have made the decision a while ago. Oh wait, I was busy grieving a friend and killing Isabella. *Sigh!*

"I'm just saying that you need to bring your a-game tonight. Give it everything you've got," she says seriously, almost as if it is an urgent matter.

Does she know something I don't?

"Have you ever seen Lyncoln not give it everything he's got?" I reply annoyed.

Lyncoln winks at her. He can be quite the charmer when he wants to be.

"I guess not," Dougall says hesitantly. Though she still seems happy enough with my decision, she seems worried. I don't get it.

"Okay, then. Next question," I say all business.

****

I'm standing before the mirror once again not recognizing my reflection. Frank is an artist, he truly is. I'm wearing a burgundy dress that is mermaid style. It is tight around my chest and down to my hips before the slit in the thigh, where it flows outward. The bodice is the best part. Along the top of my rib cage, there is an upside-down "v" of about an inch that is sheer material, so sheer you can even see my skin through it. Above that, black sparkles are placed strategically throughout the dress material making it have a torn look to it. A very classy torn look, that is.

My hair is half up and half down. My makeup is done with a smoky look to it. I have an amazing necklace and earring pair that makes me nervous to wear. I hope they aren't real and I don't bother to ask because I don't want to know. The necklace is chunky and hides what the makeup doesn't of the bruising on my neck from Isabella. Perhaps my favorite part of this outfit though, is the long black gloves I wear on my arms that match the bodice of my dress perfectly. I also have black sparkly shoes to match.

I look...like royalty! Now if only I felt the part. It seems crazy that a whole two days ago I shot Isabella, and now here I am playing dress up, heading into the final four of the Culling.

Hearing a knock on my door, I take a deep breath and open it to find Lyncoln. He is wearing a black tux, with black leather looking lapels that match amazingly well with the sparkles in my dress. He has on a burgundy vest and shirt with a black tie. The burgundy contrasts the blue in his eyes and makes them pop. He has his hands in his pockets and for a moment I forget to breathe as I wonder if this man is really my boyfriend. He is way more attractive than any of the old movie actors used to be. If I wasn't so dressed up, I would feel inadequate standing next to him. And he doesn't even try! It's just not fair.

"Wow." Lyncoln nods his approval as his gaze turns more animal like.

"Ready?" I ask. I turn to grab my matching wristlet that only holds lip gloss and tissues, and is kind of useless.

Lyncoln enters my room, letting the door slowly shut behind him, and circles around me like a vulture. "Wow."

"Like you haven't seen me in a dress before." I roll my eyes dramatically.

His gaze starts at my shoes and follows the slit up my leg, and then up my curves until his eyes find mine. I turn no less than ten shades of red. There is something so raw and powerful in the way he is looking at me. It's his "I know you" look but on steroids.

"You look amazing," he says with a slow smile that morphs into a grin.

"You look pretty good yourself." I smile back. "I have to say, I thought it was silly, but I kind of like this matching thing." I reach out and straighten his already straight tie.

He grabs my hand, holding it there, and steps closer to me. "Mhmm," he mumbles absentmindedly.

"You are acting like an animal," I say shyly as his gaze gets more intense.

"Mhmm," he mumbles again as he leans in for the kill.

"You'll make us late and Dougall will cut your throat." I try to make an effort to argue my way out of what I am sure will be a hot and heavy smoocheroo.

"Mhmm." He ignores me and his lips find mine. One hand is on my rib cage and the other is on my back. He pulls me in tight and kisses me hungrily but affectionately. When he pulls back, he smiles, saying, "Check me for lip gloss? We are going to be broadcast across the entire country, you know."

I playfully punch him and wipe off his lips, which do in fact look a little shimmery.

"I don't understand why you can't contain yourself," I say playfully, trying to be annoyed although my body temperature is sky rocketing and I would like nothing more than to skip the interview for some more kissing like that. His eyes when he comes at me like that are…feral. In a good way. Ferally awesome.

"It's because…" he says looking at me so intently I swear I can see the fire coming out of his gaze, "now you are mine. If you thought I couldn't contain myself before, you are going to be amazed at how much I am not going to be able to keep my hands off of you."

I smile like a fool and grab him by the tie for another quick peck of a kiss.

"Regs." His mood changes, getting more serious, and he pulls back like he is remembering something important.

"What?"

"Do you realize if we make it to the final two couples, your family can move to Denver to be with us?" he asks affectionately.

My family! Ashton. Mom. Dad. Here with me? With everything that has been going on lately, I haven't really had a chance to stop and think about it. I have already gotten them promoted twice, and hopefully on a leadership committee with making the final four. Coming to Denver? Having more opportunities? This is why I wanted to do this thing in the first place. It makes my heart do funny things to realize that Lyncoln knew this would be such a big deal to me. And he remembered to mention it now, before our first major event together.

"I cannot imagine my life without them," I think out loud.

He nods his head in agreement. "Me either. I love you, you love them. By default, I love them."

I panic as I think of what would happen if we don't make it any farther. "What if…" I begin before I am interrupted with a soft and tender kiss on the lips.

"We can do this, gorgeous. We will bring them to Denver. We can win the whole damn thing." He says it with that confident air that only he can pull off. "Trust me."

"Okay. I do." I smile then angle my head to the side as I say, "Thank you."

"For?"

"For believing in me…in us…and remembering my family." I wrap my arms around him and give him a hug.

With that, he gives me a light kiss on the forehead and rubs circles with his thumb on my bare back like he did the night we met. "But are you sure you don't want to change your mind? Last chance before you're stuck with me forever."

I don't even hesitate. "I'm sure."

For the first time in quite a while, I feel genuinely happy and content without having to feel a side of guilt along with it.

****

We go second, after Knox and Attie. They are already sitting down answering questions when Elle ushers us into the interview area. Frank and Gertie are there and buzz around us as they straighten us out. I shouldn't be nervous since the only thing different from earlier today is the camera in the room, and the fancy clothes, but for some reason I am. Each couple has only about ten minutes to woo over the entire country. Mom and dad and Ash will be watching at home. This is the first they will know about my decision in choosing Lyncoln too. Actually, this is the first anyone will know of my decision.

All too soon, the ten minutes has passed. When my name is called, I sit down in the appropriate chair across from Dougall. Just like with Attie, the "lady" goes first and answers a few questions on her own before her counterpart is brought out.

"Ms. Reagan Scott," Dougall greets me.

"Hello," I say warmly. I get an image of the dying former Madam President in my head. She radiated strength and kindness. I try to somehow magically channel that as I remember my family and all of Omaha are watching on the other end.

"You are from Omaha and our youngest candidate," she states.

I smile. "That is correct."

She goes on to ask me a few questions about the Culling. I answer them and then she starts asking me about Lyncoln.

"What first drew you to him?"

"He was unlike anyone I had ever met. Even in the way he walks, he is powerful and purposeful. I had never met anyone that…intense." I laugh. "He is a force of nature."

"What makes you think he will be able to lead our country?" she asks a harder question, building up for his introduction.

"Lyncoln. There is just no other like him. His life wasn't always easy," I pause and start to feel a bit emotional after this long day. I know I can't talk about his dad's murder, but I have to be as honest as I can be without giving out too much information. "He has had to go through a lot of pain. But the pain that would have crippled most people, instead made him stronger. He is hard and protective when he needs to be. If it is something he cares about, he is fiercely loyal too. He is very much a military man and has an impressive reputation, but he is so much more than that. I have so many examples and stories I could tell you, but the bottom line is, he's the man for the job. He will not only do the job, but like anything he does, he will do it greatly."

"Well said. Let's bring this man out, now shall we? Mr. Lyncoln Reed," she introduces him with a smile an open armed gesture.

He walks over and sits in the empty chair next to me. Immediately his arm goes behind my chair and I lean in closer to him, knowing this is what Dougall hounded us for this afternoon. He leans in and gives me a kiss on the forehead that has her beaming.

"So. Mr. Reed. What drew you to Ms. Scott?" she asks.

"I think the better question, Professor Dougall, is what didn't? She has a heart of gold. She works hard. She loves hard. And she is one of the most intelligent and perceptive people I have ever had the pleasure of meeting. Even Admiral Taggert is taken in with her. And if all that isn't enough, she is absolutely gorgeous too. The total package." He shrugs and steals another kiss, this time on my cheek.

I blush. This Lyncoln is definitely a charmer. He definitely brought his a-game. Dougall laughs and I know she approves.

"Can I tell you a secret?" he leans in and lazily puts an ankle across his knee.

"Of course," she smiles. She is eating this up. We are doing her proud.

"She didn't like me the first night we met," he says with a wink.

"No. I thought you hated my guts," I argue with a laugh.

"Why is that, Ms. Scott?" she inquires though loving our banter. This was not rehearsed, but she doesn't seem to mind.

"When we first met, he just seemed standoffish. He didn't act like he wanted to shake my hand, and he didn't." I shake my head smiling as I remember. It feels like it was a century ago. I remember wondering if I smelled bad or something.

"Well, Mr. Reed? What do you have to say for yourself?" Dougall asks, playing along.

"From the little that I had seen of her, I already knew at that point that she was it for me. I was afraid to meet her because I knew at that exact moment I wanted to marry this woman. I was done for," he says with a smile as he looks at me.

I blush again. We both know that at that point he knew me quite well and had seen a lot of me, not a "little". Enough that it was far from love at first sight, but we don't need to explain that. That's a detail in our story that we can tuck away for later.

"While we are on that topic, what about children?" Dougall asks.

It is expected we marry. Good thing we actually like one another. So knowing that, naturally, one of the first questions the general population would have wouldn't be about marriage, but about children.

My chest hurts as I replay Mrs. Maxwell's words to me about raising her children as presidential children. I let Lyncoln take this question so I don't falter. I don't know how I feel about having kids in this situation. It would be against the law not to though. I have always wanted kids, I just don't want to fear for their lives. I cannot even imagine how hard it would be. This is perhaps the first time of the entire Culling that my young age is to my advantage. No one expects me to start popping out babies at 18 years old. I have time. Even the Maxwells waited five years into their presidency before having kids.

"What about them? With her brains and good looks, they'll be awesome." Lyncoln smiles and it makes my heart flutter thinking again of miniature Lyncolns with blueish-brown eyes running around. I can't help but grin like a fool.

"How many?" Dougall pries.

"As many as we want. Three? Four? Maybe even five," he shrugs then playfully adds, "God sakes, can you let me marry her first, please?"

Dougall actually blushes.

She then gets to the harder questions about our views on political issues. Of course, nothing is said about the current drifter situation. I wish we could talk about that and lay it all on the line, but we can't. We answer the questions better than we have before though and piggyback off of one another making some pretty good points.

"Last question," Dougall announces as our time runs out. "Are there any issues or areas of concern that you would like to address if you become the next presidential couple? If so, what are they?"

Um, yeah, crazy lady. There is a whole war that needs to be dealt with.

I go first. "I'm interested in giving our country an upgrade in our technologies and advancements. We have some very intelligent people working on some very impactful projects that need to be implemented across the townships. We also need better meshing of those technologies in each and every township," I explain as I think of Marcia and her water advancements. I know now that because of the war, they have been holding off as to not give the drifters a new way to attack with more transportation between the townships, but that isn't a good enough excuse. We can't live in constant fear of these people. We have to keep our country moving forward. We can't cower.

"My interests are in the military, training and preparations both. I'm interested in putting units in place that rotate around to each of the townships for training, or at least a full-time unit within each township. It's time all of our townships are as well protected and trained as Denver is. It isn't fair to train our young men and just leave them in the townships to do another job until they are needed. If being a soldier is a full-time job in Denver, it should be everywhere else, too," Lyncoln explains simply and intelligently.

I am fairly certain with that he just won over all of Omaha, if not more. He has mentioned something like this to me before, how he only trusts Denver guards because they have the most training, but hearing him phrase it like that makes me feel proud to be seated next to him. Or more proud than I already am.

"Thank you, Ms. Scott and Mr. Reed," Professor Dougall says as she wraps up our time. "You honor our country with your continued service and advancement this far in the Culling, congratulations."

"Thank you," we both say simultaneously.

And just like that, we are done. I breathe a sigh of relief as we walk into the room down the hall to find refreshments and food while we will watch the next two couples on a big television screen. Feeling exhausted, I would rather just head upstairs for smooching and/or sleep, but that would be frowned upon. *Bummer sauce.*

Knox and Attie are already in the room when we arrive. We tell each other how good we did while we exchange hugs and high fives for making it through the first interview. I so wish this was the final two instead of the final four right now. I selfishly want both Attie and I to make it to the end. Now it's up to the voters.

As soon as we sit down to eat a few snacks while we wait, I begin messing with the napkin in my lap. I don't like feeling like I am competing against my friends, but I can't help but wonder how we did in comparison to them. What is just the average person sitting at home thinking about Lyncoln and me? What was our first impression? More than anything in the world, I need for us to make the final two. But that doesn't necessarily mean I want my friends to fall flat on their faces either.

Lyncoln picks up on my nervousness and places his hand in mine as he talks to Knox while Attie and I chat about our gowns. She gives me that look that only a girl can give another girl, and I know that later we will be talking about how my deciding between boys went. We somewhat pay attention to Elizabeth and Maverick on the television screen, and somewhat chitchat. It's hard to watch our friends and be torn between wanting to cheer them on and not wanting them to look too good.

Before we know it, they are also done and enter the room. We all stand to greet them and give them hugs of encouragement. Having heard our interview, Maverick laughs and gives Lyncoln a hard time about being a jerk and not wanting to shake my hand. This gets us laughing and going on about other stories from that first night when something on the television screen catches my attention.

I take a sip of my champagne and listen in wondering what it was. Something didn't seem right.

Marisol is talking about her undying love for Christopher. Cue the eye rolls. But then she says something about his dad. What does Christopher's dad do and what would that have to do with anything? This is a new development.

My mind is in overdrive, thinking fast, trying to remember what Christopher's dad does. I get a twisted feeling in my gut that something is terribly wrong. There is only one person here that has a dad with enough influence to be mentioned.

"Without further ado," Dougall says and although she's smiling, it isn't quite reaching her eyes. "Here is Mr. Henry Maxwell."

My champagne flute slips out of my hand and plummets to the ground where it breaks into thousands of tiny glass shards. Lyncoln is immediately by my side. He looks at the television where my eyes are glued and places a hand on my lower back. I grab onto his suit lapel for dear life. I feel the blood drain from my face.

This can't be happening. *This cannot be happening.*

My whole world shatters into a million pieces as Henry walks out and sits down next to Marisol.

END OF BOOK ONE

Acknowledgments

Wow. Wowdy, wow, wow. Where do I even begin?

First and foremost, I need to thank Jesus for choosing the nails so a sinner like me can get into heaven. God has blessed me with a unique set of skills that in my late twenties I am only starting to figure out what to do with. Thanks, Big G.

Next, a big thank you to my husband, my rock, my best friend. I can only write about men of a high caliber because I am married to one. You drive me bonkers, but I love the crap out of you.

Thank you to my sons, my pride and joy. I didn't understand the capacity God gave us to love until I became a mom. You motivate me to always be the best I can be.

Thank you to Bubba Gump, my English bulldog, my assistant for all things writing. More often than not, your gassy ways motivated me to hurry up and finish my paragraph. You slept and napped for me so I could stay up and keep writing. Thanks, Bubbsies.

Thank you to my parents for raising one stubborn girl and teaching me to work hard. Thank you to my mom especially for reading my manuscript at the drop of a hat and singing its praises even in the first drafts. Who would have thought when I was up all hours of the night with a flashlight plowing through books that one day I would complete one of my own?

Thank you to my friends and family who didn't laugh when I wanted to write a book. In my many times of doubt and fear, you kept me grounded. I appreciate you all. Even Meg-giggs, my first ever groupie.

Thank you to the people that assisted in my learning about the whole self-publishing world. Stephanie Churchill, you are the only real author I know...yes, "real author!" Your wisdom and willingness to take me under your wing is unexpected and refreshing in an industry that isn't always so kind.

To my beta-readers, a thank you seems inadequate. You are the reason this book is out. You are the people I trust and whose opinion I value most in this world. Sibling-in-laws, you are irreplaceable. Anita and J-Wall, you are appreciated more than you know. Not only are you educators, but you are sculptors of people. The world is a better place because of the love and grace you extend to people. Jenni, you too, even though you don't "formally" teach anymore. You came in at the last possible minute when I was exasperated and feeling down. You blessed me big time. Thank you, thank you, thank you, to you all. I would give y'all a standing ovation if I could.

A random thank you to Coach Chvala for your teaching us pinball. I hope you're teaching the angels up there. And doing play-by-play commentary, of course.

Though corny, it would be remiss to not acknowledge Amazon and KDP. It blows my mind what you allow us indie authors to do. You give the underdog a fighting chance.

And last but definitely not least, thank you to you, dear reader. I don't know how I convinced you to take a chance on my book but thank you for sticking it out until the end. I hope you loved the characters as much as I do. I wish I could grab some tea and/or coffee with every single one of you. I can't wait to hear what you have to say. And to the reader who chooses to read on to the next book, I hope for you, dear one, that you never let this scary world make you quit. I hope you never give up when laughed at. I hope you find what you want to do in this life and I hope you do the dang thang, all the circumstances be damned. Be authentic. Be crazy. Be brave. And be you.

Author's Bio

Tricia Wentworth is the award-winning author of *The Culling* series. Though she began writing at a young age, she didn't realize her love of writing would take over until after she graduated college with her teaching degree. She currently resides in Nebraska with her husband, three sons, and English bulldog. She hoards notebooks, pretty pens, books, and tea. When not reading, writing, or momming, she can be found squeezing in a run or feeding her sugar addiction by baking something ridiculously delicious.

"The Fracturing: Book 2" is available now.
"The Reckoning: Book 3" is available now.

The first Culling spinoff series book *"The Legacy: James"* is available now.

Also by the author: *Snowed In* and *Locked In*

Be sure to follow the author for release updates in addition to some teasers and snippets from her next series. Her Facebook page is where she is most active. There is also a spoiler squad group linked to her author page.

Website: **triciawentworth.com**
Facebook page: **facebook.com/triciawentworthauthor/**
Spoiler Squad: **https://www.facebook.com/groups/203737781527604**
Instagram: **authortriciawentworth**

Made in United States
North Haven, CT
30 May 2023

37147286R00318